SHARPE'S

Bernard Cornwell wa
in Essex, and now
with his wife. In add hugely suc-
cessful Sharpe novels, Bernard Cornwell is the author of the Starbuck Chronicles, the Warlord trilogy, the Grail Quest series and the Alfred series.

For more information about Bernard Cornwell and his books, please visit his website www.bernardcornwell.net or go to www.AuthorTracker.co.uk for exclusive updates.

BERNARD CORNWELL

Sharpe's Trafalgar

Richard Sharpe and
the Battle of Trafalgar,
21 October 1805

HARPER

This edition produced for The Book People Ltd,
Hall Wood Avenue, Haydock, St Helens. WA11 9UL

This novel is entirely a work of fiction.
The names, characters and incidents portrayed in it are the workof the author's imagination. Any resemblance to actual persons, living or dead, events or localities is entirely coincidental.

Harper
An imprint of HarperCollins*Publishers*
77–85 Fulham Palace Road,
Hammersmith, London W6 8JB

www.harpercollins.co.uk

This paperback edition 2006
1

First published in Great Britain by
HarperCollins*Publishers* 2000

A catalogue record for this book is available from the British Library

ISBN 978-0-00-787072-1

Set in Postscript Linotype Baskerville with Meridien display by,
Rowland Phototypesetting Ltd, Bury St Edmunds, Suffolk

Printed and bound in Great Britain by
Clays Ltd, St Ives plc

Sharpe's Trafalgar is for
Wanda Pan, Anne Knowles, Janet Eastham,
Elinor and Rosemary Davenhill,
and Maureen Shettle

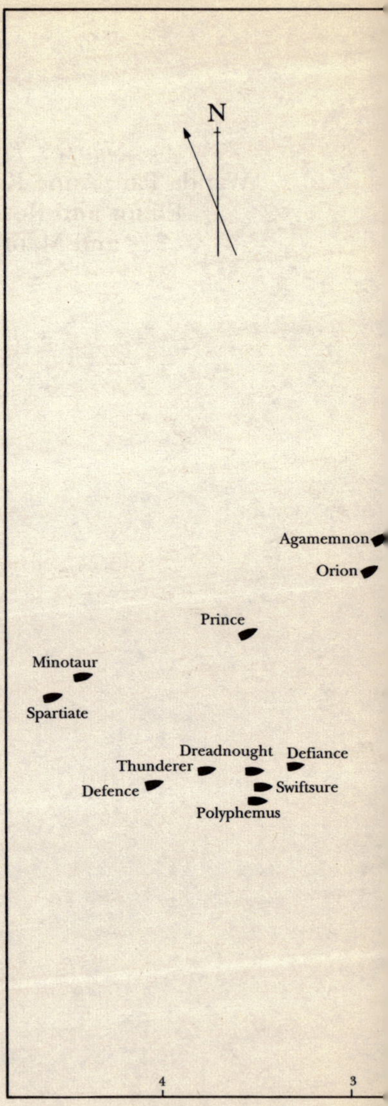
N
Agamemnon
Orion
Prince
Minotaur
Spartiate
Dreadnought
Defiance
Thunderer
Defence
Swiftsure
Polyphemus
4
3

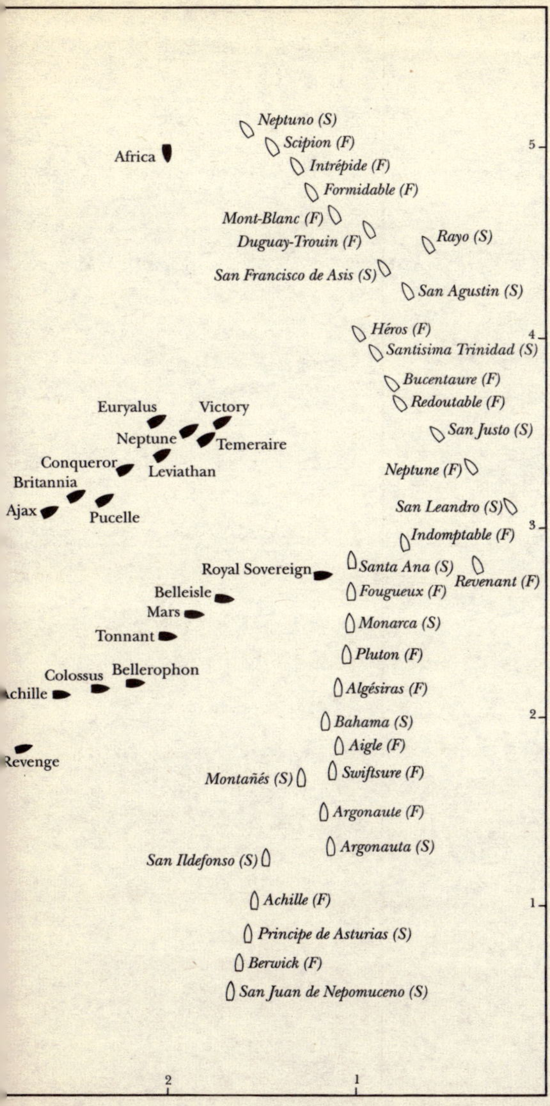

Battle of Trafalgar, 21 October 1805. The Fleets approach battle.

CHAPTER 1

'A hundred and fifteen rupees,' Ensign Richard Sharpe said, counting the money onto the table.

Nana Rao hissed in disapproval, rattled some beads along the wire bars of his abacus and shook his head. 'A hundred and thirty-eight rupees, sahib.'

'One hundred and bloody fifteen!' Sharpe insisted. 'It were fourteen pounds, seven shillings and three-pence ha'penny.'

Nana Rao examined his customer, gauging whether to continue the argument. He saw a young officer, a mere ensign of no importance, but this lowly Englishman had a very hard face, a scar on his right cheek and showed no apprehension of the two hulking bodyguards who protected Nana Rao and his warehouse. 'A hundred and fifteen, as you say,' the merchant conceded, scooping the coins into a large black cash box. He offered Sharpe an apologetic shrug. 'I get older, sahib, and find I cannot count!'

'You can count, all right,' Sharpe said, 'but you reckon I can't.'

'But you will be very happy with your purchases,' Nana Rao said, for Sharpe had just become the possessor of a hanging bed, two blankets, a teak travelling chest, a lantern and a box of candles, a hogshead of arrack, a wooden bucket, a box of soap, another of tobacco, and a brass and elmwood filtering machine which he had been assured would render water from the filthiest barrels stored in the bottom-most part of a ship's hold into the sweetest and most palatable liquid.

Nana Rao had demonstrated the filtering machine which he claimed had been brought out from London as part of the baggage of a director of the East India Company who had insisted on only the finest equipment. 'You put the water here, see?' The merchant had poured a pint or so of turbid water into the brass upper chamber. 'And then you allow the water to settle, Mister Sharpe. In five minutes it will be as clear as glass. You observe?' He lifted the upper container to show water dripping from the packed muslin layers of the filter. 'I have myself cleaned the filter, Mister Sharpe, and I will warrant the item's efficiency. It would be a miserable pity to die of mud blockage in the bowel because you would not buy this thing.'

So Sharpe had bought it. He had refused to purchase a chair, bookcase, sofa or washstand, all pieces of furniture that had been used by passengers outward bound from London to Bombay, but he had paid for the filtering machine and all the other goods because otherwise his voyage home would be excruciatingly uncomfortable. Passengers on the great merchantmen of the East India Company were expected to supply their own furniture. 'Unless you would be liking to sleep on the deck, sahib? Very hard! Very hard!' Nana Rao had laughed. He was a plump and seemingly friendly man with a large black moustache and a quick smile. His business was to purchase the furniture of incoming passengers which he then sold to those folk who were going home. 'You will leave the goods here,' he told Sharpe, 'and on the day of your embarkation my cousin will deliver them to your ship. Which ship is that?'

'The *Calliope*,' Sharpe said.

'Ah! The *Calliope*! Captain Cromwell. Alas, the *Calliope* is anchored in the roads, so the goods will need to be carried out by boat, but my cousin charges very little for such a service, Mister Sharpe, very little, and when you are happily arrived in London you can sell the items for much profit!'

Which might or, more probably, might not have been true, but was irrelevant because that same night, just two days before Sharpe was to embark, Nana Rao's godown was burned to the ground and all the goods: the beds, bookcases, lanterns, water filters, blankets, boxes, tables and chairs, the arrack, soap, tobacco, brandy and wine were supposedly consumed with the warehouse. In the morning there was nothing but ashes, smoke and a group of shrieking mourners who wailed that the kindly Nana Rao had died in the conflagration. Happily another godown, not three hundred yards from Nana Rao's ruined business, was well supplied with all the necessities for the voyage, and that second warehouse did a fine trade as disgruntled passengers replaced their vanished goods at prices that were almost double those that Nana Rao had charged.

Richard Sharpe did not buy anything from the second warehouse. He had been in Bombay for five months, much of that time spent sweating and shivering in the castle hospital, but when the fever had passed, and while he was waiting for the annual convoy to arrive from Britain with the ship that would carry him home, he had explored the city, from the wealthy houses in the Malabar hills to the pestilential alleys by the waterfront. He had found companionship in the alleyways and it was one of those acquaintances who, in return for a golden guinea, gave Sharpe a scrap of information which the ensign reckoned was worth far more than a guinea. It was, indeed, worth a hundred and fifteen rupees which was why, at nightfall, Sharpe was in another alley on the eastern outskirts of the city. He wore his uniform, though over it he had donned a swathing cloak made of cheap sacking which was thickly impregnated with mud and filth. He limped and shuffled, his body bent over with a hand outstretched as though he were begging. He muttered to himself and twitched, and sometimes turned and snarled at some innocent soul for no apparent reason. He went utterly unnoticed.

He found the house he wanted and squatted by its wall. A score of beggars, some horribly maimed, were gathered by the gate along with almost a hundred petitioners who waited for the house's owner, a wealthy merchant, to return from his place of business. The merchant came after nightfall, riding in a curtained palanquin that was carried by eight men, while another dozen men whacked the beggars out of the way with long staves, but, once the merchant's palanquin was safe inside the courtyard, the gates were left open so that the petitioners and beggars could follow. The beggars, Sharpe among them, were pushed to one side of the yard while the petitioners gathered at the foot of the broad steps that climbed to the house door. Lanterns hung from the coconut palms that arched over the yard, while from inside the big house yellow candlelight glimmered behind filigree shutters. Sharpe pushed as close to the house as he could, staying in the shadow of the palm trunks. Under the greasy cloak he had his cavalry sabre and a loaded pistol, though he hoped he would need neither weapon.

The merchant was called Panjit and he kept the petitioners and beggars waiting until he had eaten his evening meal, but then the house door was thrown open and Panjit, resplendent in a long robe of embroidered yellow silk, appeared on the top step. The petitioners called aloud while the beggars shuffled forward until they were driven back by the staves of the bodyguards. The merchant smiled then rang a small hand-bell to attract the attention of a brightly painted god who sat in a niche of the courtyard wall. Panjit bowed to the god, and then, in answer to Sharpe's prayers, a second man, this one dressed in a red silk robe, emerged from the house door.

That second man was Nana Rao. He had a wide smile, and no wonder, for he was quite untouched by fire and, as Sharpe's guinea had discovered, he was also first cousin of Panjit who was the merchant who had profited so greatly by owning the second warehouse that had replaced the goods supposedly destroyed in Nana Rao's calamitous fire. It had been a slick deception, enabling the cousins to sell the same goods twice, and tonight, replete with their swollen profits, they were choosing which men would be given the lucrative job of rowing the passengers and their belongings out to the great ships that lay in the anchorage. The chosen men would be required to pay for the privilege, thus enriching Panjit and Nana Rao even more, and the two cousins, aware of their good fortune, planned to propitiate the gods by distributing some petty coins to the beggars. Sharpe was reckoning that he could reach Nana Rao in the guise of a supplicant, then throw off the filthy cloak and shame the man into returning his money. The competent-looking bodyguards at the foot of the steps suggested that his skimpy plan might prove more complicated than he envisaged, but Sharpe guessed Nana Rao would not want his deception revealed and so would probably be happy to pay him off.

Sharpe was close to the house now. He had noticed that the empty palanquin had been carried down a narrow and dark passage that led alongside the building, evidently giving access to a courtyard at the rear of the house, and he was considering going down the passage and coming back through the building to approach Nana Rao from the rear, but any of the beggars who ventured near the passage were beaten back by the bodyguards. The petitioners were being allowed onto the steps in small groups, but the beggars were expected to wait until the main business of the evening was over.

Sharpe suspected it would be a long night, but he was content to wait with his cloak hood pulled over his face. He squatted against the wall, watching for an opportunity to dash into the passageway beside the house, but then a servant who had been guarding the outer gate pushed through the crowd and spoke in Panjit's ear. For an instant the merchant looked alarmed and a silence fell over the courtyard, but then he whispered to Nana Rao who just shrugged. Panjit clapped his hands and shouted at the bodyguards who energetically drove the petitioners back to form an open passage between the gate and the steps. Someone was plainly coming to the house and Nana Rao, nervous of their appearance, stepped into the black shadow at the back of the porch.

The way was clear now for Sharpe to go down the passage beside the house, but curiosity held him in place. There was a commotion in the alley, sounding like the jeers and scramble that always accompanied a band of constables marching through the lesser streets of London, then the outer gate was pushed fully open and Sharpe could only stare in astonishment.

A group of British sailors stood in the gate, led by a naval captain, a post captain no less, who was immaculate in cocked hat, blue frock coat, silk breeches and stockings, silver-buckled shoes and slim sword. The lantern light reflected from the heavy gold bullion of his twin epaulettes. He took off his hat, revealing thick blond hair, smiled and bowed. 'Do I have the honour,' he asked, 'of coming to the house of Panjit Lashti?'

Panjit nodded cautiously. 'This is the house,' he said in English.

The naval captain put on his cocked hat. 'I have come,' he announced in a friendly voice that had a distinct Devonshire accent, 'for Nana Rao.'

'He is not here,' Panjit answered.

The captain glanced at the red-robed figure in the porch shadows. 'His ghost will do very well.'

'I have answered you,' Panjit said, defiance now making his voice angry. 'He is not here. He is dead.'

The captain smiled. 'My name is Chase,' he said courteously, 'Captain Joel Chase of His Britannic Majesty's navy, and I would be obliged if Nana Rao would come with me.'

'His body was burned,' Panjit declared fiercely, 'and his ashes have gone to the river. Why do you not seek him there?'

'He's no more dead than you or I,' Chase said, then waved his men forward. He had brought a dozen seamen, all identically dressed in white duck trousers, red and white hooped shirts and straw hats stiffened with pitch and circled with red and white ribbons. They wore long pigtails and carried thick staves which Sharpe guessed were capstan bars. Their leader was a huge man whose bare forearms were thick with tattoos, while beside him was a Negro, every bit as tall, who carried his capstan bar as though it were a hazel wand. 'Nana Rao' – Chase abandoned the pretence that the merchant was dead – 'you owe me a deal of money and I have come to collect it.'

'What is your authority to be here?' Panjit demanded. The crowd, most of whom did not understand English, watched the sailors nervously, but Panjit's bodyguards, who outnumbered Chase's men and were just as well armed, seemed eager to be loosed on the seamen.

'My authority,' Chase said grandly, 'is my empty

purse.' He smiled. 'You surely do not wish me to use force?'

'Use force, Captain Chase,' Panjit answered just as grandly, 'and I shall have you in front of a magistrate by dawn.'

'I shall happily appear in court,' Chase said, 'so long as Nana Rao is beside me.'

Panjit shook his hands as if he was shooing Chase and his men away from his courtyard. 'You will leave, Captain. You will leave my house now.'

'I think not,' Chase said.

'Go! Or I will summon authority!' Panjit insisted.

Chase turned to the huge tattooed man. 'Nana Rao's the bugger with the moustache and the red silk robe, Bosun. Get him.'

The British seamen charged forward, relishing the chance of a scrap, but Panjit's bodyguards were no less eager and the two groups met in the courtyard's centre with a sickening crash of staves, skulls and fists. The seamen had the best of it at first, for they had charged with a ferocity that drove the bodyguards back to the foot of the steps, but Panjit's men were both more numerous and more accustomed to fighting with the long clubs. They rallied at the steps, then used their staves like spears to tangle the sailors' legs and, one by one, the pigtailed men were tripped and beaten down. The bosun and the Negro were the last to fall. They tried to protect their captain who was using his fists handily, but the British sailors had woefully underestimated the opposition and were doomed.

Sharpe sidled towards the steps, elbowing the beggars aside. The crowd was jeering at the defeated British seamen, Panjit and Nana Rao were laughing, while the petitioners, emboldened by the success of the bodyguards, jostled each other for a chance to kick the fallen men. Some of the bodyguards were wearing the sailors' tarred hats while another pranced in triumph with Chase's cocked hat on his head. The captain was a prisoner, his arms pinioned by two men.

One of the bodyguards had stayed with Panjit and saw Sharpe edging towards the steps. He came down fast, shouting that Sharpe should go back, and when the cloaked beggar did not obey he aimed a kick at him. Sharpe grabbed the man's foot and kept it swinging upwards so that the bodyguard fell on his back and his head struck the bottom step with a sickening thump that went unnoticed in the noisy celebration of the British defeat. Panjit was shouting for quiet, holding his hands aloft. Nana Rao was laughing, his shoulders heaving with merriment, while Sharpe was in the shadow of the bushes at the side of the steps.

The victorious bodyguards pushed the petitioners and beggars away from the bruised and bloodied sailors who, disarmed, could only watch as their dishevelled captain was ignominiously hustled to the bottom of the steps. Panjit shook his head in mock sadness. 'What am I to do with you, Captain?'

Chase shook his hands free. His fair hair was darkened by blood that trickled down his cheek, but he was still defiant. 'I suggest,' he said, 'that you give me Nana Rao and pray to whatever god you trust that I do not bring you before the magistrates.'

Panjit looked pained. 'It is you, Captain, who will be in court,' he said, 'and how will that look? Captain Chase of His Britannic Majesty's navy, convicted of forcing his way into a private house and there brawling like a drunkard? I think, Captain Chase, that you and I had better discuss what terms we can agree to avoid that fate.' Panjit waited, but Chase said nothing. He was beaten. Panjit frowned at the bodyguard who had the captain's hat and ordered the man to give it back, then smiled. 'I do not want a scandal any more than you, Captain, but I shall survive any scandal that this sad affair starts, and you will not, so I think you had better make me an offer.'

A loud click interrupted Panjit. It was not a single click, but more like a loud metallic scratching that ended in the solid sound of a pistol being cocked, and Panjit turned to see that a red-coated British officer with black hair and a scarred face was standing beside his cousin, holding a blackened pistol muzzle at Nana Rao's temple.

The bodyguards glanced at Panjit, saw his uncertainty, and some of them hefted their staves and moved towards the steps, but Sharpe gripped Nana Rao's hair with his left hand and kicked him in the back of the knees so that the merchant dropped hard down with a cry of hurt surprise. The sudden brutality and Sharpe's evident readiness to pull the trigger checked the bodyguards. 'I think you'd better make me an offer,' Sharpe said to Panjit, 'because this dead cousin of yours owes me fourteen pounds, seven shillings and threepence ha'penny.'

'Put the pistol away,' Panjit said, waving his bodyguards back. He was nervous. Dealing with a courteous naval captain who was an obvious gentleman was one thing, but the red-coated ensign looked wild, and the pistol's muzzle was grinding into Nana Rao's skull so that the merchant whimpered with pain. 'Just put the pistol away,' Panjit said soothingly.

'You think I'm daft?' Sharpe sneered. 'Besides, the magistrates can't do anything to me if I shoot your cousin. He's already dead! You said so yourself. He's nothing but ashes in the river.' He twisted Nana Rao's hair, making the kneeling man gasp. 'Fourteen pounds,' Sharpe said, 'seven shillings and threepence ha'penny.'

'I'll pay it!' Nana Rao gasped.

'And Captain Chase wants his money too,' Sharpe said.

'Two hundred and sixteen guineas,' Chase said, brushing off his hat, 'though I think we deserve a little more for having worked the miracle of bringing Nana Rao back to life!'

Panjit was no fool. He looked at Chase's seamen who were picking up their capstan bars and readying themselves to continue the fight. 'No magistrates?' he asked Sharpe.

'I hate magistrates,' Sharpe said.

Panjit's face betrayed a flicker of a smile. 'If you were to let go of my cousin's hair,' he suggested, 'then I think we can all talk business.'

Sharpe let go of Nana Rao, lowered the flint of the pistol and stepped back. He stood momentarily to attention. 'Ensign Sharpe, sir,' he introduced himself to Chase.

'You are no ensign, Sharpe, but a ministering angel.' Chase climbed the steps with an outstretched hand. Despite the blood on his face he was a good-looking man with a confidence and friendliness that seemed to come from a contented and good-natured character. 'You are the *deus ex machina,* Ensign, as welcome as a whore on a gundeck or a breeze in the horse latitudes.' He spoke lightly, but there was no doubting the fervency of his thanks and, instead of shaking Sharpe's hand, he embraced him. 'Thank you,' he whispered, then stepped back. 'Hopper!'

'Sir?' The huge bosun with the tattooed arms who had been laying enemies left and right before he was overwhelmed stepped forward.

'Clear the decks, Hopper. Our enemies wish to discuss surrender terms.'

'Aye aye, sir.'

'And this is Ensign Sharpe, Hopper, and he is to be treated as a most honoured friend.'

'Aye aye, sir,' Hopper said, grinning.

'Hopper commands my barge crew,' Chase explained to Sharpe, 'and those battered gentlemen are his oarsmen. This night may not go down as one of our greater victories, gentlemen' – Chase was now addressing his bruised and bleeding men – 'but a victory it still is, and I thank you.'

The yard was cleared, chairs were fetched from the house, and terms discussed.

It had been a guinea, Sharpe thought, exceedingly well spent.

'I rather liked the fellows,' Chase said.

'Panjit and Nana Rao? They're rogues,' Sharpe said. 'I liked them too.'

'Took their defeat like gentlemen!'

'They got off light, sir,' Sharpe said. 'Must have made a fortune on that fire.'

'Oldest trick in the bag,' Captain Chase said. 'There used to be a fellow on the Isle of Dogs who claimed thieves had cleaned out his chandlery on the night before some foreign ship sailed, and the victims always fell for it.' Chase chuckled and Sharpe said nothing. He had known the man Chase spoke of, and had even helped him clear the warehouse one night, but he thought it best to be silent. 'But you and I are all right, Sharpe, other than a scratch and a bruise,' Chase went on, 'and that's all that matters, eh?'

'We're all right, sir,' Sharpe agreed. The two men, followed by Chase's barge crew, were walking back through the pungent alleys of Bombay and both were carrying money. Chase had originally contracted with Rao to supply his ship with rum, brandy, wine and tobacco, and now, instead of the two hundred and sixteen guineas he had paid the merchant, he was carrying three hundred, while Sharpe had two hundred rupees, so all in all, Sharpe reckoned, it had been a good evening's work, especially as Panjit had promised to supply Sharpe with the bed, blankets, bucket, lantern, chest, arrack, tobacco, soap and filter machine, all to be delivered to the *Calliope* at dawn and at no cost to Sharpe. The two Indians had been eager to placate the Englishmen once they realized that Chase and Sharpe had no intention of telling the rest of the fleeced victims that Nana Rao still lived, and so the merchants had fed their unwanted guests, plied them with arrack, paid the money, sworn eternal friendship and bid them good night. Now Chase and Sharpe groped their way through the dark city.

'God, this place stinks!' Chase said.

'You've not been here before?' Sharpe asked, surprised.

'I've been five months in India,' Chase said, 'but always at sea. Now I'm living ashore for a week, and it stinks. My God, how the place stinks!'

'No more than London,' Sharpe said, which was true, but here the smells were different. Instead of coal fumes there was bullock-dung smoke and the rich odours of spices and sewage. It was a sweet smell, ripe even, but not unpleasant, and Sharpe was thinking back to when he had first arrived and how he had recoiled from the smell that he now thought homely and even enticing. 'I'll miss it,' he admitted. 'I sometimes wish I wasn't going back to England.'

'Which ship are you on?'

'The *Calliope*.'

Chase evidently found that amusing. 'So what do you make of Peculiar?'

'Peculiar?' Sharpe asked.

'Peculiar Cromwell, of course, the Captain.' Chase looked at Sharpe. 'Surely you've met him!'

'I haven't. Never heard of him.'

'But the convoy must have arrived two months ago,' Chase said.

'It did.'

'Then you should have made an effort to see Peculiar. That's his real name, by the way, Peculiar Cromwell. Odd, eh? He was navy once, most of the East Indiamen captains were navy, but Peculiar resigned because he wanted to become rich. He also believed he should have been made admiral without spending tedious years as a mere captain. He's an odd soul, but he sails a tidy ship, and a fast one. I can't believe you didn't make the effort to meet him.'

'Why should I?' Sharpe asked.

'To make sure you get some privileges aboard, of course. Can I assume you'll be travelling in steerage?'

'I'm travelling cheap, if that's what you mean,' Sharpe said. He spoke bitterly, for though he had paid the lowest possible rate, his passage was still costing him one hundred and seven pounds and fifteen shillings. He had thought the army would pay for the voyage, but the army had refused, saying that Sharpe was accepting an invitation to join the 95th Rifles and if the 95th Rifles refused to pay his passage then damn them, damn their badly coloured coats, and damn Sharpe. So he had cut one of the precious diamonds from the seam of his red coat and paid for the voyage himself. He still had a king's ransom in the precious stones that he had taken from the Tippoo Sultan's body in a dank tunnel at Seringapatam, but he resented using the loot to pay the East India Company. Britain had sent Sharpe to India, and Britain, Sharpe reckoned, should fetch him back.

'So the clever thing to have done, Sharpe,' Chase said, 'would have been to introduce yourself to Peculiar while he was living ashore and given the greedy bugger a present, because then he'd have assigned you to decent quarters. But if you haven't crossed Peculiar's palm with silver, Sharpe, he'll like as not have you down in lower steerage with the rats. Main-deck steerage is much better and doesn't cost a penny more, but the lower steerage is nothing but farts, vomit and misery all the way home.' The two men had left the narrow alleys and were leading the barge crew down a street that was edged with sewage-filled ditches. It was a tin-smithing quarter and the forges were already burning bright as the sound of hammers rattled the night. Pale cows watched the sailors pass and dogs barked frantically, waking the homeless poor who huddled between the ditches and the house walls. 'It's a pity you're sailing in convoy,' Chase said.

'Why, sir?'

'Because a convoy goes at the speed of its slowest boat,' Chase explained. '*Calliope* could make England in three months if she was allowed to fly, but she'll have to limp. I wish I was sailing with you. I'd offer you passage myself as thanks for your rescue tonight, but alas, I am ghost-hunting.'

'Ghost-hunting, sir?'

'You've heard of the *Revenant*?'

'No, sir.'

'The ignorance of you soldiers,' Chase said, amused. 'The *Revenant*, my dear Sharpe, is a French seventy-four that is haunting the Indian Ocean. Hides herself in Mauritius, sallies out to snap up prizes, then scuttles back before we can catch her. I'm here to stifle her ardour, only before I can hunt her I have to scrape the bottom. My ship's too slow after eight months at sea, so we scour off the barnacles to quicken her up.'

'I wish you good fortune, sir,' Sharpe said, then frowned. 'But what's that to do with ghosts?' He usually did not like asking such questions. Sharpe had once marched in the ranks of a redcoat battalion, but he had been made into an officer and so found himself in a world where almost every man was educated except himself. He had become accustomed to allowing small mysteries to slide past him, but Sharpe decided he did not mind revealing his ignorance to a man as good-natured as Chase.

'*Revenant* is the Frog word for ghost,' Chase said. 'Noun, masculine. I had a tutor for these things who flogged the language into me and I'd like to flog it out of him now.' In a nearby yard a cockerel crowed and Chase glanced up at the sky. 'Almost dawn,' he said. 'Perhaps you'll permit me to give you breakfast? Then my lads will take you out to the *Calliope*. God speed your way home, eh?'

Home. It seemed an odd word to Sharpe, for he did not have a home other than the army and he had not seen England in six years. Six years! Yet he felt no pang of delight at the prospect of sailing to England. He did not think of it as home, indeed he had no idea where home was, but wherever that elusive place lay, he was going there.

Chase was living ashore while his ship was cleaned of the weed. 'We tip her over, scrape her copper-sheathed bum clean when the tide's low, and float her off,' he explained as servants brought coffee, boiled eggs, bread rolls, ham, cold chicken and a basket of mangoes. 'Bum-scrubbing is a damned nuisance. All the guns have to be shipped and half the contents of the hold dragged out, but she'll sail like a beauty when it's done. Have more eggs than that, Sharpe! You must be hungry. I am. Like the house? It belongs to my wife's first cousin. He's a trader here, though right now he's up in the hills doing whatever traders do when they're making themselves rich. It was his steward who alerted me to

Nana Rao's tricks. Sit down, Sharpe, sit down. Eat.'

They took their breakfast in the shade of a wide verandah that looked out on a small garden, a road and the sea. Chase was gracious, generous and apparently oblivious of the vast gulf that existed between a mere ensign, the lowest of the army's commissioned ranks, and a post captain who was officially the equivalent of an army colonel, though on board his own ship such a man outranked the very powers of heaven. Sharpe had been conscious of that wide gulf at first, but it had gradually dawned on him that Joel Chase was genuinely good-natured and Sharpe had warmed to the naval officer whose gratitude was unstinting and heartfelt. 'Do you realize that bugger Panjit really could have had me in front of the magistrates?' Chase enquired. 'Dear God, Sharpe, that would have been a pickle! And Nana Rao would have vanished, and who'd have believed me if I said the dead had come back to life? Do have more ham, please. It would have meant an enquiry at the very least, and almost certainly a court martial. I'd have been damned lucky to have survived with my command intact. But how was I to know he had a private army?'

'We came out of it all right, sir.'

'Thanks to you, Sharpe, thanks to you.' Chase shuddered. 'My father always said I'd be dead before I was thirty, and I've beaten that by five years, but one day I'll jump into trouble and there'll be no ensign to pull me out.' He patted the bag which held the money he had taken from Nana Rao and Panjit. 'And between you and me, Sharpe, this cash is a windfall. A windfall! D'you think we could grow mangoes in England?'

'I don't know, sir.'

'I shall try. Plant a couple in a warm spot of the garden and who knows?' Chase poured coffee and stretched out his long legs. He was curious why Sharpe, a man in his late twenties, should only be an ensign, but he made the enquiry with an exquisite tact and once he discovered that Sharpe had been promoted from the ranks he was genuine in his admiration. 'I once had a captain who'd come up through the hawse-hole,' he told Sharpe, 'and he was damned good! Knew his business. Understood what went on in the dark places where most captains dare not look. I reckon the army's lucky in you, Sharpe.'

'I'm not sure they think so, sir.'

'I shall whisper in some ears, Sharpe, though if I don't catch the *Revenant* there'll be precious few who'll listen to me.'

'You'll catch her, sir.'

'I pray so, but she's a fast beast. Fast and slippery. All French ships are. God knows, the buggers can't sail them, but they do know how to build 'em. French ships are like French women, Sharpe. Beautiful and fast, but hopelessly manned. Have some mustard.' Chase pushed the jar across the table, then petted a skinny black kitten as he stared past the palm trees towards the sea. 'I do like coffee,' he said, then pointed out to sea. 'There's the *Calliope*.'

Sharpe looked, but all he could see was a mass of shipping far out in the harbour beyond the shallower water which was busy with scores of bumboats, launches and fishing craft.

'She's the one drying her topsails,' Chase said, and Sharpe saw that one of the far ships had hung out her topmost sails, but at this distance she looked like the other dozen East Indiamen that would sail home together to protect themselves against the privateers who haunted the Indian Ocean. From the shore they looked like naval ships, for their hulls were banded black and white to suggest that massive broadsides were concealed behind closed gunports, but the ruse would not mislead any privateer. Those ships, their hulls stuffed with the riches of India, were the greatest prizes any corsair or French naval captain could wish to take. If a man wanted to live and die rich then all he needed to do was capture an Indiaman, which is why the great ships sailed in convoy.

'Where's your ship, sir?' Sharpe asked.

'Can't see her from here.' Chase said. 'She's careened on a mudbank on the far side of Elephanta Island.'

'Careened?'

'Tipped on her side so we can polish her bum.'

'What's she called?'

Chase looked abashed. '*Pucelle*,' he said.

'*Pucelle*? Sounds French.'

'It is French, Sharpe. It means a virgin.' Chase pretended to be offended as Sharpe laughed. 'You've heard of *la Pucelle d'Orléans*?' he asked.

'No, sir.'

'The maid of Orleans, Sharpe, was Joan of Arc, and the ship was named for her and I just trust she doesn't end up like Joan, burned to a crisp.'

'But why would you name a boat for a Frenchwoman, sir?' Sharpe asked.

'We didn't. The Frogs did. She was a French boat till Nelson took her at the Nile. If you capture a ship, Sharpe, you keep the old name unless it's really obnoxious. Nelson took the *Franklin* at the Nile, an eighty-gun thing of great beauty, but the navy will be damned if it has a ship named after a traitorous bloody Yankee so we call her the *Canopus* now. But my ship kept her name, and she's a lovely beast. Lovely and fast. Oh my God, no.' He sat up straight, staring towards the road. 'Oh, God, no!' These last words were prompted by the sight of an open carriage that had slowed and now stopped just beyond the garden gate. Chase, who had been genial until this moment, suddenly looked bitter.

A man and a woman were seated in the carriage which was driven by an Indian dressed in yellow and black livery. Two native footmen, arrayed in the same livery, now hurried to open the carriage door and unfold the steps, allowing the man, who was dressed in a white linen jacket, to step down to the pavement. A beggar immediately swung on short crutches and calloused stumps towards the carriage, but one of the footmen fended the man off with a sharp kick and the coachman completed the rout with his whip. The white-jacketed man was middle-aged and had a face that reminded Sharpe of Sir Arthur Wellesley. Maybe it was the prominent nose, or perhaps it was the cold and haughty look the man wore. Or perhaps it was just that everything about him, from his carriage to the liveried servants, spoke of privilege.

'Lord William Hale,' Chase said, investing every syllable with dislike.

'Never heard of him.'

'He's on the Board of Control,' Chase explained, then saw Sharpe's raised eyebrow. 'Six men, Sharpe, who are appointed by the government to make certain that the East India Company doesn't do anything foolish. Or rather that, if it does, no blame attaches itself to the government.' He looked sourly at Lord William who had paused to speak with the woman in the carriage. 'That's his wife and I've just brought the two of them from Calcutta so they could go home on the same convoy as yourself. You should pray they aren't on the *Calliope*.'

Lord William was grey-haired and Sharpe assumed his wife would also be middle-aged, but when she lowered her white parasol Sharpe had a clear view of her ladyship and the breath was checked in his throat. She was much younger than Lord William, and her pale, slender face had a haunting beauty, almost a sadness, that struck Sharpe with the force of a bullet. He stared at her, entranced by her.

Chase smiled at Sharpe's smitten expression. 'She was born Grace de Laverre Gould, third daughter of the Earl of Selby. She's twenty years younger than her husband, but just as cold.'

Sharpe could not take his eyes from her ladyship, for she was truly beautiful; breathtakingly, achingly, untouchably beautiful. Her face was pale as ivory, sharp-shadowed as she leaned towards her husband, and framed by heavy loops of black hair that were pinned to appear artless, but which even Sharpe could tell must have taken her maid an age to arrange. She did not smile, but just gazed solemnly into her husband's face. 'She looks sad rather than cold,' Sharpe said.

Chase mocked the wistfulness in Sharpe's voice. 'What does she have to be sad about? Her beauty is her fortune, Sharpe, and her husband is as rich as he is ambitious as he is clever. She's on her way to being wife of the Prime Minister so long as Lord William doesn't put a foot wrong and, believe me, he steps as lightly as a cat.'

Lord William concluded the conversation with his wife, then gestured for a footman to open Chase's gate. 'You might have taken a house with a carriage drive,' he admonished the naval captain as he strode up the short path. 'It's devilish annoying being pestered by beggars every time one makes a call.'

'Alas, my lord, we sailors are so inept on land. I cannot entice your wife to take some coffee?'

'Her ladyship is not well.' Lord William ran up the verandah steps, gave Sharpe a careless glance, then held a hand towards Chase as if expecting to be given something. He must have noted the blood that was still crusted in Chase's fair hair, but he made no mention of it. 'Well, Chase, can you settle?'

Chase reluctantly found the big leather bag which held the coins he had taken from Nana Rao and counted out a substantial portion that he gave to Lord William. His lordship shuddered at the thought of handling the grubby currency, but forced himself to take the money and pour it into his coat's tail pockets. 'Your note,' he said, and handed Chase a scrap of paper. 'You haven't received new orders, I suppose?'

'Alas no, my lord. We are still ordered to find the *Revenant.*'

'I was hoping you'd be going home instead. It is crucial I reach London quickly.' He frowned, then, without another word, turned away.

'You did not give me a chance, my lord,' Chase said, 'to introduce my particular friend, Mister Sharpe.'

Lord William bestowed a second brief look at Sharpe and his lordship saw nothing to contradict his first opinion that the ensign was penniless and powerless, for he merely looked, calculated and glanced away without offering any acknowledgement, but in that brief meeting of eyes Sharpe had received an impression of force, confidence and arrogance. Lord William was a man who had more than his share of power, he wanted more and he would not waste time on those who had nothing to give him.

'Mister Sharpe served under Sir Arthur Wellesley,' Chase said.

'As did many thousands of others, I believe,' Lord William said carelessly, then frowned. 'There is a service you can do me, Chase.'

'I am, of course, entirely at your lordship's convenience,' Chase said politely.

'You have a barge and a crew?'

'All captains do,' Chase said.

'We must reach the *Calliope.* You could take us there?'

'Alas, my lord, I have promised Mr Sharpe the barge,'

Chase said, 'but I am sure he will gladly share it with you. He too is bound for the *Calliope*.'

'I'd be happy to help,' Sharpe said.

Lord William's expression suggested that Sharpe's help was the last thing he would ever require. 'We shall let our present arrangements stand,' he told Chase and, wasting no more time, stalked away.

Chase laughed softly. 'Share a boat with you, Sharpe? He'd rather sprout wings and fly.'

'I wouldn't mind sharing a boat with her,' Sharpe said, staring at the Lady Grace who was gazing fixedly ahead as a score of beggars whimpered a safe distance from the coachman's stinging whip.

'My dear Sharpe,' Chase said, watching the carriage draw away, 'you will be sharing that lady's company for at least four months and I doubt you will even see her. Lord William claims she suffers from delicate nerves and is averse to company. I had her on board the *Pucelle* for near a month and might have seen her twice. She sticks to her cabin, or else walks the poop at night when no one can accost her, and I will wager you a month of your wages to a year of mine that she will not even know your name by the time you reach England.'

Sharpe smiled. 'I don't wager.'

'Good for you,' Chase said. 'Like a fool I played too much whist in the last month. I promised my wife I wouldn't plunge heavily, and God punished me for it. Dear me, what a fool I am! I played almost every night between Calcutta and here and lost a hundred and seventy guineas to that rich bastard. My own fault,' he admitted ruefully, 'and I won't succumb again.' He reached out to touch the wood of the table top as if he did not trust his own resolve. 'But cash is always short, isn't it? I'll just have to capture the *Revenant* and earn myself some decent prize money.'

'You'll manage that,' Sharpe said comfortingly.

Chase smiled. 'I do hope so. I fervently hope so, but once in a while, Sharpe, the damned Frogs throw up a real seaman and the *Revenant* is in the hands of Capitaine Louis Montmorin. He's good, his men are good and his ship is good.'

'But you're British,' Sharpe said, 'so you must be better.'

'Amen to that,' Chase said, 'amen.' He wrote his English address on a scrap of paper, then insisted on walking Sharpe to the fort where the ensign collected his pack, after which the two men went past the still smoking ruins of Nana Rao's warehouse to the quay where Chase's barge waited. The naval captain shook Sharpe's hand. 'I remain entirely in your debt, Sharpe.'

'You're making too much of it, sir.'

Chase shook his head. 'I was a fool last night, and if it hadn't been for you I'd be looking an even greater fool this morning. I am beholden to you, Sharpe, and shall not forget it. We'll meet again, I'm sure of it.'

'I hope so, sir,' Sharpe said, then went down the greasy steps. It was time to go home.

The crew of Captain Chase's barge were still bruised and bloodied, but in good spirits after their night's adventure. Hopper, the bosun who had fought so stoutly, helped Sharpe down into the barge which was painted dazzling white with a red stripe around its gunwales to match the red bands painted on the white-shafted oars. 'You had breakfast, sir?' Hopper asked.

'Captain Chase looked after me.'

'He's a good man,' Hopper said warmly. 'None better.'

'You've known him long?' Sharpe asked.

'Since he was as old as Mister Collier,' the bosun said, jerking his head at a small boy, perhaps twelve years old, who sat beside him in the stern. Mister Collier was a midshipman and, once Sharpe had been safely delivered to the *Calliope*, he had the responsibility of fetching the liquor for Captain Chase's private stores. 'Mister Collier,' the bosun went on, 'is in charge of this boat, ain't that so, sir?'

'I am,' Collier said in a still unbroken voice. He held a hand to Sharpe. 'Harry Collier, sir.' He had no need to call Sharpe 'sir', for a midshipman's rank was the equivalent of an ensign, but Sharpe was much older and, besides, a friend of the captain.

'Mister Collier is in charge,' Hopper said again, 'so if he orders us to attack a ship, sir, attack we shall. Obey him to the death, ain't that right, Mister Collier, sir?'

'If you say so, Mister Hopper.'

The crew were grinning. 'Wipe those smirks off your uglies!' Hopper shouted, then spat a stream of tobacco juice over the gunwale. His two upper front teeth were missing, which made spitting the juice far easier. 'Yes, sir,' he went on, looking at Sharpe, 'I've served with Captain Chase since he was a nipper. I was with him when he captured the *Bouvines*.'

'The *Bouvines*?'

'A Frog frigate, sir, thirty-two guns, and we was in the *Spritely*, twenty-eight, and it took us twenty-two minutes first gun to last and there was blood leaking out of her scuppers when we'd finished with her. And one day, Mister Collier, sir' – he looked sternly down at the small boy whose face was almost entirely hidden by a cocked hat that was much too big for him – 'you'll be in charge of one of His Majesty's ships and it'll be your duty and privilege to knock a Froggy witless.'

'I hope so, Mister Hopper.'

The barge was travelling smoothly through water that was filthy with floating rubbish, palm fronds and the bloated corpses of rats, dogs and cats. A score of other boats, some of them heaped with baggage, were also rowing out to the waiting convoy. The luckiest passengers were those whose ships were moored at the Company's docks, but those docks were not large enough for every merchantman that would leave for home and so most of the travellers were being ferried out to the anchorage. 'I seen your goods loaded on a native boat, sir,' Hopper said, 'and told the bastards there'd be eight kinds of hell to pay if they weren't delivered shipshape. They do like their games, sir, they do.' He squinted ahead and laughed. 'See? One of the buggers is up to no good right now.'

'No good?' Sharpe asked. All he could see were two small boats that were dead in the water. One of the two boats was piled with leather luggage while the other held three passengers.

'Buggers say it'll cost a rupee to reach the ship, sir,' Hopper explained, 'then they get halfway and triple the price, and if they don't get it they'll row back to the quay. Our boys do the same thing when they pick passengers up at Deal to row them out to the Downs.' He tugged on a rudder line to skirt the two boats.

Sharpe saw that Lord William Hale, his wife and a young man were the passengers in the leading boat, while two servants and a pile of luggage were crammed into the second. Lord William was speaking angrily with a grinning Indian who seemed unmoved by his lordship's ire.

'His bloody lordship will just have to pay up,' Hopper said, 'or else get rowed ashore.'

'Take us close,' Sharpe said.

Hopper glanced at him, then shrugged as if to suggest that it was none of his business if Sharpe wanted to make a fool of himself. 'Ease oars!' he shouted and the crew lifted their dripping blades from the water to let the barge glide on until it was within a few feet of the stranded boats. 'Back water!' Hopper snapped and the oars dipped again to bring the elegant boat to a stop.

Sharpe stood. 'You have trouble, my lord?'

Lord William frowned at Sharpe, but said nothing, while his wife managed to suggest that an even more noxious stench than the others in the harbour had somehow approached her delicate nostrils. She just stared sternwards, ignoring the Indian crew, her husband and Sharpe. It was the third passenger, the young man who was dressed as soberly as a curate, who stood and explained their trouble. 'They won't move,' he complained.

'Be quiet, Braithwaite, be quiet and sit down,' his lordship snapped, disdaining Sharpe's assistance.

Not that Sharpe wanted to help Lord William, but his wife was another matter and it was for her benefit that Sharpe drew his pistol and cocked the flint. 'Row on!' he ordered the Indian, who answered by spitting overboard.

'What in God's name are you doing?' Lord William at last acknowledged Sharpe. 'My wife's aboard! Have a care with that gun, you fool! Who the devil are you?'

'We were introduced not an hour ago, my lord,' Sharpe said. 'Richard Sharpe is the name.' He fired and the pistol ball splintered a timber of the boat just on the water line between the recalcitrant skipper and his passengers. Lady Grace put a hand to her mouth in alarm, but the ball had harmed no one, merely holed the boat so that the Indian had to stoop to plug the damage with a thumb. Sharpe began to reload. 'Row on, you bastard!' he shouted.

The Indian glanced behind as if judging the distance to the shore, but Hopper ordered his crew to back water and the barge slowly moved behind the two boats, cutting them off from land. Lord William seemed too astonished to speak, but just stared indignantly as

Sharpe rammed a second bullet down the short barrel.

The Indian did not want another ball cracking into his boat and so he suddenly sat and shouted at his men who began pulling hard on their oars. Hopper nodded approvingly. 'Twixt wind and water, sir. Captain Chase would be proud of you.'

'Between wind and water?' Sharpe asked.

'You holed the bastard on the water line, sir. It'll sink him if he doesn't keep it stopped up.'

Sharpe gazed at her ladyship who, at last, turned to look at her rescuer. She had huge eyes, and perhaps they were the feature that made her seem so sad, but Sharpe was still astonished by her beauty and he could not resist giving her a wink. She looked quickly away. 'She'll remember my name now,' he said.

'Is that why you did it?' Hopper asked, then laughed when Sharpe did not answer.

Lord William's boat drew up to the *Calliope* first. The servants, who were in the second boat, were expected to scramble up the ship's side as best they could while seamen hauled the baggage up in nets, but Lord William and his wife stepped from their boat onto a floating platform from which they climbed a gangway to the ship's waist. Sharpe, waiting his turn, could smell bilge water, salt and tar. A stream of dirty water emerged from a hole high up in the hull. 'Pumping his bottoms, sir,' Hopper said.

'You mean she leaks?'

'All ships leak, sir. Nature of ships, sir.'

Another launch had gone alongside the *Calliope*'s bows and sailors were hoisting nets filled with struggling goats and crates of protesting hens. 'Milk and eggs,' Hopper said cheerfully, then barked at his crew to lay to their oars so Sharpe could be put alongside. 'I wish you a fast, safe voyage, sir,' the bosun said. 'Back to old England, eh?'

'Back to England,' Sharpe said, and watched as the oars were raised straight up as Hopper used the last of the barge's momentum to lay her sweetly alongside the floating platform. Sharpe gave Hopper a coin, touched his hat to Mister Collier, thanked the boat's crew and stepped up onto the platform from where he climbed to the main deck past an open gunport in which a polished cannon muzzle showed.

An officer waited just inside the entry port. 'Your name?' he asked peremptorily.

'Richard Sharpe.'

The officer peered at a list. 'Your baggage is already aboard, Mister Sharpe, and this is for you.' He took a folded sheet of paper from a pocket and gave it to Sharpe. 'Rules of the ship. Read, mark, learn and explicitly obey. Your action station is gun number five.'

'My what?' Sharpe asked.

'Every male passenger is expected to help defend the ship, Mister Sharpe. Gun number five.' The officer waved across the deck which was so heaped with baggage that none of the guns on the farther side could be seen. 'Mister Binns!'

A very young officer hurried through the piled baggage. 'Sir?'

'Show Mister Sharpe to the lower-deck steerage. One of the seven by sixes, Mister Binns, seven by six. Mallet and nails, look lively, now!'

'This way, sir,' Binns said to Sharpe, darting aft. 'I've got the mallet and nails, sir.'

'The what?' Sharpe asked.

'Mallet and nails, sir, so you can nail your furniture to the deck. We don't want it sliding topsy-turvy if we gets rough weather, sir, which we shouldn't, sir, not till we reach the Madagascar Straits and it can be lumpy there, sir, very lumpy.' Binns hurried on, vanishing down a dark companionway like a rabbit down its burrow.

Sharpe followed, but before he reached the companionway he was accosted by Lord William Hale who stepped from behind a pile of boxes. The young man in the sepulchral clothes stood behind his lordship. 'Your name?' Hale demanded.

Sharpe bristled. The sensible course was to knuckle under, for Hale was evidently a formidable man in London, but Sharpe had acquired an acute dislike of his lordship. 'The same as it was ten minutes ago,' he answered curtly.

Lord William looked into Sharpe's face which was sunburned, hard and slashed by the wicked scar. 'You are impertinent,' Lord William said, 'and I do not abide impertinence.' He glanced at the grubby white facings on Sharpe's jacket. 'The 74th? I am acquainted with Colonel Wallace and I shall let him know of your insubordination.' So far Lord William had not raised his voice which was chilling enough anyway, but now a note of indignation did creep in. 'You could have killed me with that pistol!'

'Killed you?' Sharpe asked. 'No, I couldn't. I wasn't aiming at you.'

'You will write to Colonel Wallace now, Braithwaite,' Lord William said to the young man in the black clothes, 'and make sure the letter goes ashore before we sail.'

'Of course, my lord. At once, my lord,' Braithwaite said. He was evidently Lord William's secretary and he shot Sharpe a look of pitying condescension, suggesting that the ensign had come up against forces far too strong for him.

Lord William stepped aside, allowing Sharpe to catch up with the young Binns who had been watching the confrontation from the companionway.

Sharpe was not worried by Lord William's threat. His lordship could write a thousand letters to Colonel Wallace and much good it would do him for Sharpe was no longer in the 74th. He wore the uniform for he had no other clothes to wear, but once he was back in Britain he would join the 95th with its odd new uniform of a green jacket. He did not like the idea of wearing green. He had always worn red.

Binns waited at the foot of the companionway. 'Lower deck, sir,' he said, then pushed through a canvas screen into a dark, humid and foul-smelling space. 'This is steerage, sir.'

'Why's it called steerage?'

'They used to steer the boats from here, sir, in the old days, before there was wheels. Gangs of men hauling on ropes, sir, must have been hell.' It still looked hellish. A few lanterns guttered, struggling against the gloom in which a score of sailors were nailing up canvas screens to divide the foetid space into a maze of small rooms. 'One seven by six,' Binns shouted, and a sailor gestured to the starboard side where the screens were already in place. 'Take your pick, sir,' Binns said, 'as you're one of the first gentlemen aboard, but if you wants my advice I'd be as near aft as you can go, and it's best not to share with a gun, sir.' He gestured at an eighteen-pounder cannon that half filled one cabin. The weapon was lashed to the deck and pointed at a closed gunport. Binns ushered Sharpe into the empty cubicle next door where he dropped a linen bag on the floor. 'That's a mallet and nails, sir, and as soon as your dunnage is delivered you can secure everything shipshape.' He tied back one side of the canvas box, thus allowing a little dim lantern light to seep into the cabin, then tapped the deck with his foot. 'All the money's down below, sir,' he said cheerfully.

'The money?' Sharpe asked.

'A cargo of indigo, sir, saltpetre, silver bars and silk. Enough to make us all rich a thousand times over.' He grinned, then left Sharpe to contemplate the tiny space that would be his home for the next four months.

The rear wall of his cabin was the curving side of the ship. The ceiling was low, and crossed by heavy black beams in which some hooks rusted. The floor was the deck, thickly scarred with old nail-holes where previous passengers had hammered down their chests. The remaining three walls were made of dirty canvas, but it was a heaven compared to the accommodation he had been given when he had sailed from Britain to India. Then, a private, he had been content with a hammock and fourteen inches of space in which to swing it.

He squatted in the cabin's entrance, where a lantern offered some light, and unfolded the ship's rules. They were printed, though some additions had been inked in afterwards. He was forbidden to go on the quarterdeck unless invited by the ship's captain or the officer of the watch, and to that prohibition someone had added the warning that, even if he was so invited, he was never to come between the captain and the weather rail. Sharpe did not even know what the weather rail was. Upon going on deck he was required to touch his hat to the quarterdeck, even if the captain was not in sight. Gambling was forbidden. The purser would hold divine service, weather permitting, each Sunday and passengers were required to attend unless excused by the ship's surgeon. Breakfast would be supplied at eight o'clock in the morning, dinner at midday, tea would be served at four o'clock and supper at eight. All male passengers were required to acquaint themselves with the quarter bill which allocated their action stations. No unshielded flames were to be lit below decks and all lanterns must be extinguished by nine o'clock at night. Smoking was forbidden because of the danger of fire, and passengers who chewed tobacco were to use the spittoons. Spitting on the deck was strictly forbidden. No passenger was to climb the rigging without permission of a ship's officer. Passengers in steerage, like Sharpe, were prohibited from entering the great cabin or the roundhouse unless invited. There would be no foul language aboard.

'Christ all-bloody-mighty,' a sailor grumbled as he struggled with Sharpe's barrel of arrack. Two other seamen were carrying his bed and another pair were bringing his chest. 'Got any rope, sir?' one of them asked.

'No.'

The sailor produced a length of hemp rope and showed Sharpe how to secure the wooden chest and the heavy hogshead which virtually filled the small space. Sharpe gave the sailor a rupee as thanks, then hammered the nails through the chest's corners into the deck and roped the barrel to one of the beams on the ship's side. The bed was a wooden cot, the size of a coffin, which he hung from the hooks in the beams. He suspended the bucket alongside. 'It's best to piss through the after gunport when it ain't underwater,' the sailor had told him, 'and save your bucket for solids, if you sees my meaning, sir. Or go on deck and use the heads which are forrard, but not in heavy seas, sir, for you're likely to go overboard and no one will be any the wiser. Specially at night, sir. Many a good man has gone to see the angels through being caught short on a bad night.'

A woman was protesting loudly at the accommodation on the deck's far side, while her husband was meekly asserting that they could afford no better. Two small children, hot and sweating, were bawling. A dog barked until it was silenced by a kick. Dust sifted from the overhead beam as a passenger in the main-deck steerage hammered in a staple or a nail. Goats bleated.

The bilge pump clattered and sucked and gulped and spat filthy water into the sea.

Sharpe sat on the chest. There was just enough light for him to read the paper that Captain Chase had pressed on him. It was a letter of introduction to Chase's wife at the captain's house near Topsham in Devon. 'Lord knows when I'll see Florence and the children again,' Chase had said, 'but if you're in the west country, Sharpe, do go and introduce yourself. The house ain't much. A dozen acres, run-down stable block and a couple of barns, but Florence will make you welcome.'

No one else would, Sharpe thought, for no one waited for him in England; no hearth would blaze for his return and no family would greet him. But it was home. And, like it or not, he was going there.

CHAPTER 2

That evening, when the last boats had delivered their passengers and baggage to the convoy, the *Calliope*'s bosun shouted for the topmen to go aloft. Thirty other seamen came to the lower deck and shipped the capstan bars, then began to trudge round and round, inching up the great anchor cable that came through the hawse-hole, along the lower deck and down into the ship's belly. The cable seeped a foul-smelling mud that two seamen ineffectually tried to wash overboard with pails of water, but much of the diluted mud swilled aft into the steerage compartments. The topsails were dropped, then the headsails were unfurled as the anchor came clear of the bottom and the ship's head swung away from land as the mainsails were dropped. The steerage passengers were not allowed to leave their quarters until the sails were hoisted and Sharpe sat on his trunk listening to the rush of feet overhead, the scraping of ropes along the deck and the creak of the ship's timbers. It was a half-hour after the anchor had been hauled that Binns, the young officer, shouted that the deck was clear, and Sharpe could go up the stairs to see that the ship had still not cleared the harbour. A red swollen sun, streaked by black clouds, hovered above the roofs and palm trees of Bombay. The scent of the land came strong. Sharpe leaned on the gunwale and stared at India. He doubted he would see it again and was sad to be leaving. The rigging creaked and the water gurgled down the ship's side. On the quarterdeck, where the richer passengers took the air, a woman waved to the distant shore. The ship tilted to a stronger gust of wind and a cannon near Sharpe scraped on the deck until it was checked by its lashings.

The channel veered nearer the shore, taking the ship close to a temple with a brightly coloured tower carved with monkeys, gods and elephants. The big driver sail on the mizzen was just being loosed and its canvas slapped and cracked, then bellied with the wind to lean the ship further over. Behind the *Calliope* the other great ships of the convoy were turning away from the anchorage, showing white water at their stems and filling their high masts and tangled rigging with creamy yellow sails. An East India Company frigate that would escort the convoy as far as the Cape of Good Hope sailed just ahead of the *Calliope.* The frigate's bright ensign, thirteen stripes of red and white with the union flag in the upper staff quadrant, streamed bright in the sun's red glow. Sharpe looked for Captain Joel Chase's ship, but the only Royal Navy vessel he could see was a small schooner with four cannon.

The *Calliope*'s seamen tidied the deck, stowing the loose sheets in wooden tubs and checking the lashings of the ship's boats that were stored on the spare spars which ran like vast rafters between the quarterdeck and the forecastle. A dark-skinned man in a fishing canoe paddled out of the ship's way, then gaped up at the great black and white wall that roared past him. The temple was fading now, lost in the glare of the sun, but Sharpe stared at the tower's black outline and wished again that he was not leaving. He had liked India, finding it a playground for warriors, princes, rogues and adventurers. He had found wealth there, been commissioned there, fought in its hills and on its ancient battlements. He was leaving friends and lovers there, and more than one enemy in his grave, but for what? For Britain? Where no one waited for him and no adventurers rode from the hills and no tyrants lurked behind red battlements.

One of the wealthy passengers came down the steep steps from the quarterdeck with a woman on his arm. Like most of the *Calliope*'s passengers he was a civilian and was elegantly dressed in a long dark-green coat, white breeches and an old-fashioned tricorne. The woman on his arm was plump, dressed in gauzy white, fair-haired, and laughing. The two spoke a foreign language, one Sharpe did not know. German? Dutch? Swedish? Everything the foreign couple saw, from the lashed guns to the crates of hens to the first seasick passengers leaning over the rail, amused them. The man was explaining the ship to his companion. 'Boom!' he cried, pointing to one of the guns, and the woman laughed, then staggered as a gust of wind made the big ship lurch. She whooped in mock alarm and clung to the man's elbow as they staggered on forrard.

'Know who that is?' It was Braithwaite, Lord William Hale's secretary, who had sidled alongside Sharpe.

'No.' Sharpe was brusque, instinctively disliking anyone connected with Lord William.

'That was the Baron von Dornberg,' Braithwaite said, evidently expecting Sharpe to be impressed. The secretary watched the baron help his lady up to the forecastle where another gust of wind threatened to snatch her wide-brimmed hat.

'Never heard of him,' Sharpe said churlishly.

'He's a nabob.' Braithwaite spoke the word in awe, meaning that the baron was a man who had made himself fabulously rich in India and was now carrying his wealth back to Europe. Such a career was a gamble. A man either died in India or became wealthy. Most died. 'Are you carrying goods?' Braithwaite asked Sharpe.

'Goods?' Sharpe asked, wondering why the secretary was making such an effort to be pleasant to him.

'To sell,' Braithwaite said impatiently, as though Sharpe was being deliberately obtuse. 'I've got peacock feathers,' he went on, 'five crates! The plumes fetch a rare price in London. Milliners buy them. I'm Malachi Braithwaite, by the way.' He held out his hand. 'Lord William's confidential secretary.'

Sharpe reluctantly shook the offered hand.

'I never did send that letter,' Braithwaite said, smiling meaningfully. 'I told him I did, but I didn't.' Braithwaite leaned close to make these confidences. He was a few inches taller than Sharpe, but much thinner, and had a lugubrious face with quick eyes that never seemed to look at Sharpe for long before darting sideways, almost as though Braithwaite expected to be attacked at any second. 'His lordship will merely assume your colonel never received the letter.'

'Why didn't you send it?' Sharpe asked.

Braithwaite looked offended at Sharpe's curt tone. 'We're to be shipmates,' he explained earnestly, 'for how long? Three, four months? And I don't travel in the stern like his lordship, but have to sleep in the steerage, and lower steerage at that! Not even main-deck steerage.' He plainly resented that humiliation. The secretary was dressed as a gentleman, with a fashionable high stock and an elaborately tied cravat, but the cloth of his black coat was shiny, the cuffs were frayed and the collar of his shirt was darned. 'Why should I make unnecessary enemies, Mister Sharpe?' Braithwaite asked. 'If I scratch your back, then maybe you can do me a service.'

'Such as?'

Braithwaite shrugged. 'Who knows what eventuality might arise?' he asked airily, then turned to watch the Baron von Dornberg come back down the forecastle steps. 'They say he made a fortune in diamonds,' Braithwaite murmured to Sharpe, 'and his servant isn't expected to travel in steerage, but has a place in the great cabin.' He spat that last information, then composed his face and stepped forward to intercept the baron. 'Malachi Braithwaite, confidential secretary to Lord William Hale,' he introduced himself as he raised his hat, 'and most honoured to meet your lordship.'

'The honour and pleasure are entirely mine,' the Baron von Dornberg answered in excellent English, then returned Braithwaite's courtesy by removing his tricorne hat and making a low bow. Straightening, he looked at Sharpe and Sharpe found himself staring into a familiar face, though now that face was decorated with a big waxed moustache. He looked at the baron, and the baron looked astonished for a second, then recovered himself and winked at Sharpe.

Sharpe wanted to say something, but feared he would laugh aloud and so he simply offered the baron a stiff nod.

But von Dornberg would have none of Sharpe's formality. He spread his powerful arms and gave Sharpe a bear-like embrace. 'This is one of the bravest men in the British army,' he told his woman, then whispered in Sharpe's ear. 'Not a word, I beg you, not a pippy squeak.' He stepped back. 'May I name the Baroness von Dornberg? This is Mister Richard Sharpe, Mathilde, a friend and an enemy from a long time ago. Don't tell me you travel in steerage, Mister Sharpe?'

'I do, my lord.'

'I am shocked! The British do not know how to treat their heroes. But I do! You shall come and dine with us in the captain's cuddy. I shall insist on it!' He grinned at Sharpe, offered Mathilde his arm, inclined his head to Braithwaite and walked on.

'I thought you said you didn't know him!' Braithwaite said, aggrieved.

'I didn't recognize him with his hat on,' Sharpe said. He turned away, unable to resist a grin. The Baron von Dornberg was no baron, and Sharpe doubted he had traded for any diamonds, no matter how many he carried, for von Dornberg was a rogue. His true name was Anthony Pohlmann and he had once been a sergeant in the Hanoverian army before he deserted for the richer service of an Indian prince, and his talent for war had brought him ever swifter promotion until, for a time, he had led a Mahratta army that was feared throughout central India. Then, one hot day, his forces met a much smaller British army between two rivers at a village called Assaye, and there, in an afternoon of dusty heat and red-hot guns and bloody slaughter, Anthony Pohlmann's army had been shredded by sepoys and Highlanders. Pohlmann himself had vanished into the mystery of India, but now he was here on the *Calliope* as a celebrated passenger.

'How did you meet him?' Braithwaite demanded.

'Can't remember now,' Sharpe said vaguely. 'Somewhere or other. Can't really remember.' He turned to stare at the shore. The land was black now, punctured by sparks of firelight and outlined by a grey sky smeared with a city's smoke. He wished he was back there, but then he heard Pohlmann's loud voice and turned to see the German introducing his woman to Lady Grace Hale.

Sharpe stared at her ladyship. She was above him, on the quarterdeck, seemingly oblivious of the folk crowded on the main deck below. She offered Pohlmann a limp hand, inclined her head to the fair-haired woman and then, without a word, turned regally away. 'That is Lady Grace,' Braithwaite told Sharpe in an awed voice.

'Someone told me she was ill?' Sharpe suggested.

'Merely highly strung,' Braithwaite said defensively. 'Very fine-strung women are prone to fragility, I think, and her ladyship is fine-strung, very fine-strung indeed.' He spoke warmly, unable to take his eyes from Lady Grace, who stood watching the receding shore.

An hour later it was dark, India was gone and Sharpe sailed beneath the stars.

'The war is lost,' Captain Peculiar Cromwell declared, 'lost.' He made the statement in a harsh, flat voice, then frowned at the tablecloth. It was the *Calliope*'s third day out from Bombay and she was running before a gentle wind. She was, as Captain Chase had told Sharpe, a fast ship and the East India Company frigate had ordered Cromwell to shorten sail during the day because she was in danger of outrunning the slower ships. Cromwell had grumbled at the order, then had taken so much canvas from the yards that the *Calliope* now sailed at the convoy's rear.

Anthony Pohlmann had invited Sharpe to take supper in the cuddy where Captain Cromwell nightly presided over those wealthier passengers who had paid to travel in the luxurious stern cabins. The cuddy was in the poop, the highest part of the ship, just forward of the two roundhouse cabins that were the largest, most lavish and most expensive. Lord William Hale and the Baron von Dornberg occupied the roundhouse, while beneath them, on the main deck of the ship, the great cabin had been divided into four compartments for the ship's other wealthy passengers. One was a nabob and his wife who returned to their Cheshire home after twenty profitable years in India, another was a barrister who had been travelling after practising in the Supreme Court in Bengal, the third was a grey-haired major from the 96th who was retiring from the army, while the last cabin belonged to Pohlmann's servant who alone among the stern passengers was not invited to eat in the cuddy.

It was the Scottish major, a stocky man called Arthur Dalton, who frowned at Peculiar Cromwell's declaration that the war was lost. 'We've beaten the French in India,' the major protested, 'and their navy is on its knees.'

'If their navy is on its knees,' Cromwell growled, 'why are we sailing in convoy?' He stared belligerently at Dalton, waiting for an answer, but the major declined to take up the cudgels and Cromwell looked triumphantly about the cuddy. He was a tall and heavy-set man with black hair streaked badger white that he wore past his shoulders. He had a long jaw, big yellow teeth and belligerent eyes. His hands, large and powerful, were permanently blackened from the tarred rigging. His uniform coat was cut from a thick blue broadcloth and heavily crusted with brass buttons decorated with the Company's symbol which was supposed to show a lion holding a crown, but which everyone called 'the cat and the cheese'. Cromwell shook his ponderous head. 'The war is lost,' he declared again. 'Who rules the continent of Europe?'

'The French,' the barrister answered lazily, 'but it won't last. All flash and fire, the French, but there ain't no substance in them. No substance at all.'

'The whole coast of Europe,' Cromwell said icily, ignoring the lawyer's scorn, 'is in enemy hands.' He paused as a shuddering, grating and scraping noise echoed through the cabin. It punctuated the conversation sporadically and it had taken Sharpe a few moments to realize that it was the sound of the tiller ropes that ran two decks beneath him. Cromwell glanced up at a telltale compass that was mounted on the ceiling, then, deciding all was in order, resumed his argument. 'Europe, I tell you, is in enemy hands. The Americans, damn their insolence, are hostile, so our home ocean, sir, is an enemy sea. An enemy sea. We sail there because we have more ships, but ships cost money, and for how long will the British people pay for ships?'

'There are the Austrians,' Major Dalton suggested, 'the Russians?'

'The Austrians, sir!' Cromwell scoffed. 'No sooner do the Austrians field an army than it is destroyed! The Russians? Would you trust the Russians to free Europe when they cannot liberate themselves? Have you been to Russia, sir?'

'No,' Major Dalton admitted.

'A land of slaves,' Cromwell said derisively.

Lord William Hale might have been expected to contribute to this conversation for, as one of the six members of the East India Company's Board of Control, he must have been familiar with the thinking of the British government, but he was content to listen with a faintly amused smile, though he did raise an eyebrow at Cromwell's assertion that the Russians were a nation of slaves.

'The French, sir,' Cromwell went on hotly, 'face a rabble of enemies on their eastern frontiers, but none on their west. They can therefore concentrate their armies, sure in the knowledge that no British army will ever touch their shore.'

'Never?' the merchant, a solid man called Ebenezer Fairley, asked sarcastically.

Cromwell swung his heavy gaze on this new opponent. He contemplated Fairley for a while, then shook his head. 'The British, Fairley, do not like armies. They keep a small army. A small army can never defeat Napoleon. Ergo, Napoleon is safe. Ergo, the war is lost. Good God, man, they might already have invaded Britain!'

'I pray not,' Major Dalton said fervently.

'Their army was ready,' Cromwell boomed with a strange relish in this talk of British defeat, 'and all they needed was for their navy to command the channel.'

'Which it cannot do,' the barrister intervened quietly.

'And even if they did not invade this year,' Cromwell went on, ignoring the lawyer, 'then in time they will succeed in building a navy fit to defeat ours, and when that day comes Britain will have to seek peace. Britain will revert to its natural posture, and its natural posture is to be a small and insignificant island poised off a great continent.'

Lady Grace spoke for the first time. Sharpe had been pleased and surprised to see her at supper, for Captain Chase had suggested that she eschewed company, but she seemed content to be in the cuddy though so far she had taken as little part in the conversation as her husband. 'So we are doomed to defeat, Captain?' she suggested.

'No, ma'am,' Cromwell answered, softening his pugnacity now that he addressed a titled passenger. 'We are doomed to a realistic settlement of peace just as soon as the jackanapes politicians recognize what is plain in front of their faces.'

'Which is?' Fairley demanded.

'That the French are more powerful than us, of course!' Cromwell growled. 'And until we make peace the prudent man makes money, for we shall need money in a world run by the French. That is why India is important. We should suck the place dry before the French take it from us.' Cromwell snapped his fingers to instruct the stewards to remove the plates which had held a ragout of salted beef. Sharpe had eaten clumsily, finding the thick silverware unwieldy, and wishing he had dared take out his folding pocket knife which he used at meals when his betters were not present.

Mathilde, the Baroness von Dornberg, smiled gratefully as the captain replenished her wine glass. The baroness, who was almost certainly nothing of the sort, sat on Captain Cromwell's left while opposite her was Lady Grace Hale. Pohlmann, resplendent in a lace-fringed silk coat, sat next to Lady Grace while Lord William was to the left of Mathilde. Sharpe, as the least important person present, was at the lower end of the table.

The cuddy was an elegant room panelled with wood that had been painted pea-green and gold, while a brass chandelier, bereft of candles, hung from a beam alongside the wide skylight. If the room had not been gently rocking, sometimes shifting a wine glass on the table, Sharpe might have thought himself ashore.

He had said nothing all evening, content to gaze at Lady Grace who, white-faced and aloof, had ignored him since the moment he had been named to her. She had politely offered him a gloved hand, given him an expressionless glance, then turned away. Her husband had frowned at Sharpe's presence, then imitated his wife by pretending the ensign did not exist.

A dessert of oranges and burnt sugar was served. Pohlmann eagerly spooned the rich sauce into his mouth, then looked at Sharpe. 'You think the war is lost, Sharpe?'

'Me, sir?' Sharpe was startled at being addressed.

'You, Sharpe, yes, you,' Pohlmann said. 'Do you think the war is lost?'

Sharpe hesitated, wondering whether the wisest course was to say something harmless and let the conversation go on again without him, but he had been offended by Cromwell's defeatism. 'It certainly isn't over, my lord,' he said to Pohlmann.

Cromwell recognized the challenge. 'What do you mean by that, sir, eh? Explain yourself.'

'A fight ain't lost till it's finished, sir,' Sharpe said, 'and this one ain't done.'

'An ensign speaks,' Lord William murmured scornfully.

'You think a rat has a chance against a terrier?' Cromwell demanded, just as scornfully.

Pohlmann held up a hand to stop Sharpe from responding. 'I think Ensign Sharpe knows a good deal about fighting, Captain,' the German said. 'When I first met him he was a sergeant, and now he is a commissioned officer.' He paused, letting that statement cause its stir of surprise. 'What does it take for a sergeant to become an officer in the British army?'

'Damned luck,' Lord William said laconically.

'It takes an act of outstanding bravery,' Major Dalton observed quietly. He raised his wine glass to Sharpe. 'Honoured to make your acquaintance, Sharpe. I didn't place the name when we were introduced, but I recall you now. I'm honoured.'

Pohlmann, enjoying his mischief, toasted Sharpe with a sip of wine. 'So what was your act of outstanding bravery, Mister Sharpe?'

Sharpe reddened. Lady Grace was staring at him, the first notice she had taken of him since the company had sat to dinner.

'Well, Sharpe?' Captain Cromwell insisted.

Sharpe was tongue-tied, but was rescued by Dalton. 'He saved Sir Arthur Wellesley's life,' the major said quietly.

'How? Where?' Pohlmann demanded.

Sharpe caught the German's eye. 'At a place called Assaye, sir.'

'Assaye?' Pohlmann said, frowning slightly. It had been at Assaye that his army and his ambitions had been wrecked by Wellesley. 'Never heard of it,' he said lightly, leaning back in his chair.

'And you were first over the wall at Gawilghur, Sharpe,' the major said. 'Isn't that right?'

'Me and Captain Campbell were first across, sir. But it were lightly defended.'

'Is that where you fetched the scar, Sharpe?' the major enquired, and the whole table gazed at Sharpe. He looked uncomfortable, but there was no denying the power of his face, nor the suggestion of violence that was contained in the scar. 'It wasn't a bullet, was it?' the major insisted. 'No bullet makes that kind of scar.'

'It were a sword, sir,' Sharpe answered. 'Man called Dodd.' He looked at Pohlmann as he spoke and Pohlmann, who had once commanded and heartily disliked the renegade Dodd, half smiled.

'And does Mister Dodd still live?' the German asked.

'He's dead, sir,' Sharpe said flatly.

'Good.' Pohlmann raised his glass to Sharpe.

The major turned to Cromwell. 'Mister Sharpe is a very considerable soldier, Captain. Sir Arthur told me that if you find yourself in a bad fight then you can ask for no one better at your side.'

The news that General Wellesley had said any such thing pleased Sharpe, but Captain Cromwell had not been deflected from his argument and was now frowning at the ensign. 'You think,' the captain demanded, 'that the French can be defeated?'

'We're at war with them, sir,' Sharpe retorted, 'and you don't go to war unless you mean to win.'

'You go to war,' Lord William said icily, 'because small-minded men can see no alternative.'

'And if every war has a winner,' Cromwell said, 'it must by ineluctable logic also have a loser. If you want my advice, young man, leave the army before some politician has you killed in an ill-considered attack on France. Or, more likely, the French invade Britain and kill you along with the rest of the redcoats.'

The ladies withdrew a short while later and the men drank a glass of port, but the atmosphere was stiff and Pohlmann, plainly bored, excused himself from the company and gestured that Sharpe should follow him back to the starboard roundhouse cabin where Mathilde was now sprawled on a silk-covered sofa. Facing her on a matching sofa was an elderly man who was talking animatedly in German when Pohlmann entered, but who immediately stood and bowed his head respectfully. Pohlmann seemed surprised to see him and gestured the man to the door. 'I won't need you tonight,' he said in English.

'Very good, my lord,' the man, evidently Pohlmann's servant, answered in the same language, then, with a glance at Sharpe, left the cabin. Pohlmann peremptorily ordered Mathilde to take some air on the poop, then, when she had gone, he poured two large brandies and gave Sharpe a mischievous grin. 'My heart,' he said, clasping a dramatic hand to his breast, 'almost flopped over and died when I first saw you.'

'Would it matter if they knew who you were?' Sharpe asked.

Pohlmann grinned. 'How much credit will merchants give Sergeant Anthony Pohlmann, eh? But the Baron von Dornberg! Ah! They queue to give the baron credit. They trip over their fat feet to pour guineas into my purse.'

Sharpe looked about the big cabin that was furnished with two sofas, a sideboard, a low table, a harp and an enormous teak bed with ivory inlays on the headboard. 'But you must have done well in India,' Sharpe said.

'For a former sergeant, you mean?' Pohlmann laughed. 'I do have some loot, my dear Sharpe, but not as much as I would have liked and nowhere near as much as I lost at Assaye, but I cannot complain. If I am careful I shall not need to work again.' He looked at the hem of Sharpe's red coat where the jewels made small lumps in the threadbare cloth. 'I see you did well in India too, eh?'

Sharpe was aware that the fraying, thinning cloth of his coat was increasingly an unsafe place to hide the diamonds, emeralds and rubies, but he did not want to discuss them with Pohlmann so gestured at the harp instead. 'You play?'

'*Mein Gott,* no! Mathilde plays. Very badly, but I tell her it is wonderful.'

'She's your wife?'

'Am I a numbskull? A blockhead? Would I marry? Ha! No, Sharpe, she was whore to a rajah and when he tired of her I took her over. She is from Bavaria and wants babies, so she is a double fool, but she will keep my bed warm till I see home and then I shall find something younger. So you killed Dodd?'

'Not me, a friend killed him.'

'He deserved to die. A very horrid man.' Pohlmann shuddered. 'And you? You travel alone?'

'Yes.'

'In the rat hole, eh?' He looked at the hem of Sharpe's coat. 'You keep your jewels until you reach England and travel in steerage. But more important, my cautious friend, will you reveal who I am?'

'No,' Sharpe said with a smile. The last time he had seen Pohlmann the Hanoverian had been hiding in a peasant's hut in the village of Assaye. Sharpe could have arrested him and gained credit for capturing the commander of the beaten army, but he had always liked Pohlmann and so he had looked the other way and let the big man escape. 'But I reckon my silence is worth something, though,' Sharpe added.

'You want Mathilde every other Friday?' Pohlmann, assured that his secret was safe with Sharpe, could not hide his relief.

'A few invitations to supper, perhaps?'

Pohlmann was surprised by the modesty of the demand. 'You so like Captain Cromwell's company?'

'No.'

Pohlmann laughed. 'Lady Grace,' he said softly. 'I saw you, Sharpe, with your tongue lolling like a dog. You like them thin, do you?'

'I like her.'

'Her husband doesn't,' Pohlmann said. 'We hear them through the partition.' He jerked his thumb at the wall which divided the big roundhouse. The bulkhead was made from thin wooden panelling which could be struck down into the hold if only one passenger travelled in the lavish quarters. 'The captain's steward tells me their cabin is twice as big as this one and divided into two. He has one part and she the other. They are like, what do you say? Dog and cat?'

'Cat and dog,' Sharpe said.

'He barks and she hisses. Still, I wish you joy. The gods alone know what they must make of us. They probably think we are bull and cow. Shall we join Mathilde on deck?' Pohlmann took two cigars from the sideboard. 'The captain says we should not smoke on board. We must chew tobacco instead, but he can roger himself.' He lit the cigars, handed one to Sharpe and then led him out onto the quarterdeck and up the stairs to the poop deck. Mathilde was standing at the rail, staring down at a seaman who was lighting the lamp in the binnacle, the only light which was allowed on the ship after dark, while Lady Grace was at the taffrail, standing beneath the huge stern lantern that would not be lit on this voyage so long as there was a danger of the *Revenant* or another French ship seeing the convoy. 'Go and talk to her.' Pohlmann leered, digging an elbow into Sharpe's ribs.

'I've got nothing to say to her.'

'So you are not really brave after all,' Pohlmann said. 'I dare say you wouldn't think twice about charging a line of guns like those I had at Assaye, but a beautiful woman makes you shiver, yes?'

Lady Grace stood solitary and slim, wrapped in a cloak. A maid attended her, but the girl stood at the side of the deck as though she was nervous of her ladyship. Sharpe was also nervous. He wanted to talk to her, but he knew he would stumble over his words, so instead he stood beside Pohlmann and stared forrard past the great bulk of the sails to where the rest of the convoy was just visible in the gathering night. Far forrard, on the fo'c'sle, a violin was being played and a group of sailors danced the hornpipe.

'Were you really promoted from the ranks?' a cold voice asked and Sharpe turned to see that Lady Grace had appeared at his side.

He instinctively touched his forelock. For a moment he felt struck dumb and his tongue seemed stuck to his palate, but then he managed to nod. 'Yes, ma'am. Milady.'

She looked into his eyes and was tall enough not to need to look up. Her big eyes were dim in the twilight, but at supper Sharpe had seen they were green. 'It must be a difficult circumstance,' she said, still using a distant voice as though she was being reluctantly forced into this conversation.

'Yes, ma'am,' Sharpe said again, and knew he was sounding like a fool. He was tense, a muscle was twitching in his left leg, his mouth was dry and his belly felt sour, the same sensations that a man got when he was waiting for battle. 'Before it happened, ma'am,' he blurted out, wanting to say anything other than a monosyllabic response, 'I wanted it badly, but afterwards? I reckon I shouldn't have wanted it at all.'

Her face was expressionless. Beautiful, but

expressionless. She ignored Pohlmann and Mathilde, but just stared down at the quarterdeck before looking back to Sharpe. 'Who makes it most difficult,' she asked, 'the men or the officers?'

'Both, ma'am,' Sharpe said. He saw that the smoke from his cigar was annoying her and so he tossed it overboard. 'The men don't think you're a proper officer, and the other officers . . . well, it's like a working dog ending up on the hearth rug. The lap dogs don't like it.'

She half smiled at that. 'You must tell me,' she said in a voice which still suggested she was merely making polite conversation, 'just how you saved Arthur's life.' She paused, and Sharpe saw there was a nervous tic in her left eye that caused it to quiver every few seconds. 'He's a cousin,' she went on, 'but quite far removed. None of the family thought he'd amount to anything.'

It had taken Sharpe a second or two to realize that she meant Sir Arthur Wellesley, the cold man who had promoted Sharpe. 'He's the best general I've ever seen, ma'am,' Sharpe said.

'And you would know?' she asked sceptically.

'Yes, ma'am,' Sharpe said firmly, 'I would know.'

'So how did you save his life?' she insisted.

Sharpe hesitated. The aroma of her perfume was heady. He was about to say something vague of battle, confusion and blurred memory, but just then Lord William appeared on the quarterdeck and, without a word, Lady Grace turned to the poop stairs. Sharpe watched her go, conscious of his heart thumping against his ribs. He was still trembling. He had been dizzied by her.

Pohlmann was laughing softly. 'She likes you, Sharpe.'

'Don't be daft.'

'She is panting for you,' Pohlmann said.

'My dear Sharpe! My dear Sharpe!' It was the Scotsman, Major Dalton, climbing from the quarterdeck. 'There you are! You vanished! I would speak with you, Sharpe, if you can be kind enough to spare me a few moments. Like you, Sharpe, I was at Assaye, but I'm still utterly confused as to what happened there. We must talk, indeed we must. My dear baron, baroness' – he took off his hat and bowed – 'my compliments, and perhaps you will forgive two soldiers reminiscing?'

'I will forgive you, Major,' Pohlmann said expansively, 'but I will also leave you, for I know nothing of soldiering, nothing! Your conversation would be one long mystery to me. Come, my *Liebchen*, come.'

So Sharpe talked of battle, and the ship trembled to the sea, and the tropical darkness fell.

'Number four gun!' Lieutenant Tufnell, the *Calliope*'s first officer, shouted. 'Fire!'

The eighteen-pounder leaped back, jerking to a halt as its breeching rope took the vast strain of the weapon's recoil. Scraps of paint flew from the taut hemp, for Captain Cromwell was insistent that the gun tackles, like every other piece of equipment on deck, were painted white. It was for that reason that only one gun was being fired, for Cromwell did not want to disturb the other thirty-one cannons that had polished barrels and freshly painted tackle, so each gun crew, half made up of the ship's crew and half of passengers, was taking it in turn to fire number four gun. The eighteen-pounder, its muzzle blackened by powder, hissed as the barrel was sponged out. A great cloud of smoke drifted in the wind to keep the ship company.

'Shot fell short, sir!' Binns, the young officer, piped from the poop where, equipped with a telescope, he watched the fall of shot. The *Chatham Castle*, another ship of the convoy, was periodically loosing empty casks in its wake to serve as targets for the *Calliope*'s gun.

It was the turn of number five gun's crew to fire. The seaman in charge was a wizened man with long grey hair that he wore tied in a great bun into which he had stuck a marlin spike. 'You' – he pointed at Malachi Braithwaite who, to his great displeasure, was expected to serve on a gun crew despite being private secretary to a peer – 'shove two of them black bags down the gun when I gives the word. Him' – he pointed at a lascar seaman – 'rams it and you' – he peered at Braithwaite again – 'puts the shot in and the blackie rams that as well and none of you landlubbers gets in his way, and you' – he looked at Sharpe – 'aims the piece.'

'I thought that was your job,' Sharpe said.

'I'm half blind, sir.' The seaman offered Sharpe a toothless grin then turned on the other three passengers. 'The rest of you,' he said, 'helps the other blackies haul the gun forrard on those two lines there, and once you've done that you stand out the bleeding way and cover your ears. If it comes to a fight the best thing you can do is fall to your knees and pray to the Almighty that we surrender. You'll fire the gun, sir?' he asked Sharpe. 'And you knows as to stand to one side unless you want to be buried at sea. Bag of reeds here, sir, lanyard there, sir, and it's best to fire on the uproll if you don't want to make us look like lubberly fools. You ain't going to hit nothing, sir, because no one ever does. We only practise because the Company says we must, but we ain't never fired a gun in anger and I hopes and prays we never will.'

The cannon was equipped with a flintlock, just like a musket, which fired the powder packed inside a hollow reed which was inserted in the touch-hole and so carried the flame down to the main charge. Once the gun was loaded all Sharpe had to do was aim it, stand aside, and jerk the lanyard which triggered the lock.

Braithwaite and the lascar put the powder and shot into the barrel, the lascar rammed it down, Sharpe pushed a sharpened wire through the touch-hole to pierce the canvas powder bag, then slid the reed into place. The other crew members clumsily hauled the gun until its barrel protruded through the main deck's gunwale. There were handspikes available, great club-like wooden levers that could be used to turn the gun left or right, but none of the crews used them. They were not seriously trying to aim the gun, merely going through the obligatory motions of practice so that the logbook could confirm that the Company regulations had been fulfilled.

'There's your target!' Captain Cromwell called and Sharpe, standing on the gun carriage, saw an impossibly small cask bobbing on the distant waves. He had no idea what the range was, and all he could do was wait until the cask floated into line then pause until a wave rolled the ship upwards when he skipped smartly aside and jerked the lanyard. The flintlock snapped forward and a small jet of fire whipped up from the touch-hole, then the gun hammered back on its small wheels and its smoke billowed halfway up the mainsail as the powder flame licked and curled in the pungent white cloud. The big breeching rope quivered, scattering more flecks of paint, and Mister Binns called excitedly from the poop, 'A hit, sir, a hit! A hit! Plumb, sir! A hit!'

'We heard you the first time, Mister Binns,' Cromwell growled.

'But it's a hit, sir!' Binns protested, thinking that no one believed him.

'Up to the main cap!' Cromwell snapped at Binns. 'I told you to be quiet. If you cannot learn to curb your tongue, boy, then go and shriek at the clouds. Up!' He pointed to the very top of the mainmast. 'And you will stay there until I can abide your malodorous presence again.'

Mathilde was applauding enthusiastically from the quarterdeck. Lady Grace was also there and Sharpe had been acutely aware of her presence as he aimed the gun. 'That was bleeding luck,' the old seaman said.

'Pure luck,' Sharpe agreed.

'And you've cost the captain ten guineas,' the old man chuckled.

'I have?'

'He has a wager with Mister Tufnell that no one would ever hit the target.'

'I thought gambling was forbidden on board.'

'There's lots that's forbidden, sir, but that don't mean it don't happen.'

Sharpe's ears were ringing from the terrible sound of the gun as he stepped away from the smoking weapon. Tufnell, the first lieutenant, insisted on shaking his hand and refused to countenance Sharpe's insistence that the shot had been pure luck, then Tufnell stepped aside for Captain Cromwell had come down from the quarterdeck and was advancing on Sharpe. 'Have you fired a cannon before?' the captain enquired fiercely.

'No, sir.'

Cromwell peered up into the rigging, then looked for his first officer. 'Mister Tufnell!'

'Sir?'

'A broken horse! There, on the main topsail!' Cromwell pointed. Sharpe followed the captain's finger and saw that one of the footropes that the topmen would stand on when they were furling the sail had parted. 'I will not command a ragged ship, Mister Tufnell,' Cromwell snarled. 'This ain't a Thames hay barge, Mister Tufnell, but an Indiaman! Have it spliced, man, have it spliced!'

Tufnell sent two seamen aloft to mend the broken

line, while Cromwell paused to glower at the next crew firing the gun. The cannon recoiled, the smoke blossomed, and the ball skipped across the waves a good hundred yards from the bobbing cask.

'A miss!' Binns shouted from the top of the mainmast.

'I have an eye for an irregularity,' Cromwell said in his harsh, low voice, 'as I've no doubt you do, Mister Sharpe. You see a hundred men on parade and doubtless your eye goes to the one sloven with a dirty musket. Am I right?'

'I hope so, sir.'

'A broken horse can kill a man. It can tumble him to the deck, putting misery into a mother's heart. Her son put his foot down and there was nothing beneath him but void. Do you want your mother to have a broken heart, Mister Sharpe?'

Sharpe decided this was no time to explain that he had long been orphaned. 'No, sir.'

Cromwell glared around the main deck which was crowded with the men who formed the gun crews. 'What is it that you notice about these men, Mister Sharpe?'

'Notice, sir?'

'They are in shirtsleeves, Mister Sharpe. All except you and me are in shirtsleeves. I keep my coat on, Sharpe, because I am captain of this ship and it is meet and right that a captain should appear formally dressed before his crew. But why, I ask myself, does Mister Sharpe keep on his wool jacket on a hot day? Do you believe you are captain of this scow?'

'I just feel the cold, sir,' Sharpe lied.

'Cold?' Cromwell sneered. He put his right foot on a crack between the deck planks and, when he lifted the shoe, a string of melting tar adhered to his sole. 'You are not cold, Mister Sharpe, you are sweating.

Sweating! So come with me, Mister Sharpe.' The captain turned and led Sharpe up to the quarterdeck. The passengers watching the gunnery made way for the two men and Sharpe was suddenly conscious of Lady Grace's perfume, then he followed Cromwell down the companionway into the great cabin where the captain had his quarters. Cromwell unlocked his door, pushed it open and gestured that Sharpe should go inside. 'My home,' the captain grunted.

Sharpe had expected that the captain would have one of the stern cabins with their big wide windows, but it was more profitable to sell such accommodation to passengers and Cromwell was content with a smaller cabin on the larboard side. It was still a comfortable home. A bunk bed was built into a wall of bookshelves while a table, hinged to the bulkhead, was smothered in unrolled charts that were weighted down with three lanterns and a pair of long-barrelled pistols. The daylight streamed in through an opened porthole, above which the sea's reflection rippled on the white painted ceiling. Cromwell unlocked a small cupboard to reveal a barometer and, beside it, what appeared to be a fat pocket watch hanging from a hook. 'Three hundred and twenty-nine guineas,' Cromwell told Sharpe, tapping the timepiece.

'I've never owned a watch,' Sharpe said.

'It is not a watch, Mister Sharpe,' Cromwell said in disgust, 'but a chronometer. A marvel of science. Between here and Britain I doubt it will lose more than two seconds. It is that machine, Mister Sharpe, that tells us where we are.' He blew a fleck of dust from the chronometer's face, tapped the barometer, then carefully closed and locked the cupboard. 'I keep my treasures safe, Mister Sharpe. You, on the other hand, flaunt yours.'

Sharpe said nothing, and the captain waved at the

cabin's only chair. 'Sit down, Mister Sharpe. Do you wonder about my name?'

Sharpe sat uneasily. 'Your name?' He shrugged. 'It's unusual, sir.'

'It is peculiar,' Peculiar Cromwell said, then gave a harsh laugh that betrayed no amusement. 'My people, Mister Sharpe, were fervent Christians and they named me from the Bible. "The Lord has chosen thee to be a peculiar people unto himself," the book of Deuteronomy, chapter fourteen, verse two. It is not easy, Mister Sharpe, living with such a name. It invites ridicule. In its time that name has made me a laughing stock!' He said these last words with extraordinary force, as though resenting all the folk who had ever mocked him, but Sharpe, perched on the edge of the chair, could not imagine anyone mocking the harsh-voiced, heavy-faced Peculiar Cromwell.

Cromwell sat on his bunk bed, placed his elbows on the charts and fixed his eyes on Sharpe. 'I was put aside for God, Mister Sharpe, and it makes for a lonely life. I was denied a proper education. Other men go to Oxford or Cambridge, they are immersed in knowledge, but I was sent to sea for my parents believed I would be beyond earthly temptation if I was far from any shore. But I taught myself, Mister Sharpe. I learned from books' – he waved at the shelves – 'and discovered that I am well named. I am peculiar, Mister Sharpe, in my opinions, apprehensions and conclusions.' He shook his head sadly, rippling his long hair which rested on the shoulders of his heavy blue coat. 'All around me I espy educated men, rational men, conventional men and, above all, sociable men, but I have discovered that no such creature ever did a great thing. It is among the lonely, Mister Sharpe, that true greatness occurs.' He scowled, as though that burden was almost too heavy to bear. 'You too, I think, are a peculiar man,' Cromwell went on. 'You have been plucked by destiny from your natural place among the dregs of society and have been translated into an officer. And that' – he leaned forward and jabbed a finger at Sharpe – 'must make for loneliness.'

'I have never lacked friends,' Sharpe said, evading the embarrassing conversation.

'You trust yourself, Mister Sharpe,' Cromwell boomed, ignoring Sharpe's words, 'as I have learned to trust myself in the knowledge that no one else can be trusted. We have been set aside, you and I, as lonely men doomed to watch the traffic of those who are not peculiar. But today, Mister Sharpe, I am going to insist that you put your mistrust aside. I shall demand that you trust me.'

'In what, sir?'

Cromwell paused as the tiller ropes creaked and groaned beneath him, then glanced up at a telltale compass fixed above the bunk. 'A ship is a small world, Mister Sharpe,' he said, 'and I am appointed the ruler of that world. Upon this vessel I am lord of all, and the power of life and death is granted to me, but I do not crave such power. What I crave, Mister Sharpe, is order. Order!' He slapped a hand on the charts. 'And I will not abide thievery on my ship!'

Sharpe sat up in indignation. 'Thievery! Are you . . .'

'No!' Cromwell interrupted him. 'Of course I am not accusing you. But there will be thievery, Mister Sharpe, if you continue to flaunt your wealth.'

Sharpe smiled. 'I'm an ensign, sir, lowest of the low. You said yourself I'd been plucked out of my place, and you know there's no money down there. I'm not wealthy.'

'Then what, Mister Sharpe, is sewn into the seams of your garment?' Cromwell asked.

Sharpe said nothing. A king's ransom was sewn into

the hems of his coat, the tops of his boots and the waistband of his trousers, and the jewels in his coat were showing because of the frailty of the red-dyed cloth.

'Sailors are keen-eyed fellows, Mister Sharpe,' Cromwell growled. He looked irritated when the gun fired from the main deck, as though the sound had interrupted his thinking. 'Sailors have to be keen-eyed,' he continued, 'and mine are clever enough to know that a soldier hides his plunder on his person, and they're keen-eyed enough to note that Mister Sharpe does not take off his coat, and one night, Mister Sharpe, when you go forrard to the heads, or when you take the air on the deck, a keen-eyed sailor will come at you from behind. A belaying pin? A strike at your skull? A splash in the night? Who would miss you?' He smiled, revealing long yellow teeth, then touched the hilt of one of the pistols on the table. 'If I were to shoot you now, strip your body and then push you through the scuttle, who would dare contradict my story that you had attacked me?'

Sharpe said nothing.

Cromwell's hand stayed on the pistol. 'You have a chest in your cabin?'

'Yes, sir.'

'But you don't trust my sailors. You know they will break through its lock in a matter of seconds.'

'They would too,' Sharpe said.

'But they will not dare break into my chest!' Cromwell declared, gesturing beneath the table where a vast iron-bound teak chest stood. 'I want you to yield me your treasure now, Mister Sharpe, and I will sign for it and I will store it, and when we reach our destination you will be given it back. It is a normal procedure.' He at last removed his hand from the gun and reached onto the bookshelf, taking down a small box that was filled with papers. 'I have some money belonging to Lord William Hale in that chest, see?' He handed one of the papers to Sharpe who saw that it acknowledged receipt of one hundred and seventy guineas in native specie. The paper had been signed by Peculiar Cromwell and, on Lord William's behalf, by Malachi Braithwaite, MA Oxon. 'I have possessions of Major Dalton,' Cromwell said, producing another piece of paper, 'and jewels belonging to the Baron von Dornberg.' He showed Sharpe that receipt. 'And more jewels belonging to Mister Fazackerly.' Fazackerly was the barrister. 'This' – Cromwell kicked the chest – 'is the safest place on the ship, and if one of my passengers is carrying valuables then I want those valuables out of temptation's way. Do I make myself plain, Mister Sharpe?'

'Yes, sir.'

'But you are thinking that you do not trust me?'

'No, sir,' Sharpe said, who was thinking just that.

'I told you,' Cromwell growled, 'it is a normal procedure. You entrust your valuables to me and I, as a captain in the service of the East India Company, give you a receipt. If I were to lose the valuables, Mister Sharpe, then the Company would reimburse you. The only way you can lose them is if the ship sinks or if it is taken by enemy action, in which case you must have recourse to your insurers.' Cromwell half smiled, knowing full well that Sharpe's treasure would not be insured.

Sharpe still said nothing.

'Thus far, Mister Sharpe,' Cromwell said in a low voice, 'I have requested you to comply with my wishes. If needs be, I can insist.'

'No need to insist, sir,' Sharpe said, for, in truth, Cromwell was right in suggesting that every sharp-eyed sailor in the ship would note the badly hidden jewels. Each and every day Sharpe was aware of the stones, and they were a burden to him and would stay a burden until he could sell them in London, and that burden would be lifted if he yielded the stones into the Company's keeping. Besides, he had been reassured by the fact that Pohlmann had entrusted so many jewels to the captain's keeping. If Pohlmann, who was nobody's fool, trusted Cromwell then Sharpe surely could.

Cromwell gave him a small pair of scissors and Sharpe cut the hem of his coat. He did not reveal the stones in his waistband, nor in his boots, for they were not obvious to even a searching glance, but he did place on the table a growing heap of rubies, diamonds and emeralds that he stripped from the red coat's seams.

Cromwell separated the stones into three piles, then weighed each pile on a small and delicate balance. He carefully noted the results, locked the jewels away, then gave Sharpe a receipt which both he and Sharpe had signed. 'I thank you, Mister Sharpe,' Cromwell said gravely, 'for you have made my mind easier. The purser will find a seaman who can sew up your coat,' he added, standing.

Sharpe also stood, ducking his head under the low beams. 'Thank you, sir.'

'I've no doubt I'll see you at dinner soon. The baron seems fond of your company. You know him well?'

'I met him once or twice in India, sir.'

'He seems a strange man, not that I know him at all. But an aristocrat? Dirtying his hands with trade?' Cromwell shuddered. 'I suppose they do things differently in Hanover.'

'I imagine they do, sir.'

'Thank you, Mister Sharpe.' Cromwell tucked his keys into a pocket and nodded to indicate that Sharpe could leave.

Major Dalton was on the quarterdeck, revelling in the gun practice. 'No one's matched your marksmanship,

Sharpe,' the Scotsman said. 'I'm proud of you! Upholding the honour of the army.'

Lady Grace gave Sharpe one of her disinterested glances, then turned back to look at the horizon. 'Tell me, sir,' Sharpe said to the major, 'would you trust an East India captain?'

'If you can't trust such a man, Sharpe, then the world is coming to an end.'

'We wouldn't want that, sir, would we?'

Sharpe gazed at Lady Grace. She stood beside her husband, lightly touching his arm to keep her balance on the swaying deck. Dog and cat, he thought.

And he felt like being scratched.

CHAPTER 3

The boredom on the ship was palpable.

Some passengers read, but Sharpe, who still found reading difficult, obtained no relief from the few books he borrowed from Major Dalton, who spent his time making notes for a memoir he planned to write about the war against the Mahrattas. 'I doubt anyone will read it, Sharpe,' the major admitted modestly, 'but it would be a pity if the army's successes were not recorded. You would oblige me with your best recollections?'

Some of the men passed the time by practising with small arms or fighting mock duels with sword and sabres up and down the main deck until they were running with sweat. During the second week of the voyage there was a sudden enthusiasm for target practice, using the ship's heavy sea-service muskets to fire at empty bottles hurled into the waves, but after five days Captain Cromwell declared that the fusillades were depleting the *Calliope*'s powder stores and the pastime ceased. Later that week a seaman claimed to have spied a mermaid at dawn and for a day or two the passengers hung on the rails vainly searching the empty sea for another glimpse. Lord William scornfully denied the existence of such creatures, but Major Dalton had seen one when he was a boy. 'It was exhibited in Edinburgh,' he told Sharpe, 'after the poor creature had washed ashore on Inchkeith Rock. It was a very dark room, I remember, and she was somewhat hairy. Bedraggled, really. She was very ill-smelling, but I recall her tail and seem to remember she was very well endowed above.' He blushed. 'Poor lass, she was dead as a bucket.'

A strange sail was sighted one morning and there was an hour's excitement as the gun crews mustered, the convoy clumsily closed up and the Company frigate set her studdingsails to investigate the stranger, which turned out to be an Arab dhow on course for Cochin and certainly no threat to the big Indiamen.

The passengers in the stern, the rich folk who inhabited the roundhouse and the great cabin, played whist. Another group played the game in steerage, but Sharpe had never learned to play and, besides, was not tempted to wager. He was aware that large sums were being won and lost, and though it was forbidden by the Company rules, Captain Cromwell made no objection. Indeed he sometimes played a hand himself. 'He wins,' Pohlmann told Sharpe, 'he always wins.'

'And you lose?'

'A little.' Pohlmann shrugged as though it did not matter.

Pohlmann was sitting on one of the lashed guns. He often came and talked with Sharpe, usually about Assaye where he had suffered such a great defeat. 'Your William Dodd,' he told Sharpe, 'claimed that Sir Arthur was a cautious general. He isn't.' He always called Dodd 'your William Dodd', as though the renegade redcoat had been a colleague of Sharpe's.

'Wellesley's bull-headed,' Sharpe said admiringly. 'He sees a chance and snatches it.'

'And he's gone home to England?'

'Sailed last year,' Sharpe said. Sir Arthur, as befitted his rank, had sailed on the *Trident*, Admiral Rainier's flagship, and was probably in Britain by now.

'He will be bored at home,' Pohlmann said.

'Bored? Why?'

'Because our dour Captain Cromwell is right. Britain cannot fight France in Europe. She can fight her at the ends of the world, but not in Europe. The French army, my dear Sharpe, is a horde. It is not like your army. It doesn't depend on jailbirds, failures and drunkards, but is conscripted. It is therefore huge.'

Sharpe grinned. 'The jailbirds, failures and drunkards cooked your goose.'

'So they did,' Pohlmann acknowledged without taking offence, 'but they cannot stand against the vast armies of France. No one can. Not now. And when the French decide to build a proper navy, my friend, then you will see the world dance to their tunes.'

'And you?' Sharpe asked. 'Where will you be dancing?'

'Hanover?' Pohlmann suggested. 'I shall buy a big house, fill it with women and watch the world from my windows. Or perhaps I shall live in France. The women are more beautiful there and I have learned one thing in my life, Sharpe, and that is that women do like money. Why do you think Lady Grace married Lord William?' He jerked his head towards the quarterdeck where Lady Grace, accompanied by her maid, walked up and down. 'How goes your campaign with the lady?'

'It doesn't,' Sharpe grunted, 'and there isn't a campaign.'

Pohlmann laughed. 'Then why do you accept my invitations to supper?'

The truth, and Sharpe knew it, was that he was obsessed with the Lady Grace. From the moment he woke in the morning until he finally slept he thought of little but her. She seemed untouchable, unemotional, unapproachable, and that only made his obsession worse. She had spoken to him once, then never again, and when Sharpe did meet her at suppertime in the captain's cuddy and tried to engage her in conversation she turned away as though his presence offended her.

Sharpe thought of her constantly, and constantly watched for her, though he took good care not to show his obsession. But it was there, gnawing at him, filling the tedious hours as the *Calliope* thumped her way across the Indian Ocean. The winds stayed kind and each day the first officer, Lieutenant Tufnell, reported on the convoy's progress: seventy-two miles, sixty-eight miles, seventy miles, always about the same distance.

The weather was fine and dry, yet even so the ship seemed to be rotting with damp below the decks. Even in the tropic winds that blew the convoy southwestwards some water slopped through the closed lower gunports, and the lower-deck steerage where Sharpe slept was never dry; his blankets were damp, the timbers of the ship were dank, indeed the whole *Calliope*, wherever the sun did not shine, was weeping with water, stinking and decaying, fungus-ridden and rat-infested. Seamen constantly manned the ship's four pumps and the water slopped out of the elm tubes into gutters on the lower deck which led the stinking bilge water overboard, but however much they pumped, more always needed to be sucked out of the hull.

The goats had an infection and most died in the first fortnight so there was no fresh milk for the steerage passengers. The fresh food was soon used up, and what was left was salted, tough, rancid and monotonous. The water was foul, discoloured and stank, useful only for making strong tea, and though Sharpe's filtering machine removed some of the impurities, it did nothing to improve the taste, and after two weeks the filter was so clogged with brown muck that he hurled the machine into the ocean. He drank arrack and sour beer or, in Captain Cromwell's cuddy, the wine which was little better than vinegar.

Breakfast was at eight every morning. The steerage

passengers were divided into groups of ten and the men took it in turn to fetch each mess a cauldron of burgoo from the galley in the forecastle. The burgoo was a mixture of oatmeal and scraps of beef fat that had simmered all night on the galley stove. Dinner was at midday and was another burgoo, though this sometimes had larger scraps of meat or fibrous pieces of dried fish floating in the burned and lumpy oatmeal. On Sundays there was salt fish and ship's biscuits that were as hard as stone, yet even so were infested with weevils that needed to be tapped out. The biscuits had to be chewed endlessly so that it was like masticating a dried brick that was occasionally enlivened by the juice of an insect that had escaped the tapping. Tea was served at four, but only to the passengers who travelled in the stern of the ship, while the steerage passengers had to wait for supper, which was more dried fish, biscuits and a hard cheese in which red worms made miniature tunnels. 'Human beings should not be expected to eat such things,' Malachi Braithwaite said, shuddering after one particularly evil supper. He had joined Sharpe on the main deck to watch the sun set in red-gold splendour.

'You ate them on the way out, didn't you?' Sharpe asked.

'I travelled out as a private secretary to a London merchant,' Braithwaite said grandly, 'and he accommodated me in the great cabin and fed me at his own expense. I told his lordship as much, but he refuses the expense.' He sounded hurt. Braithwaite was a proud man, but poor, and very aware of any insults to his self-esteem. He spent his afternoons in the roundhouse where, he told Sharpe, Lord William was compiling a report for the Board of Control. The report would suggest the future governance of India and Braithwaite enjoyed the work, but late every afternoon he was dismissed back to the lower deck and his gnawing misery. He was ashamed of being made to travel steerage, he hated being one of the gun crews and he detested fetching the mess cauldrons, believing that chore put him in the place of a menial servant, no better than Lord William's valet or Lady Grace's maid. 'I am a secretary,' he protested once to Sharpe. 'I was at Oxford!'

'How did you become Lord William's secretary?' Sharpe now asked him.

Braithwaite thought about the question as though a trap lay within it, then decided it was safe to answer. 'His original secretary died in Calcutta. Of snake-bite, I believe, and his lordship was kind enough to offer me the position.'

'Now you regret taking it?'

'Indeed I do not!' Braithwaite said sharply. 'His lordship is a prominent man. He is intimate with the Prime Minister.' This was confided in an admiring tone. 'Indeed the report we work on will not just be for the Board of Control, but will go directly to Pitt himself! Much depends on his lordship's conclusions. Maybe even a cabinet post? His lordship could well become Foreign Secretary within a year or two, and what would that make me?'

'An overworked secretary,' Sharpe said.

'But I will have influence,' Braithwaite insisted earnestly, 'and his lordship will have one of the grandest houses in London. His wife will preside over a salon of wit and vast influence.'

'If she'll ever talk to anyone,' Sharpe commented drily. 'She don't say a word to me.'

'Of course she doesn't,' Braithwaite said crossly. 'She is accustomed to nothing but the highest discourse.' The secretary looked to the quarterdeck, but if he hoped to see Lady Grace he was disappointed. 'She is an angel, Sharpe,' he blurted out. 'One of the best women I have ever had the privilege of meeting. And with a mind to match! I have a degree from Oxford, Mister Sharpe, yet even I cannot match her ladyship's knowledge of the Georgics.'

Whatever the hell they were, Sharpe thought. 'She is a rare-looking woman,' he said mildly, wondering whether that would provoke Braithwaite into another burst of candour.

It did. 'Rare-looking?' Braithwaite asked sarcastically. 'She is a beauty, Mister Sharpe, the very quintessence of feminine virtue, looks and intelligence.'

Sharpe laughed. 'You're in love with her, Braithwaite.'

The secretary gave Sharpe a withering look. 'If you were not a soldier with a reputation for savagery, Sharpe, I should deem that statement impertinent.'

'I might be the savage,' Sharpe said, rubbing salt into the secretary's wounded pride, 'but I'm the one who had supper with her tonight.'

Though Lady Grace had neither spoken with him that night, nor even appeared to notice his presence in the cuddy where the food was scarcely better than the slop provided in steerage. The richer passengers were served the dead goats that were stewed and served in a vinegar sauce and Captain Cromwell was particularly fond of peas and pork, though the peas were dried to the consistency of bullets and the meat was salted to the texture of ancient leather. There was a suet pudding most nights, then port or brandy, coffee, cigars and whist. Eggs and coffee were served for breakfast, luxuries that never appeared in steerage, but Sharpe was not invited to share breakfast with the privileged folk.

On the nights when he ate in steerage Sharpe would go on deck afterwards and watch the sailors dancing to a four-man orchestra of two violins, a flute and a drummer who beat his hands on the end of a half-barrel. One night there was a sudden and violent downpour of rain that drummed on the sails. Sharpe stood bare-chested, head back and mouth agape to drink the clean water, but most of the rain which fell on the ship seemed to find its way between decks that became ever more rank. Everything seemed to rot, rust or grow fungus. On Sundays the purser held divine service and the four-man orchestra played while the passengers, the richer standing on the quarterdeck and the less privileged beneath them on the main deck, sang 'Awake, my soul, and with the sun thy daily stage of duty run'. Major Dalton sang gustily, beating time with his hand. Pohlmann seemed amused by the services, while Lord William and his wife, contravening the captain's orders, did not bother to attend. When the hymn was done the purser read a toneless prayer that Sharpe and those other passengers who were paying attention found alarming. 'O most glorious and gracious Lord God, who dwellest in heaven, but beholdest all things below; Look down, we beseech thee, and hear us, calling out of the depths of misery and out of the jaws of this death which is ready now to swallow us up. Save, Lord, or else we perish.'

Yet they did not perish and the sea and the miles slipped endlessly by, untouched by any speck of land or hostile sail. At noon the officers solemnly sighted the sun with their sextants, then hurried to Captain Cromwell's cabin to work out the mathematics, though, in the middle of the third week, a day at last came when the sky was so thick with cloud that no sight could be taken. Captain Cromwell was overheard to remark that the *Calliope* was in for a blow, and all day he strode about the quarterdeck with a look of grim pleasure. The wind rose slowly but surely, making the passengers stagger on the canted deck and hold onto their hats.

Many of those who had overcome their early seasickness now succumbed again, and the spray breaking on the ship's bluff bows rattled on the sails as it flew down the deck. Late in the afternoon it began to rain so heavily that grey veils hid all but the closest vessels of the convoy.

Sharpe was again invited to be Pohlmann's guest for supper and, when he went below to change into his least dirty shirt and to pull on his coat that had been neatly mended by a foretop man, he found the steerage slopping with water and vomit. Children cried, a tethered dog yelped. Braithwaite was draped over a gun, heaving dry. Every time the ship dipped to the wind water forced its way through the locked gunports and rippled across the deck, and when she buried her bows into the sea a veritable flood came through the hawseholes and rolled down the sopping planks.

Water cascaded down the companionway as Sharpe climbed back to the remains of the daylight. He staggered across the quarterdeck where six men hung onto the wheel and banged through the poop door where he was thrown across the small hallway before cannoning back into the cuddy where only the captain, Major Dalton, Pohlmann, Mathilde and Lord William and Lady Grace waited. The other three passengers were all either seasick or were eating in their own cabins.

'You're the baron's guest again?' Cromwell asked pointedly.

'You surely do not mind Mister Sharpe being my guest?' Pohlmann enquired hotly.

'He eats from your purse, Baron, not mine,' Cromwell growled, then waved Sharpe into his usual chair. 'For God's sake, sit, Mister Sharpe.' He held up a massive hand, then paused as the ship rolled. The bulkheads shifted alarmingly and the cutlery slid across the table.

'May the good Lord bless these victuals,' Cromwell said, 'and make us grateful for their sustenance, in the name of the Lord, amen.'

'Amen,' Lady Grace said distantly. Her husband looked pale and gripped the table's edge as if it might alleviate the boat's quick motion. Lady Grace, on the other hand, was quite unaffected by the weather. She wore a red dress, cut low, and had a string of pearls around her slim neck. Her dark hair was piled at her crown and held in place with pearl-encrusted pins.

Fiddles had been placed about the table so that the knives, forks, spoons, glasses, plates and cruets would not slide off, but the lurching of the ship made the meal a perilous experience. Cromwell's steward served a thick soup first. 'Fresh fish!' Cromwell boasted. 'All caught this morning. I have no idea what kind of fish they were, but no one has yet died of an unknown fish on my ship. They've died of other things, of course.' The captain eagerly spooned the bony gruel into his mouth, expertly holding the plate so that the contents did not spill as the ship tilted. 'Men fall from the upper works, folk die of fever and I've even had a passenger kill herself for unrequited love, but I've never had one die of fish poison.'

'Unrequited love?' Pohlmann asked, amused.

'It happens, Baron, it happens,' Cromwell said with relish. 'It is a well-attested phenomenon that a sea voyage spurs the baser instincts. You will forgive me mentioning the matter, milady,' he added hastily to Lady Grace, who ignored his coarseness.

Lord William took one taste of the fish soup and turned away, leaving his plate to slop itself empty on the table. Lady Grace managed a few spoonfuls, but then, disliking the taste, pushed the malodorous mess away. The major ate heartily, Pohlmann and Mathilde greedily and Sharpe warily, not wanting to disgrace himself with a display of ill manners in front of Lady Grace. Fish bones were caught in his teeth and he tried to extricate them subtly, for he had seen Lady Grace shudder whenever Pohlmann spat them onto the table.

'Cold beef and rice next,' the captain announced, as though he were offering a treat. 'So tell me, Baron, how did you make your fortune? You traded, is that right?'

'I traded, Captain, yes.'

Lady Grace looked up sharply, frowned, then pretended the conversation did not interest her. The wine decanters rattled in their metal cage. The whole ship creaked, groaned and shuddered whenever a stronger wave exploded at her bows.

'In England,' Cromwell said pointedly, 'the aristocracy do not trade. They think it beneath them.'

'English lords have land,' Pohlmann said, 'but my family lost its estates a hundred years ago, and when one does not possess land one must work for a living.'

'Doing what, pray?' Cromwell demanded. His long wet hair lay lank on his shoulders.

'I buy, I sell,' Pohlmann said, evidently unworried by the captain's inquisition.

'And successfully, too!' Captain Cromwell appeared to be making conversation to take his guests' minds off the ship's pitching and rolling. 'So now you take your profits home, and quite right too. So where is home? Bavaria? Prussia? Hesse?'

'Hanover,' Pohlmann said, 'but I have been thinking that perhaps I should buy a house in London. Lord William can give me advice, no doubt?' He smiled across the table at Lord William who, for answer, abruptly stood, clutched a napkin to his mouth and bolted from the cuddy. Spray spattered on the closed panes of the skylight and some dripped through onto the table.

'My husband is a poor sailor,' Lady Grace said calmly.

'And you, my lady, are not?' Pohlmann asked.

'I like the sea,' she said, almost indignantly. 'I have always liked the sea.'

Cromwell laughed. 'They say, my lady, that those who would go to sea for pleasure would visit hell as a pastime.'

She shrugged, as if what others said made no difference to her. Major Dalton took up the burden of the conversation. 'Have you ever been seasick, Sharpe?'

'No, sir, I've been lucky.'

'Me neither,' Dalton said. 'My mother always believed beefsteak was a specific against the condition.'

'Beefsteak, fiddlesticks,' Cromwell growled. 'Only rum and oil will serve.'

'Rum and oil?' Pohlmann asked with a grimace.

'You force a pint of rum down the patient's throat and follow it with a pint of oil. Any oil will do, even lamp oil, for the patient will void it utterly, but next day he'll feel lively as a trivet.' Cromwell turned a jaundiced eye on Lady Grace. 'Should I send the rum and oil to your cabin, my lady?'

Lady Grace did not even bother to reply. She gazed at the panelling where a small oil painting of an English country church swayed to the ship's motion.

'So how long will this storm last?' Mathilde asked in her accented English.

'Storm?' Cromwell cried. 'You think this is a storm? This, ma'am, is nothing but a blow. Nothing but a morsel of wind and rain that will do no harm to man or ship. A storm, ma'am, is violent, violent! This is gentle to what we might meet off the Cape.'

No one had the stomach for a dessert of suet and currants, so instead Pohlmann suggested a hand of whist in his cabin. 'I have some fine brandy, Captain,' he said, 'and if Major Dalton is willing to play we can make a foursome? I know Sharpe won't play.' He indicated himself and Mathilde as the other players, then smiled at Lady Grace. 'Unless I could persuade you to play, my lady?'

'I don't,' she said in a tone suggesting that Pohlmann had invited her to wallow in his vomit. She stood, somehow managing to stay graceful despite the lurching of the ship, and the men immediately pushed their chairs back and stepped aside to let her leave the cabin.

'Stay and finish your wine, Sharpe,' Pohlmann said, leading his whist players out.

Sharpe was left alone in the cuddy. He finished his wine, then fetched the decanter from its metal frame on the sideboard, and poured himself another glass. Night had fallen and the frigate, anxious that the convoy should not scatter in the darkness, was firing a gun every ten minutes. Sharpe told himself he would stay for three guns, then make his way into the foetid hold and try to sleep.

Then the door opened and Lady Grace came back into the cuddy. She had a scarf about her neck, hiding the pearls and the smooth white skin of her shoulders. She gave Sharpe an unfriendly glance and ignored his awkward greeting. Sharpe expected her to leave straightaway, assuming she had merely come to fetch something she had left in the cuddy, but to his surprise she sat in Cromwell's chair and frowned at him. 'Sit down, Mister Sharpe.'

'Some wine, my lady?'

'Sit down,' she said firmly.

Sharpe sat at the opposite end of the table. The empty brass chandelier swung from the beam, reflecting flashes of the candlelight that came from the two shielded lanterns on the bulkheads. The flickering flames accentuated the high bones of Lady Grace's face.

'How well do you know the Baron von Dornberg?' she asked abruptly.

Sharpe blinked, surprised by the question. 'Not well, my lady.'

'You met him in India?'

'Yes, ma'am.'

'Where?' she demanded peremptorily. 'How?'

Sharpe frowned. He had promised not to give away Pohlmann's identity, so he would need to treat Lady Grace's insistence tactfully. 'I served with a Company exploring officer for a while, ma'am,' he said, 'and he frequently rode behind enemy lines. That's when I met P— the baron.' He thought for a second or two. 'I maybe met him four times, perhaps five?'

'Which enemy?'

'The Mahrattas, ma'am.'

'So he was a friend to the Mahrattas?'

'I imagine so, ma'am.'

She stared at him as if she was weighing the truth of his words. 'He seems very attached to you, Mister Sharpe.'

Sharpe almost swore as the wine glass slid away from him and fell over the fiddle. The glass smashed on the floor, splashing wine across the canvas rug. 'I did him a service, ma'am, the last time we met. It was after a fight.'

'He was on the other side?' she interrupted him.

'He was with the other side, ma'am,' Sharpe said carefully, disguising the truth that Pohlmann had been the general commanding the other side. 'And he was caught up in the rout. I could have captured him, I suppose, but he didn't seem to pose any harm, so I let him go. He's grateful for that, I'm sure.'

'Thank you,' she said, and seemed about to stand.

'Why, ma'am?' Sharpe asked, hoping she would stay.

She relaxed warily, then stared at him for a long time,

evidently considering whether to answer, then let go of the table and shrugged. 'You heard the captain's conversation with the baron tonight?'

'Yes, ma'am.'

'They appear as strangers to each other?'

'Indeed they do,' Sharpe agreed, 'and Cromwell told me as much himself.'

'Yet almost every night, Mister Sharpe, they meet and talk. Just the two of them. They come in here after midnight and sit across the table from each other and talk. And sometimes the baron's manservant is here with them.' She paused. 'I frequently find it hard to sleep and if the night is fine I will go on deck. I hear them through the skylight. I don't eavesdrop,' she said acidly, 'but I hear their voices.'

'So they know each other a great deal better than they pretend?' Sharpe said.

'So it would seem,' she answered.

'Odd, ma'am,' Sharpe said.

She shrugged as if to suggest that Sharpe's opinion was of no interest to her. 'Perhaps they merely play backgammon,' she said distantly.

She again looked as though she would leave and Sharpe hurried to keep the conversation going. 'The baron did tell me he might go to live in France, ma'am.'

'Not London?'

'France or Hanover, he said.'

'But you can hardly expect him to confide in you,' she said scornfully, 'on the basis of your very slight acquaintance.' She stood.

Sharpe pushed back his chair and hurried to open the door. She nodded thanks for his courtesy, but a sudden wave heaved the *Calliope* and made Lady Grace stagger and Sharpe instinctively put a hand out to check her and the hand encircled her waist and took her weight so that she was leaning against him with her face just inches from his. He felt a terrible desire to kiss her and he knew she would not object for, though the ship steadied, she did not step away. Sharpe could feel her slender waist beneath the soft material of her dress. His mind was swimming because her eyes, so large and serious, were on his, and once again, as he had the very first time he glimpsed her, he sensed a melancholy in her face, but then the quarterdeck door banged open and Cromwell's steward swore as he carried a tray towards the cuddy. Lady Grace twisted from Sharpe's arm and, without a word, went through the door.

'Raining buckets, it is,' the steward said. 'A bloody fish would drown on deck, I tell you.'

'Bloody hell,' Sharpe said, 'bloody hell.' He picked the decanter up by the neck, tipped it to his mouth and drained it.

The wind and rain stayed high throughout the night. Cromwell had shortened sail at nightfall and those few passengers who braved the deck at dawn found the *Calliope* plunging beneath low dark clouds from which black squalls hissed across a white-capped sea. Sharpe, lacking a greatcoat, and unwilling to soak his coat or shirt, went on deck bare-chested. He turned towards the quarterdeck and respectfully bowed his head in acknowledgement of the unseen captain, then half ran and half walked towards the forecastle where the breakfast burgoo waited to be fetched. He found a group of sailors at the galley, one of them the grey-haired commander of number five gun, who greeted Sharpe with a tobacco-stained grin. 'We've lost the convoy, sir.'

'Lost it?'

'Gone to buggery, ain't it?' The man laughed. 'And not by accident if I knows a thing about it.'

'And what do you know about it, Jem?' a younger man asked.

'More'n you know, and more'n you'll ever learn.'

'Why no accident?' Sharpe asked.

Jem ducked his head to spit tobacco juice. 'The captain's been at the wheel since midnight, sir, so he has, and he's been steering us hard south'ards. Had us on deck in dark of night, hauling the sails about. We be running due south now, sir, instead of sou'west.'

'The wind changed,' a man observed.

'Wind don't change here!' Jem said scornfully. 'Not at this time of year! Wind here be steady as a rock out of the nor'east. Nine days in ten, sir, out the nor'east. You don't need to steer a ship out of Bombay, sir. You clear the Balasore Roads, hang your big rags up the sticks, and this wind'll blow you to Madagascar straight as a ball down a tavern alley, sir.'

'So why has he turned south?' Sharpe asked.

'Because we're a fast ship, sir, and it was grating Peculiar's nerves to be tied to them slow old tubs of the convoy. You watch him, sir, he'll have us hanging our shirts in the rigging to catch the wind and we'll fly home like a seagull.' He winked. 'First ship home gets the best prices for the cargo, see, sir?'

The cook ladled the burgoo into Sharpe's cauldron and Jem opened the forecastle door for Sharpe who almost collided with Pohlmann's servant, the elderly man who had been so relaxed on his master's sofa on the first night Sharpe had visited the cabin.

'*Pardonnez-moi,*' the servant said instinctively, stepping hastily back so that Sharpe did not spill the burgoo down his grey clothes.

Sharpe looked at him. 'Are you French?'

'I'm Swiss, sir,' the man said respectfully, then stood aside, though he still looked at Sharpe, who thought the man's eyes were not like a servant's eyes. They were like Lord William's eyes, confident, clever and knowing. 'Good morning, sir,' the servant said respectfully, offering a slight bow, and Sharpe stepped past him and carried the steaming burgoo down the rain-slicked main deck towards the aft companionway.

Cromwell chose that moment to appear at the quarterdeck rail and, just as Jem had forecast, he wanted every stitch of sail aloft. He bellowed at the topmen to start climbing, then took a speaking trumpet from the rail and hailed the first lieutenant who was making his way forward. 'Fly the jib boom spritsail, Mister Tufnell. Lively now! Mister Sharpe, you'll oblige me by getting dressed. This is an Indiaman, not some sluttish Tyne collier.'

Sharpe went below to eat breakfast and when he came back to the deck, properly dressed, Cromwell had gone to the poop from where he was watching north for fear that the Company frigate might appear to order him back to the convoy, but neither Cromwell, nor the men aloft, saw any sign of the other ships. It appeared that Cromwell had escaped the convoy and could now let *Calliope* show her speed. And show it she did, for every sail that had been handed at nightfall was now back on the yards, stretching to the wet wind, and the *Calliope* seemed to churn the sea to cream as she raced southwards.

The wind moderated during the day and the clouds scudded themselves ragged so that by nightfall the sky was again clear and the sea was blue green instead of grey. There was an air of ebullience on board, as though by freeing itself of the convoy the *Calliope* had brightened everyone's life. There was the sound of laughter in steerage, and cheers when Tufnell rigged wind scoops to air out the foetid decks. Passengers joined the seamen in dances below the forecastle as the sun sank in a blaze of orange and gold.

Pohlmann brought Sharpe a cigar before supper. 'I won't invite you to eat with us tonight,' he said. 'Joshua

Fazackerly is donating the wine, which means he will feel entitled to bore us all with his legal recollections. It will likely prove a tedious meal.' He paused, blowing a plume of smoke towards the mainsail. 'You know why I liked the Mahrattas? There were no lawyers among them.'

'No law, either,' Sharpe said.

Pohlmann gave him a sideways glance. 'True. But I like corrupt societies, Richard. In a corrupt society the biggest rogue wins.'

'So why go home?'

'Europe is being corrupted,' Pohlmann said. 'The French talk loudly of law and reason, but beneath the talk there is nothing but greed. I understand greed, Richard.'

'So where will you live?' Sharpe asked. 'London, Hanover or France?'

'Maybe in Italy? Maybe Spain? No, not Spain. I could not stomach the priests. Maybe I shall go to America? They say rogues do well there.'

'Or perhaps you'll live in France?'

'Why not? I have no quarrel with France.'

'You will if the *Revenant* finds us.'

'The *Revenant*?' Pohlmann asked innocently.

'French warship,' Sharpe said.

Pohlmann laughed. 'It would be like, how do you say? Finding a needle in a haystack? Although I have always thought it would be easy to find a needle in a haystack. Simply take a girl onto the stack and make love, and you could be quite certain the needle will find her bum. Have you ever made love on a haystack?'

'No.'

'I don't recommend it. It is like those beds the Indian magicians sleep on. But if you do, Richard, make sure you are the one on top.'

Sharpe gazed out across the darkening ocean. There

were no whitecaps any more, just an endless vista of slow-heaving waves. 'How well do you know Cromwell?' He blurted the question out, torn between a reluctance to raise the German's suspicions and a desire not to believe in those suspicions at all.

Pohlmann gave Sharpe a glance full of curiosity and not a little hostility. 'I scarcely know the man,' he answered stiffly. 'I met him once or twice when he was ashore in Bombay, because it seemed sensible if we were to get decent accommodation, but otherwise I know him about as well as you do. Why do you ask?'

'I was wondering if you knew him well enough to find out why he left the convoy?'

Pohlmann laughed, his suspicions allayed by Sharpe's explanation. 'I don't think I know him that well, but Mister Tufnell tells me we are to sail to the east of Madagascar while the convoy goes to the west. We shall make faster time, he reckons, and be home at least two weeks ahead of the other ships. And that will increase the value of the cargo in which the captain has a considerable interest.' Pohlmann drew on the cigar. 'You disapprove of his initiative?'

'There's safety in numbers,' Sharpe said mildly.

'There's safety in speed, too. Tufnell says we should make at least ninety miles a day now.' The German threw the remains of his cigar overboard. 'I must change for supper.'

There was something wrong, Sharpe reckoned, but he could not place it. If Lady Grace was right, then Pohlmann and the captain talked frequently, but Pohlmann claimed he scarcely knew Cromwell, and Sharpe was inclined to believe her ladyship, though for the life of him he could not see how it affected anyone other than Pohlmann and Cromwell.

Two days later land was sighted far to the west. The shout from the masthead brought a rush of passengers to the starboard rail, though no one could see the land unless they were willing to climb into the high rigging, but a belt of thick cloud on the horizon showed where the distant coast lay. 'Cape East on Madagascar,' Lieutenant Tufnell announced, and all day the passengers stared at the cloud as though it portended something significant. The cloud was gone the following day, though Tufnell told Sharpe they were still following the Madagascar coast which now lay well beyond the horizon. 'The next landfall will be the African shore,' Tufnell said, 'and there we'll find a quick current to carry us round to Cape Town.'

The two men spoke on the darkened quarterdeck. It was well past midnight on the second day since the sighting of Cape East and the third night in succession that Sharpe had gone in the small hours to the quarterdeck in hope that Lady Grace would be on the poop. He needed to ask permission to be on the quarterdeck, but the watch officer had welcomed his company every night, unaware why Sharpe wanted to be there. The Lady Grace had not appeared on either of the first two nights, but as Sharpe now stood beside the lieutenant he heard the creak of a door and the sound of soft shoes climbing the stairs to the poop deck. Sharpe waited until the lieutenant went to talk with the helmsman, then he turned and went to the poop deck himself.

A thin sabre-curve of moon glistened on the sea and offered just enough light for Sharpe to see Lady Grace, swathed in a dark cloak, standing beside the stern lantern. She was alone, with no maid to chaperone her, and Sharpe joined her, standing a pace to her left with his hands, like hers, on the rail and he stared, like her, at the smooth, moon-silvered wake that slipped endlessly into the dark. The great mizzen driver sail loomed pale above them.

Neither spoke. She glanced at him when he joined her, but did not walk away. She just stared at the ocean.

'Pohlmann,' Sharpe said very quietly, for two panes of the cuddy's skylight were open and he did not want to be overheard if anyone was below, 'claims he does not know Captain Cromwell.'

'Pohlmann?' Lady Grace asked, frowning at Sharpe.

'The Baron von Dornberg is no baron, my lady.' Sharpe was breaking his word to Pohlmann, but he did not care, not when he was standing close enough to smell Lady Grace's perfume. 'His name is Anthony Pohlmann and he was once a sergeant in a Hanoverian regiment that was hired by the East India Company, but he deserted. He became a freelance soldier instead, and a very good one. He was the commander of the enemy army at Assaye.'

'Their commander?' She sounded surprised.

'Yes, ma'am. He was the enemy general.'

She stared at the sea again. 'Why have you protected him?'

'I like him,' Sharpe said. 'I've always liked him. He once tried to make me an officer in the Mahratta army and I confess I was tempted. He said he'd make me rich.'

She smiled at that. 'You want to be rich, Mister Sharpe?'

'It's better than being poor, milady.'

'Yes,' she said, 'it is. So why are you telling me about Pohlmann now?'

'Because he lied to me, ma'am.'

'Lied to you?'

'He told me he didn't know the captain, and you told me that he does.'

She turned to him again. 'Perhaps I lied to you?'

'Did you?'

'No.' She glanced at the cuddy's skylight, then walked

to the far corner of the deck where a small signal cannon was lashed to the gunwale. She stood in the corner between the cannon and the taffrail and Sharpe, after a moment's hesitation, joined her there. 'I don't like it,' she said quietly.

'Don't like what, ma'am?'

'That we're sailing to the east of Madagascar. Why?'

Sharpe shrugged. 'Pohlmann tells me we're trying to race ahead of the convoy. Get to London first and bring the cargo to market.'

'No one sails outside Madagascar,' she said, 'no one! We're losing the Agulhas Current, which means we'll make slower time. And by coming this way we go much closer to the Île-de-France.'

'Mauritius?' Sharpe asked.

She nodded. Mauritius, or the Île-de-France, was the enemy base in the Indian Ocean, an island fortress for raiders and warships with a main harbour protected by treacherous coral reefs and stone forts. 'I told William all this,' she said bitterly, 'but he laughed at me. What would I know? Cromwell knows his business, he says, and I should just leave well alone.' She fell silent and Sharpe was suddenly and awkwardly aware that she was crying. The realization astonished him, for one moment she had been as aloof as ever, and now she was weeping. She stood with her hands on the rail as the tears ran silently down her cheeks. 'I hated India,' she said after a while.

'Why, milady?'

'Everything dies in India,' she said bitterly. 'Both my dogs died, and then my son died.'

'Oh, God, I'm sorry.'

She ignored his sympathy. 'And I almost died. Fever, of course.' She sniffed. 'And there were times when I wished I would die.'

'How old was your son?'

'Three months,' she said softly. 'He was our first and he was so small and perfect, with little fingers and he was just beginning to smile. Just beginning to smile and then he rotted away. Everything rots in India. It turns black and it rots!' She began to cry harder, her shoulders heaving with sobs and Sharpe simply turned her and drew her towards him and she went to him and wept onto his shoulder.

She calmed after a while. 'I'm sorry,' she whispered and half stepped away, but seemed content to let him keep his hands on her shoulders.

'There's no need to be sorry,' Sharpe said.

Her head was lowered and Sharpe could smell her hair, but then she raised her face and looked at him. 'Have you ever wanted to die, Mister Sharpe?'

He smiled at her. 'I always reckoned that would be a terrible waste, my lady.'

She frowned at that answer, then, quite suddenly, she laughed and her face, for the first time since Sharpe had met her, was filled with life and he thought he had never seen, nor ever would see, a woman so lovely. So lovely that Sharpe leaned forward and kissed her. She pushed him away and he stepped back, mortified, readying incoherent apologies, but she was only extricating her arms that had been trapped between their bodies and once they were free she snaked them round his neck and pulled his face to hers and kissed him so fiercely that Sharpe tasted blood from her lip. She sighed, then placed her cheek against his. 'Oh, God,' she said softly, 'I wanted you to do that since the moment I first saw you.'

Sharpe hid his astonishment. 'I thought you hadn't noticed me.'

'Then you are a fool, Richard Sharpe.'

'And you, my lady?'

She pulled her head back, leaving her arms about his

neck. 'Oh, I'm a fool. I know that. How old are you?'

'Twenty-eight, milady, as near as I know.'

She smiled and he thought he had never seen a face so transformed by joy, then she leaned forward and kissed him lightly on the lips. 'My name is Grace,' she said quietly, 'and why only as near as you know?'

'I never knew my mother or father.'

'Never? So who raised you?'

'I wasn't really raised, ma'am. Sorry. Grace.' He blushed as he said it, for though he could imagine kissing her, and though he could imagine laying her on a bed, he could not accustom himself to using her name. 'I was in a foundling home for a few years, one that were attached to a workhouse, and after that I fended for myself.'

'I'm twenty-eight too,' she said, 'and I don't think I've ever been happy. That's why I'm a fool.' Sharpe said nothing, but just stared at her in disbelief. She saw his incredulity and laughed. 'It's true, Richard.'

'Why?'

There was a murmur of voices from the quarterdeck and a sudden glow of light as the compass in the lantern-lit binnacle was unshielded. Lady Grace stepped away from Sharpe and he from her, and both instinctively turned to stare at the sea. The binnacle light vanished. Lady Grace said nothing for a while and Sharpe wondered if she was regretting what had happened, but then she spoke softly. 'You're like a weed, Richard. You can grow anywhere. A big, strong weed and you've probably got thorns and stinging leaves. But I was like a rose in a garden: trained and cut back and pampered, but not allowed to grow anywhere except where the gardener wanted me.' She shrugged. 'I'm not seeking your pity, Richard. You should never waste pity on the privileged. I'm just talking to find out why I'm here with you.'

'Why are you?'

'Because I'm lonely,' she answered firmly, 'and unhappy and because you intrigue me.' She reached out and touched a very gentle finger to the scar on his right cheek. 'You're a horribly good-looking man, Richard Sharpe, but if I met you in a London street I'd be very frightened of your face.'

'Bad and dangerous,' Sharpe said, 'that's me.'

'And I'm here,' Lady Grace went on, 'because there is a joy in doing things we know we should not do. What Captain Cromwell calls our baser instincts, I suppose, and I suppose it will end in tears, but that does not preclude the joy.' She frowned at him. 'You look very cruel sometimes. Are you cruel?'

'No,' Sharpe said. 'Perhaps to the King's enemies. Perhaps to my enemies, but only if they're as strong as I am. I'm a soldier, not a bully.'

She touched the scar again. 'Richard Sharpe, my fearless soldier.'

'I was terrified of you,' Sharpe admitted. 'From the moment I saw you.'

'Terrified?' She seemed genuinely puzzled. 'I thought you despised me. You looked at me so grimly.'

'I never said I didn't despise you,' Sharpe said in mock seriousness, 'but from the moment I saw you I wanted to be with you.'

She laughed. 'You can be with me here,' she said, 'but only on fine nights. I come here when I can't sleep. William sleeps in the stern cabin,' she explained, 'and I sleep on the sofa in the day cabin. My maid uses a truckle bed there.'

'You don't sleep with him?' Sharpe dared to ask.

'I have to go to bed with him,' she admitted, 'but he takes laudanum every night because he insists he cannot sleep. He takes too much and he sleeps like a hog, so when he's asleep I go to the day cabin.' She shuddered.

'And the drug makes him costive, which makes him even more bad-tempered.'

'I have a cabin,' Sharpe said.

She looked at him, unsmiling, and Sharpe feared he had offended her, but then she smiled. 'To yourself?'

He nodded. 'You'll like it. It's seven foot by six with walls of damp wood and clammy canvas.'

'And you swing in your lonely hammock there?' she asked, still smiling.

'Hammock be blowed,' Sharpe said, 'I've a proper hanging cot with a damp mattress.'

She sighed. 'And not six months ago a man offered me a palace with walls of carved ivory, a garden of fountains, and a pavilion with a bed of gold. He was a prince, and I must say he was very delicate about it.'

'And were you?' Sharpe asked, suddenly jealous of the man. 'Were you delicate?'

'I froze him.'

'You're good at that.'

'And in the morning,' she said, 'I will have to be good at it again.'

'Yes, my lady, you will.'

She smiled, acknowledging that he understood the necessary deception. 'But it won't be light,' she said, 'for another three hours.'

'Four, more like.'

'And I've been wanting to explore the ship,' she said. 'All I ever see is the roundhouse, the cuddy and the poop deck.'

He took her hand. 'It'll be pitch black below.'

'I think that would probably help,' she said gravely. She took her hand from his. 'You go first,' she said, 'and I'll follow. I'll meet you on the main deck.'

And so he waited below the break of the quarterdeck and she did follow and he led her below and there they forgot their suspicions of Pohlmann and Cromwell.

Who, most probably, Sharpe thought when the dawn came and he lay astonished and alone again in his bed, had been playing backgammon. He closed his eyes, amazed at his happiness and praying that this voyage could last for ever.

CHAPTER 4

Two mornings later a sail was sighted, the first since the *Calliope* had left the convoy. It was dawn and the sky above unseen Madagascar was still dark when a topman saw the first sunlight reflect from a distant sail off the starboard bow. Captain Cromwell, summoned from his cabin by Lieutenant Tufnell, appeared agitated. He was wearing a flannel nightgown and his long hair was twisted into a bun at the nape of his neck. He stared at the strange ship's sails through an ancient telescope. 'It ain't a native ship,' Sharpe heard him say. 'They're proper topsails. Christian canvas, that.' Cromwell ordered the main-deck guns to be unlashed. Powder was brought up from the magazines while Cromwell changed into his usual uniform. Tufnell went to the mainmast crosstrees equipped with a telescope. He stared for a long time, then shouted that he thought the distant vessel was a whaler. Cromwell seemed relieved, but left the powder charges on deck just in case the strange ship proved to be a privateer.

It was the best part of an hour before the distant ship could be seen from the *Calliope*'s deck and its presence brought the passengers on deck to stare at the stranger. Like the glimpse of land, this was a break in the journey's tedium and Sharpe gazed with the rest, though he had an advantage over most of the passengers, for he possessed a telescope. The instrument was a marvel, a beautiful spyglass made by Matthew Berge of London and inscribed with the date of the battle of Assaye. Sir Arthur Wellesley had given the telescope to Sharpe, with his thanks engraved above the date, though he had been his usual distant and diffident self as he handed the glass over. 'I would not have you think I was unmindful of the service you did me,' the general had said awkwardly.

'I was just glad to be there, sir,' Sharpe had answered just as awkwardly.

Sir Arthur had forced himself to say something more. 'Remember, Mister Sharpe, that an officer's eyes are more valuable than his sword.'

'I'll remember that, sir,' Sharpe said, reflecting that the general would have been dead without Sharpe's sabre. Still, he supposed the advice was good. 'And thank you, sir,' Sharpe had said and remembered being obscurely disappointed with the telescope. He had reckoned that a good sword would have been a better reward for saving the general's life.

Sir Arthur had frowned, but Campbell, one of his aides, had tried to be friendly. 'So you're off to join the Rifles, Sharpe?'

'I am, sir.'

Sir Arthur had cut the conversation short. 'You'll be happy there, I'm sure. Thank you, Mister Sharpe. Good day to you.'

And thus Sharpe had become the ungrateful possessor of a telescope that would have been the envy of richer men. He trained it now on the strange ship, which, to his untutored eye, looked a good deal smaller than the *Calliope.* She was certainly no warship, but appeared to be a small merchantman.

'She's a Jonathon!' Tufnell called from aloft, and Sharpe edged the glass leftwards and saw a faded ensign flying at the far ship's stern. The flag looked very like the red-and-white-striped banner of the East India Company, but then the wind lifted it and he saw the stars in its upper quadrant and realized she was an American.

Major Dalton had come down to the main deck and now stood beside Sharpe who politely offered the Scotsman the use of the telescope. The major stared at the American ship. 'She's carrying powder and shot to Mauritius,' he said.

'How do you know, sir?'

'Because that's what they do. No French merchantman dare sail in these waters, so the damned Americans supply Mauritius with weaponry. And they have the nerve to call themselves neutral! Still, I've no doubt they turn a fine profit, which is all that matters to them. This is a very fine glass, Sharpe!'

'It was a gift, Major.'

'A handsome one.' Dalton handed the glass back and frowned. 'You look tired, Sharpe.'

'Not been sleeping that well, Major.'

'I pray you're not sickening. The Lady Grace is also looking very peaky. I do hope there isn't ship fever on board. I recall a brigantine coming into Leith when I was a child and there can't have been more then three men alive on her, and they were near death's door. They couldn't land, of course, poor things. They had to anchor off and let the sickness run its course, which left them all dead.'

The American, confident that the *Calliope* presented no threat, sailed close to the great Indiaman and the two ships inspected each other as they passed in mid ocean. The American ship was half the *Calliope*'s length and her main deck was crammed with the longboats that her crew used to stalk and kill whales. 'Doubtless she'll drop her cargo on Mauritius,' Major Dalton observed, 'then head for the Southern Ocean. A hard life, Sharpe.'

The American crew returned the *Calliope*'s waves,

then she was past and the folk on board the Indiaman could read the whaler's name and hailing port, which were painted in blue and gold on handsome stern boards. 'The *Jonah Coffin* out of Nantucket,' Dalton said. 'What extraordinary names they do pick!'

'Like Peculiar Cromwell?'

'There is that!' Dalton laughed. 'But I can't imagine our captain painting his name on his boat's stern, can you? By the way, Sharpe, I've donated a pickled tongue for dinner.'

'Generous of you, sir.'

'And I owe you a recompense for all the help you've been to me,' Dalton said, referring to his long conversations with Sharpe about the war against the Mahrattas which the major planned to write about in his retirement, 'so why don't you join us at noon? The captain's agreed to let us eat on the quarterdeck!' Dalton sounded excited, as if dining in the open air would prove a special treat.

'I don't want to intrude, Major.'

'No intrusion, no intrusion! You shall be my guest. I've also donated some wine and you can help drink it. Red coat, I fear, Sharpe. Dinner might be a mere cold collation, but Peculiar rightly insists there are no shirt-sleeves on the quarterdeck.'

Sharpe had an hour before the dinner was to be served and he went below to brush the red coat and, to his astonishment, found Malachi Braithwaite seated on his travelling chest. The secretary was becoming ever more morose as the voyage continued and now looked up at Sharpe with resentful eyes.

'Lost your own quarters, Braithwaite?' Sharpe asked brusquely.

'I wanted to see you, Sharpe.' The secretary seemed nervous, unable to meet Sharpe's eyes.

'You could have found me on deck,' Sharpe said and

waited, but Braithwaite said nothing, just watched as Sharpe draped the red coat over the edge of the hanging cot and began to brush it vigorously. 'Well?' Sharpe asked.

Braithwaite still hesitated. His right hand was fiddling with a loose thread hanging from the sleeve of his faded black coat, but he finally summoned the courage to look at Sharpe, opened his mouth to speak, then lost his courage and closed it again. Sharpe scrubbed at a patch of dirt and finally the secretary found his voice. 'You entertain a woman at nights,' he blurted out accusingly.

Sharpe laughed. 'What if I do? Didn't they teach you about women at Oxford?'

'A particular woman,' Braithwaite said in a tone so filled with resentment that he sounded like a spitting serpent.

Sharpe put the brush on top of his barrel of arrack and turned on the secretary. 'If you've got something to say, Braithwaite, then bloody say it.'

The secretary reddened. The fingers of his right hand were now drumming on the edge of the chest, but he forced himself to continue the confrontation. 'I know what you're doing, Sharpe.'

'You don't know a bloody thing, Braithwaite.'

'And if I inform his lordship, as I should, then you can be assured that you will have no career in His Majesty's army.' It had taken almost all Braithwaite's courage to voice the threat, but he was encouraged by a rancour that was eating him like a tapeworm. 'You'll have no career, Sharpe, none!'

Sharpe's face betrayed no emotion as he stared at the secretary, but he was privately appalled that Braithwaite had discovered his secret. Lady Grace had been in this squalid cabin for two nights running, coming long after dark and leaving well before dawn, and Sharpe had thought no one had noticed. They had both believed they were being discreet, but Braithwaite had seen and now he was bitter with envy. Sharpe picked up the brush. 'Is that all you've got to say?'

'And I'll ruin her too,' Braithwaite hissed, then started violently back as Sharpe threw down the brush and turned on him. 'And I know you deposited valuables with the captain!' the secretary went on hurriedly, holding up both hands as if to ward off a blow.

Sharpe hesitated. 'How do you know that?'

'Everyone knows. It's a ship, Sharpe. People talk.'

Sharpe looked into the secretary's shifty eyes. 'Go on,' he said softly.

'My silence can be purchased,' Braithwaite said defiantly.

Sharpe nodded as though he were considering the bargain. 'I'll tell you how I'll buy your silence, Braithwaite, a silence, by the way, about nothing because I don't know what you're talking about. I reckon Oxford addled your brain, but let's suppose, just for a minute, that I think I know what you're suggesting. Shall we agree to that?'

Braithwaite nodded cautiously.

'And a ship is a very small place, Braithwaite,' Sharpe said, seating himself beside the gangly secretary, 'and you can't escape me on board this ship. And that means that if you open your sordid mouth to tell anyone anything, if you say even one bloody word, then I'll kill you.'

'You don't understand . . .'

'I do understand,' Sharpe interrupted, 'so shut your mouth. In India, Braithwaite, there are men called *jettis* who kill by wringing their victims' necks like chickens.' Sharpe put his hands on Braithwaite's head and began to twist it. 'They twist it all the bloody way round, Braithwaite.'

'No!' the secretary gasped. He fumbled at Sharpe's hands with his own, but he lacked the strength to free himself.

'They twist it till their victim's eyes are staring out over his arse and his neck gives way with a crack.'

'No!' Braithwaite could barely speak, for his neck was being twisted hard round.

'It's not really a crack,' Sharpe went on in a conversational tone, 'more a kind of grating creak, and I've often wondered if I could do it myself. It's not that I'm afraid of killing, Braithwaite. I wouldn't have you think that. I've killed men with guns, with swords, with knives and with my bare hands. I've killed more men, Braithwaite, than you can imagine in your worst nightmare, but I've never wrung a man's neck till it creaked. But I'll start with you. If you do anything to hurt me, or anything to hurt any lady I know, then I'll twist your head like a cork in a bloody bottle, and it'll hurt. My God, it'll hurt.' Sharpe gave the secretary's neck a sudden jerk. 'It'll hurt more than you know, and I promise you that it will happen if you say so much as one single bloody word. You'll be dead, Braithwaite, and I won't give a rat's droppings about doing it. It'll be a real pleasure.' He gave the secretary's neck a last twist, then let go.

Braithwaite gasped for breath, massaging his throat. He gave Sharpe a scared glance, then tried to stand, but Sharpe hauled him back onto the chest. 'You're going to make me a promise, Braithwaite,' Sharpe said.

'Anything!' All the fight had gone from the man now.

'You'll say nothing to anybody. And I'll know if you do, I'll know, and I'll find you, Braithwaite. I'll find you and I'll wring your scrawny neck like a chicken.'

'I won't say a word!'

'Because your accusations are false, aren't they?'

'Yes.' Braithwaite nodded eagerly. 'Yes, they are.'

'You're having dreams, Braithwaite.'

'I am, I am.'

'Then go. And remember I'm a killer, Braithwaite. When you were at Oxford learning to be a bloody fool I was learning how to kill folk. And I learned well.'

Braithwaite fled and Sharpe stayed seated. Damn, he thought, damn and damn and damn again. He reckoned he had frightened the secretary into silence, but Sharpe was still scared. For if Braithwaite had found out, who else might discover their secret? Not that it mattered for Sharpe, but it mattered mightily to Lady Grace. She had a reputation to lose. 'You're playing with fire, you bloody fool,' he told himself, then retrieved his brush and finished cleaning his coat.

Pohlmann seemed surprised that Sharpe should be a guest at dinner, but he greeted him effusively and shouted at the steward to fetch another chair onto the quarterdeck. A trestle table had been placed forward of the *Calliope*'s big wheel, spread with white linen and set with silverware. 'I was going to invite you myself,' Pohlmann told Sharpe, 'but in the excitement of seeing the Jonathon I quite forgot.'

There was no precedence at this table, for Captain Cromwell was not dining with his passengers, but Lord William made sure he took the table's head, then cordially invited the baron to sit beside him. 'As you know, my dear baron, I am compiling a report on the future policy of His Majesty's government towards India and I would value your opinion on the remaining Mahratta states.'

'I'm not sure I can tell you much,' Pohlmann said, 'for I hardly knew the Mahrattas, but of course I shall oblige you as best I can.' Then, to Lord William's evident irritation, Mathilde took the chair on his left and called for Sharpe to sit next to her.

'I'm the major's guest, my lady.' Sharpe explained his reluctance to sit beside Mathilde, but Dalton shook his head and insisted Sharpe take the offered chair.

'I have a handsome man on either of my sides now!' Mathilde exclaimed in her eccentric English, earning a look of withering condescension from Lord William. Lady Grace, denied a seat beside her husband, stayed standing until Lord William coldly nodded to the chair beside Pohlmann which meant she would be sitting directly opposite Sharpe. In a superb piece of dumb play she glanced at Sharpe, then raised her eyebrows towards her husband, who shrugged as though there was nothing he could do to alleviate the misfortune of being made to sit opposite a mere ensign, and so the Lady Grace sat. Not eight hours before she had been naked in Sharpe's hanging bed, but now her disdain of him was cruelly obvious. Fazackerly, the barrister, asked permission to sit beside her and she smiled at him graciously as though she was relieved to have a dinner companion who could be relied on to make civilized conversation.

'Sixty-nine miles,' Lieutenant Tufnell said, joining the passengers and announcing the results of the noon sight. 'We'd hoped to do better, much better, but the wind frets.'

'My wife,' Lord William said, shaking out his napkin, 'claims we would make faster progress if we sailed inside Madagascar. Is she right, Lieutenant?' His voice suggested that he hoped she was not.

'She is indeed right, my lord,' Tufnell said, 'for there is a prodigious current down the African coast, but the Madagascar Straits are liable to be very stormy. Very stormy. And the captain deemed we might do better outside, which we will if the wind stirs itself.'

'You see, Grace?' Lord William looked at his wife. 'The captain evidently knows his business.'

'I thought we were in a hurry to be first back to London,' Sharpe observed to Tufnell.

The first lieutenant shrugged. 'We anticipated stronger winds. Now, shall I carve? Major, perhaps you will pass the coleslaw? Sharpe? That is a chitney in the covered dish, or should I say chatna? Chutney, perhaps? Baron, you might pour some wine? We're indebted to Major Dalton for the wine and for this very fine tongue.'

The guests murmured their appreciation of Dalton's generosity, then watched as Tufnell carved. The first lieutenant passed the plates up the table and, as a stronger wave heaved the ship, one of the plates slipped from Major Dalton's hand to spill its thick slices of pickled tongue onto the linen cloth. '*Lapsus linguae,*' Fazackerly said gravely, and was rewarded with instant laughter.

'Very good!' Lord William said. 'Very good!'

'Your lordship is too kind,' the barrister acknowledged with an inclination of his head.

Lord William leaned back in his chair. 'You did not laugh, Mister Sharpe,' he observed silkily. 'Perhaps you do not approve of puns?'

'Puns, my lord?' Sharpe knew he was being made a fool, but did not see any way out except to let it happen.

'*Lapsus linguae,*' Lord William said, 'means a slip of the tongue.'

'I'm glad you told me,' a strong voice came from the far end of the table, 'because I didn't know what it meant either. And it's not much of a joke even when you do know.' The speaker was Ebenezer Fairley, the wealthy merchant who was returning with his wife after making his fortune in India.

Lord William looked at the nabob, who was a corpulent man of blunt and straightforward views. 'I doubt, Fairley,' Lord William said, 'that Latin is a desideratum in business, but knowledge of it is an attribute of a gentleman, just as French is the language of diplomacy, and we shall need all the gentlemen and diplomacy that we can muster if this new century is to be a time of peace. The aim of civilization is to subdue barbarity' – he flicked a scornful glance at Sharpe – 'and cultivate prosperity and progress.'

'You think a man cannot be a gentleman unless he speaks Latin?' Ebenezer Fairley asked indignantly. His wife frowned, perhaps feeling that her husband should not be belligerent with an aristocrat.

'The arts of civilization,' Lord William said, 'are the highest achievements and every gentleman should aim high. And officers' – he did not look at Sharpe, but everyone around the table knew who he meant – 'should be gentlemen.'

Ebenezer Fairley shook his head in astonishment. 'You surely wouldn't deny the King's commission to men who can't speak Latin?'

'Officers should be educated,' Lord William insisted, 'properly educated.'

Sharpe was about to say something utterly tactless when a foot descended on his right shoe and pressed hard. He glanced at Lady Grace who was taking no notice of him, but it was her foot nonetheless. 'I quite agree with you, my dear,' Lady Grace said in her coldest voice, 'uneducated officers are a disgrace to the army.' Her foot slid up Sharpe's ankle.

Lord William, unaccustomed to his wife's approval, looked mildly surprised, but rewarded her with a smile. 'If the army is to be anything other than a rabble,' he decreed, 'it must be led by men of breeding, taste and manners.'

Ebenezer Fairley grimaced in disgust. 'If Napoleon lands his army in Britain, my lord, you won't care whether our officers talk in Latin, Greek, English or Hottentot, so long as they know their business.'

Lady Grace's foot pressed harder on Sharpe's, warning him to be circumspect.

Lord William sneered. 'Napoleon will not land in Britain, Fairley. The navy will see to that. No, the Emperor of France' – he invested the title with a superb scorn – 'will strut and posture for a year or so yet, but he'll make a mistake sooner or later and then there'll be another government in France. How many have we had in the last few years? We've had a republic, a directorate, a consulate and now an empire! An empire of what? Of cheese? Of garlic? No, Fairley, Bonaparte won't last. He's an adventurer. A cutthroat. He's safe so long as he wins victories, but no mere cutthroat wins for ever. He'll be defeated one day, and then we shall have serious men in Paris with whom we can do serious business. Men with whom we can make peace. It'll come soon enough.'

'I trust your lordship's right,' Fairley said dubiously, 'but for all we know this fellow Napoleon might have crossed the Channel already!'

'His navy will never put to sea,' Lord William insisted. 'Our navy will see to that.'

'I have a brother in the navy,' Tufnell said mildly, 'and he tells me that if the wind blows too strong from the east then the blockade ships run for shelter and the French are free to leave port.'

'They haven't sailed in ten years,' Lord William observed, 'so I think we can sleep safe in our beds.' Lady Grace's foot slid up and down Sharpe's calf.

'But if the Emperor doesn't invade Britain,' Pohlmann asked, 'who will defeat France?'

'My money's on the Prussians. On the Prussians and Austrians.' Lord William seemed very certain.

'Not the British?' Pohlmann asked.

'We don't have a dog in the European rat pit,' Lord William said. 'We should save our army' – he glanced at Sharpe – 'such as it is, to protect our trade.'

'You think we'd be wasted fighting the French?' Sharpe asked. Lady Grace's foot pressed warningly on his.

Lord William contemplated Sharpe for a moment, then shrugged. 'The French army would destroy ours in a day,' he said with a sneer. 'You might have seen some victories over Indian armies, Sharpe, but that is hardly the same as facing the French.'

The foot pressed harder on Sharpe's instep.

'I think we would acquit ourselves nobly,' Major Dalton averred, 'and the Indian armies were not to be despised, my lord, not to be despised at all.'

'Fine troops!' Pohlmann said warmly, then hastily added, 'Or so I'm told.'

'It isn't the quality of the troops,' Lord William said, nettled, 'but their leadership. Good Lord! Even Arthur Wellesley beat the Indians! He's a distant cousin of yours, ain't he, my dear?' He did not wait for his wife to answer. 'And he was never very bright. A dunce at school.'

'You were at school with him, my lord?' Sharpe asked, interested.

'Eton,' Lord William said curtly. 'And my younger brother was there with Wellesley who was no damn good at Latin. He left early, I believe. Wasn't up to the place.'

'He learned to cut throats, though,' Sharpe said.

'Didn't he just!' the major agreed eagerly. 'You were at Argaum, Sharpe. Did you see him muster those sepoys? Line broken, enemy raining shot like hail, cavalry lurking on the flank and there's your cousin, ma'am, cool as you like, bringing the fellows back into line.'

'Arthur is a very distant cousin,' Grace said, smiling

at Dalton, 'though I am glad of your good opinion of him, Major.'

'And of Sharpe's good opinion, I hope?' Dalton said.

Lady Grace shuddered as if to suggest that it would demean her even to consider an opinion of Sharpe's, and at the same time she kicked him on the shin so that he almost grinned. Lord William regarded Sharpe coldly. 'You only like Wellesley, Sharpe, because he made you an officer. Which is properly loyal of you, but scarcely discriminating.'

'He also had me flogged, my lord.'

That brought silence to the table. Lady Grace alone knew Sharpe had been flogged, for she had drawn her long white fingers across the scars on his back, but the rest of the table stared at him as though he were some strange creature just dragged up on one of the seamen's fishing lines. 'You were flogged?' Dalton asked in astonishment.

'Two hundred lashes,' Sharpe said.

'I'm sure you deserved it,' Lord William said, amused.

'As it happens, my lord, I didn't.'

'Oh come, come.' Lord William frowned. 'Every man says that. Ain't that right, Fazackerly? Have you ever known a guilty man accept responsibility for his crime?'

'Never, my lord.'

'It must have hurt dreadfully,' Lieutenant Tufnell said sympathetically.

'That,' Lord William said, 'is the point of it. You can't win battles without discipline, and you can't have discipline without the lash.'

'The French don't use the lash,' Sharpe said mildly, staring up at the big mainsail and the tangle of canvas and rigging that rose higher still, 'and you tell me, my lord, that they would destroy us in a day.'

'That is a question of numbers, Sharpe, numbers. Officers should also know how to count.'

'I can manage up to two hundred,' Sharpe said, and was rewarded with another kick.

They finished the meal with dried fruit, then the men drank brandy, and Sharpe slept for much of the afternoon in a hammock slung under the spare spars that ran lengthwise above the main deck and on which the ship's boats were stored during the voyage. He dreamed of battle. He was running away, pursued by a giant Indian with a spear. He woke drenched in sweat and immediately looked for the sun, for he knew he could not meet Grace until it was dark. Well dark. Until the ship was sleeping and only the night watch was on deck, but Braithwaite, he knew, would be watching and listening in that dark. What the hell was he to do about Braithwaite? He dared not tell Lady Grace about the man's allegations, for they would terrify her.

He ate in steerage, then paced the main deck as darkness fell. And still he must wait until Lord William had finished playing whist or backgammon and had finally taken his drops of laudanum and gone to bed. The ship's bell rang the night past and Sharpe waited in the black shadows between the vast mainmast and the bulkhead which supported the front end of the quarterdeck. It was where he waited for Lady Grace, for she could come there unseen by any of the crew on the quarterdeck. She used the stairs that went from the roundhouse down to the great cabin, then through a door which led to the main-deck steerage. She crept between the canvas screens and so out through another door on to the open deck. Then, taking her hand, Sharpe would lead her down into the warm stink of the lower-deck steerage and to his narrow cot where, with a greed that astonished them both, they would cling to each other as though they drowned. The very thought of her made Sharpe dizzy. He was besotted by her, drunk with her, insane for her.

He waited. The rigging creaked. The great mast shifted imperceptibly with gusts of wind. He could hear an officer pacing the quarterdeck, hear the slap of hands on the wheel spokes and the grating of the rudder ropes. The ensign flapped at the stern, the sea ran down the ship's flanks and still Sharpe waited. He stared up at the stars visible through the sails and thought they looked like the bivouac fires of a great army encamped across the sky.

He closed his eyes, wishing she would come and wishing that the voyage could last for ever. He wished they could be lovers on a ship sailing in an endless night beneath a spread of stars, for once the *Calliope* reached England she would go away from him. She would go to her husband's house in Lincolnshire and Sharpe would go to Kent to join a regiment he had never seen.

Then the door opened and she was there, crouching beside him in her vast boat cloak. 'Come to the poop deck,' she whispered.

He wanted to ask why, but he bit the question back for there had been an urgency in her voice and he reckoned that if it was important to her then it was important to him too, and so he let her take his hand and lead him back into the main-deck steerage. These berths cost the same as the lower deck, but they were much drier and airier. It was pitch black, for no lights were allowed after nine o'clock except in the roundhouse day cabins where deadlights could be fixed across the small portholes. Lady Grace twined her fingers in his as they groped and felt their way to the door leading to the great cabin, then up the stairs. 'As I left my cabin,' she whispered to him at the top of the stairs, 'I saw Pohlmann go into the cuddy.'

She led him to the door which opened onto the back of the quarterdeck and they stepped out, risking the eyes of the helmsman and the duty officer, but if they were seen no one remarked it. They climbed to the poop deck and Lady Grace gestured at the skylight above the cuddy cabin from which, in contravention of Captain Cromwell's orders, a faint light gleamed.

Creeping softly as children who have stayed up long after their bedtime, Sharpe and Lady Grace went close to the skylight. Four of its ten panes were propped open and Sharpe could hear the murmur of men's voices. Lady Grace peeped over the edge, then drew back. 'They're there,' she mouthed in his ear.

Sharpe looked through one of the dirty panes and saw three men's heads bent over the long table. One was Cromwell, the second Pohlmann and Sharpe did not recognize the third. They seemed to be examining a chart, then Pohlmann straightened up and Sharpe ducked back. The smell of cigar smoke came through the open panes.

'*Morgen früh,*' said a voice, only it was not Pohlmann who spoke in German, but another man. Sharpe risked leaning forward again and saw it was Pohlmann's servant, the man who spoke French and claimed to be Swiss.

'*Morgen früh,*' Pohlmann repeated.

'These things ain't certain, Baron,' Cromwell said.

'You have done well this far, my friend, so I am sure all will go well tomorrow,' Pohlmann answered and Sharpe heard the clink of glasses, then he and Grace shrank back because a hand came into sight to close the open panes. The dim light was extinguished and a moment later Sharpe heard Cromwell's growling voice talking to the helmsman on the quarterdeck.

'We can't go down now,' Grace whispered in his ear.

They went to the dark corner between the signal cannon and the taffrail and there, crouched in the shadows, they kissed, and only then did Sharpe ask if she had heard the German words.

'They mean "tomorrow morning",' Grace said.

'And the man who said them first,' Sharpe said, 'is supposed to be Pohlmann's servant. What's a servant doing drinking with his master? I've heard him speak French, too, but he claims to be Swiss.'

'The Swiss, dearest,' Lady Grace said, 'speak German and French.'

'They do?' Sharpe asked. 'I thought they talked Swiss.' She laughed. Sharpe was sitting with his back against the gunwale and she was straddling his lap, her knees either side of his chest. 'I don't know,' he went on, 'maybe they were just saying that we turn west tomorrow? We've been sailing south for days, we have to go west soon.'

'Not too soon,' she said. 'I would like this voyage to last for ever.' She leaned forward and kissed his nose. 'I thought you were going to be appallingly rude to William at dinner.'

'I held my tongue, didn't I?' he asked. 'But only because my shin's black and blue.' He touched a finger to her face, marvelling at the delicacy of her looks. 'I know he's your husband, my love, but he's stuffed to his muzzle with rubbish. Wanting officers to speak Latin! What use is Latin?'

Lady Grace shrugged. 'If the enemy is coming to kill you, Richard, who do you want defending you? A properly educated gentleman who can construe Ovid, or some barbarian cutthroat with a back like a washboard?'

Sharpe pretended to think. 'If you put it like that, of course, then I'll take the Ovid fellow.' She laughed, and it seemed to Sharpe that this was a woman born to happiness, not misery. 'I missed you,' he said.

'I missed you,' she answered.

He put his hands under the big black cloak to find that she was naked under her nightgown and then they forgot the next morning, forgot Cromwell, forgot Pohlmann and forgot the mysterious servant, for the *Calliope* was shrouded in the night, sailing beneath a slivered moon as it carried its star-crossed lovers to nowhere.

Captain Peculiar Cromwell was on the quarterdeck all next morning, pacing from larboard to starboard, glowering at the binnacle, pacing again, and his restlessness infected the ship so that the passengers became nervous and constantly glanced at the captain as if expecting him to lose his temper. Speculation flew round the main deck until it was finally agreed that Cromwell was expecting a storm, but the captain made no preparations. No sail was shortened or lashings inspected.

Ebenezer Fairley, the nabob who had responded so angrily to Lord William's assertions about Latin, came down to the main deck in search of Sharpe. 'I was hoping, Mister Sharpe, that you were not upset by those fools at dinner yesterday,' he boomed.

'By Lord William? No.'

'Man's a halfwit,' Fairley said savagely, 'saying we should speak Latin! What's the use of Latin? Or of Greek? He makes me ashamed to be an Englishman.'

'I took no offence, Mister Fairley.'

'And his wife's no better! Treats you like dirt, don't she? And she won't even speak to my wife.'

'She's a beauty, though,' Sharpe said wistfully.

'A beauty?' Fairley sounded disgusted. 'Well, aye, I suppose if you like getting splinters every time you touch her.' He sniffed. 'But what have either of them ever done except learn Latin? Have they ever planted a field of wheat? Set up a factory? Dug a canal? They were born, Sharpe, that's all that ever happened to them, they were born.' He shuddered. 'I tell you,

Sharpe, I'm not a radical man, not me! But there are times when I wouldn't mind seeing a guillotine outside Parliament. I could find business for it, I tell you.' Fairley, a tall and heavy-faced man, glanced up at Cromwell. 'Peculiar's in an itchy mood.'

'Folk say there's a storm coming.'

'God save the ship, then,' Fairley said, 'because I'm carrying three thousand pounds of cargo in this bottom, but we should be safe. I chose the *Calliope*, Mister Sharpe, because she has a reputation. A good one. Fast and seaworthy, she is, and Peculiar's a good seaman for all his scowls. This hold, Mister Sharpe, is fair stuffed with valuables because the ship's got a good name. You can't beat a good name in business. Did they really flog you?'

'They did, sir.'

'And you became an officer?' Fairley shook his head in rueful admiration. 'I've made a fortune in my time, Sharpe, a rare fortune, and you don't make a fortune without knowing men. If you want to work for me just say the word. I might be going home to rest my backside, but I've still got a business to run and I need good men I can trust. I do business in India, in China and wherever in Europe the damned French let me, and I need capable men. I can only promise you two things, Sharpe, that I'll work you like a dog and pay you like a prince.'

'Work for you, sir?' Sharpe was astonished.

'You don't speak Latin, do you? There's an advantage. And you don't know trade either, but you can learn that a damned sight easier than you can learn Latin.'

'I like being a soldier.'

'Aye, I can see that. And Dalton tells me you're good at it. But one day, Sharpe, some halfwit like William Hale will make peace with the French because he's too damned scared of defeat and on that day the army will spit you out like a biscuit weevil.' He felt inside a waistcoat pocket stretched tight across a paunch that remained undiminished by the ship's execrable food. 'Here.' He passed Sharpe a slip of pasteboard. 'It's what my wife calls a *carte de visite.* Call on me when you want a job.' The card gave Fairley's address, Pallisser Hall. 'I grew up near that house,' Fairley said, 'and my father used to clean out its gutters with his bare hands. Now it's mine. I bought his lordship out.' He smiled, pleased with himself. 'There's no storm coming. Peculiar's got fleas in his trousers, that's all. And so he should.'

'He should?'

'I'm not happy that we lost the convoy, Sharpe. I don't approve, but on board ship it's Peculiar's word that counts, not mine. You don't buy a dog and bark yourself, Sharpe.' He fished a pocket watch out and clicked open its lid. 'Almost dinner time. The remnants of that tongue, no doubt.'

Midday came and still nothing explained Cromwell's nervousness. Pohlmann appeared on deck, but went nowhere near the captain, and a few minutes later Lady Grace, attended by her maid, took the air before going to the cuddy for dinner. The wind was lighter than it had been for days, making the *Calliope* rock in the swell, and some pale-faced passengers were clinging to the lee rail. Lieutenant Tufnell was reassuring. There was no storm coming, he said, for the glass in the captain's cabin was staying high. 'The wind'll be back,' he told the passengers on the main deck.

'Are we turning west today?' Sharpe asked.

'Tomorrow, probably,' Tufnell said, 'southwest, anyway. I rather think our gamble hasn't paid off and that we should have gone through the Straits. Still, we're a quick sailor and we should make up the time in the Atlantic.'

'Sail ho!' a lookout called from the mainmast. 'Sail on the larboard bow!'

Cromwell snatched up a speaking trumpet. 'What kind of sail?'

'Topsail, sir, can't see more.'

Tufnell frowned. 'A topsail means a European ship. Perhaps another Jonathon?' He looked up at Cromwell. 'You want to wear ship, sir?'

'We shall stand on, Mister Tufnell, we stand on.'

'Wear ship?' Sharpe asked.

'Turn away from whoever it is,' Tufnell said. 'It don't matter if it's a Jonathon, but we don't want to be playing games with a Frenchie.'

'The *Revenant*?' Sharpe suggested.

'Don't even say the name,' Tufnell answered grimly, reaching out to touch the wooden rail to avert the ill fortune of Sharpe's suggestion. 'But if we wore now we could outrun her. She's coming upwind, whoever she is.'

The lookout shouted again. 'She's a French ship, sir.'

'How do you know?' Cromwell called back.

'Cut of her sails, sir.'

Tufnell looked pained. 'Sir?' he appealed to Cromwell.

'The *Pucelle* is a French-made ship, Mister Tufnell,' Cromwell snapped. 'Most likely it's the *Pucelle*. We stand on.'

'Powder on deck, sir?' Tufnell asked.

Cromwell hesitated, then shook his head. 'Probably another whaler, Mister Tufnell, probably another whaler. Let us not become unduly excited.'

Sharpe forgot his dinner and climbed to the foredeck where he trained his telescope on the approaching ship. It was still hull down, but he could see two layers of sails above the skyline and make out the flattened shape of the foresails as they fought to gain a purchase on the wind. He lent the glass to the sailors who crowded the foredeck and none liked what they saw. 'That ain't the *Pucelle*,' one grunted. 'She's got a dirty streak on her fore topsail.'

'Could have washed the sail,' another suggested. 'Captain Chase ain't a man to let dirt stay on a sail.'

'Well, if it ain't the *Pucelle*,' the first man said, 'it's the *Revenant*, and we shouldn't be standing on. Shouldn't be standing on. Don't make sense.'

Tufnell had gone to the maintop with his own telescope. 'French warship, sir!' he called down to the quarterdeck. 'Black hoops on the mast!'

'The *Pucelle* has black hoops,' Cromwell shouted back. 'Can you see her flag?'

'No, sir.'

Cromwell stood irresolute for a moment, then gave an order to the helmsman so that the *Calliope* clumsily turned towards the west. Sailors ran to man the sheets, trimming the great sails to the wind's new angle.

'She's turning with us, sir!' Tufnell shouted.

The *Calliope* was going faster now and her bluff bows were thumping into the waves, and each thump sent a tremor through her tons of oak timbers. The passengers were silent. Sharpe stared through the telescope and saw that the far ship's hull was above the horizon now and it was painted black and yellow like a wasp.

'French colours, sir!' Tufnell shouted.

'Peculiar left it too bloody late,' a seaman near Sharpe said. 'Bloody man thinks he can walk on water.'

Sharpe turned and stared across the main deck at Peculiar Cromwell. Maybe, he thought, the captain had been expecting this. *Morgen früh*, Sharpe thought, *morgen früh*, only the rendezvous had come a few minutes late, but then he dismissed the idea. Surely Cromwell had not expected this? But then Sharpe saw Pohlmann gazing forrard with a glass and he remembered that Pohlmann had once commanded French officers. Had he stayed in touch with the French after Assaye? Was he allied with the French? No, Sharpe thought, no. It seemed unthinkable, but then Lady Grace came to the quarterdeck rail and she stared straight at Sharpe, looked pointedly at Cromwell, then back to Sharpe and he knew she was thinking the same unthinkable thought. 'Are we going to fight?' a passenger asked.

A seaman laughed. 'Can't fight a French seventy-four! And she'll have big guns, not like our eighteen-pounders.'

'Can we outrun her?' Sharpe asked.

'If we're lucky.' The man spat overboard.

Cromwell kept giving the helmsman orders, demanding a point closer to the wind or three points off the wind, and to Sharpe it seemed that the captain was trying to coax the last reserves of speed from the *Calliope*, but the sailors on the foredeck were disgusted. 'Just slows us down,' one of them explained. 'Every time you turn the rudder it slows you. He should leave well alone.' He looked at Sharpe. 'I should hide that glass, sir. Some Frenchie would like that, and yon ship has the legs of us.'

Sharpe ran below. He would have to fetch his jewels from Cromwell's cabin, but there were other things he also wanted to save and so he stuffed the precious telescope inside his shirt and tied his red officer's sash across it, then he pulled on his red coat, buckled his sword belt and pushed the pistol into his trouser pocket. Other passengers were trying to hide their more valuable possessions, the children were crying, and then, far away, muffled by distance and the ship's hull, Sharpe heard a gun.

He climbed back to the main deck and asked Cromwell's permission to be on the quarterdeck. Cromwell nodded, then looked with amusement at Sharpe's sabre. 'Expecting a fight, Mister Sharpe?'

'Can I retrieve my valuables from your cabin, Captain?' Sharpe asked.

Cromwell scowled. 'All in good time, Sharpe, all in good time. I'm busy now and will thank you to let me try and save the ship.'

Sharpe went to the rail. The French ship still looked a long way off, but now Sharpe could see the seas breaking white at the enemy's stem and a shredding puff of smoke drifting just ahead of its bows. 'They fired' – Major Dalton, his heavy claymore at his waist, joined Sharpe at the rail – 'but the ball fell a long mile short. Tufnell says they weren't trying to hit us, they just want us to heave to.'

Ebenezer Fairley came to Sharpe's other side. 'We should have stayed with the convoy,' he spat in disgust.

'A ship like that,' Dalton said, gazing at the French warship's massive flank which was thick with gunports, 'could have chewed up the whole convoy.'

'We'd have sacrificed the Company frigate,' Fairley said. 'That's what the frigate is for.' He drummed nervous fingers on the rail. 'She's a fast sailor.'

'So are we,' Major Dalton said.

'She's bigger,' Fairley said brusquely, 'and bigger ships sail faster than small ones.' He turned. 'Captain!'

'I am busy, Fairley, busy.' Cromwell did not look at the merchant.

'Can you outrun her?'

'If I am left in peace to practise my trade, perhaps.'

'What about my cash?' Lord William demanded. He had joined his wife on deck.

'The French,' Cromwell decreed, 'do not make war on private individuals. The ship and its cargo might be lost, but they will respect private property. If I have time, my lord, I will unlock my cabin. But for now, gentlemen, perhaps you will all let me sail this ship without yapping at me?'

Sharpe glanced at Lady Grace, but she ignored him and he looked back at the French warship. Fairley thumped the rail in his frustration. 'That bloody Frenchman will make a tidy profit,' the merchant said bitterly. 'This hull and cargo must be worth sixty thousand pound. Sixty thousand! Maybe more.'

Twenty for the French, Sharpe thought, twenty for Pohlmann and twenty for Cromwell, a captain who fervently believed the war was lost and that the French would win. A captain who had declared that a man must make his fortune before the French took over the world. And twenty thousand pounds was a real fortune, a sum on which a man could live for ever. 'They've still got to catch us,' Sharpe tried to reassure Fairley, 'and they'll have to get the ship and its cargo back to France. That won't be easy.'

Fairley shook his head. 'Doesn't work like that, Mister Sharpe. They'll take us to Mauritius and sell the cargo there. There are plenty of neutrals ready to buy this cargo. And like as not they'll sell the ship too. Next thing you know she'll be called the *George Washington* and be sailing out of Boston.' He spat across the rail. The tiller ropes creaked as Cromwell demanded yet another correction.

'What about us?' Sharpe asked.

'They'll send us home,' Fairley said, 'eventually. Don't know about you or the major, seeing as you're in uniform. They might put you in prison.'

'They'll parole us, Sharpe,' Dalton reassured the younger man, 'and we'll live at liberty in Port Louis. I hear it's a pleasant kind of place. And a good-looking young fellow like you will find a surfeit of bored young ladies.'

The *Revenant*, for it could be no other ship, fired

again. Sharpe saw a monstrous billow of white smoke appear high on her bows and a few seconds later the sound of the cannon came rumbling across the water. A fountain of white spray showed a half-mile short of the *Calliope*.

'Closer,' Dalton grunted.

'We should fire back,' Fairley growled.

'She's too big for us,' Dalton said sadly.

The two ships were on converging courses and the *Calliope* was still ahead, but Cromwell's frequent course corrections were slowing her. 'A few shots into her rigging might slow her down,' Fairley suggested.

'We'll soon be showing her our stern,' Dalton said. 'No guns will bear.'

'Then move a gun,' Fairley said angrily. 'Good God, there must be something we can do!'

The *Revenant* fired again and this time the ball bounced across the waves like a stone skipping across a pond and finally sank a quarter-mile short of the *Calliope*. 'The gun's getting warmer,' Dalton said. 'Another minute or two and she'll be thumping us.'

Lady Grace abruptly walked across the deck to stand between Dalton and Sharpe. 'Major' – she spoke very loudly, so that her husband would know she talked to the respectable Dalton and not to Sharpe – 'you think he will catch us?'

'I pray not, ma'am,' Dalton said, removing his cocked hat. 'I pray not.'

'We won't fight?' she asked.

'We cannot,' Dalton said.

She was wearing wide skirts that, because of her closeness to Sharpe, crushed up against his trousers and he felt her fingers tap his leg. He surreptitiously dropped his hand and she clutched it fiercely, unseen by anyone. 'But the French will treat us well?' she asked Dalton.

'I am sure they will, my lady,' the major said, 'and

there are a score of gentlemen aboard this ship ready to protect you.'

Grace dropped her voice to scarce above a whisper and, at the same time, gripped Sharpe's fingers so hard that it hurt. 'Look after me, Richard,' she murmured, then turned and walked back to her husband.

Major Dalton followed her, evidently eager to add more reassurance, and Ebenezer Fairley offered Sharpe a crooked grin. 'So that's how it is, eh?'

'What is?' Sharpe asked, not looking at the merchant.

'My family always had good ears. Good ears and good eyes. You and her, eh?'

'Mister Fairley . . .' Sharpe began to protest.

'Don't be daft, lad. I'm not going to say a word. But you're a sly one, aren't you? And so's she. Good for you, lad, and good for her too. So she ain't as bad as I thought, eh?' He frowned suddenly as Cromwell demanded another tweak of the wheel. 'Cromwell!' Fairley turned angrily on the captain. 'Stop fiddling with the rudder, man!'

'I'll thank you to go below, Mister Fairley,' Cromwell said calmly. 'This is my quarterdeck.'

'A fair piece of the cargo is mine!'

'If you do not go below, Fairley, I shall have the bosun escort you.'

'Damn your insolence,' Fairley growled, but obediently left the deck.

The *Revenant* fired again and this time the round shot sank within a few yards of the *Calliope*'s counter and close enough to spray the gilded stern with water. Cromwell had seen the fountain of water show above his taffrail and its proximity made up his mind. 'Haul down the colours, Mister Tufnell.'

'But, sir . . .'

'Haul down the colours!' Cromwell bellowed angrily at Tufnell. 'Point her upwind,' he added to the helmsman. The ensign came flapping down from the mizzen gaff and, at the same time, the *Calliope* turned her bows right round into the wind so that all the great sails hammered against the masts and rigging like demented wings. 'Furl sails!' Cromwell shouted. 'Lively now!'

The wheel turned to and fro by itself, responding to the surges of water that beat against the rudder. Cromwell glowered at his passengers on the quarterdeck. 'I apologize,' he snarled, sounding anything other than apologetic.

'My cash,' Lord William demanded.

'Is safe!' Cromwell snapped. 'And I have work to do before the Frenchies arrive.' He stalked off the deck.

It took a few minutes for the *Revenant* to catch up with the *Calliope*, but then the French warship hove to off the starboard quarter and lowered a boat. The rail of the French ship was thick with men who stared at their rich prize. All French seamen dreamed of a fat Indiaman loaded with valuables, but Sharpe doubted that any Frenchman had ever gained a prize as easily as this. This ship had been given to the French. He could not prove it, but he was certain of it, and he turned to stare at Pohlmann who, catching his eye, offered a rueful shrug.

Bastard, Sharpe thought, bastard. But for now he had other things to worry about. He must stay near her ladyship and he must be wary of Braithwaite, but, above all, he had to survive. Because there had been treachery and Sharpe wanted revenge.

CHAPTER 5

Sharpe went to Cromwell's cabin as the *Revenant* was lowering the first of her boats. The cabin door was ajar, but Cromwell was not inside. Sharpe tried to lift the big chest's lid, but it was locked. He went back to the quarterdeck, but the captain was not there either and the first French longboat was already pulling towards the *Calliope.*

Sharpe hurried back to the captain's cabin where he found Lord William standing irresolute. His lordship disliked speaking to Sharpe, but forced himself to sound civil. 'Have you seen Cromwell?'

'He's disappeared,' Sharpe said curtly as he stooped to the chest. The large size of the keyhole suggested the lock was Indian-made, which was good, for Indian locks were simple to pick, but he knew it could well be a European lock with an Indian faceplate which could prove trickier. He fished in his pocket and brought out a short length of bent steel that he inserted into the lock.

'What's that?' Lord William asked.

'A picklock,' Sharpe said. 'I've always carried one. Before I became respectable I used to earn my living this way.'

Lord William sniffed. 'Hardly something to boast about, Sharpe.' He paused, expecting Sharpe to answer, but the only sound was the small scraping of the pick against the lock's levers. 'Maybe we should wait for Cromwell?' Lord William suggested.

'He's got valuables of mine in here,' Sharpe said, probing with the steel to discover the levers. 'And the bloody Frogs will be here soon. Move, you awkward bastard!' This last was to the first lever rather than to Lord William.

'You will find a bag of cash in there, Sharpe,' Lord William said. 'It was too large to conceal, so I permitted Cromwell . . .' His voice tailed away as he realized he was explaining too much. He hesitated as the first lever clicked dully, then watched as Sharpe, holding that lever back with the blade of his folding knife, worked on the second. 'You say you entrusted valuables to Cromwell?' Lord William enquired, sounding surprised, as if he could not imagine Sharpe possessing anything worthy of such protection.

'I did,' Sharpe said, 'more fool me.' The second lever slipped back and Sharpe heaved up the chest's heavy lid.

The stench of old unwashed clothes assailed him. He grimaced, then threw aside a filthy boat cloak and layers of dirty shirts and undergarments. Cromwell, it seemed, washed nothing aboard the *Calliope*, but simply let the laundry accrete in the chest until he reached shore. Sharpe tossed more and more garments aside until he had reached the chest's bottom. There were no jewels. No diamonds, no rubies, no emeralds. No bag of cash. 'The bastard,' he said bitterly, and unceremoniously pushed past Lord William to seek Cromwell on deck.

He was too late. The captain was already at the main-deck entry port where he was greeting a tall French naval officer who was resplendent in a gilded blue coat, red waistcoat, blue breeches and white stockings. The Frenchman took off his salt-stained cocked hat as a courtesy to Cromwell. 'You yield the ship?' he asked in good English.

'Don't have much bloody choice, do I?' Cromwell

said, glancing at the *Revenant*, which had opened four of her gunports to deter anyone aboard the *Calliope* from attempting a futile resistance. 'Who are you?'

'I am Capitaine Montmorin.' The Frenchman bowed. 'Capitaine Louis Montmorin and you have my sympathy, monsieur. And you are?'

'Cromwell,' Cromwell grunted.

Montmorin, the French captain of whom Captain Joel Chase had spoken so admiringly, now talked to his seamen who had followed him up the *Calliope*'s side to fill the ship's waist. Once he had given them their orders he looked back to Cromwell. 'Do I have your word, Captain, that neither you nor your officers will attempt anything rash?' He waited until Cromwell had offered a grudging nod, then smiled. 'Then your crew will go to the forecastle, you and your officers will retire to your quarters and all passengers will return to their cabins.' He left Cromwell by the entry port and climbed to the quarterdeck. 'I apologize for the inconvenience, ladies and gentlemen,' he said courteously, 'but you must go to your cabins. You, gentlemen' – he had turned to look at Sharpe and Dalton who were the only men on the quarterdeck in military uniform – 'you are British officers?'

'I am Major Dalton.' Dalton stepped forward, then gestured to Sharpe who still stood beside the wheel. 'And that is my colleague, Mister Sharpe.'

Dalton had begun to draw his claymore to offer a formal surrender, but Montmorin frowned and shook his head as if to suggest he required no such gesture. 'Do you give me your word that you will obey my orders, Major?'

'I do,' Dalton said.

'Then you may keep your swords.' Montmorin smiled, but his elegant courtesy was given an edge of steel by three French marines in blue coats who now climbed to the quarterdeck and pointed their muskets at Dalton.

The major stepped back, gesturing that Sharpe should join him. 'Stay with me,' he said softly.

Montmorin had now registered Lady Grace's presence and he greeted her by removing his hat again and offering a sweeping bow. 'I am sorry, ma'am, that you should be inconvenienced.' Lady Grace appeared not to notice the Frenchman's existence, but Lord William spoke to Montmorin in fluent French, and whatever he said seemed to amuse the French captain who bowed a second time to Lady Grace. 'No one,' Montmorin announced in a loud voice, 'will be molested. So long as you co-operate with the prize crew. Now, ladies and gentlemen, to your cabins if you please.'

'Captain!' Sharpe called. Montmorin turned and waited for Sharpe to speak. 'I want Cromwell,' Sharpe said and started towards the quarterdeck steps. Cromwell looked alarmed, but then a French marine barred Sharpe's path.

'To your cabin, monsieur,' Montmorin insisted.

'Cromwell!' Sharpe called and he tried to force his way past the marine, but a second bayonet faced him and Sharpe was driven back.

Pohlmann and Mathilde, alone among the stern passengers, had not been on the quarterdeck when the Frenchmen came aboard, but now they emerged and with them was the Swiss servant who was no longer dressed in sombre grey but wore a sword like any gentleman. He greeted Montmorin in fluent French and the *Revenant*'s captain offered the so-called servant a deep bow, and then Sharpe saw no more because the French marines were ushering the passengers off the deck and Sharpe reluctantly followed Dalton to the major's cabin, which was twice the size of Sharpe's quarters and partitioned with wood instead of canvas. It was furnished with a bed, bureau, chest and chair. Dalton gestured that Sharpe should sit on the bed, hung his sword and belt on the back of the door and uncorked a bottle. 'French brandy,' he said unhappily, 'to console ourselves for a French victory.' He poured two glasses. 'I thought you'd be more comfortable here than down in the ship's cellar, Sharpe.'

'It's kind of you, sir.'

'And to be truthful,' the elderly major said, 'I'd be glad of some company. I fear these next hours are liable to be tedious.'

'I fear they will, sir.'

'Mind you, they can't keep us cooped up for ever.' He handed Sharpe a glass of brandy, then peered through the porthole. 'More boats arriving, more men. Horrible-looking rogues. I don't know about you, Sharpe, but I thought Cromwell didn't try over-hard to escape. Not that I'm any sailor, of course, but Tufnell told me there were other sails we might have set. Skyscrapers, I think he called them. Can that be right? Skyscrapers and studdingsails?'

'I don't think Peculiar tried at all, sir,' Sharpe said morosely. Indeed, Sharpe believed that this empty spot of an empty ocean had been a rendezvous and that Cromwell had deliberately lost the convoy and then purposefully sailed here in the knowledge that the *Revenant* would be waiting for him. The English captain had put on a feeble display of attempting to escape, and a meagre show of defiance when Montmorin came aboard, but Sharpe still reckoned the *Calliope* had been sold long before the *Revenant* hove into sight.

'But we're not seamen, you and I,' Dalton said, then frowned as boots tramped on the deck above, evidently inside Pohlmann's quarters in the roundhouse. Something heavy fell on the deck, then there was a scraping sound. 'Dear me,' Dalton said, 'now they're looting us.'

He sighed. 'Lord knows how long it'll be before we'll be paroled and I did so hope to be home by autumn.'

'It'll be cold in Edinburgh, sir,' Sharpe said.

Dalton smiled. 'I'll have forgotten what it's like to feel the cold. What place do you call home, Sharpe?'

Sharpe shrugged. 'I've only ever lived in London and Yorkshire, sir, and I don't know that either's home. The army's my real home.'

'Not a bad home, Sharpe. You could do much worse.'

The brandy made Sharpe's head swim and he refused a second glass. The ship, oddly silent, rocked in a long swell. Sharpe edged to the porthole to see that the French seamen had taken the spare spars from the *Calliope*'s main deck and were now floating the great lengths of timber across to the *Revenant*, towing them behind longboats, while other craft were carrying back casks of wine, water and food. The French warship was at least half as long again as the *Calliope* and her decks were much higher. Her gunports were all closed now, but she still looked sinister as she rose and fell on the ocean swell. The copper at her water line looked bright, suggesting she had recently scraped her bottom clean.

Footsteps sounded in the narrow passageway and there was a sudden knock on the door. 'Come!' Major Dalton called, expecting one of his fellow passengers, but it was Capitaine Louis Montmorin who ducked under the low door, followed by an even taller man dressed in the same red, blue and white uniform. The two tall Frenchmen made the cabin seem very small.

'You are the senior English officer aboard?' Montmorin asked Dalton.

'Scottish,' Dalton bristled.

'*Pardonnez-moi.*' Montmorin was amused. 'Permit me to name Lieutenant Bursay.' The captain indicated the huge man who loomed just inside the door. 'Lieutenant Bursay will be captain of the prize crew that will take this ship to Mauritius.' The lieutenant was a gross-looking creature with an expressionless face that had been first scarred by smallpox, then by weapons. His right cheek was pitted blue with powder burns, his greasy hair hung lank over his collar and his uniform was stained with what looked like dried blood. He had huge hands with blackened palms, suggesting he had once earned his living in the high rigging, while at his side hung a broad-bladed cutlass and a long-barrelled pistol. Montmorin spoke to the lieutenant in French, then turned back to Dalton. 'I have told him, Major, that in all matters concerning the passengers he is to consult with you.'

'*Merci, Capitaine,*' Dalton said, then looked at the huge Bursay. '*Parlez-vous anglais?*'

Bursay offered Dalton a flat stare for a few seconds. '*Non,*' he finally grunted.

'But you speak French?' Montmorin asked Dalton.

'Passably,' Dalton conceded.

'That is good. And you may be assured, monsieur, that no harm will come to any passenger so long as you all obey Lieutenant Bursay's orders. Those orders are very simple. You are to stay below decks. You may go anywhere in the ship, except on deck. There will be armed men guarding every hatchway, and those men have orders to shoot if any of you disobey those simple orders.' He smiled. 'It will be three, perhaps four days to Mauritius? Longer, I fear, if the wind does not improve. And, monsieur, allow me to tell you how sincerely I regret your inconvenience. *C'est la guerre.*'

Montmorin and Bursay left and Dalton shook his head. 'This is a sad business, Sharpe, a sad business.'

The noise overhead, from Pohlmann's cabins, had stopped and Sharpe looked up. 'Do you mind if I make a reconnaissance, sir?'

'A reconnaissance? Not on deck, I hope? Good Lord, Sharpe, do you think they'd really shoot us? It seems very uncivilized, don't you think?'

Sharpe did not answer, but instead went out into the passageway and, followed by Dalton, climbed the narrow stairs to the roundhouse. The door to the cuddy was open and inside Sharpe found a disconsolate Lieutenant Tufnell staring at an almost empty room. The chairs had been taken, the chintz curtains removed and the chandelier carried away. Only the table which was fixed to the deck and had presumably been too heavy to move in a hurry still remained. 'The furniture belonged to the captain,' Tufnell said, 'and they've stolen it.'

'What else have they stolen?' Dalton asked.

'Nothing of mine,' Tufnell said. 'They've taken cordage and spars, of course, and some food, but they've left the cargo. They can sell that, you see, in Mauritius.'

Sharpe went back into the passage and so to Pohlmann's door which, though shut, was not locked and all his suspicions were confirmed when he pushed open the door, for the cabin was empty. The two silk-covered sofas were gone, Mathilde's harp had disappeared, the low table was no more and only the sideboard and the bed, both monstrously heavy, were still nailed to the deck. Sharpe crossed to the sideboard and pulled open its doors to find it had been stripped of everything except empty bottles. The sheets, blankets and pillows were gone from the bed, leaving only a mattress. 'Damn him,' Sharpe said.

'Damn who?' Dalton had followed Sharpe into the cabin.

'The Baron von Dornberg, sir.' Sharpe decided not to reveal Pohlmann's true identity, for Dalton would doubtless demand to know why Sharpe had not uncovered the impostor before, and Sharpe did not think that he could answer that question satisfactorily. Nor did he know whether such a revelation could have saved the ship, for Cromwell was just as guilty as Pohlmann. Sharpe led the major and Tufnell down the stairs to Cromwell's quarters to find them swept as clean as Pohlmann's cabin. The dirty clothes were gone, the books had been taken from the shelves and the chronometer and barometer were no longer in the small cupboard. The big chest had vanished. 'And damn goddamn bloody Cromwell too,' Sharpe said. 'Damn him to hell.' He did not even bother to look in the cabin occupied by Pohlmann's 'servant', for he knew that would be as bare as this. 'They sold the ship, sir,' he said to Dalton.

'They did what?' The major looked appalled.

'They sold the ship. The baron and Cromwell. Damn them.' He kicked the table leg. 'I can't prove it, sir, but it was no accident we lost the convoy, and no accident that we met the *Revenant*.' He rubbed his face tiredly. 'Cromwell believes the war is lost. He thinks we're going to be living under French sufferance, if not French rule, so he sold himself to the winners.'

'No!' Lieutenant Tufnell protested.

'I can't believe it, Sharpe,' the major said, but his face showed that he did believe it. 'I mean, the baron, yes! He's a foreigner. But Cromwell?'

'I've no doubt it was the baron's idea, sir. He probably talked to all the convoy's captains when they were waiting in Bombay and found his man in Cromwell. Now they've stolen the passengers' jewellery, sold the ship and deserted. Why else has the baron gone to the *Revenant*? Why didn't he stay with the rest of the passengers?' He almost called him Pohlmann, but remembered just in time.

Dalton sat on the empty table. 'Cromwell was looking after a watch for me,' he said sadly. ' Rather a valuable one that belonged to my dear father. It kept uncertain time, but it was precious to me.'

'I'm sorry, sir.'

'Nothing we can do,' Dalton said bleakly. 'We've been fleeced, Sharpe, fleeced!'

'Not by Cromwell, surely!' Tufnell said in wonderment. 'He was so proud of being English!'

'It's just that he loves money more than his country,' Sharpe said sourly.

'And you told me yourself that he could have tried harder to evade the *Revenant*,' Dalton pointed out to Tufnell.

'He could, sir, he could,' Tufnell admitted, appalled at Cromwell's betrayal.

They went to Ebenezer Fairley's cabin and the merchant grunted when he heard Sharpe's tale, but did not seem unduly surprised. 'I've seen folk beggar their own families for a slice of profit. And Peculiar was always a greedy man. Come in, the three of you. I've got brandy, wine, rum and arrack that needs drinking before those French buggers find it.'

'I hope Cromwell was not carrying any of your valuables?' Dalton asked solicitously.

'Do I look like a blockhead?' Fairley demanded. 'He tried! He even told me I had to give him my valuables under Company rules, but I told him not to be such a damned fool!'

'Quite,' Dalton said, thinking of his father's watch. Sharpe said nothing.

Fairley's wife, a plump and motherly woman, expressed a hope that the French would provide supper. 'It'll be nothing fancy, mother,' Fairley warned his wife, 'not like we've been getting in the cuddy. It'll be burgoo, don't you reckon, Sharpe?'

'I imagine so, sir.'

'God knows how their lordships will like that!' Fairley

said, jerking his head up towards Lord William's cabin before offering Sharpe a sly glance. 'Not that her ladyship seems to mind mucking it.'

'I doubt she'll like burgoo,' Dalton said earnestly.

It was almost nightfall before the French had emptied the *Calliope* of all they wanted. They took powder, cordage, spars, food, water and all the *Calliope*'s boats, but left the cargo intact for that, like the ship itself, would be sold in Mauritius. The last boat rowed back to the warship, then the Frenchman loosed her topsails and chanting seamen hauled out the foresails to catch the wind and turn the ship westwards as the other sails were loosed. Men waved from the quarterdeck as the black and yellow ship drew away.

'Gone towards the Cape of Good Hope,' Tufnell said morosely. 'Looking for the China traders, I don't doubt.'

The *Calliope*, now with the French tricolour hoisted above the Company ensign, began to move. She went slowly at first, for her prize crew was small and it took them over half an hour to loose all the Indiaman's sails, but by dusk the great ship was sailing smoothly eastwards in a light wind.

Two of the *Calliope*'s own seamen were allowed to bring supper to the passengers and Fairley invited the major, Tufnell and Sharpe to eat in his cabin. The meal was a pot of boiled oats thickened with salt beef fat and dried fish that Fairley declared was the best meal he had yet eaten on board. He saw his wife's distaste. 'You ate worse than this when we were first married, mother.'

'I cooked for you when we were first married!' she answered indignantly.

'You think I've forgotten?' Fairley asked, then spooned another mouthful of burgoo.

The light was fading in the cabin as they ate supper,

but none of the prize crew bothered to ascertain whether any of the passengers were using lanterns and so Fairley lit every lamp he could find and hung them in the stern windows. 'There are supposed to be British ships in this ocean,' he declared, 'so let them see us.'

'Give me some lanterns,' Sharpe said, 'and I'll hang them in the baron's window.'

'Good lad,' Fairley said.

'And you might as well sleep there, Sharpe,' the major said. 'I can give you a blanket.'

'We'll give you a blanket, lad, and sheets,' Fairley insisted, and his wife opened a travelling chest and handed Sharpe a heap of bedding while Fairley fetched two lanterns from the passageway outside his cabin. 'Do you need a tinderbox?'

'I have one,' Sharpe said.

'At least you get a good cabin for a day or two,' Fairley said, 'though God knows how we'll make out in Mauritius. Bed bugs and French lice, I dare say. I was in Calais once for a night and I've never seen a room so filthy. You remember that, mother? You were costive for a week afterwards.'

'Henry!' Mrs Fairley remonstrated.

Sharpe climbed the stairs and took possession of Pohlmann's big empty cabin. He lit the two lanterns, placed them on the stern seat, then made the bed. The tiller ropes creaked. He opened one of the windows, banging the frame to loosen the swollen wood, and stared down at the *Calliope*'s flattened wake. A thin moon lit the sea and silvered some small clouds, but no ships were visible. Above him a Frenchman laughed on the poop deck. Sharpe took off his sabre and coat, but he was too tense to sleep and so he just lay on the bed and stared at the white-painted planks above him and thought of Grace next door. He supposed that she and her husband would sleep apart, as they had on every other night, and he wondered how he could let her know that he was now ensconced in luxury.

Then he became aware of raised voices coming from the neighbouring quarters and he swung off the bed and crouched beside the thin wooden partition. There were at least three men in the foremost cabin, all speaking in French. Sharpe could make out Lord William's voice, which sounded angry, but he had no idea of what was being said. Perhaps his lordship was complaining about the food, and that thought made Sharpe smile. He went back to the bed and just then Lord William yelped. It was an odd sound, like a dog. Sharpe was on his feet again, bracing himself against the slow roll of the ship. There was a silence. Once more Sharpe crouched by the flimsy wooden partition and heard a French voice saying a word over and over. Bee-joo, it sounded like. Lord William spoke, his voice muffled, then grunted as if he had been hit in the belly and had all the wind driven from him.

Sharpe heard the door between Lord William's two cabins open and close. There was a click as the locking hook was dropped into its eye. A Frenchman's voice sounded again, this time from the stern cabin that shared the wide window with Sharpe's makeshift quarters. Lady Grace answered him in French, apparently protesting, then she screamed.

Sharpe stood. He expected to hear Lord William intervene, but there was silence, then Grace gave a second scream which was abruptly stifled and Sharpe hurled himself at the partition. He could have gone into the corridor and back into the next-door cabin, but breaking down the panelled partition was the quickest way to reach Grace and so he hammered it with his shoulder and the thin wood splintered and Sharpe tore his way through, bellowing as though he went into battle.

Which he did, for Lieutenant Bursay was on the bed

where he was holding down Lady Grace. The tall lieutenant had torn her dress open at the neck and was now trying to rip it further while, at the same time, keeping one hand over her mouth. He turned to see Sharpe, but he was much too slow, for Sharpe was already on the lieutenant's broad back with his left hand tangled in Bursay's greasy hair. He hauled the Frenchman's head back and chopped the side of his right hand onto the lieutenant's neck. He hit him once, twice, then Bursay heaved Sharpe off and twisted to swing a huge fist. Someone hammered on the cabin door, but Bursay had locked it.

Bursay had taken off his coat and sword belt, but he seized the cutlass handle, dragged the blade free and slashed at Sharpe. Lady Grace was hunched at the head of the bed, clutching the remnants of her dress to her neck. There were pearls scattered on the bed. Bursay had evidently come to plunder Lord William's possessions and found Grace the most delectable.

Sharpe threw himself back through the ruins of the bulkhead. His own sabre was on the bed and he dragged it from the scabbard and swung the blade as the big Frenchman clambered through the splintered panels. Bursay parried the stroke, then, as the sound of the blades still echoed in the cabin, he charged at Sharpe.

Sharpe tried to spear the sabre into Bursay's belly, but the lieutenant contemptuously swatted the steel away and punched the hilt of the cutlass into Sharpe's head. The blow made Sharpe reel, scattering his vision with sparks and darkness as he fell backwards. He rolled desperately to his right as the cutlass chopped down into the deck, then he swung the sabre in a wild, back-handed and clumsy stroke that did no damage, but served to make Bursay step back. Sharpe scrambled to his feet, his head still ringing, and heard the locked door between Lord William's two cabins being broken down. Bursay grinned. He was so tall that he had to stoop beneath the deck beams, but he was confident, for he had hurt Sharpe, who was staggering slightly. The cutlass hilt had drawn blood which trickled from Sharpe's forehead down his cheek. He shook his head, trying to clear his vision, knowing that this brute of a man was just as savage and quick as he was himself. The lieutenant ducked under a beam and lunged at Sharpe, who parried, then Bursay snarled and charged, the cutlass sweeping like a reaping hook, and Sharpe threw himself back against the cabin's forward bulkhead and the Frenchman knew he had won, except that Sharpe bounced back from the wall, his sabre held like a spear, and stretched forward so that the curved tip ripped into Bursay's throat. Sharpe swerved to his left to avoid the cutlass's heavy riposte and it seemed to him that his thrust had not done any real damage, for he had felt no resistance to the blade, but Bursay was wavering and blood was pouring down his coat. The Frenchman's right arm fell so that the cutlass tip struck the deck. He stared at Sharpe with an expression of puzzlement and put his left hand to his neck where the blood was pulsing dark and then, with a lurch, he fell to his knees and made a gurgling sound. A marine kicked through the shattered bulkhead and stared wide-eyed at the big lieutenant, who was looking up at Sharpe in faint surprise. Then, as if pole-axed, Bursay fell hard forward and a wash of blood spilt across the deck and vanished between the cracks.

The marine raised his musket, but just then an authoritative voice snapped in French and the man lowered the gun. Major Dalton thrust the marine aside and saw Bursay's body which was still twitching. 'You did this?' the major asked, kneeling and lifting the lieutenant's head, then dropping it swiftly as more blood welled from the wound in the neck.

'What else was I to do with him?' Sharpe asked belligerently. He wiped the sabre's tip on the hem of his coat, then pushed past the marine and peered through the broken bulkhead to see that Lady Grace was still crouched on the bed, her hands at her throat, shaking. 'It's all right, my lady,' he said, 'it's over.'

She stared at him. Dalton spoke in French to the marine, evidently ordering the man to report to the quarterdeck, then Lord William peered round the shattered partition, saw the corpse and looked up at Sharpe's bloodied face. 'What . . .' he began, but then was bereft of words. There was a graze on Lord William's cheek where he had been struck by Bursay. The Frenchman was unmoving now. Lady Grace was still sobbing, gasping huge breaths, then whimpering.

Sharpe tossed his sabre onto Pohlmann's bed, and stepped past Lord William. 'It's all right, my lady,' he said again, 'he's dead.'

'Dead?'

'He's dead.'

A silk embroidered dressing gown, presumably Lord William's, was hung over the foot of the bed and Sharpe tossed it to Lady Grace. She draped it about her shoulders, then began shaking again. 'I'm sorry,' she sobbed, 'I'm sorry.'

'Nothing for you to be sorry about, my lady,' Sharpe said.

'You will leave this cabin, Sharpe,' Lord William said coldly. He was shaking slightly and a trickle of blood traced his jawbone.

Lady Grace turned on her husband. 'You did nothing!' she spat at him. 'You did nothing!'

'You're hysterical, Grace, hysterical. The man hit me!' he protested to anyone who would listen. 'I tried to stop him, he hit me!'

'You did nothing!' Lady Grace said again.

Lord William summoned Lady Grace's maid who, like him, had been under the marine's guard in the day cabin. 'Calm her down, for Christ's sake,' he told the girl, then jerked his head to indicate that Sharpe should leave the bedroom.

Sharpe stepped back through the ruined bulkhead to discover that most of the great cabin's passengers had come upstairs and were now staring at Bursay's corpse. Ebenezer Fairley shook his head in wonder. 'When you do a job, lad,' the merchant said, 'you do it proper. Can't be a drop of blood left in him! Most of it's dripped down onto our bed.'

'I'm sorry,' Sharpe said.

'Not the first blood I've seen, lad. And worse things happen at sea, they tell me.'

'You should all leave!' Lord William had come into Pohlmann's quarters. 'Just leave!' he snapped pettishly.

'This ain't your room,' Fairley growled, 'and if you were a half a man, my lord, neither Sharpe nor this corpse would be here.'

Lord William gaped at Fairley, but just then Lady Grace, her hair ragged, stepped over the splinters of the partition. Her husband tried to push her back, but she shook him off and stared down at the corpse, then up at Sharpe. 'Thank you, Mister Sharpe,' she said.

'Glad I could be of service, my lady,' Sharpe replied, then turned and braced himself as Major Dalton led a Frenchman into the crowded cabin. 'This is the new captain of the ship,' Dalton said. 'He's an *officier marinier*, which I think is the equivalent of our petty officer.'

The Frenchman was an older man, balding, with a face weathered and browned by long service at sea. He had no uniform, for he was not a wardroom officer, but evidently a senior seaman who seemed quite unmoved by Bursay's death. It was plain that the marine had already explained the circumstance for he asked no questions, but simply made a clumsy and embarrassed bow to Lady Grace and muttered an apology.

Lady Grace acknowledged the apology in a voice still shaking from fear. '*Merci, monsieur.*'

The *officier marinier* spoke to Dalton who translated for Sharpe's benefit. 'He regrets Bursay's actions, Sharpe. He says the man was an animal. He was a petty officer till a month ago, when Montmorin promoted him. He told him he was on his honour to behave like a gentleman, but Bursay had no honour.'

'I'm forgiven?' Sharpe asked, amused.

'You defended a lady, Sharpe,' Dalton said, frowning at Sharpe's light tone. 'How can any reasonable man object?'

The Frenchman made arrangements for a sheet of canvas to be nailed over the broken partition and for the lieutenant's body to be taken away. He also insisted that the lanterns be removed from the window.

Sharpe stood the lanterns on the empty sideboard. 'I'll sleep in here,' he announced, 'just in case any other bloody Frenchman gets lonely.' Lord William opened his mouth to protest, then thought better of it. The corpse was taken away and a piece of frayed sailcloth nailed over the partition. Then Sharpe slept in Pohlmann's bed as the ship sailed on, taking him to captivity.

The next two days were tedious. The wind was light so the ship rolled and made slow progress, so slow that Tufnell guessed it would take nearer six days to reach Mauritius, and that was good, for it meant there was more time for a British warship to see the great captured Indiaman wallowing in the long swells. None of the passengers could go on deck and the heat in the cabins was stifling. Sharpe passed the time as best he could. Major Dalton lent him a book called *Tristram Shandy*, but Sharpe could make neither head nor tail of it. Just lying and staring at the ceiling was more rewarding. The barrister tried to teach Sharpe backgammon, but Sharpe was not interested in gambling and so Fazackerly went off to find more willing prey. Lieutenant Tufnell showed him how to tie some knots, and that passed some hours between the meals which were all burgoo enlivened with dried peas. Mrs Fairley embroidered a shawl, her husband growled and paced and fretted, Major Dalton attempted to compile an accurate account of the battle at Assaye which needed Sharpe's constant advice, the ship sailed slowly on and Sharpe did not see Lady Grace during the daytime.

She came to his cabin on the second night, arriving while he was asleep and waking him by putting a hand on his mouth so he did not cry out. 'The maid's asleep,' she whispered, and in the silence that followed Sharpe could hear Lord William's drug-induced snores beyond the makeshift canvas screen.

She lay beside Sharpe, one leg across his, and did not speak for a long time. 'When he came in,' she finally whispered, 'he said he wanted my jewels. That was all. My jewels. Then he told me he was going to cut William's throat if I didn't do what he wanted.'

'It's all right,' Sharpe tried to soothe her.

She shook her head abruptly. 'And then he told me that he hated all aristos. That was what he said, "aristos", and said we should all be guillotined. He said he was going to kill us both and claim that William had attacked him and that I had died of a fever.'

'He's the one feeding the fishes now,' Sharpe said. He had heard a splash the previous morning and knew it was Bursay's body being launched into eternity.

'You don't hate aristos, do you?' Grace asked after a long pause.

'I've only met you, your husband and Sir Arthur. Is he an aristo?'

She nodded. 'His father's the Earl of Mornington.'

'So I like two out of three,' Sharpe said. 'That's not bad.'

'You like Arthur?'

Sharpe shrugged. 'I don't know that I like him, but I'd like him to like me. I admire him.'

'But you don't like William?'

'Do you?'

She paused. 'No. My father made me marry him. He's rich, very rich, and my family isn't. He was reckoned a good match, a very good match. I liked him once, but not now. Not now.'

'He hates me,' Sharpe said.

'He's frightened of you.'

Sharpe smiled. 'He's a lord, though, isn't he? And I'm nothing.'

'You're here, though,' Grace said, kissing him on the cheek, 'and he isn't.' She kissed him again. 'And if he found me here I would be ruined. My name would be a disgrace. I would never see society again. I might never see anyone again.'

Sharpe thought of Malachi Braithwaite and was grateful that the secretary was mewed up in the steerage where he could not add to his suspicions of Sharpe and Lady Grace. 'You mean your husband would kill you?' Sharpe asked her.

'He'd like to. He might.' She thought about it. 'But he'd probably have me declared mad. It isn't difficult. He'd hire expensive doctors who'd call me an hysterical lunatic and a judge would order me locked away. I'd spend the rest of my short life shut in a wing of the Lincolnshire house being spoon-fed medicines. Only the medicines would be mildly poisonous so that, mercifully, I wouldn't live long.'

Sharpe turned to look at her, though it was so dark that he could see little but the blur of her face. 'He could really do that?' he asked.

'Of course,' she said, 'but I stay safe by behaving very correctly, and by pretending that William doesn't take whores and mistresses. And, of course, he wants an heir. He was overjoyed when our son was born, but has hated me ever since he died. Which doesn't stop him trying to give me another.' She paused. 'So my best hope of staying alive is to give him a son and to behave like an angel, and I swore I would do both, but then I saw you and I thought why not lose my wits?'

'I'll look after you,' Sharpe promised.

'Once we're off this boat,' she said quietly, 'I doubt we'll ever meet again.'

'No,' Sharpe protested, 'no.'

'Shh,' she whispered, and covered his mouth with hers.

By dawn she was gone. The view from the stern window was unchanged. No British warship was in pursuit, there was just the endless Indian Ocean stretching away to a hazed horizon. The wind was fresher so that the ship rolled and thumped, dislodging the chess pieces that Major Dalton had arrayed on the stern seat in a plan of the battle of Assaye. 'You must tell me,' the major said, 'what happened when Sir Arthur was unhorsed.'

'I think you must ask him, Major.'

'But you know as much as he, surely?'

'I do,' Sharpe agreed, 'but I doubt he's fond of telling the story, or of having it told. You might do better to say he fought off a group of the enemy and was rescued by his aides.'

'But is that true?'

'There's truth in it,' Sharpe said and would say no more. Besides, he could not remember exactly what had happened. He remembered sliding off his horse and slashing the sabre in hay-making cuts; he remembered Sir Arthur being dazed and standing in the shelter of a cannon's wheel and he remembered killing, but what he remembered clearest of all was the Indian swordsman who had deserved to kill him, for the man had swung his *tulwar* in a scything stroke that had struck the nape of Sharpe's neck. That stroke should have beheaded Sharpe, but he had been wearing his hair in the soldier's queue, bound around a leather bag that would normally have been filled with sand, only instead Sharpe had concealed the great ruby from the Tippoo Sultan's hat in the bag and the big jewel had stopped the *tulwar* cold. The blow had released the ruby and Sharpe remembered how, when the vicious fight was over, Sir Arthur had picked up the stone and held it out to him with a puzzled expression. The general had been too confused to recognize what it was and probably thought it was nothing but a prettily coloured pebble that Sharpe had collected. Goddamn Cromwell had the pretty pebble now.

'What was Sir Arthur's horse called?' Dalton asked.

'Diomed,' Sharpe said. 'He was very fond of that horse.' He could remember the gush of blood that spilt onto the dry ground when the pike was pulled from Diomed's chest.

Dalton questioned Sharpe till late afternoon, making notes for his memoir. 'I have to do something with my retirement, Sharpe. If ever I see Edinburgh again.'

'Are you not married, sir?'

'I was. A dear lady. She died.' The major shook his head, then stared wistfully through the stern window. 'We had no children,' he said softly, then frowned as a sudden rush of feet sounded from the quarterdeck. A voice could be heard shouting, and a heartbeat later the *Calliope* yawed to larboard and the sails hammered like guns firing. One by one the sails were sheeted home and the ship, after momentarily wallowing in the swells, was sailing smooth again, only this time she was beating up into the wind on a course as near northerly as the small crew could hold. 'Something's excited the Frenchies,' the major said.

No one knew what had caused the northwards turn, for no other ship was visible from the cabin portholes, though it was possible a lookout high in the rigging had seen some topsails on the southern horizon. The motion of the ship was more uncomfortable now for she was slamming into the waves and heeling over. Then, when the supper was carried to the passengers, the *officier marinier* ordered that no lights were to be shown, and promised that anyone who disobeyed him would be thrust down into the ship's hold where foetid seawater slopped and rats ruled.

'So there is another ship,' Dalton said.

'But has she seen us?' Sharpe wondered.

'Even if she has,' Dalton said gloomily, 'what can we do?'

Sharpe prayed it was the *Pucelle*, Captain Chase's French-built warship that was as quick a sailor as the *Revenant*. 'There is one thing,' he said.

'What?'

'I need Tufnell,' Sharpe said, and he went down to the officers' quarters in the great cabin and hammered on the lieutenant's door and, after a brief conversation, took the lieutenant and Dalton to Ebenezer Fairley's cabin.

The merchant was robed for bed and had a tasselled nightcap falling over the left side of his face, but he listened to Sharpe, then grinned. 'Come on in, lad. Mother! You'll have to get up again. We've got some mischief to make.'

The problem was a lack of tools, but Sharpe had his

pocket knife, Tufnell had a short dagger and the major produced a dirk and the three men first pulled up the painted canvas carpet in Fairley's sleeping cabin, then attacked a floorboard.

The board was made of oak over two inches thick. It was old oak, seasoned and hard, but Sharpe could see no alternative except to make a hole in the deck and hope that it was in the right place. The men took it in turns to hack and scratch and carve and cut the wood, while Mrs Fairley produced a kitchen steel from a travelling chest and periodically sharpened the three blades that were slowly, so very slowly, digging through the plank.

They made two cuts, a foot apart, and it took till well past midnight to cut through the board and lift the section out. They worked in the dark, but once the hole was made Fairley lit a lantern that he shielded with one of his wife's cloaks and the three men peered into the darkness below. At first Sharpe could see nothing. He could hear the grating of the tiller rope, but he could not see it, and then, when Fairley dropped the lantern into the hole, he saw the great hemp rope just a foot or so away. Every few seconds the taut rope would move an inch or more and the creaking sound would echo through the stern.

The rope was fastened to the tiller which was the bar that turned the *Calliope*'s great rudder. From the tiller the rope went to both sides of the ship where it ran through pulleys before returning to the centre of the ship where two more pulleys led the rope up to the ship's wheel which was really two wheels, one in front of the other, so that as many men as possible could heave on the spokes when the ship was in heavy seas and high winds. The twin wheels were connected by a hefty wooden drum round which the tiller rope was tightly wound so that a turn of the wheel pulled on the rope and transferred the motion to the tiller bar. Cut that rope and the *Calliope* would be rudderless for a while.

'But when to cut it, eh?' Fairley asked.

'Wait for daylight,' Dalton suggested.

'It'll take some cutting,' Sharpe said, for the rope was near three inches thick. It ran in a space between the main and lower decks and Fairley put the canvas carpet back into place, not only to disguise the hole, but to keep the rats from coming up into his cabin.

'How long will it take to replace that rope?' the merchant asked Tufnell.

'A good crew could do it in an hour.'

'They'll have some good seamen,' the merchant said, 'so we'd best not waste their efforts now. We'll see what morning brings.'

That night brought no Lady Grace. Perhaps, Sharpe thought, she had already looked into Pohlmann's cabin and found Sharpe absent. Or perhaps Lord William was awake and watchful, wondering if a rescue was closing on the night-shrouded *Calliope*, so Sharpe wrapped himself in a blanket and slept until a fist knocked on his door to announce the breakfast burgoo. 'There's a ship on the starboard bow, sir,' the seaman who had brought the cauldron said softly. 'You can't see it from here, but she's there all right. One of ours, too.'

'Navy?'

'We reckons she is, sir. So it's a race to Mauritius now.'

'How close is she?'

'Seven, eight miles? Fair ways, sir, and she has to tack to cut us off so it'll be precious close, sir.' He lowered his voice even more. 'The Froggies have taken down their ensign, so we're flying our old colours, but that won't help 'em if it's a warship. She'll come and look at us anyway. Ensigns don't mean nothing when there's prize money to be gained.'

The news had spread through the ship, elating the passengers and alarming the French crew who tried to coax their prize into showing her best speed, but to the passengers in the stern, who could neither see the other ship nor determine what happened on the *Calliope*'s deck, it was a slow and agonizing morning. Lieutenant Tufnell suggested that the two ships must be on converging courses and that the *Calliope* had the advantage of the wind, but it was bitterly frustrating not knowing for sure. They all wanted to cut the tiller rope, but knew that if they severed it too soon the French might have time to make a repair.

No dinner was served at midday and perhaps it was that small hardship which persuaded Sharpe that the rope was best cut. 'We can't tell when the best moment is,' he argued, 'so let's give the buggers a headache now.'

No one demurred. Fairley pulled back the carpet and Sharpe thrust his sabre into the hole and sawed the blade back and forth on the rope. The rope kept moving, not by much, but enough to ensure that it was difficult keeping the sabre on the same spot, but Sharpe grunted and sweated as he tried to find the leverage to bring all his strength onto the blade.

'Shall I try?' Tufnell asked.

'I'm managing,' Sharpe said. He could not see the rope, but he knew he had the blade deep in its fibres now, for the blade was being tugged back and forth with the rudder's small movements. His right arm was on fire from the wrist to the shoulder, but he kept the blade sawing and suddenly felt the tension vanish as the ravaged hemp unravelled. The rudder squealed on its pintles as Sharpe drew the sabre back through the hole and collapsed in exhaustion against the foot of Fairley's bed.

The *Calliope*, with no pressure on the rudder to resist

her weather-helm, swung ponderously into the wind. There were frantic shouts on deck, the sound of bare feet going to the sheets and then the blessed noise of the sails slatting and banging as they flapped uselessly in the wind.

'Cover the hole,' Fairley ordered, 'quick! Before the buggers see it.'

Sharpe moved his feet so they could drop the carpet into place. The ship jerked as the French used the headsails to bring her round, but without the rudder's pressure she stubbornly went back into irons, and the sails again hammered at the masts. The helmsman would be spinning the wheel that suddenly had no load, and then there was a rush of feet going down the companionways and Sharpe knew the French were at last exploring the tiller lines.

There was a knock on Fairley's door and, without waiting to be bidden, Lord William entered the cabin. 'Does anyone know,' he asked, 'what precisely is happening?'

'We cut the tiller ropes,' Fairley said, 'and I'll thank your lordship to keep quiet about it.' Lord William blinked at that brusque request, but before he could say anything there was the sound of a distant gun. 'I reckon that's the end of it,' Fairley said happily. 'Come on, Sharpe, let's go and see what you wrought.' He held out a big hand and hauled Sharpe to his feet.

None of the prize crew tried to stop them going on deck, indeed the Frenchmen were already hauling down the *Calliope*'s original ensign which they had hoped would fool their pursuer into thinking that the Indiaman was still under British command.

And now they really were under British command for, coming slowly towards the *Calliope* and furling her sails as she glided ever nearer, was another great bluff-sided warship painted yellow and black. Her beakhead was a riot of gilded wood supporting a figurehead that showed an ecstatic-faced lady graced with a halo, carrying a sword and dressed in silver-painted armour, though her breastplate was curiously truncated to reveal a pinkly naked bosom. 'The *Pucelle*,' Sharpe said in delight. Joan of Arc had come to the rescue of the British.

And the *Calliope*, for the second time in five days, was taken.

CHAPTER 6

The first *Pucelle* crewman to board the *Calliope* was Captain Joel Chase himself who scrambled nimbly up the merchantman's side to the cheers of the liberated passengers. The *officier marinier,* having no sword to surrender, stoically offered Chase a marlin spike instead. Chase grinned, took the spike, then gallantly returned it to the *officier marinier* who resignedly led his men into imprisonment below decks while Chase doffed his hat, shook hands with the passengers on the main deck and tried to answer a dozen questions all at once. Malachi Braithwaite stood apart from the happy passengers, staring morosely at Sharpe on the quarterdeck. The secretary had been sequestered in steerage ever since the French took the ship and he must have been suffering pangs of jealousy at the thought of Sharpe being in the stern with Lady Grace.

'There's a happy naval captain,' Ebenezer Fairley said. He had come to stand beside Sharpe on the quarterdeck and was staring down at the throng of steerage passengers surrounding Chase. 'He's just made a fortune in prize money, but mind you he'll have to fight for it proper now.'

'What do you mean?'

'You think the lawyers won't want their share?' Fairley asked sourly. 'The East India Company will have lawyers saying that the Frogs never took the ship properly so it can't be a prize, and Chase's prize agent will have another set of lawyers arguing the opposite and between them they'll keep the court busy for years and make themselves rich and everyone else poor.' He sniffed. 'I suppose I could hire a lawyer or two myself, seeing as how a deal of the cargo is mine, but I won't bother. Yon captain's welcome to the prize so far as I'm concerned. I'd rather he got the cash than some blood-sucking lawyer.' Fairley grimaced. 'I once had a good idea on how we could mightily improve the prosperity of Britain, Sharpe. My notion was that every man of property could kill one lawyer a year without fear of penalty. Parliament wasn't interested, but then, Parliament's full of blood-suckers.'

Captain Chase extricated himself from the main-deck throng and climbed to the quarterdeck where the first person he saw was Sharpe. 'My dear Sharpe!' Chase cried, his face lighting up. 'My dear Sharpe! We are equal now, eh? You rescue me, I rescue you. How are you?' He clasped Sharpe's hand in both his, was introduced to Fairley, then glimpsed Lord William Hale. 'Oh God, I'd forgotten he was on board. How are you, my lord? You're well? Good, good!' In fact Lord William had not answered the captain, though he was eager to speak with him privately, but Chase spun away and took Tufnell's arm and the two seamen embarked on a long discussion about how the *Calliope* had first fallen prey to the *Revenant*. A party of *Calliope* sailors went below to mend the tiller ropes, while some Pucelles, led by Hopper, the big man who commanded Captain Chase's gig, hoisted a British ensign above the French flag.

Lord William, visibly irritated at being ignored by Chase, was waiting to catch the captain's attention, but something Tufnell said caused Chase to ignore his lordship and turn back to the other passengers. 'I want to know everything you can tell me,' Chase said urgently, 'about the man posing as the Baron von Dornberg's servant.'

Most of the passengers looked puzzled. Major Dalton commented that the baron had been a decent sort of chap, a bit loud-mouthed, but that no one had really remarked on the servant. 'He kept himself to himself,' Dalton said.

'He spoke French to me once,' Sharpe said.

'He did?' Chase spun round eagerly.

'Only the once,' Sharpe said, 'but he spoke English and German too. Claimed he was Swiss. But I don't know that he was really a servant at all.'

'What do you mean?'

'He was wearing a sword, sir, when he left the ship. Not many servants wear swords.'

'Hanoverian servants might,' Fairley said. 'Foreign folk, strange ways.'

'So what do we know about the baron?' Chase asked.

'He was a buffoon,' Fairley growled.

'He was decent enough,' Dalton protested, 'and he was generous.'

Sharpe could have provided a far more detailed answer, but he was still reluctant to admit that he had deceived the *Calliope* for so long. 'It's a strange thing, sir,' he said instead to Chase, 'and I didn't really think about it until after the baron had left the ship, but he looked just like a fellow called Anthony Pohlmann.'

'Did he, Sharpe?' Dalton asked, surprised.

'Same build,' Sharpe said. 'Not that I ever saw Pohlmann except through a telescope.' Which was not true, but Sharpe had to cover his tracks.

'Who,' Chase interrupted, 'is Anthony Pohlmann?'

'He's a Hanoverian soldier, sir, who led the Mahratta armies at Assaye.'

'Sharpe,' Chase said seriously, 'are you sure?'

'He looked like him,' Sharpe replied, reddening, 'very like.'

'God save me,' Chase said in his Devonian accent, then frowned in thought. Lord William approached him again, but Chase distractedly waved his lordship away and Lord William, already insulted by the captain's disregard, looked even more offended. 'But the main point,' Chase went on, 'is that von Dornberg and his servant, if he is a servant, are now on the *Revenant*. Hopper!'

'Sir?' the bosun called from the main deck.

'I want all Pucelles back on board fast, but you wait with my barge. Mister Horrocks! Here, please!' Horrocks was the *Pucelle*'s fourth lieutenant who would command the small prize crew, just three men, that Chase would leave aboard the *Calliope*. The men were not needed to sail the ship, for Tufnell and the *Calliope*'s own seamen could do that, but they were to stay aboard the Indiaman to register Chase's claim on the vessel which would now sail to Cape Town where the French prisoners would be given into the care of the British garrison and the ship could be revictualled for its journey back to Britain and the waiting lawyers. Chase gave Horrocks his orders, stressing that he was to accede to Lieutenant Tufnell in all matters of sailing the *Calliope*, but he also instructed Horrocks to select twenty of the *Calliope*'s best seamen and press them into the *Pucelle*. 'I don't like doing it,' he told Sharpe, 'but we're short-handed. Poor fellows won't be happy, but who knows? Some may even volunteer.' He did not sound hopeful. 'What about you, Sharpe? Will you sail with us?'

'Me, sir?'

'As a passenger,' Chase hurriedly explained. 'We're going your way, as it happens, and you'll reach England far quicker by sailing with me than staying aboard this scow. Of course you want to come. Clouter!' he called to one of his barge crew in the ship's waist. 'You'll bring Mister Sharpe's dunnage on deck. Lively now! He'll show you where it is.'

Sharpe protested. 'I should stay here, sir,' he said. 'I don't want to be in your way.'

'Don't have time to discuss it, Sharpe,' Chase said happily. 'Of course you're coming with me.' The captain at last turned to Lord William Hale who had been growing ever more angry at Chase's lack of attention. Chase walked away with his lordship as Clouter, the big black man who had fought so hard on the night Sharpe had first met Chase, climbed to the quarterdeck. 'Where do we go, sir?' Clouter asked.

'The dunnage will wait for a while,' Sharpe answered. He did not want to leave the *Calliope*, not while Lady Grace was aboard, but first he would have to invent some pressing excuse to refuse Chase's invitation. He could think of none offhand, but the thought of abandoning Lady Grace was unbearable. If the worst came to the worst, he decided, he would risk offending Chase by simply refusing to change ships.

Chase was now pacing up and down beneath the poop, listening to Lord William who was doing most of the talking. Chase was nodding, but eventually the captain seemed to shrug resignedly, then turned abruptly to rejoin Sharpe. 'Damn,' he said bitterly, 'damn and double damn. You still standing here, Clouter? Go and fetch Mister Sharpe's dunnage! Nothing too heavy. No pianofortes or four poster beds.'

'I told him to wait,' Sharpe said.

Chase frowned. 'You're not going to argue with me, are you, Sharpe? I have quite enough troubles. His bloody lordship claims he needs to reach Britain swiftly and I couldn't deny that we're on our way into the Atlantic.'

'The Atlantic?' Sharpe asked, astonished.

'Of course! I told you I was going your way. And besides, that's where the *Revenant* is gone. I'll swear on it. I'm even risking my reputation on it. And Lord William tells me he is carrying government despatches, but is he? I don't know. I think he just wants to be on a larger and safer ship, but I can't refuse him. I'd like to, but I can't. Damn his eyes. You're not listening to this, are you, Clouter? These are words for your superiors and betters. Damn! So now I'm hoisted with bloody Lord William Hale and his bloody wife, their bloody servants and his bloody secretary. Damn!'

'Clouter,' Sharpe said energetically, 'lower-deck steerage, larboard side. Hurry!' He almost sang as he jumped down the stairs. Grace was going with him!

Sharpe hid his elation as he made his farewells. He was sorry to part from Ebenezer Fairley and from Major Dalton, both of whom pressed invitations on him to visit their homes. Mrs Fairley clasped Sharpe to her considerable bosom and insisted he took a bottle of brandy and another of rum with him. 'To keep you warm, dear,' she said, 'and to stop Ebenezer from guzzling them.'

A longboat from the *Pucelle* carried the pressed men away from the *Calliope.* They were mostly the youngest seamen and they went to replace those of Chase's crew who had succumbed to disease during the *Pucelle*'s long cruise. They looked morose, for they were exchanging good wages for poor. 'But we'll cheer them up,' Chase said airily. 'There's nothing like a dose of victory to cheer a tar.'

Lord William had insisted that his expensive furniture be taken to the *Pucelle*, but Chase exploded in anger, saying that his lordship could either travel without furniture or not travel at all, and his lordship had icily given way, though he did convince Chase that his collection of official papers must go with him. Those were all brought from his cabin and taken to the *Pucelle*, then Lord William and his wife left the *Calliope* without making any farewells. Lady Grace looked utterly distraught as she left. She had been weeping and was now making a huge effort to appear dignified, but she could not help giving Sharpe a despairing glance as she was lowered by a rope and tackle into Chase's barge. Malachi Braithwaite clambered down the *Calliope*'s side after her and gave Sharpe a venomously triumphant look as if to suggest that he would now enjoy Lady Grace's company while Sharpe was marooned on the *Calliope.* Lady Grace gripped the gunwale of the barge with a white-knuckled hand, then the wind snatched at her hat, lifting its brim, and as she caught the hat she saw Sharpe swing out of the entry port and begin to clamber down the ship's side and, for a heartbeat, an expression of pure joy showed on her face. Braithwaite, seeing Sharpe come down the ladder, gaped in astonishment and looked as though he wanted to protest, but his mouth just opened and closed like a gaffed fish. 'Make space, Braithwaite,' Sharpe said, 'I'm keeping you company.'

'Goodbye, Sharpe! Write to me!' Dalton called.

'Good luck, lad!' Fairley boomed.

Chase descended the ladder last and took his place in the sternsheets. 'All together now!' Hopper shouted and the oarsmen dug in their red and white blades and the barge slid away from the *Calliope.*

The stench of the *Pucelle* reached across the water. It was the smell of a huge crew crammed into a wooden ship, the stink of unwashed bodies, of body waste, of tobacco, tar, salt and rot, but the ship herself loomed high and mighty, a great sheer wall of gunports, crammed with men, powder and shot.

'Goodbye!' Dalton called a last time.

And Sharpe joined the hunter, seeking revenge, going home.

'I hate having women on board,' Chase said savagely. 'It's bad luck, you know that? Women and rabbits, both bring bad luck.' He touched the polished table in his day cabin to avert the ill fortune. 'Not that there aren't women on board already,' he admitted. 'There's at least six Portsmouth whores down below who I'm not supposed to know about, and I suspect one of the gunners has his wife hidden away, but that ain't the same as having her ladyship and her maid out on the open deck feeding the crew's filthy fantasies.'

Sharpe said nothing. The elegant cabin stretched the whole width of the ship and was lit by a wide stern window through which he could see the far-off *Calliope* already hull down on the horizon. The windows were curtained in flowered chintz which matched the cushions spread along the window seat, and the deck was carpeted with canvas painted in a black and white chequerboard pattern. There were two tables, a sideboard, a deep leather armchair, a couch and a revolving bookcase, though the air of genteel domesticity was somewhat spoiled by the presence of two eighteen-pounder cannons that pointed towards red-painted gunports. Forward of the day cabin, and on the ship's starboard side, were Chase's sleeping quarters, while forward on the larboard side was a dining cabin that could seat a dozen in comfort. 'And I'll be damned if I'll move out for Lord goddamn bloody Hale,' Chase grumbled, 'though he plainly expects me to. He can go back to the first lieutenant's quarters and his damned wife can go into the second lieutenant's cabin, which is how they sailed from Calcutta. Lord knows why they sleep apart, but they do. I shouldn't have told you that.'

'I didn't hear it,' Sharpe said.

'The bloody secretary can go in Horrocks's cabin,' Chase decided. Horrocks was the lieutenant who had been made prize master of the *Calliope*. 'And the first lieutenant can have the master's cabin. He died three days ago. No one knows why. He tired of life, or life tired of him. God alone knows where the second will go. He'll turf out the third, I suppose, who'll kick out someone else, and so on down to the ship's cat that will get chucked overboard, poor thing. God, I hate having passengers, especially women! You'll have my quarters.'

'Your quarters?' Sharpe asked in astonishment.

'Sleeping cabin,' Chase said, 'through that door there. Good Lord above, Sharpe, I've got this damn great room!' He gestured about the lavish day cabin with its elegant furniture, framed portraits and curtained windows. 'My steward can hang my cot in here, and yours can go in the small cabin.'

'I can't take your cabin!' Sharpe protested.

'Of course you can! It's a damned poky little hole, anyway, just right for an insignificant ensign. Besides, Sharpe, I'm a fellow who likes some company and as captain I can't go to the wardroom without an invitation and the officers don't invite me much. Can't blame them. They want to relax, so I end up in lonely state. So you can entertain me instead. D'you play chess? No? I shall teach you. And you'll take supper with me tonight? Of course you will.' Chase, who had taken off his uniform coat, stretched out in a chair. 'Do you really think the baron might have been Pohlmann?'

'He was,' Sharpe said flatly.

Chase raised an eyebrow. 'So sure?'

'I recognized him, sir,' Sharpe admitted, 'but I didn't tell any of the *Calliope*'s officers. I didn't think it was important.'

Chase shook his head, more in amusement than disapproval. 'It wouldn't have done any good if you had told them. And Peculiar would probably have killed you if you had, and as for the others, how were they to know what was happening? I only hope to God I do!' He straightened to find a piece of paper on the larger table. 'We, that is His Britannic Majesty's navy, are looking for a gentleman named Vaillard. Michel Vaillard. He's a bad lad, our Vaillard, and it seems he is trying to return to Europe. And how better to travel than disguised as a servant? No one looks at servants, do they?'

'Why are you searching for him, sir?'

'It seems, Sharpe, that he has been negotiating with the last of the Mahrattas who are terrified that the British will take over what's left of their territory, so Vaillard has concluded a treaty with one of their leaders, Holkar?' He looked at the paper. 'Yes, Holkar, and Vaillard is taking the treaty back to Paris. Holkar agrees to talk peace with the British, and in the meantime Monsieur Vaillard, presumably with the help of your friend Pohlmann, arranges to supply Holkar with French advisers, French cannon and French muskets. This is a copy of the treaty.' He flicked the paper over to Sharpe who saw that it was in French, though someone had helpfully written a translation between the lines. Holkar, the ablest of the Mahratta war leaders and a man who had evaded the army of Sir Arthur Wellesley, but who was now being pressed by other British forces, had undertaken to open peace negotiations and, under their cover, raise an enormous army which would be equipped by his allies, the French. The treaty even listed those princes in British territory who could be relied on to rebel if such an army attacked out of the north.

'They've been clever, Vaillard and Pohlmann,' Chase said. 'Used British ships to go home! Quickest way, you see. They suborned your fellow, Cromwell, and must have sent a message to Mauritius arranging a rendezvous.'

'How did we get a copy of their treaty?' Sharpe asked.

'Spies?' Chase guessed. 'Everything became vigorous after you left Bombay. The admiral sent a sloop to the Red Sea in case Vaillard decided to go overland and he sent the *Porcupine* to overhaul the convoy and told me to keep my eyes skinned as well, because stopping that damned Vaillard is our most important job. Now we know where the bloody man is, or we think we do, so I'll have to pursue him. They're going back to Europe and we are too. It's back home for us, Sharpe, and you're going to see just how fast a French-built warship can sail. The trouble is that the *Revenant*'s just as quick and she's the best part of a week in front of us.'

'And if you catch her?'

'We beat her to smithereens, of course,' Chase said happily, 'and make certain Monsieur Vaillard and Herr Pohlmann go to the fishes.'

'And Captain Cromwell with them,' Sharpe said vengefully.

'I think I'd rather take him alive,' Chase said, 'and hang him from the yardarm. Nothing cheers up a jack tar's spirit so much as seeing a captain swinging on a generous length of Bridport hemp.'

Sharpe looked through the stern window to see the *Calliope* was just a smudge of sails on the horizon. He felt like a cask thrown into a fast river, being swept away to some unknown destination on a journey over which he had no control, but he was glad it was happening, for he was still with Lady Grace. The very thought of her sparked a warm feeling in his breast, though he knew it was a madness, an utter madness, but he could not escape it. He did not even want to escape it.

'Here's Mister Harold Collier,' Chase said, responding to a knock on the door that brought into the cabin the diminutive midshipman who had commanded the boat that had carried Sharpe out to the *Calliope* so long ago in Bombay Harbour. Now Mister Collier was ordered to show Sharpe the *Pucelle.*

The boy was touchingly proud of his ship while Sharpe was awed by it. It was a vast thing, much bigger than the *Calliope,* and young Harry Collier rattled off its statistics as he took Sharpe through the lavish dining cabin where another eighteen-pounder squatted. 'She's 178 feet long, sir, not counting her bowsprit, of course, and 48 in the beam, sir, and 175 feet to the main truck which is the very top of the mainmast, sir, and mind your head, sir. She was French-built out of two thousand oak trees and she weighs close to two thousand tons, sir – mind your head – and she's got seventy-four guns, sir, not counting the carronades, of course, and we've six of them, all thirty-two-pounders, and there's six hundred and seventeen men aboard, sir, not counting the marines.'

'How many of those?'

'Sixty-six, sir. This way, sir. Mind your head, sir.'

Collier led Sharpe onto the quarterdeck where eight long guns lay behind their closed ports. 'Eighteen-pounders, sir,' Collier squeaked, 'the babies on the ship. Just six a side, sir, including the four in the stern quarters.' He slithered down a perilously steep companionway to the main deck. 'This is the weather deck, sir. Thirty-two guns, sir, all twenty-four-pounders.' The centre of the main deck, or weather deck, was open to the sky, but the forward and aft sections of the deck were planked over where the forecastle and quarterdeck were built. Collier led Sharpe forward, weaving nimbly between the huge guns and the mess tables rigged between them, ducking under hammocks where men of the off-duty watch slept, then swerving around the anchor capstan and down another ladder into the stygian darkness of the lower deck, which held the ship's biggest guns, each throwing a ball of thirty-two pounds. 'Thirty of these big guns, sir,' he said proudly, 'mind your head, sir, fifteen a side, and we're lucky to have so many. There's a shortage of these big guns, they tell us, and some ships are even driven to put eighteen-pounders on their lower deck, but not Captain Chase, he wouldn't abide that. I told you to mind your head, sir.'

Sharpe rubbed the bruise on his forehead and tried to work out the weight of shot that the *Pucelle* could fire, but Collier was ahead of him. 'We can throw 972 pounds of metal with each broadside, sir, and we've got two sides,' he added helpfully, 'as you may have noticed. And we've got the six carronades, sir, and they can throw thirty-two pounds apiece plus a cask of musket balls as well, which will make a Frenchman weep, sir. Or so I'm told, sir. Mind your head, sir.' Which meant, Sharpe thought, that this one ship could throw more round shot in a single broadside than all the combined batteries of the army's artillery at the battle of Assaye. It was a floating bastion, a crushing killer of the high seas, and this was not even the largest warship afloat. Some ships, Sharpe knew, carried over a hundred guns, and again Collier had the answers, trained in them because, like all midshipmen, he was preparing for his lieutenant's examination. 'The navy's got eight first rates, sir, that's ships with a hundred or more guns – watch that low beam, sir – fourteen second rates, which carry about ninety or more cannon, and a hundred and thirty of these third rates.'

'You call this a third rate?' Sharpe asked, astonished.

'Down here, sir, watch your head, sir.' Collier vanished into another companionway, sliding down the ladder's uprights, and Sharpe followed more slowly, using the rungs, to find himself in a dark, dank, low-ceilinged deck that stank foully and was dimly lit by a scatter of glass-shielded lanterns. 'This is the orlop deck, sir. Mind your head. It's called the cockpit as well, sir. Watch that beam, sir. We're just about under water here, sir, and the surgeon has his rooms down there, beyond the magazines, and we all prays, sir, we never end under his knife. This way, sir. Mind your head.' He showed Sharpe the cable tiers where the anchor ropes were flaked down, the two leather-curtained magazines that were guarded by red-coated marines, the spirit store, the surgeon's lair where the walls were painted red so that the blood did not show, the dispensary, and the midshipmen's cabins that were scarce bigger than dog kennels, then he took Sharpe down a final ladder into the massive hold where the ship's stores were piled in vast heaps of casks. Only the bilge lay beneath and a mournful sucking, interrupted by a clatter, told Sharpe that men were even now pumping it dry. 'We hardly ever stop the six pumps,' the midshipman said, 'because as tight as you build 'em, sir, the sea do get in.' He kicked at a rat, missed, then scrambled back up the ladder. He showed Sharpe the galley beneath the forecastle, introduced him to master-at-arms, cooks, bosuns, gunner's mates, the carpenter, then offered to take Sharpe up the mainmast.

'I'll not bother today,' Sharpe said.

Collier took him to the wardroom where he was named to a half-dozen officers, then back to the quarterdeck and aft, past the great double wheel, to a door that led directly into Captain Chase's sleeping cabin. It was, as the captain had said, a small room, but it was panelled with varnished wood, had a canvas carpet on the floor and a scuttle to let in the daylight. Sharpe's sea chest took up one wall, and Collier now helped him rig the hanging cot. 'If you're killed, sir,' the boy said earnestly, 'then this will be your coffin.'

'Better than the one the army would give me,' Sharpe said, throwing his blankets into the cot. 'Where's the first lieutenant's cabin?' he asked.

'Forrard of this one, sir.' Collier indicated the forward bulkhead. 'Just beyond there, sir.'

'And the second lieutenant's?' Sharpe asked, knowing that was where Lady Grace would be sleeping.

'Weather deck, sir. Aft. By the wardroom,' Collier said. 'There's a hook for your lantern there, sir, and you'll find the captain's quarter gallery is aft through that door, sir, and on the starboard side.'

'Quarter gallery?' Sharpe asked.

'Latrine, sir. Drops direct into the sea, sir. Very hygienic. Captain Chase says you're to share it, sir, and his steward will look after you, you being his guest.'

'You like Chase?' Sharpe asked, struck by the warmth in the midshipman's voice.

'Everyone likes the captain, sir, everyone,' Collier said. 'This is a happy ship, sir, which is more than I can say for many, and permit me to remind you that captain's supper is at the end of the first dogwatch. That's four bells, sir, seeing as how the dogwatches are only two hours apiece.'

'What is it now?'

'Just past two bells, sir.'

'So how long till four bells?'

Collier's small face showed astonishment that anyone should need to ask such a question. 'An hour, sir, of course.'

'Of course,' Sharpe said.

Chase had invited six other guests to join him for supper. He could hardly avoid asking Lord William Hale and his wife, but he confided in Sharpe that Haskell, the first lieutenant, was a terrible snob who had flattered Lord William all the way from Calcutta to Bombay. 'So he can damn well do it again now,' Chase said, glancing at his first lieutenant, a tall, good-looking man, who was bending close to Lord William and evidently drinking in every word. 'And this is Llewellyn Llewellyn,' Chase said, drawing Sharpe towards a red-faced man in a scarlet uniform coat. 'A man who does nothing by halves and is the captain of our marines, which means that if the Frogs board us I'm relying on Llewellyn Llewellyn and his rogues to throw them overboard. Is your name really Llewellyn Llewellyn?'

'We are descended from the lineage of ancient kings,' Captain Llewellyn said proudly, 'unlike the Chase family, which, unless I am very much mistaken, were mere servants of the hunt.'

'We hunted the bloody Welsh out,' Chase said, smiling. It was plain that the two were old friends who took a delight in mutual insult. 'This is my particular friend, Llewellyn, Richard Sharpe.'

The marine captain shook Sharpe's hand energetically and expressed the hope that the ensign would join him and his men for some musketry training. 'Maybe you can teach us something?' the captain suggested.

'I doubt it, Captain.'

'I could use your help,' Llewellyn said enthusiastically. 'I've a lieutenant, of course, but the lad's only sixteen. Doesn't even shave! Not sure he can wipe his own bum. It's good to have another redcoat aboard, Sharpe. It raises the tone of the ship.'

Chase laughed, then drew Sharpe on to meet the last guest, the ship's surgeon, who was a plump man called Pickering. Malachi Braithwaite had been talking to the surgeon and he looked uncomfortable as Sharpe was introduced. Pickering, whose face was a mass of broken blood vessels, shook Sharpe's hand. 'I trust we never meet professionally, Ensign, for there ain't a great deal

I can do except carve you up and mutter a prayer. I do the latter very prettily, if that's a consolation. I say, she does look better.' The surgeon had turned to look at Lady Grace who was in a low-cut dress of very pale blue with an embroidered collar and hem. There were diamonds at her throat and more diamonds in her black hair which was pinned so high that it brushed the beams of Chase's cabin whenever she moved. 'I hardly saw her when she was aboard before,' Pickering said, 'but she seems a good deal more lively now. Even so, she's unwelcome.'

'Unwelcome?' Sharpe asked.

'Monstrous ill luck to have women on board, monstrous ill luck.' Pickering reached up and superstitiously touched a beam. 'But I must say she's decorative. There'll be some odious things being said in the fo'c'sle tonight, I can tell you. Ah well, we must survive what the good Lord sends us, even if it is a woman. Our captain tells us you are a celebrated soldier, Sharpe!'

'He does?' Sharpe asked. Braithwaite had stepped back, signifying he wanted no part in the conversation.

'First into the breach and all that sort of stuff,' Pickering said. 'As for me, my dear fellow, as soon as the guns begin to sound I scamper down to the cockpit where no French shot can reach me. You know what the trick of a long life is, Sharpe? Stay out of range. There! Good medical advice, and free!'

The food at Captain Chase's table was a great deal better than that which Peculiar Cromwell had supplied. They began with sliced smoked fish, served with lemon and real bread, then ate a roast of mutton which Sharpe suspected was goat, but which nevertheless tasted wonderful in its vinegar sauce, and finished with a concoction of oranges, brandy and syrup. Lord William and Lady Grace sat either side of Chase, while the first lieutenant sat next to her ladyship and tried to persuade her to drink more wine than she wished. The red wine was called blackstrap and was sour, while the insipid white was called Miss Taylor, a name that puzzled Sharpe until he saw the label on one of the bottles: Mistela. Sharpe was at the far end of the table where Captain Llewellyn questioned him closely about the actions he had seen in India. The Welshman was intrigued by the news that Sharpe was going to join the 95th Rifles. 'The concept of a rifled barrel might work on land,' Llewellyn said, 'but it'll never serve at sea.'

'Why not?'

'Accuracy's no good on a ship! The things are always heaving up and down to spoil your aim. No, the thing to do is to pour a lot of fire onto the enemy's deck and pray not all of it is wasted. Which reminds me, we've got some new toys aboard. Seven-barrel guns! Monstrous things! They spit out seven half-inch balls at once. You must try one.'

'I'd like that.'

'I'd like to see some seven-barrel guns in the fighting tops,' Llewellyn said eagerly. 'They could do some real damage, Sharpe, real damage!'

Chase had overheard Llewellyn's last remark, for he intervened from the table's far end. 'Nelson won't allow muskets in the fighting tops, Llewellyn. He says they set the sails on fire.'

'The man is wrong,' Llewellyn said, offended, 'just plain wrong.'

'You know Lord Nelson?' Lady Grace asked the captain.

'I served under him briefly, milady,' Chase said enthusiastically, 'too briefly. I had a frigate then, but, alas, I never saw action under his lordship's command.'

'I pray God we see no action now,' Lord William said piously.

'Amen,' Braithwaite said, breaking his silence. He

had spent most of the meal gazing dumbly at Lady Grace and flinching whenever Sharpe spoke.

'By God I hope we do see action!' Chase retorted. 'We have to stop our German friend and his so-called servant!'

'Do you think you can catch the *Revenant*?' Lady Grace asked.

'I hope so, milady, but it'll be touch and go. He's a good seaman, Montmorin, and the *Revenant*'s a quick ship, but her bottom will be a deal more fouled than ours.'

'It looked clean to me,' Sharpe said.

'Clean?' Chase sounded alarmed.

'No green copper at the water line, sir. All bright.'

'Wretched man,' Chase said, meaning Montmorin. 'He's scrubbed his hull, hasn't he? Which will make him harder to catch. And I made a wager with Mister Haskell that we'd meet with him on my birthday.'

'And when is that?' Lady Grace asked.

'October 21st, ma'am, and by my reckoning we should be somewhere off Portugal by then.'

'She won't be off Portugal,' the first lieutenant suggested, 'for she won't be sailing direct to France. She'll put into Cadiz, sir, and my guess is we'll catch her during the second week in October, somewhere off Africa.'

'Ten guineas rides on the result,' Chase said, 'and I know I have forsworn gambling, but I shall happily pay you so long as we do catch her. Then we'll have a rare fight, milady, but let me assure you that you will be safe below the water line.'

Lady Grace smiled. 'I am to miss all the entertainment aboard, Captain?'

That brought laughter. Sharpe had never seen her ladyship so relaxed in company. The candles glinted off her diamond earrings and necklace, from the jewels on her fingers and from her bright eyes. Her vivacity was captivating the whole table, all except for her husband who wore a slight frown as though he feared his wife had drunk too much of the blackstrap or the Miss Taylor. Sharpe was assailed with the jealous thought that perhaps she was responding to the handsome and genial Chase, but just as he felt that envy she glanced down the table and briefly caught his eye. Braithwaite saw it and stared down at his plate.

'I have never entirely understood,' Lord William said, breaking the moment's mood, 'why you fellows insist on taking your ships up close to the enemy and battering their hulls. Easier, surely, to stand off and destroy their rigging from a distance?'

'That's the French way, my lord,' Chase said. 'Bar shot, chain shot and round shot, fired on the uproll and intended to take out our sticks. But once they've dismasted us, once we're lying like a log in the water, they still have to take us.'

'But if they have masts and sails and you do not,' Lord William pointed out, 'why can they not just pour their broadsides into your stern?'

'You assume, my lord, that while our notional Frenchman is trying to unmast us, we are doing nothing.' Chase smiled to soften his words. 'A ship of the line, my lord, is nothing more than a floating artillery battery. Destroy the sails and you still have a gun battery, but dismount the cannons, splinter its decks and kill the gunners and you have denied the ship its very purpose of existence. The French try to give us a long-range haircut, while we get up close and mangle their vitals.' He turned to Lady Grace. 'This must be tiresome, milady, men talking of battle.'

'I have become used to it these past weeks,' Grace said. 'There was a Scottish major on the *Calliope* who was ever trying to persuade Mister Sharpe to tell us such tales.'

She turned to Sharpe. 'You never did tell us, Mister Sharpe, what happened when you saved my cousin's life.'

'My wife has become excessively interested in one of her remoter cousins,' Lord William interrupted, 'ever since he gained some small notoriety in India. Extraordinary how a dull fellow like Wellesley can rise in the army, isn't it?'

'You saved Wellesley's life, Sharpe?' Chase asked, ignoring his lordship's sarcasm.

'I don't know about that, sir. I probably just kept him from being captured.'

'Is that how you got that scar?' Llewellyn asked.

'That was at Gawilghur, sir.' Sharpe wished the conversation would veer away to another subject and he tried desperately to think of something to say which might steer it in a new direction, but his mind was floundering.

'So what happened?' Chase demanded.

'He was unhorsed, sir,' Sharpe said, reddening, 'in the enemy ranks.'

'He was not by himself, surely?' Lord William asked.

'He was, sir. Except for me, of course.'

'Careless of him,' Lord William suggested.

'And how many enemy?' Chase asked.

'A good few, sir.'

'And you fought them off?'

Sharpe nodded. 'Didn't have much choice really, sir.'

'Stay out of range!' the surgeon boomed. 'That's my advice! Stay out of range!'

Lord William complimented Captain Chase on the concoction of oranges and Chase boasted of his cook and steward, and that started a general discussion on the problem of reliable servants that only ended when Sharpe, as the junior officer present, was asked to give the loyal toast.

'To King George,' Sharpe said, 'God bless him.'

'And damn his enemies,' Chase added, tossing back the glass, 'especially Monsieur Vaillard.'

Lady Grace pushed her chair back. Captain Chase tried to stop her retiring, saying that she was most welcome to breathe the cigar smoke that was about to fill the cabin, but she insisted on leaving and so the whole table stood.

'You will not object, Captain, if I walk on your deck for a while?' Lady Grace asked.

'I should be delighted to have it so honoured, milady.'

Brandy and cigars were produced, but the company did not stay long. Lord William suggested a hand of whist, but Chase had lost too much on his first voyage with his lordship and explained he had decided to give up playing cards altogether. Lieutenant Haskell promised a lively game in the wardroom, and Lord William and the others followed him down to the weather deck and then aft. Chase bade his visitors a good night, then invited Sharpe into the day cabin at the stern. 'One last brandy, Sharpe.'

'I don't want to keep you up, sir.'

'I'll turf you out when I'm tired. Here.' He gave Sharpe a glass, then led the way into the more comfortable day cabin. 'Lord, but that William Hale is a bore,' he said, 'though I confess I was surprised by his wife. Never seen her so lively! Last time she was aboard I thought she was going to wilt and die.'

'Maybe it was the wine tonight?' Sharpe suggested.

'Maybe, but I hear tales.'

'Tales?' Sharpe asked warily.

'That you not only rescued her cousin, but that you rescued her? To the detriment of one French lieutenant who now sleeps with his ancestors?'

Sharpe nodded, but said nothing.

Chase smiled. 'She seems the better for the

experience. And that secretary of his is a gloomy bird, isn't he? Scarce a damn word all night and he's an Oxford man!' To Sharpe's relief Chase left the subject of Lady Grace and instead enquired whether Sharpe would consider putting himself under Captain Llewellyn's command and so become an honorary marine. 'If we do catch the *Revenant*,' Chase said, 'we'll be trying to capture her. We might hammer her into submission' – he put out a hand and surreptitiously touched the table – 'but we still might have to board her. We'll need fighting men if that happens, so can I count on your help? Good! I'll tell Llewellyn that you're now his man. He's a thoroughly first-rate fellow, despite being a marine and a Welshman, and I doubt he'll pester you overmuch. Now, I must go on deck and make certain they're not steering in circles. You'll come?'

'I will, sir.'

So Sharpe was now an honorary marine.

The *Pucelle* used every sail that Chase could cram onto her masts. He even rigged extra hawsers to stay the masts so that yet more canvas could be carried aloft and hung from spars that jutted out from the yards. There were studdingsails and skyscrapers, staysails, royals, spritsails and topsails, a cloud of canvas that drove the warship westwards. Chase called it hanging out his laundry, and Sharpe saw how the crew responded to their captain's enthusiasm. They were as eager as Chase to prove the *Pucelle* the fastest sailor on the sea.

And so they flew westwards until, deep in a dark night, the sea became lumpy and the ship rolled like a drunk and Sharpe was woken by the rush of feet on the deck. The cot, in which he was alone, swung wildly and he fell hard when he rolled out of it. He did not bother to dress, but just put on a boat cloak that Chase had lent him, then let himself out of the door onto the quarterdeck where he could see almost nothing, for clouds were obscuring the moon, yet he could hear orders being bellowed and hear the voices of men high in the rigging above him. Sharpe still did not understand how men could work in the dark, a hundred feet above a pitching deck, clinging to thin lines and hearing the wind's shriek in their ears. It was a bravery, he reckoned, as great as any that was needed on a battlefield.

'Is that you, Sharpe?' Chase's voice called.

'Yes, sir.'

'It's the Agulhas Current,' Chase said happily, 'sweeping us round the tip of Africa! We're shortening sail. It'll be rough for a day or two!'

Daylight revealed broken seas being whipped ragged white by the wind. The *Pucelle* pitched into the steep waves, sometimes shattering them into clouds of drenching spray that rose above the foresail and rained down in streams from the canvas, yet still Chase pushed his ship and drove her and talked to her. He still gave suppers in his quarters, for he enjoyed company in the evening, but any shift of wind would drive him from the table onto the quarterdeck. He watched each cast of the log eagerly and jotted down the ship's speed, and rejoiced when, as the African coast curved westwards, he was able to hoist his full laundry again and feel the long hull respond to the wind's force.

'I think we'll catch her,' he told Sharpe one day.

'She can't be going this fast,' Sharpe guessed.

'Oh, she probably is! But my guess is that Montmorin won't have dared go too close to land. He'll have been forced far to the south in case he was spotted by our ships out of Cape Town. So we're cutting the corner on him! Who knows, we may be only a score or so of miles behind him?'

The *Pucelle* was seeing other ships now. Most were small native trading vessels, but they also passed two

British merchantmen, an American whaler and a Royal Navy sloop with which there was a brisk exchange of signals. Connors, the third lieutenant who had the responsibility of looking after the ship's signals, ordered a man to haul a string of brightly coloured flags up into the rigging, then put a telescope to his eye and called out the sloop's answering message. 'She's the *Hirondelle*, sir, out of Cape Town.'

'Ask if she's seen any other ships of the line.'

The flags were found, sorted and hoisted, and the answer came back no. Chase then sent a long message telling the *Hirondelle*'s captain that the *Pucelle* was pursuing the *Revenant* into the Atlantic. In time that news would reach the admiral in Bombay who must already have been wondering what had happened to his precious seventy-four.

Land was spotted the next day, but it was distant and obscured by a squall of rain that rattled on the sails and bounced from the decks which were scrubbed clean every morning by grinding sand into the timber beneath blocks of stone the size of bibles. Holy-stoning, the men called it. Still the *Pucelle* drove on with every last scrap of canvas hoisted, sailing as though the devil himself was on her tail. The wind stayed strong, but for long days it brought stinging rain so that everything below deck became damp and greasy. Then, on another day of driving rain and gusting wind, they passed Cape Town, though Sharpe could see nothing of the place except a misty glimpse of a great flat-topped mountain half shrouded in cloud.

Captain Chase ordered new charts spread on the big table in his day cabin. 'I have a choice now,' he told Sharpe. 'Either I head west into the Atlantic, or ride the current up the African coast until we find the southeast trades.'

The choice seemed obvious to Sharpe: ride the current, but he was no sailor. 'I take a risk,' Chase explained, 'if I stay inshore. I get the land breezes and I have the current, but I also risk fog and I might get a westerly gale. Then we're on a lee shore.'

'And a lee shore means?' Sharpe asked.

'We're dead,' Chase said shortly, and let the chart roll itself up with a snap. 'Which is why the Sailing Directions insist we go west,' he added, 'but if we do then we risk being becalmed.'

'Where do you think the *Revenant* is?'

'She's out west. She's avoiding land. At least I hope she is.' Chase stared out of the stern window at the white-fretted wake. He looked tired now, and older, because his natural ebullience had been drained from him by days and nights of broken sleep and unbroken worry. 'Maybe she stayed inshore?' he mused. 'She could have hoisted false colours. But the *Hirondelle* didn't see her. Mind you, in these damned squalls a fleet could go within a couple of miles of us and we wouldn't see a thing.' He pulled on his tarpaulin coat, ready to go back on deck. 'Up the coast, I think.' He spoke to himself. 'Up the coast and God help us if there's a blow out of the west.' He picked up his hat. 'God help us anyway if we don't find the *Revenant.* Their lordships of the Admiralty don't look mercifully on captains who abandon their station to chase wild geese halfway round the world. And God help us if we do find it and that fellow really is a Swiss servant and not Vaillard after all! And the first lieutenant's right. He won't be sailing to France, but making for Cadiz. It's closer. Much closer.' He shrugged. 'I'm sorry, Sharpe, I'm not very good company for you.'

'I'm having a better time than I ever dared expect when I embarked on the *Calliope.*'

'Good,' Chase said, going to the door, 'good. And time to turn north.'

Sharpe was busy enough. In the morning he paraded with the marines, and then there was practice, endless practice, for Captain Llewellyn feared his men would become stale if they were not busy. They fired their muskets in all weathers, learning how to shield their locks from the rain. They fired from the decks and from the upperworks, and Sharpe fired with them, using one of the Sea Service muskets which was similar to the weapon he had fired when he was a private, but with a slightly shorter barrel and an old-fashioned flat lock which looked crude, but, as Llewellyn explained, was easier to repair at sea. The weapons were susceptible to salt air and the marines spent hours cleaning and oiling the guns, and more hours practising with bayonets and cutlasses. Llewellyn also insisted that Sharpe try his new toys, the seven-barrel guns, and so Sharpe fired one into the sea from the forecastle and thought his shoulder must be broken, so violent was the kick of the seven half-inch barrels. It took over two minutes to reload, but the marine captain would not see that as a disadvantage. 'Fire one of those down onto a Frog deck, Sharpe, and we're making some proper misery!' Most of all, Llewellyn wanted to board the *Revenant* and could not wait to launch his red-coated men onto the enemy's deck. 'Which is why the men have to stay spry, Sharpe,' he would say, then he would order groups to race from the forecastle to the quarterdeck, back to the forecastle, then up the forward mast by the larboard ratlines and down by the starboard ones. 'If the Frogs board us,' he said, 'we have to be able to get round the ship quickly. Don't dawdle, Hawkins! Hurry, man, hurry! You're a marine, not a slug!'

Sharpe equipped himself with a cutlass that suited him far better than the cavalry sabre he had worn ever since the battle of Assaye. The cutlass was straight-bladed, heavy and crude, but it felt like a weapon that could do serious damage. 'You don't fence with them,' Llewellyn advised him, 'because it ain't a weapon for the wrist. It's a full arm blade. Hack the buggers down! Keep your arms strong, Sharpe, eh? Climb the masts every day, do the cutlass drill, keep strong!'

Sharpe did climb the masts. He found it terrifying, for every small motion on deck was magnified as he went higher. At first he did not try to reach the topmost parts of the rigging, but he became adept at clambering up to the maintop, which was a wide platform built where the lower mast was joined to the upper. The sailors reached the maintop by using the futtock shrouds which led to the platform's outer edge, but Sharpe always wriggled through the small hatchway beside the mast rather than risk the frightening climb up the futtock shrouds where a man must hang upside down from the tarred ropes. Then, a week after they had turned north, on a day when the sea was frustratingly calm and the wind fitful, Sharpe decided to attempt the futtock shrouds and so show that a soldier could do what any midshipman made look simple. He climbed the lower ratlines which were easy for they leaned like a ladder against the mast, but then he came to the place where the futtock shrouds went out and backwards above his head. He would have to climb upside down, but he was determined to do it and so he reached back with his hands and hauled himself upwards. Then, halfway to the maintop's platform, his feet slipped off the ratlines and he hung there, suspended fifty feet above the deck, and he felt his fingers, hooked like claws, slipping on the wet ropes and he dared not swing his legs for fear of falling and so he stayed, paralysed by fear, until a topman, swinging down through the web of rigging with the agility of a monkey, grabbed his waistband and hauled him into the maintop. 'Lord, sir, you don't want to be going that a way.

That be for matelots, not lobsters. Use the lubber's hole, sir, that's what it be for, lubbers.'

Sharpe was still too scared to speak. All he could think of was the sensation of his fingers slipping over the rough tarred rope, but at last he managed to gasp a thank you and promised to reward the man with a pound of tobacco from his stores.

'Almost lost you there, Sharpe!' Chase said cheerfully when Sharpe regained the quarterdeck.

'Terrifying,' Sharpe said, and looked at his hands that were scored deep with tar.

Lady Grace had also seen his near fall. She had not been near Sharpe now for the best part of a week, and her distance worried him. She had exchanged glances with him once or twice, and those swift looks had seemed to be filled with a mute appeal, but there had been no chance to talk with her and she had not risked coming to his cabin in the heart of the night. Now she was standing on the lee side of the quarterdeck, close to her husband who was speaking with Malachi Braithwaite, and she seemed to hesitate before approaching Sharpe, but then, with a visible effort, she made herself cross the deck. Malachi Braithwaite watched her, while her husband frowned at a sheaf of papers.

'We make slow progress today, Captain Chase,' she said stiffly.

'We have a current, milady, which invisibly helps us, but I do wish the wind would pipe up.' Chase frowned at the sails. 'Some folk believe whistling encourages the wind, but it never seems to work.' He whistled two bars of 'Nancy Dawson', but the wind stayed light. 'See?'

Lady Grace stared at Chase, apparently at a loss for words, and the captain suddenly sensed that she was in some distress. 'Milady?' he enquired with a concerned frown.

'You could perhaps show me on a chart where we are, Captain?' she blurted out.

Chase hesitated, confused by the sudden request. 'It will be a pleasure, milady,' he said. 'The charts are in my day cabin. Will his lordship . . .'

'I shall be quite safe in your cabin, Captain,' Lady Grace said.

'The ship's yours, Mister Peel,' Chase said to the second lieutenant, then led Lady Grace under the break of the poop to the door on the larboard side which led into the dining cabin. Lord William saw them and frowned, making Chase pause. 'You wish to see the charts, my lord?' the captain asked.

'No, no,' Lord William said, and returned to the papers.

Braithwaite watched Sharpe, and Sharpe knew he must not arouse the secretary's suspicions, but he did not believe Lady Grace truly wanted to see the charts and so, ignoring Braithwaite's hostile gaze, he went to his sleeping cabin which lay beyond the starboard door under the poop deck. He knocked on the farther door, which led from the sleeping cabin into the day cabin, but there was no answer and so he let himself into the big stern cabin. 'Sharpe!' Chase showed a small flash of irritation for, friendly as he was, his quarters were sacrosanct and he had not responded to the knock on the door.

'Captain,' Lady Grace said, laying a hand on his arm, 'please.'

Chase, who had been unrolling a chart, looked from her to Sharpe and from Sharpe back to Lady Grace again. He let the chart roll up with a snap. 'I clean forgot to wind the chronometers this morning,' he said. 'Would you forgive me?' He went past Sharpe into the dining cabin, ostentatiously closing the door with a deliberately loud click.

'Oh God, Richard.' Lady Grace ran to him and hugged him. 'Oh, God!'

'What's the matter?'

For a few seconds she did not speak, but then realized she had little time if tongues were not to wag about herself and the captain. 'It's my husband's secretary,' she said.

'I know all about him.'

'You do?' She stared at him wide-eyed.

'He's blackmailing you?' Sharpe guessed.

She nodded. 'And he watches me.'

Sharpe kissed her. 'Leave him to me. Now go, before anyone starts a rumour.'

She kissed him fiercely, then went back onto the deck scarce two minutes after she had left it. Sharpe waited until Chase, who had wound his chronometers at dawn as he always did, came back to the day cabin. Chase rubbed his face tiredly, then looked at Sharpe. 'Well, I never,' he said, then sat in his deep armchair. 'It's called playing with fire, Sharpe.'

'I know, sir.' Sharpe was blushing.

'Not that I blame you,' Chase said. 'Good Lord, don't think that! I was a dog myself until I met Florence. A dear woman! A good marriage tends a man to steadiness, Sharpe.'

'Is that advice, sir?'

'No,' Chase smiled, 'it's a boast.' He paused, thinking now of his ship rather than of Sharpe and Lady Grace. 'This thing isn't going to explode, is it?'

'No,' Sharpe said.

'It's just that ships are oddly fragile, Sharpe. You can have the people content and working hard, but it doesn't take much to start dissent and rancour.'

'It won't explode, sir.'

'Of course not. You said so. Well! Dear me! You do surprise me. Or maybe you don't. She's a beauty, I'll say that, and he's a very cold fish. I think, if I wasn't so securely married, I'd be envious of you. Positively envious.'

'We're just acquaintances,' Sharpe said.

'Of course you are, my dear fellow, of course you are!' Chase smiled. 'But her husband might be affronted by a mere' – he paused – 'acquaintanceship?'

'I think that's safe to say, sir.'

'Then make sure nothing happens to him, for he's my responsibility.' Chase spoke those words in a harsh voice, then smiled. 'Other than that, Richard, enjoy yourself. But quietly, I beg you, quietly.' Chase said the last few words in a whisper, then stood and went back to the quarterdeck.

Sharpe waited a half-hour before leaving the stern quarters, doing his best to allay any suspicions that Braithwaite must inevitably have, but the secretary had left the quarterdeck by the time Sharpe reappeared, and that perhaps was a good thing for Sharpe was in a cold fury.

And Malachi Braithwaite had made himself an enemy.

CHAPTER 7

The wind was still low the next morning and the *Pucelle* seemed hardly to be moving in a greasy sea that slid in long low swells from the west. It was hot again, so that the seamen went bare-chested, some showing the livid cross-hatching of scars where their backs had been subjected to the lash. 'Some wear it as a badge of pride,' Chase told Sharpe, 'though I hope not on this ship.'

'You don't flog?'

'I must,' Chase said, 'but rarely, rarely. Maybe twice since I took command? That's twice in three years. The first was for theft and the other was for striking a petty officer who probably deserved to be struck, but discipline is discipline. Lieutenant Haskell would like me to flog more, he thinks it would make us more efficient, but I don't think it needful.' He stared morosely at the sails. 'No damn wind, no damn wind! What the hell does God think he's doing?'

If God would not send a wind, Chase would practise the guns. Like many naval captains he carried extra powder and shot, bought at his own expense, so that his crew could practise. All morning he had the guns going, every port open, even the ones in his great cabin, so that the ship was constantly surrounded by a pungent white-grey smoke through which it moved with a painful slowness.

'This could mean bad luck,' Peel, the second lieutenant, told Sharpe. He was a friendly man, round-faced, round-waisted and invariably cheerful. He was also untidy, a fact that irritated the first lieutenant, and the bad blood between Peel and Haskell made the wardroom a tense and unhappy place. Sharpe sensed the unhappiness, knew that it upset Chase and was aware of the ship's preference for Peel, who was far more easy-going than the tall, unsmiling Haskell.

'Why bad luck?'

'Guns lull the wind,' Peel explained seriously. He was wearing a blue uniform coat far more threadbare than Sharpe's red jacket, though the second lieutenant was rumoured to be wealthy. 'It is an unexplained phenomenon,' Peel said, 'that gunfire depletes wind.' He pointed at the vast red ensign at the gaff as proof and, sure enough, it hung limp. The flag was not hoisted every day, but at times like this, when the wind was lazily tired, Chase reckoned that an ensign served to show small variations in the breeze.

'Why is it red?' Sharpe asked. 'That sloop we saw had a blue one.'

'It depends which admiral you serve,' Peel explained. 'We take orders from a rear admiral of the red, but if he was blue we'd fly blue and if he was white, white, and if he was yellow he wouldn't command any ships anyway. Simple, really.' He grinned. The red flag, which had the union flag in its upper corner, stirred sluggishly as a rare gust of warm air disturbed its folds. Off to the east, where the gust came from, there were heaps of clouds which Peel said were over Africa. 'And you'll note the water's discoloured,' he added, pointing over the side to a muddy brown sea, 'which means we're off a river mouth.'

Chase timed the gun crews, promising an extra tot of rum to the fastest men. The sound of the guns was astonishing. It pounded the eardrums and shivered the ship before fading slowly into the immensity of sea and sky. The gunners tied scarves about their ears to diminish the shock of the noise, but many of them were still prematurely deaf. Sharpe, curious, went down to the lower deck where the big thirty-two-pounders lurked and he stood in wonder as the guns were fired. He had his fingers in his ears, yet, even so, the whole dark space, punctuated with bright shafts of smoky sunlight which pierced through the open gunports, reverberated with each gun's firing. The sound seemed to punch him in the abdomen, it rang in his head, it filled the world. One after the other, the guns hammered back. Each barrel was close to ten feet long and each gun weighed nearly three tons, and each shot strained the gun's breeching rope taut as an iron bar. The breeching rope was a great cable, fixed with eyebolts to the ship's ribs, that looped through a ring at the gun's breech. Half-naked gunners, sweat glistening on their skins, leaped to sponge out the vast barrels while the gun's chief stopped the venthole with a leather-encased thumb. Men put in powder bags and shot, rammed them home, then hauled the weapon's muzzle out through the gunport with the rope-and-pulley tackles fixed on either side of the carriage.

'You're not aiming at anything!' Sharpe had to shout to the fifth lieutenant who commanded one group of guns.

'We ain't marksmen,' the lieutenant, who was called Holderby, shouted back. 'If it comes to battle we'll be so close to the bastards that we can't miss! Twenty paces at most, and usually less.' Holderby paced down the gundeck, ducking under beams, touching men's shoulders at random. 'You're dead!' he shouted. 'You're dead!' The chosen men grinned and sat gratefully on the shot gratings. Holderby was thinning the crews, as they would be thinned by battle, and watching how well the 'survivors' manned their big guns.

The guns, like those on the *Calliope*, were all fired by flintlocks. The army's field artillery, none of it so big as these guns, was fired with a linstock, a slow match that glowed red as it burned, but no naval captain would dare have a glowing red-hot linstock lying loose on a gundeck where so much powder lay waiting to explode. Instead the guns had flintlocks, though, if the flintlock failed, a linstock was suspended in a nearby tub half-filled with water. The flintlock's trigger was a lanyard which the gunner would twitch, the flint would fall, the spark flash and then the powder-packed reed in the touch-hole hissed and a four- or five-inch flame leaped upwards before the world was consumed by noise as another flame, twice as long as the gun's barrel, seared into the instant cloud of smoke as the gun crashed back.

Sharpe climbed to the deck, and from the deck to the maintop, for only from there could he see beyond the massive bank of smoke to where the shots fell. They fell ragged, some seemingly going as much as a mile before they splashed into the sullen sea, others ripping the surface into spray only a hundred yards from the ship. Chase, as the lieutenant had said, was not training his men to be marksmen, but to be fast. There were gunners aboard who boasted they could lay a ball onto a floating target tub at half a mile, but the secret of battle, Chase insisted, was getting close and releasing a storm of shot. 'It doesn't have to be aimed,' he had told Sharpe. 'I use the ship to aim the guns. I lay the guns alongside the enemy and let them massacre the bastard. Speed, speed, speed, Sharpe. Speed wins battles.'

It was just like musketry, Sharpe realized. On land the armies came together and, as often as not, it was the side that could fire its muskets fastest that would win. Men did not aim muskets, because they were so inaccurate. They pointed their muskets, then fired so that their bullet was just one amongst a cloud of balls that spat towards the enemy. Send enough balls and the enemy would weaken. Lay two ships close together and the one that fired fastest should win in the same way, and so Chase harried his gunners, praising the swift ones and chivvying the laggards, and all morning the sea about the ship quivered to the vibration of the guns. A long track of wavering and thinning powder smoke lay behind the ship, proof that she made some progress, though it was frustratingly slow. Sharpe had brought his telescope up the mast and now trained it eastwards in hope of seeing land, but all he could see was a dark shadow beneath the cloud. He shortened the barrel and trained the glass downwards to see Malachi Braithwaite pacing up and down the quarterdeck, flinching every time a gun cracked.

What to do about Braithwaite? In truth Sharpe knew exactly what to do, but how to do it on a ship crammed with over seven hundred men was the problem. He collapsed the telescope and put it into a pocket, then, for the first time, climbed from the maintop up above the main topsail to the crosstrees, a much smaller platform than the maintop, where he perched beneath the main topgallant sail. Yet another sail rose above that, the royal, up somewhere in the sky, though not so high that men did not climb to it, for there was a lookout poised above the royal's yard, contentedly chewing tobacco as he stared westwards. The deck looked small from here, small and narrow, but the air was fresh for the ever-present stink of the ship and the rotten-egg stench of the powder smoke did not reach this high.

The tall mast trembled as two guns fired together. A freak breath of wind blew the smoke away and Sharpe saw the sea rippling in a frantic fan pattern away from the guns' blasts. Grass did that in front of a field gun, except that the grass became scorched and sometimes caught fire. The sea settled and the smoke thickened.

'Sail!' the man above Sharpe bellowed to the deck, the hail so loud and sudden that Sharpe jumped in fright. 'Sail on the larboard beam!'

Sharpe had to think which side of the ship was larboard and which starboard, but managed to remember and trained his telescope out towards the west, but he could see nothing except a hazy line where the sea met the sky.

'What do you see?' Haskell, the first lieutenant, called up through a speaking trumpet.

'Royals and tops,' the man shouted, 'same course as us, sir!'

The gunfire ceased, for Chase now had something else to worry about. The gunports were closed and the big guns lashed tight as a half-dozen men scurried up the rigging to add their eyes to the lookout's gaze. Sharpe could still see nothing on the western horizon, even with the help of the telescope. He was proud of his eyesight, but being at sea demanded a different kind of vision to looking for enemies on land. He swept the glass left and right, still unable to find the strange ship, then a sudden tiny blur of dirty white broke the horizon; he lost it, edged the glass back, and there she was. Just a blur, nothing but a blur, but the man above him, without any glass, had seen it and could distinguish one sail from another.

A man settled beside Sharpe on the crosstrees. 'It's a Frenchie,' he said.

Sharpe recognized him as John Hopper, the big bosun of the captain's gig. 'You can't tell at this distance, surely?' Sharpe asked.

'Cut of the sails, sir,' Hopper said confidently. 'Can't mistake it.'

'What is it, Hopper?' Chase, bareheaded and in shirt-sleeves, hauled himself onto the platform.

'It could be her, sir, it really could,' Hopper said. 'She's a Frenchie, right enough.'

'Damn wind,' Chase said. 'May I, Sharpe?' He held out his hand for the telescope, then trained it west. 'Damn it, Hopper, you're right. Who spotted her?'

'Pearson, sir.'

'Triple his rum ration,' Chase said, then closed the glass, returned it to Sharpe, and slithered back to the deck in a manner that scared Sharpe witless. 'Boats!' Chase shouted, running towards the quarterdeck. 'Boats!'

Hopper followed his captain and Sharpe watched as the ship's boats were lowered over the side and filled with oarsmen. They were going to tow the ship, not west towards the strange sail, but north in an attempt to get ahead of her.

The men rowed all through the afternoon. They sweated and tugged until their arms were agony. Very slight ripples at the *Pucelle*'s flank showed that they were making some progress, but not enough, it seemed to Sharpe, to gain any headway on the far sail. The small breaths of wind that had relieved the heat earlier in the day seemed to have died away completely so that the sails hung lifeless and the ship was enveloped in an odd silence. The loudest noises were the footfalls of the officers on the quarterdeck, the shouts of the men urging on the tired oarsmen and the creak of the wheel as it spun backwards and forwards in the lolling swell.

Lady Grace, attended by her maid and carrying a parasol against the hot sun, appeared on the quarter-deck and stared westwards. Captain Chase claimed the strange sail was now visible from the deck, but she could not see it, even with a telescope. 'They probably haven't seen us,' Chase suggested.

'Why not?' she asked.

'Our sails have clouds behind them' – he gestured to the great cloud range that piled above Africa – 'and with any luck our canvas just blends into the sky.'

'You think it's the *Revenant*?'

'I don't know, milady. She could be a neutral merchantman.' Chase tried to sound neutral himself, but his suppressed excitement made it plain he believed the far ship was indeed the *Revenant.*

Braithwaite was standing under the break of the poop, watching to see if Sharpe joined her ladyship, but Sharpe did not move. He looked east and saw cat's-paws of ripples on the water, the first signs of a freshening wind. The ripples chased and skittered across the long swells, obstinately refusing to come near the *Pucelle*, but then they seemed to gather together and slide over the sea and suddenly the sails filled, the rigging creaked and the towing lines dipped towards the water.

'The land wind,' Chase said, 'and about time!' He went to the quartermaster at the wheel who at last had some purchase on the rudder. 'Can you feel it?'

'Aye aye, sir.' The helmsman paused to spit a stream of tobacco juice into a big brass spittoon. 'Ain't much though,' he added, 'no more than if a little old lady was breathing on the sails, sir.'

The wind faltered, shivering the sails, then lazily caught again and Chase turned to watch the sea. 'Get the boats in, Mister Haskell!'

'Aye aye, sir!'

'Tot of rum for the oarsmen!'

'Aye aye, sir.' Haskell, who believed Chase spoiled his men, sounded disapproving.

'Double tot of rum for the oarsmen,' Chase said to annoy Haskell, 'and wind for us and death to the French!' His spirits had risen in the belief that he had found his quarry. Now he must stalk her. 'We'll close the angle on her during the night,' he told Haskell. 'Every inch of canvas! And no lights on board. And we'll wet the sails.' A canvas hose was rigged to a pump and used to douse the sails with sea water. Chase explained to Sharpe that wet sails caught more of a light wind than dry, and it did seem as if the soaked canvas worked better. The ship moved perceptibly, though below decks, where the gunsmoke lingered, no wind cleared the air.

The wind freshened at dusk and the *Pucelle* once again heeled to its pressure. Night fell and officers went round the ship to make certain that not a single lantern was alight anywhere on board except for one feeble, red-shielded binnacle lamp that gave the helmsman a glimpse of the compass. The course was changed a few points westwards in hope of closing on the far ship. The wind rose still more so that the sea could be heard coursing down the ship's black and yellow flanks.

Sharpe slept, woke, slept again. No one disturbed his night. He was up before dawn and found that the rest of the ship's officers, even those who should have been sleeping, were on the quarterdeck. 'She'll see us before we see her,' Chase said, meaning that the rising sun would silhouette the *Pucelle*'s topsails against the horizon, and for a few minutes he considered rousting the off-duty watch to help the topmen bring in everything above the mains, but he reckoned the loss of speed would be a worse result and so he kept his canvas aloft. The men with the best eyesight were all high in the rigging. 'If we're lucky,' Chase confided in Sharpe, 'we may catch her by nightfall.'

'That soon?'

'If we're lucky,' the captain said again, then reached out and touched the wooden rail.

The eastern sky was grey now, streaked with cloud,

but soon a leak of pink, like the dye from a redcoat's jacket seeping in the rain onto uniform trousers, suffused the grey. The ship quivered to the seas, left a white wake, raced. The pink turned red, and deeper red, glowing like a furnace over Africa. 'They'll have seen us by now,' Chase said, and took a speaking trumpet from the rail. 'Keep your eyes sharp!' he called to the lookouts, then flinched. 'That was unnecessary,' he chided himself, then corrected the damage by raising the trumpet again and promising a week's worth of rum ration to the man who first sighted the enemy. 'He deserves to be dead drunk,' Chase said.

The east flared to brilliance and became too bright to look at as the sun at last inched above the horizon. Night had gone, the sea was spread naked under the burning sky and the *Pucelle* was alone.

For the distant sail had vanished.

Captain Llewellyn was angry. Everyone on board was irritated. The loss of the other ship had caused morale to plummet on the *Pucelle* so that small mistakes were constantly being made. The bosun's mates were lashing out with their rope ends, officers were snarling, the crew was sullen, but Captain Llewellyn Llewellyn was genuinely angry and apprehensive.

Before the ship sailed from England he had taken aboard a crate of grenades. 'They're French ones,' he told Sharpe, 'so I've no idea what's in them. Powder, of course, and some kind of fulminate. They're made of glass. You light it, you throw it and you pray that it kills someone. Devilish things, they are, quite devilish.'

But the grenades were lost. They were supposed to be in the forward magazine deep on the orlop deck, but a search by Llewellyn's lieutenant and two sergeants had failed to find the devices. To Sharpe the loss of the grenades was just another blow of ill fortune on a day that seemed ill-starred for the *Pucelle*, but Llewellyn reckoned it was far more serious than that. 'Some fool might have put them in the hold,' he said. 'We bought them from the *Viper* when she was being refitted. They took them in an action off Antigua and their captain didn't want them. Reckoned they were too dangerous. If Chase finds them in the hold he'll crucify me, and I don't blame him. Their proper place is in a magazine.'

A dozen marines were organized into a search party and Sharpe joined them in the deep hold where the rats ruled and the ship's stink was foully concentrated. Sharpe had no need to be there, Llewellyn had not even asked him to help, but he preferred to be doing something useful rather than endure the bad-tempered disappointment that had soured the deck ever since daybreak.

It took three hours, but eventually a sergeant found the grenades in a box that had the word 'biscuit' stencilled on its lid. 'God knows what's in the magazines, then,' Llewellyn said sarcastically. 'They're probably full of salt beef. That bloody man Cowper!' Cowper was the ship's purser, in charge of the *Pucelle*'s supplies. The purser was not quite an officer, but was generally treated as one, and he was thoroughly disliked. 'It's the fate of pursers,' Llewellyn had told Sharpe, 'to be hated. It is why God put them on earth. They are supposed to supply things, but rarely can, and if they do then the things are usually the wrong size or the wrong colour or the wrong shape.' Pursers, like the army's sutlers, could trade on their own account, and their venality was famous. 'Cowper probably hid them,' Llewellyn said, 'thinking he could sell them to some benighted savage. Bloody man!' Now, having cursed the purser, the Welshman took one of the grenades from the box and handed it to Sharpe. 'Packed with scrap metal, see? That thing could go off like case shot!'

Sharpe had never handled a grenade before. The old British ones, long discarded for being ineffective, had resembled a miniature shell that had been launched from a bowl-like attachment at the front of a musket, but this French weapon was made of a dark-green glass. The light was poor in the hold, but he held the grenade close to one of the marine's lanterns and saw that the interior of the glass globe, which was about the size of a decent suet pudding, was packed with scraps of metal. A fuse protruded from one side, sealed with a ring of melted wax. 'You light the fuse,' Llewellyn said, 'throw the damn thing, and I suppose the glass container shatters when it falls. The lit fuse communicates to the powder and that's the end of a Frenchman.' He paused, frowning at the glass ball. 'I hope.' He took the grenade back and fondled it like a baby. 'I wonder if Captain Chase would let us try one. If we had men standing by with buckets of water?'

'Make a dirty mark on his nice clean deck?' Sharpe asked.

'I suppose he won't,' Llewellyn said sadly. 'Still, if it comes to a battle I'll give some to the boys up the masts and they can hurl them onto the enemy decks. They have to be good for something.'

'Chuck 'em overboard,' Sharpe advised.

'Dear me, no! I don't want to hurt the fish, Sharpe!'

Llewellyn, hugely relieved by the discovery, had the precious grenades taken to the forward magazine and Sharpe followed the marines up the ladder to the orlop deck which, being beneath the water line, was almost as dark as the hold. The marines went forrard, while Sharpe went towards the stern, intending to climb to Chase's dining cabin for midday dinner, but he could not use the companionway up to the lower deck for a man in a faded black coat was clambering unsteadily down the ladder. Sharpe instinctively waited, then saw that it was Malachi Braithwaite who so cautiously descended the rungs. Sharpe stepped swiftly back into the surgeon's cabin where the red-painted walls and table waited for battle's casualties and from there he watched Braithwaite take a lantern from a hook beside the companionway. The secretary fumbled with a tinderbox, blew on the charred linen to make a flame and lit the oil lamp. He put the lamp on the deck, then grunted as he heaved up the aft hatch of the hold to release a stench of bilge water and rot. Braithwaite shuddered, nerved himself, then took the lantern and clambered down into the ship's depths.

Sharpe followed. There were moments in life, he thought, when fate played into his hands. There had been such a moment when he met Sergeant Hakeswill and joined the army, and another on the battlefield at Assaye when a general had been unhorsed, and now Braithwaite was alone in the hold. Sharpe stood by the hatch and watched Braithwaite's lantern bob as the secretary went slowly down the ladder, and then went aft towards the place where the officers' dunnage was stored.

Sharpe dropped down the ladder and carefully pulled the hatch shut behind him. He went stealthily, though any noise his shoes made on the rungs was masked by the creak of the great pine masts which protruded down through all the decks to be rooted in the elmwood keel. The sound of the flexing masts was magnified in the hold, which also reverberated to the squelching clatter of the ship's six pumps, the sound of the sea and the grating screech of the rudder turning on its pintles.

This after part of the hold was isolated from the forward part of the ship by a great heap of water butts and vinegar barrels that stretched from the planking above the bilge to the beams of the orlop deck twelve feet above. Those beams were supported by great shafts of oak that, in the dim lantern light, looked like the pillars of an old, smoke-darkened church. Braithwaite threaded his way between the oak pillars, climbing the gentle rise of the ship's hull towards a stack of shelves at the very back of the hold that shielded a small space in the stern that was known as the lady hole because it provided the safest place on board during a battle. There was nothing valuable kept on the shelves, merely the officers' unwanted dunnage, but Lord William had brought so much luggage to the *Pucelle* that some of it had to be stored here, and Sharpe, crouching in the shadow of some casks of pungent salt beef, watched the secretary climb a short ladder to find a leather case which he hauled from the top shelf and carried awkwardly back to the deck. He took a key from his pocket and unlocked the case which proved to be crammed with papers. Nothing there, Sharpe thought, for any light-fingered seamen to filch, though he did not doubt that some of them would already have picked the case's lock in hope of better spoils. Braithwaite leafed through the papers, found what he wanted, relocked the case and carried it back up the ladder where he clumsily pushed it past the wooden bar that kept the shelf's contents from spilling in a high sea. The secretary was muttering to himself and snatches of his words carried to Sharpe. 'I'm an Oxford man, not a slave! It could have waited till we reached England. Get in there, damn you!'

The case was finally stowed away, Braithwaite came down the ladder, pocketed the sheet of paper, collected his lantern and started back towards the larger ladder that lay alongside the mizzenmast and led to the closed hatch. He did not see Sharpe. He thought he was alone in the hold until a hand suddenly grasped his collar. 'Hello, Oxford man,' Sharpe said.

'Jesus!' Braithwaite swore and shuddered. Sharpe took the lantern from the secretary's nerveless hand and placed it on top of a cask, then spun Braithwaite round and pushed him hard so that he fell onto the deck.

'I had an interesting conversation with her ladyship the other day,' Sharpe said. 'It seems you're blackmailing her.'

'You're being ridiculous, Sharpe, ridiculous.' Braithwaite thrust himself backwards until he could go no further, then sat with his back against the water casks where he brushed at the dirt on his trousers and coat.

'Do they teach blackmail at Oxford?' Sharpe asked. 'I thought they only taught you useless things like Latin and Greek, but I'm wrong, am I? They give lectures in blackmail and housebreaking, maybe? Pocket-slitting on the side, perhaps?'

'I don't know what you're talking about.'

'You know what I'm talking about, Braithwaite.' Sharpe said. He picked up the lantern and walked slowly towards the terrified secretary. 'You're blackmailing Lady Grace. You want her jewels, don't you, and maybe more? You'd like her in your bed, wouldn't you? You'd like to go where I've been, Braithwaite.'

Braithwaite's eyes widened. He was scared, but he was not so witless as to miss the significance of Sharpe's words. Sharpe had admitted the adultery, and that meant Braithwaite was about to die, for Sharpe could not afford to let him live and tell the tale. 'I just came to fetch a memorandum, Sharpe,' the secretary babbled in apparent panic, 'that's all. I came to fetch this paper. Just a memorandum, Sharpe, for Lord William's report. Let me show you,' and he put a hand in his pocket to fetch the paper and brought out, not a memorandum, but a small pistol. It was the kind of gun designed to be carried in a purse or pocket for use against cutthroats or highwaymen and Braithwaite, his hand shaking, dragged back the flint. 'I've carried this ever since you threatened me, Sharpe.' His voice was suddenly more confident as he levelled the pistol.

Sharpe dropped the lantern.

It hit the deck, there was a shudder of light, then the smash of glass and utter darkness. Sharpe twisted aside, half expecting to hear the pistol crack, but Braithwaite had retained enough nerve to hold his fire.

'You've got one shot, Oxford man,' Sharpe said. 'One shot, then it's my turn.'

Silence, except for the clatter of the pumps and the noise of the masts and the scratching of rats' feet in the bilge.

'I'm used to this,' Sharpe said. 'I've crawled in the darkness before, Braithwaite, and killed men. Cut their gizzards. I did it outside Gawilghur on a dark night. Cut two men's throats, Braithwaite, slit them back to the spine.' He was crouching behind a cask so that if Braithwaite did fire then the secretary would merely inflict a wound on a barrel of salt beef. Sharpe kept his body behind the cask and reached out with his left hand, scraping his nails on the plank deck. 'I slit their gizzards, Oxford man.'

'We can come to an agreement, Sharpe,' Braithwaite said nervously. He had not moved since the hold went dark. Sharpe knew that, for he would have heard. He reckoned Braithwaite was waiting until he went close and then he would fire. Just like ship-to-ship fighting. Let the bugger get close, then fire.

'What kind of agreement, Oxford man?' Sharpe asked, then scratched the deck again, making little noises that would be magnified by the secretary's fear. He found a shard of broken lantern glass and scraped it on the wood.

'You and I should be friends, Sharpe,' Braithwaite said. 'You and I? We ain't like them. My father is a parson. He doesn't make much. Three hundred a year? That may sound like a competence to you, but it's nothing, Sharpe, nothing. Yet people like William Hale are born to fortunes. They abuse us, Sharpe, they grind us down. They think we're dirt.'

Sharpe tapped the glass scrap against the lantern's metal, then scratched it on wood to make a noise like rats' claws. He reached as far as he could, tapping the glass closer to Braithwaite. Braithwaite would be listening, trying to make sense of the small noises, trying to contain a rising terror.

'By what justification,' Braithwaite asked, his voice a tone higher, 'can mere birth bestow such good fortune on one man and deny it to another? Are we lesser men because our parents were poor? Must we forever tug the forelock because their ancestors were brutes in plate armour who stole a fortune? You and I should combine, Sharpe. I beg you, think on it.'

Sharpe was lying flat on the deck now, reaching towards Braithwaite, grinding the glass on the rough planking, taking the sound ever nearer to the secretary who tried to see something, anything, in the stygian darkness.

'I never wrote to Colonel Wallace as I was ordered to,' Braithwaite said in desperation. 'That was a favour to you, Sharpe. Can you not apprehend that we're on the same side?' He paused, waiting for an answer to come from the pitch darkness, but there was only the small scraping sound on the deck in front of him. 'Speak, Sharpe!' Braithwaite pleaded. 'Or kill Lord William.' Braithwaite's voice was almost sobbing with fear now. 'Her ladyship will thank you, Sharpe. You'd like that, wouldn't you? Sharpe? Answer me, Sharpe, for God's sake, answer me!'

Sharpe tapped the glass fragment on the deck. He could hear Braithwaite's hoarse breathing. The secretary lunged out a foot, hoping to find Sharpe, but the shoe struck nothing. 'I beg you, Sharpe, think of me as a friend! I mean you no harm. How could I? When I so admire your achievements? Her ladyship misconstrued my words, nothing else. She is finely strung, Sharpe, and I am your friend, Sharpe, your friend!'

Sharpe tossed the glass scrap so that it rattled among the casks somewhere in the hold's starboard side. Braithwaite gave a yelp of terror, but held his fire, then sobbed as he heard more small noises. 'Talk to me, Sharpe. We are not brutes, you and I. We have things in common, we should talk. Talk to me!'

Sharpe gathered a handful of the broken glass, paused, then threw them towards the secretary who, as the small scraps struck him, screamed and thrust the pistol blindly forward and pulled the trigger. The small gun flashed blindingly in the hold and the bullet smacked harmlessly into a timber. Sharpe stood and walked forward, waited for the echo of the shot to die away. 'One bullet, Oxford man,' he said, 'then it was my turn.'

'No!' Braithwaite flailed wildly in the dark, but Sharpe kicked him hard, then dropped on him, pinioned his arms and turned the secretary over so that he lay on his belly.

Sharpe sat on the small of Braithwaite's back. 'Now tell me, Oxford man,' he asked softly, 'just what you wanted of Lady Grace?'

'I've written it all down, Sharpe.'

'Written what down, Oxford man?' Sharpe had Braithwaite's arms held tight.

'Everything! About you and Lady Grace. I've left the letter among Lord William's papers with instructions to open it if anything should happen to me.'

'I don't believe you, Oxford man.'

Braithwaite gave a sudden heave, trying to release his arms. 'I'm not a fool, Sharpe. You think I wouldn't take precautions? Of course I've left a letter.' He paused. 'Just let me go,' he went on, 'and we can discuss this.'

'So if I let you go,' Sharpe said, still holding tight to Braithwaite's arms, 'you'll fetch the letter back from Lord William?'

'Of course I will. I promise.'

'And you'll apologize to Lady Grace? Tell her you were wrong about your suspicions?'

'Of course I'll do that. Willingly! Gladly!'

'But you weren't wrong, Oxford man,' Sharpe said, stooping close to Braithwaite's head, 'her and me are lovers. Sweat and nakedness in the dark, Oxford man. I couldn't have you telling lies to her, saying it never happened, could I? And now you know my secret I'm not sure I can let you go after all.'

'But there's a letter, Sharpe!'

'You lie like a bloody rug, Braithwaite. There's no letter.'

'There is!' Braithwaite cried in despair.

Sharpe was holding the secretary's arms above his back, pushing them painfully forward, and now he shoved them hard to dislocate both at the shoulders. Braithwaite gave a whimper of pain, then screamed for help as Sharpe gripped one of his ears and turned his head sideways. Sharpe was trying to find a purchase with his right hand on Braithwaite's face and Braithwaite attempted to bite him, but Sharpe smacked his face, then gripped a handful of hair and ear and twisted the head hard. 'God knows how they did it,' Sharpe said, 'those bloody *jettis*, but I watched them, so it must be possible.' He wrenched Braithwaite's head again and the secretary's frantic protest was stilled as his throat was constricted. His breath became a harsh gasping, but still he fought back, trying to heave Sharpe from his back, and Sharpe, amazed that the *jettis* had made this look so easy, clamped his hands on Braithwaite's head and wrenched it with all his strength. The secretary's breathing became a scratchy whimper, hardly audible over the cacophony of creaking and clanking in the hold, but he still twitched and so Sharpe took a deep breath, then twisted a second time and was rewarded with a small grating scrunch that he reckoned was the spine twisting out of alignment in Braithwaite's neck.

The secretary was still now. Sharpe put a finger on Braithwaite's neck, trying and failing to find a pulse. He waited. Still no pulse, no twitches, no breathing, and so Sharpe felt around the deck until he discovered the pistol which he put into his pocket, then he stood and heaved the dead man onto his shoulder and staggered forward, pitched left and right by the motion of the ship, until he blundered into the mizzen ladder. He dropped the body there, climbed the ladder and heaved open the hatch to the astonishment of a seaman who was passing. Sharpe nodded a greeting, closed the hatch on the corpse and on the rats that scrabbled in the dark, then climbed on into the daylight. He chucked the pistol out of his cabin's scuttle. No one noticed.

Dinner was salt pork, peas and biscuits. Sharpe ate well.

Captain Chase assumed that the *Revenant*, if indeed it was the *Revenant* that had been glimpsed on the horizon, had seen the *Pucelle*'s topsails the previous day despite the cloud bank, and so had turned westwards in the night. 'That'll slow her down,' he insisted, recovering some of his usual optimism. The wind was fair, for even though the *Pucelle* had now drawn far enough offshore to lose the advantage of the current, they were in the latitudes where the southeast trades blew. 'The wind can only get stronger,' Chase said, 'and the barometer's rising, which is good.'

Flying fish skittered away from the *Pucelle*'s hull. The ill feeling that had pervaded the ship all morning dissipated beneath the warm sun and under the captain's renewed optimism. 'We know she's no faster than us,' Chase said, 'and we're on the inside of the bend from now to Cadiz.'

'How far is that?' Sharpe asked. He was taking the air on the quarterdeck after sharing dinner with Chase.

'Another month,' Chase said, 'but we ain't out of trouble yet. We should do well as far as the equator, but after that we could be becalmed.' He drummed his fingers on the rail. 'But with God's help we'll catch her first.'

'You haven't seen my secretary, have you, Chase?' Lord William appeared on deck to interrupt the conversation.

'Not a sign of him,' Chase said happily.

'I need him,' Lord William said petulantly. Lord William had persuaded Chase to allow him to use his dining cabin as an office. Chase had been reluctant to yield the room with its lavish table, but had decided it was better to keep Lord William happy rather than have him scowling about the ship in frustration.

Chase turned to the fifth lieutenant, Holderby. 'Did his lordship's secretary take dinner in the wardroom?' he asked.

'No, sir,' Holderby said, 'haven't seen the fellow since breakfast.'

'Have you seen him, Sharpe?' his lordship enquired coldly. He did not like talking to Sharpe, but condescended to ask the question.

'No, my lord.'

'I asked him to fetch a memorandum about our original agreement with Holkar. Damn him, I need it!'

'Perhaps he's still looking for it,' Chase suggested.

'Or he's seasick, my lord?' Sharpe added. 'The wind's freshened.'

'I've looked in his cabin,' Lord William complained, 'and he's not there.'

'Mister Collier!' Chase summoned the midshipman who was pacing up and down the weather deck. 'We have a missing secretary. The tall gloomy fellow who dresses in black. Look below decks for him, will you? Tell him he's wanted in my dining cabin.'

'Aye aye, sir,' Collier said and dived below to start his search.

Lady Grace, attended by her maid, strolled onto the deck and stood a studious distance from Sharpe. Lord William turned on her. 'Have you seen Braithwaite?'

'Not since this morning,' Lady Grace said.

'The wretched man has disappeared.'

Lady Grace shrugged, suggesting that Braithwaite's fate was none of her concern, then turned to watch the flying fish skim over the waves.

'I do hope the bugger hasn't fallen overboard,' Chase said. 'He's got a long swim if he has.'

'He had no business being on deck,' Lord William said in annoyance.

'I doubt he's drowned, my lord,' Chase said reassuringly. 'If he had fallen then someone would have seen him.'

'What do you do then?' Sharpe asked.

'Stop the ship and make a rescue,' Chase said, 'if we can. Did I ever tell you about Nelson in the *Minerva*?'

'Even if you had,' Sharpe said, 'you'd tell me again.'

Chase laughed. 'Back in 'ninety-seven, Sharpe, Nelson commands the *Minerva*. Fine frigate! He was being pursued by two Spanish ships of the line and a frigate when some halfwit falls overboard. Tom Hardy was aboard, wonderful man, he captains the *Victory* now, and Hardy took a boat to rescue the fellow. See the picture, Sharpe? *Minerva* fleeing for her life, close pursued by three Spaniards and Hardy and his boat crew, with the wet fellow aboard, can't row hard enough to catch up. So what does Nelson do? He backs his topsails! Can you credit it? Backs his topsails. By God, he said, I won't lose Hardy. Now the Dons can't make head nor tail of this. Why's the fellow stopping? They think he must have reinforcements coming, so the silly buggers haul their own wind. Hardy catches up, gets aboard, and the *Minerva* takes off like a scalded cat! What a great man Nelson is.'

Lord William scowled and stared westwards. Sharpe gazed up at the mainsail, trying to trace a rope from its beginning, through blocks and tackles, down to the belaying pins beside the gunwales. Hammocks were being aired over the netting racks in which they were stuffed during battle to stop musket bullets. A solitary sea bird, white and long-winged, curved close to the ship then soared away into the blue. Mister Cowper, the purser, was counting the boarding pikes racked around the mainmast's trunk. He licked a pencil, made a note in a book, shot a scared look at Chase and waddled away. Holderby, who had the deck, ordered a bosun's mate forrard to ring the ship's bell. Chase, still thinking about Nelson, smiled.

'Captain! Sir! Captain!' It was Harry Collier, erupting into sight on the weather deck from beneath the quarterdeck.

'Calm down, Mister Collier,' Chase said. 'The ship isn't on fire, is it?'

'No, sir. It's Mister Braithwaite, sir, he's dead, sir!' Everyone on the quarterdeck stared down at the small boy.

'Go on, Mister Collier,' Chase said. 'He can't have just died! Men don't just die. Well, the master did, but he was old. Braithwaite was young. Did he fall? Was he strangled? Did he kill himself? Enlighten me.'

'He fell in the hold, sir, looks like he broke his neck. Off the ladder, sir.'

'Careless,' Chase said, and turned away.

Lord William frowned, did not know what to say, so turned on his heel and stalked back towards the dining cabin, then thought better of it and hurried back to the railing. 'Midshipman?'

'Sir?' Collier hauled off his cocked hat. 'My lord?'

'Was there a piece of paper in his hand?'

'I didn't see, sir.'

'Then pray look, Mister Collier, pray look,' Lord William said, 'and bring it to my cabin if you find such a thing.' He walked away again. Lady Grace looked at Sharpe who met her eye, kept his expression neutral, then turned to gaze up the mainmast.

The body was brought onto the deck. It was plain that poor Braithwaite had slipped off the ladder and fallen, breaking his neck in the process, but it was strange, the surgeon commented with a frown, that the secretary had dislocated both his arms.

'Caught them in the ladder's rungs?' Sharpe suggested.

'That could be so, that could be so,' Pickering allowed. He did not seem convinced, but nor was he minded to probe the mystery. 'But at least it was a quick end.'

'One hopes so,' Sharpe said piously.

'Probably struck his head on a barrel.' Pickering twisted the corpse's head, looking for a mark, but finding none. He stood up, dusting his hands. 'Happens once every voyage,' he said cheerfully, 'sometimes more. We have practical jokers, Mister Sharpe, who like to grease the rungs with soap. Usually when they believe the purser might be using a ladder. It usually ends with a broken leg and much hilarity, but our Mister Braithwaite was less fortunate.' He wrenched the dislocated arms back into place. 'Ugly sort of bugger, wasn't he?'

Braithwaite's body was stripped and then placed in his sleeping cot and the sailmaker sewed a stretch of old, frayed sailcloth as a lid for the makeshift coffin. The final stitch, as was customary, was threaded through the corpse's nose to make certain he was truly dead. Three eighteen-pounder cannon balls had been placed in the coffin that was laid on a plank beside the starboard entry port.

Chase read the service for the dead. The *Pucelle*'s officers, hats off, stood respectfully about the makeshift coffin which had been covered with a British flag. Lord William and Lady Grace stood beside the entry port. 'We therefore commit his body to the deep,' Chase read solemnly, 'to be turned into corruption, looking for the resurrection of the body when the sea shall give up her dead, through our Lord Jesus Christ; who at his coming shall change our vile body that it might be like his glorious body, according to the mighty working whereby he is able to subdue all things to himself.' Chase closed the prayer book and looked at Lord William who nodded his thanks, then spoke a few well-chosen words that described Braithwaite's excellent moral character, his assiduity as a confidential secretary and Lord William's fervent hopes that Almighty God would receive the secretary's soul into a life of eternal bliss. 'His loss,' Lord William finished, 'is a sad, sad blow.'

'So it is,' Chase said, then nodded at the two seamen who crouched beside the plank and they obediently lifted it so that the coffin slid out from beneath the flag. Sharpe heard the edge of the cot strike against the sill of the entry port, then there was a splash.

Sharpe looked at Lady Grace, who looked back, expressionless.

'Hats on,' Chase said.

The officers went away to their duties while the seamen carried away the flag and plank. Lady Grace turned towards the quarterdeck steps and Sharpe, left alone, went to the rail and stared down into the sea.

'The Lord giveth' – Lord William Hale was suddenly beside Sharpe – 'and the Lord taketh away. Blessed be the name of the Lord.'

Sharpe, astonished that his lordship should deign to speak to him, was silent for a few seconds. 'I'm sorry about your secretary, my lord.'

Lord William looked at Sharpe who was again struck by his lordship's resemblance to Sir Arthur Wellesley. The same cold eyes, the same hooked nose that looked like a hawk's beak, but something in Lord William's face now suggested amusement, as though his lordship was privy to information that Sharpe did not possess. 'Are you really sorry, Sharpe?' Lord William asked. 'That's good of you. I spoke well of him just now, but what else could I say? In truth he was a narrow man, envious, inefficient and inadequate to his duties and I doubt the world will much regret his passing.' Lord William pulled his hat on as if to walk away, then turned back to Sharpe. 'It occurs to me, Sharpe, that I never thanked you for the service you did for my wife on the *Calliope*. That was remiss of me, and I apologize. I also thank you for that service, and will thank you further if we do not speak of it again.'

'Of course, my lord.'

Lord William walked away. Sharpe watched him, wondering if there was some game being played that he was unaware of. He remembered Braithwaite's claim to have left a letter among Lord William's papers, then dismissed that idea as a lie. Sharpe reckoned he was seeing dangers where there were none and so he shrugged the conversation away and climbed, first to the quarterdeck and then to the poop where he stood at the taffrail and watched the wake dissipate in the sea.

He heard the footsteps behind him and knew who they belonged to before she came to the rail where, like him, she stared at the sea. 'I've missed you,' she said softly.

'And I you,' Sharpe said. He gazed at the ship's wake which rippled the place where a shrouded body sank under a stream of bubbles towards an unending darkness.

'He fell?' Lady Grace asked.

'So it seems,' Sharpe said, 'but it must have been a very quick death, which is a blessing.'

'Indeed it is,' she said, then turned to Sharpe. 'I find the sun tiresomely hot.'

'Maybe you should go below. My cabin is cooler, I think.'

She nodded, looked into his eyes for a few seconds, then abruptly turned and went.

Sharpe waited five minutes, then followed.

The *Pucelle*, if anyone could have seen her from out where the flying fish splashed down into the waves, looked beautiful that afternoon. Warships were not elegant. Their hulls were massive, making their masts seem disproportionately short, but Captain Chase had hung every sail high in the wind and those royals, studdingsails and skyscrapers added enough bulk aloft to balance the big yellow and black hull. The gilding on her stern and the silver paint on her figurehead reflected the sun, the yellow on her flanks was bright, her deck was scrubbed pale and clean, while the water broke white at her stem and foamed briefly behind. Her seventy-four massive guns were hidden.

The rot and damp and rust and stench could not be detected from the outside, but inside the ship the stink was no longer noticed. In the forecastle the ship's last three goats were milked for the captain's supper. In the bilge the water slopped. Rats were born, fought and died in the hold's deep darkness. In the magazine a gunner sewed powder bags for the guns, oblivious of a whore who plied her trade between the two leather screens that protected the magazine's door from an errant spark. In the galley the cook, one-eyed and syphilitic, shuddered at the smell of some badly salted beef, but put it in the cauldron anyway, while in his cabin at the stern of the weather deck Captain Llewellyn dreamed of leading his marines in a glorious charge that would capture the *Revenant*. Four bells of the afternoon watch sounded. On the quarterdeck a seaman cast the log, a lump of wood, and let the line trail fast from its reel. He counted the knots in the line as they vanished over the rail, chanting the numbers aloud while an officer peered at a pocket watch. Captain Chase went to his day cabin and tapped the barometer. Still rising. The off-duty watch slept in their hammocks, swaying together like so many cocoons. The carpenter scarfed a piece of oak into a gun carriage while in Chase's sleeping cabin an ensign and a lady lay in each other's arms.

'Did you kill him?' Lady Grace asked Sharpe in a whisper.

'Would it matter if I did?'

She traced a finger down the scar on his face. 'I hated him,' she whispered. 'From the day he came into William's employment he just watched me. He would drool.' She shuddered suddenly. 'He told me if I went to his cabin he would keep silent. I wanted to slap him. I almost did, but I thought he'd tell William everything if I struck him, so I just walked away. I hated him.'

'And I killed him,' Sharpe said softly.

She said nothing for a while, then she kissed the tip of his nose. 'I knew you did. The very moment William asked me where he was I knew you had killed him. Was it really quick?'

'Not very,' Sharpe admitted. 'I wanted him to know why he was dying.'

She thought about that for a while, then decided she did not mind if Braithwaite's end had been slow and painful. 'No one's killed for me before,' she said.

'I'd carve my way through a bloody army for you, lady,' Sharpe said, then again remembered Braithwaite's claim that he had left a letter for Lord William and again dismissed his fears, reckoning that the claim had been nothing more than a desperate effort by a doomed man to cling onto life. He would not mention it to Lady Grace.

The sun westered, casting the intricate shadow of shrouds and halliards and sails and masts on the green sea. The ship's bell counted the half-hours. Three seamen were brought before Captain Chase, accused of various sins, and all three had their rum rations suspended for a week. A marine drummer boy cut his hand playing with a cutlass and the surgeon bandaged it, then clipped him about the ear for being a bloody little fool. The ship's cats slept by the galley stove. The purser smelt a cask of water, recoiled from its stench, but chalked a sign on the barrel decreeing that it was drinkable.

And just after the sun set, when the west was a furnace blaze, a last bright ray was reflected off a distant sail.

'Sail on the larboard quarter!' the lookout shouted. 'Sail on the larboard quarter.'

Sharpe did not hear the cry. At that moment he would not have heard the last trump, but the rest of the ship heard the news and seemed to quiver with excitement. For the hunt was not lost, it still ran, and the quarry was again in sight.

CHAPTER 8

The happy days followed.

The far ship was indeed the *Revenant.* Chase had never seen the French warship at close quarters and, try as he might, he could not bring the *Pucelle* near enough to see her name, but some of the seamen pressed from the *Calliope* recognized the cut of the Frenchman's spanker sail. Sharpe stared through his glass and could see nothing strange about that vast sail which hung at the stern of the enemy ship, but the seamen were certain it had been ill-repaired and, as a consequence, hung unevenly. Now the Frenchman raced the *Pucelle* homewards. The ships were almost twins and neither could gain an advantage on the other without the help of weather and the god of winds sent them an equal share.

The *Revenant* was to the west and the two ships sailed northwest to clear the great bulge of Africa and Chase reckoned that would grant the *Pucelle* an advantage once they were north of the equator for then the Frenchman must come eastwards to make his landfall. At night Chase worried he would lose his prey, but morning after morning she was there, ever on the same bearing, sometimes hull down, sometimes nearer, and none of Chase's seamanship could close the gap any more than Montmorin's skills could open it. If Chase edged westwards to try and narrow the distance between them then the French ship would inch ahead and Chase would revert to his previous course and curse the lost ground. He prayed constantly that Montmorin would turn eastwards to offer battle, but Montmorin resisted the temptation. He would take his ship to France, or at least to a harbour belonging to France's ally, Spain, and the men he carried would spur the French into another attempt to make India a British graveyard.

'He'll still have to get through our blockade,' Chase said after supper one evening, then shrugged and tempered his optimism. 'Though that shouldn't be difficult.'

'Why not?' Sharpe asked.

'It ain't a close blockade off Cadiz,' Chase explained. 'The big ships stay well out to sea, beyond the horizon. There'll only be a couple of frigates inshore and Montmorin will brush those aside. No, we have to catch him.' The captain frowned. 'You can't move a pawn sideways, Sharpe!'

'You can't?' They spoke during the first watch which, perversely, ran from eight in the evening until midnight, a time when Chase craved company, and Sharpe had become accustomed to sharing brandy with the captain who was teaching him to play chess. Lord William and Lady Grace were frequent guests, and Lady Grace enjoyed playing the game and was evidently good at it, for she always made Chase frown and fidget as he stared at the board. Lord William preferred to read after supper, though he did once deign to play against Chase and checkmated him inside fifteen minutes. Holderby, the fifth lieutenant, was a keen player, and when he was invited for supper he liked helping Sharpe play against Chase. Sharpe and Lady Grace scrupulously ignored each other during those evenings.

The trade winds blew them northwards, the sun shone, and Sharpe would ever remember those weeks as bliss. With Braithwaite dead, and Lord William Hale immersed in the report he was writing for the British government, Sharpe and Lady Grace were free. They used circumspection, for they had no choice, yet Sharpe still suspected the ship's crew knew of their meetings. He dared not use her cabin, for fear that Lord William might demand entrance, but she would go to his, gliding across the darkened quarterdeck in a black cloak and usually waiting for the brief commotion as the watch changed until she slipped through Sharpe's unlocked door which lay close enough to the first lieutenant's quarters, where Lord William slept, for folk to assume it was there she went, but even so it was hard to remain unseen by the helmsmen. Johnny Hopper, the bosun of Chase's crew, grinned at Sharpe knowingly, and Sharpe had to pretend not to notice, though he also reckoned the secret was safe with the crew for they liked him and universally disliked the contemptuous Lord William. Sharpe and Grace told each other that they were being discreet, but night after night and even sometimes by day they risked discovery. It was reckless, but neither could resist. Sharpe was delirious with love, and he loved her all the more because she made light of the vast gulf that separated them. She lay with him one afternoon, when a scrap of sunlight spearing through a chink in the scuttle's deadlight was scribing an oval shape on the opposite bulkhead, and she mentally added up the number of rooms in her Lincolnshire house. 'Thirty-six,' she decided, 'though that doesn't include the front hall or the servants' quarters.'

'We never counted them at home either,' Sharpe said, and grunted when she dug his ribs with an elbow. They lay on blankets spread on the floor, for the hanging cot was too narrow. 'So how many servants have you got?' he asked.

'In the country? Twenty-three, I think, but that's just in the house. And in London? Fourteen, and then there are the coachmen and stable boys. I've no idea how many of those there are. Six or seven perhaps?'

'I lose count of mine, too,' Sharpe said, then flinched. 'That hurt!'

'Shh!' she whispered. 'Chase will hear. Did you ever have a servant?'

'A little Arab boy,' Sharpe said, 'who wanted to come to England with me. But he died.' He lay silent, marvelling at the touch of her skin on his. 'What does your maid think you're doing?'

'Lying down in the dark with orders not to be disturbed. I say the sun gives me a headache.'

He smiled. 'So what will you do when it rains?'

'I'll say the rain gives me a headache, of course. Not that Mary cares. She's in love with Chase's steward, so she's glad I don't need her. She haunts his pantry.' Grace ran a finger down Sharpe's belly. 'Maybe they'll run away to sea together?'

Sometimes it seemed to Sharpe that he and Grace had run away to sea, and they played a game where they pretended the *Pucelle* was their private ship and its crew their servants and that they would forever be sailing forgiving seas under sunny skies. They never spoke of what waited at journey's end, for then Grace must go back to her lavish world and Sharpe to his place, and he did not know whether he would ever see her again. 'We are like children, you and I,' Grace said more than once, a note of wonder in her voice, 'irresponsible, careless children.'

In the mornings Sharpe exercised with the marines, in the afternoons he slept, and in the evening he ate his supper with Chase, then waited impatiently until Lord William was in his laudanum-induced sleep and Grace could come to his door. They would talk, sleep, make love, talk again. 'I haven't had a bath since Bombay,' she said one night with a shudder.

'Nor have I.'

'But I'm used to having baths,' she said.

'You smell good to me.'

'I stink,' she said. 'I stink, and the whole ship stinks. And I miss walking. I love to walk in the country. If I had my way I would never see London again.'

'You'd like the army,' Sharpe said. 'We're always going for long walks.'

She lay silent for a while, then stroked his hair. 'I dream sometimes of William's death,' she said softly. 'Not when I'm asleep, but when I'm awake. That's dreadful.'

'It's human,' Sharpe said. 'I think of it too.'

'I wish he'd fall overboard,' she said. 'Or slip down a ladder. He won't though.' Not without help, Sharpe thought, and he pushed that idea away. Killing Braithwaite was one thing – the private secretary had been a blackmailer – but Lord William had done nothing except be haughty and married to a woman Sharpe loved. Yet Sharpe did think of killing him, though how it could be done he did not know. Lord William was hardly likely to descend into the hold and he was never on deck in the dark of the night when a man might be pushed over the side. 'If he died,' Grace said quietly, 'I'd be wealthy. I would sell the London house and live in the country. I'd make a great library with a fireplace, walk the dogs, and you could live with me. I'd be Mrs Richard Sharpe.'

For a moment Sharpe thought he had misheard her, then he smiled. 'You'd miss society,' he said.

'I hate society,' she said vehemently. 'Vapid conversation, stupid people, endless rivalry. I shall be a recluse, Richard, with books from the floor to the ceiling.'

'And what will I do?'

'Make love to me,' she said, 'and glower at the neighbours.'

'I reckon I could manage that,' Sharpe said, knowing it was a dream, except that all it would take was one man's death to make the dream come true. 'Is there a gunport in your husband's cabin?' he asked, knowing he should not ask the question.

'Yes, why?'

'Nothing,' he said, but he had been wondering whether he could go into the cabin at night and overpower Lord William and heave him through the gunport, but then he dismissed the idea. Lord William's cabin, like Sharpe's, was under the poop and close to the ship's wheel, and Sharpe doubted he could commit murder and dispose of the body without alerting the officer on watch. Even the creak of the opening gunport would be too loud.

'He's never ill,' Grace said on another afternoon when she had risked coming to Sharpe's cabin. 'He's never ill.'

Sharpe knew what she was thinking and he was thinking it himself, but he doubted Lord William would have the decency to die of some convenient disease. 'Perhaps he'll be killed in the fight with the *Revenant*,' Sharpe said.

Grace smiled. 'He'll be down below, my love, safe beneath the water line.'

'He's a man!' Sharpe said, surprised. 'He'll have to fight.'

'He's a politician, my dear, and he assassinates, he does not fight. He will tell me his life is too precious to be risked, and he will really believe it! Though when we reach England he will modestly claim to have played a part in the *Revenant*'s defeat and I, like a loyal wife, will sit there and smile while the company admires him. He is a politician.'

Footsteps sounded outside the cabin, in the space behind the wheel and under the overhang of the poop. Sharpe listened apprehensively, expecting the steps to go away as they usually did, but this time they came right to his door. Grace clutched his hand, then shuddered as a knock sounded. Sharpe did not respond, then the bolted door shook as someone tried to force it open. 'Who is it?' Sharpe called, pretending to have been asleep.

'Midshipman Collier, sir.'

'What do you want?'

'You're wanted in the captain's quarters, sir.'

'Tell him I'll be there in a minute, Harry,' Sharpe said. His heart was racing.

'You should go,' Grace whispered.

Sharpe dressed, buckled his sword belt, leaned over to kiss her, then slipped out of the door. Chase was standing by the larboard shrouds, gazing at the dot on the horizon that was the *Revenant*. 'You wanted me, sir?' Sharpe asked.

'Not me, Sharpe, not me,' Chase said. 'It's Lord William who wants you.'

'Lord William?' Sharpe could not keep the surprise from his voice.

Chase raised an eyebrow as if to suggest that Sharpe had brought this trouble on himself, then jerked his head towards his dining cabin. Sharpe felt a rising panic, subdued it by telling himself Braithwaite had not left a damning letter, straightened his red coat, then went to the dining cabin's door beneath the poop.

Lord William's voice invited him to come in, Sharpe obeyed and was negligently waved towards a chair. Lord William was alone in the room, sitting at the long table which was covered with books and papers. He was writing, and the scratch of his pen seemed ominous. He wrote for a long time, ignoring Sharpe. The skylight above the table was open and the wind rustled the papers on the table. Sharpe stared at his lordship's grey hair, not one out of place.

'I am writing a report,' Lord William broke the silence, making Sharpe jump with guilty surprise, 'about the political situation in India.' He dipped the nib in an inkwell, drained it carefully, then wrote another sentence before placing the pen on a small silver stand. His cold eyes were pouchy and glassy, probably from the laudanum that he took each night, but they were still filled with their usual distaste for Sharpe. 'I would not normally turn to a junior officer for assistance, but I have small choice under the present circumstances. I would like your opinion, Sharpe, on the fighting abilities of the Mahrattas.'

Sharpe felt a pang of relief. The Mahrattas! Ever since entering the cabin he had been thinking of Braithwaite and his claim to have written a damned letter, but all Lord William wanted was an opinion on the Mahrattas! 'Brave men, my lord,' Sharpe said.

Lord William shuddered. 'I suppose I deserve a vulgar opinion, since I requested it of you,' he said tartly, then steepled his fingers and looked at Sharpe over his well-manicured nails. 'It is evident to me, Sharpe, that we must eventually take over the administration of the whole Indian continent. In time that will also become evident to the government. The major obstacles to that ambition are the remaining Mahratta states, particularly those governed by Holkar. Let me be specific. Can those states prevent us from annexing their territory?'

'No, my lord.'

'Be explicit, please.' Lord William had drawn a clean sheet of paper towards him and had the pen poised.

Sharpe took a deep breath. 'They are brave men, my lord,' he said, risking an irritated glance, 'but that ain't enough. They don't understand how to fight in our way. They think the secret is artillery, so what they do, sir, is line up all their guns in a great row and put the infantry behind them.'

'We don't do that?' Lord William asked, sounding surprised.

'We put the guns at the sides of the infantry, sir. That way, if the other infantry attacks, we can rake them with crossfire. Kill more men that way, my lord.'

'And you,' Lord William said acidly as his pen raced over the paper, 'are an expert on killing. Go on, Sharpe.'

'By putting their guns in front, sir, they give their own infantry the idea that they're protected. And when the guns fall, sir, which they always do, the infantry lose heart. Besides, sir, our lads fire muskets a good deal faster than theirs, so once we're past the guns it's really just a matter of killing them.' Sharpe watched the pen scratch, waited until his lordship dipped it into the inkwell again. 'We like to get close, my lord. They shoot volleys at a distance, and that's no good. You have to march up close, very close, till you can smell them, then start firing.'

'You're saying their infantry lack the discipline of ours?'

'They lack the training, sir.' He thought about it. 'And no, they're not as disciplined.'

'And doubtless,' Lord William said pointedly, 'they do not use the lash. But what if their infantry was properly led? By Europeans?'

'It can be good then, sir. Our sepoys are as good, but the Mahrattas don't take well to discipline. They're raiders. Pirates. They hire infantry from other states, and a man never fights so well when he's not fighting for his own. And it takes time, my lord. If you gave me a company of Mahrattas I'd want a whole year to get them ready. I could do it, but they wouldn't like it. They'd rather be horsemen, my lord. Irregular cavalry.'

'So you do not think we need take Monsieur Vaillard's errand to Paris too seriously?'

'I wouldn't know, my lord.'

'No, you wouldn't. Did you recognize Pohlmann, Sharpe?'

The question took Sharpe utterly by surprise. 'No,' he blurted with too much indignation.

'Yet you must have seen him' – Lord William paused to sort through the papers – 'at Assaye.' He found the name which, Sharpe suspected, he had never forgotten.

'Only through a telescope, my lord.'

'Only through a telescope.' Lord William repeated the words slowly. 'Yet Chase assures me you were very certain in your identification of him. Why else would this man-of-war be racing through the Atlantic?'

'It just seemed obvious, my lord,' Sharpe said lamely.

'The workings of your mind are a constant mystery to me, Sharpe,' Lord William said, writing as he spoke. 'I shall, of course, moderate your opinions by talking to more senior men when I reach London, but your jejune thoughts will make a first draft possible. Perhaps I shall talk to my wife's distant cousin, Sir Arthur.' The pen scratched steadily. 'Do you know where my wife is this afternoon, Mister Sharpe?'

'No, my lord,' Sharpe said, and was about to ask how he could be expected to know, but bit his tongue in case he heard the wrong answer.

'She has a habit of vanishing,' Lord William said, his grey eyes now steady on Sharpe.

Sharpe said nothing. He felt like a mouse under a cat's gaze.

Lord William turned to look at the bulkhead which divided the dining cabin from Sharpe's cabin. He could have been gazing at the picture of Chase's old frigate, the *Spritely*, which hung there. 'Thank you, Sharpe,' he said, looking back at last. 'Close the door firmly, will you? The latch is imperfectly aligned with its socket.'

Sharpe left. He was sweating. Did Lord William know?

Had Braithwaite really written a letter? Jesus, he thought, Jesus. Playing with fire. 'Well?' Captain Chase had come to stand beside him, an amused expression on his face.

'He wanted to know about the Mahrattas, sir.'

'Don't we all?' Chase enquired sweetly. He looked up at the sails, leaned to see the compass, smiled. 'The ship's orchestra is giving a concert tonight on the forecastle,' he said, 'and we're all invited to attend after supper. Do you sing, Sharpe?'

'Not really, sir.'

'Lieutenant Peel sings. It's a pleasure to hear him. Captain Llewellyn should sing, being Welsh, but doesn't, and the lower-deck larboard gun crews make a splendid choir, though I shall have to order them not to sing the ditty about the admiral's wife for fear of offending Lady Grace, yet even so it should be a wonderful evening.'

Grace had left his cabin. Sharpe closed the door, shut his eyes and felt the sweat trickle beneath his shirt. Playing with fire.

Two mornings later there was an island visible far off to the south and west. The *Revenant* must have passed quite close to the island in the night, but at dawn she was well to its north. Cloud hung above the small scrap of grey which was all Sharpe could see of the island's summit through his telescope. 'It's called St Helena,' Chase told him, 'and belongs to the East India Company. If we weren't otherwise engaged, Sharpe, we'd make a stop there for water and vegetables.'

Sharpe gazed at the ragged scrap of land isolated in an immensity of ocean. 'Who lives there?'

'Some miserable Company officials, a handful of morose families, and a few wretched black slaves. Clouter was a slave there. You should ask him about it.'

'You freed him?'

'He freed himself. Swam out to us one night, climbed the anchor cable and hid away till we were at sea. I've no doubt the East India Company would like him back, but they can whistle in the wind for him. He's far too good a seaman.'

There were a score of black seamen like Clouter aboard, another score of lascars, and a scattering of Americans, Dutchmen, Swedes, Danes and even two Frenchmen. 'Why would a man be called Clouter?' Sharpe asked.

'Because he clouted someone so hard that the man didn't wake up for a week,' Chase said, amused, then took the speaking trumpet from the rail and hailed Clouter who was among the men lounging on the forecastle. 'Would you like me to put in to St Helena, Clouter? You can visit your old friends.'

Clouter mimed cutting his throat and Chase laughed. It was small gestures like that, Sharpe reckoned, that made the *Pucelle* a happy ship. Chase was easy in command and that ease did not diminish his authority, but simply made the men work harder. They were proud of their ship, proud of their captain and Sharpe did not doubt they would fight for him like fiends, but Capitaine Louis Montmorin had the same reputation and when the two ships met it would doubtless prove a grim and bloody business. Sharpe watched Chase for he reckoned he had still a lot to learn about the subtle business of leading men. He saw that the captain did not secure his authority by recourse to punishment, but rather by expecting high standards and rewarding them. He also hid his doubts. Chase could not be certain that Pohlmann's servant really was Michel Vaillard, and he did not know for sure that he could catch the *Revenant* even if the Frenchman was aboard, and if he failed then the lords of the Admiralty would take a dim view of his initiative in taking the *Pucelle* so far from her proper station. Sharpe knew Chase worried about those things, yet the crew never received a hint of their captain's doubts. To them he was certain, decisive and confident, and so they trusted him. Sharpe noted it and resolved to imitate it, and then he wondered whether he really would stay in the army. Perhaps Lord William would die? Perhaps Lord William would have a sleepless night and stroll the poop deck in the dark?

And then, Sharpe wondered, what? A library with a fireplace? Grace happy with books, and he with what? And, as he asked himself those questions, he would sheer away from their answers, for they involved a murder that Sharpe feared. A man could kill a secretary and pass it off as a fall from a ladder, but a peer of England was not so easily destroyed. Nor had Sharpe any right to kill Lord William. He probably would, he thought, if the chance came, but he knew it would be wrong and he dimly apprehended that such a wrong would leave a scar on his future. He often surprised himself by realizing he had a conscience. Sharpe knew plenty of men, dozens, who would kill for the price of a pot of ale, yet he was not among them. There had to be a reason, and selfishness was not enough. Even love was not enough.

Provoke Lord William to a duel? He thought about that, but he suspected Lord William would never stoop to fight a mere ensign. Lord William's weapons were more subtle; memoranda to the Horse Guards, letters to senior officers, quiet words in the right ears and at their end Sharpe would be nothing. So forget it, Sharpe told himself, let the dream go, and he tried to lose himself in the work of the ship. He and Llewellyn were holding a competition among the marines to see who could fire the most musket shots in three minutes and the men were improving, though none could yet match

Sharpe. He practised them, encouraged them, swore at them, and morning after morning they filled the ship's forecastle deck with powder smoke until Sharpe reckoned the marines were as good as any redcoat company. He practised with the cutlass, fighting Llewellyn up and down the weather deck, slashing and hacking, parrying and slicing until the sweat ran down his face and chest. Some of the marines practised with boarding pikes which were eight-foot ash staffs tipped with slender steel spikes that Llewellyn claimed were marvellously effective for clearing narrow passageways on enemy ships. The Welshman also encouraged the use of boarding axes which had vicious blades on short handles. 'They're clumsy,' Llewellyn admitted, 'but, by God, they put the fear of Christ into the Froggies. A man don't fight long with one of those buried in his skull, Sharpe, I can tell you. It cools his ardour, it does.'

They crossed the equator and, because everyone aboard had crossed it before, there was no need to put them through the ordeal of being dressed in women's clothes, shaved with a cutlass and dipped in sea water. Nevertheless one of the seamen dressed himself as Neptune and went round the ship with a makeshift trident and demanded tribute from men and officers alike. Chase ordered a double rum ration, hung out a larger studdingsail that the sailmaker had stitched, and watched the *Revenant* on the northwestern horizon.

Then the calms came. For a week the two ships made scarce forty miles, but just lay on a glassy sea in which their reflections were almost mirror perfect. The sails hung and the powder smoke belched by gun practice made a cloud about each ship that did not shift so that, from a distance, the *Revenant* looked like a patch of fog rigged with masts and sails. Lieutenant Haskell tried to time the Frenchman's volleys by watching the cloud twitch in his telescope. 'Only one shot every three minutes and twenty seconds,' he finally concluded.

'They're not trying their hardest,' Chase said. 'Montmorin's not going to let me know how well his men are trained. You may be assured they're a good deal faster than that.'

'How fast are we?' Sharpe asked Llewellyn.

The Welshman shrugged. 'On a good, day, Sharpe? Three broadsides in five minutes. Not that we ever fire a broadside proper. Fire all the guns together, Sharpe, and the bloody ship would fall to bits! But we fire in a ripple, see? One gun after the other. Pretty to watch, it is, and after that the guns fire as they're loaded. The faster crews will easily do three shots in five minutes, but the bigger guns are slower. But our lads are good. There aren't many Frenchmen who can do three shots in five minutes.'

Some days Chase tried to tow the ship closer to the *Revenant*, but the Frenchman was also using his boats to tow and so the foes kept their stations. One day a freak breeze carried the *Revenant* almost beyond the horizon, leaving the *Pucelle* stranded, but next day it was the British ship's turn to be wafted northwards while the *Revenant* lay becalmed. The *Pucelle* ghosted along, drawing nearer and nearer to the enemy, the ripples of her passage scarcely disturbing the glasslike sea, and foot by foot, yard by yard, cable by cable, she gained on the *Revenant* despite the best efforts of the French oarsmen who were out ahead in their ship's longboats. Still the *Pucelle* closed the gap until at last Captain Chase had the tompion pulled from the barrel of his forward larboard twenty-four-pounder. The gun was already loaded, for all the guns were left charged, and the gunner took off the lead touch-hole cover and screwed a flintlock into place. The captain had gone to the forward end of the weather deck, where the *Pucelle*'s goats were penned, and crouched beside the open gunport.

'We'll load with chain after the first shot,' he decided.

Chain shot looked at first glance like ordinary round shot, but the ball was split into two halves and when it left the gun the halves separated. They were joined by a short length of chain and the two hemispheres whirled through the air, the chain between them, to slice and tear at the enemy's rigging. 'Long range for chain shot,' the gunner told Chase.

'We'll get closer,' Chase said. He was hoping to disable the *Revenant*'s sails, then close and finish her with solid shot. 'We'll get closer,' he said again, stooping to the gun and staring at the enemy that was now almost within range. The gilding on her stern reflected the sunlight, the tricolour hung limp from the mizzen gaff and her rail was crowded with men who must have been wondering why the wind was fickle enough to favour the British. Sharpe was staring through a telescope, hoping for a glimpse of Peculiar Cromwell's long hair and blue coat, or of Pohlmann and his servant, but he could not make out the individuals who stood watching the *Pucelle* glide closer. He could see the ship's name on her stern, see the water being pumped from her bilges and the copper, now pale green, at her water line.

Then the longboats towing the *Revenant* were suddenly called back. Chase grunted. 'They probably plan to tow her head round,' he suggested, 'to show us her broadside. Drummer!'

A marine boy stepped forward. 'Sir?'

'Beat to quarters,' Chase said, then held up a hand. 'No, belay that! Belay!'

The wind was not so fickle after all, and the *Revenant*'s boats had not been recalled to turn the ship, but rather because Montmorin had seen the flickering cat's-paws of wind ruffling the water at his stern. Now her sails lifted, stretched and tightened and the Frenchman was suddenly sliding ahead, just out of cannon range. 'Damn,' Chase said mildly, 'damn and blast his French luck.' The flintlock was dismounted, the tompion hammered into the muzzle, the gunport closed and the twenty-four-pounder secured.

Next day the *Revenant* pulled ahead again, the beneficiary of an unfair breeze, and by the end of the week of calms the two ships were again almost an horizon apart, though now the French ship was directly ahead of the *Pucelle*. 'Far enough,' Chase said bitterly, 'to see her safe into harbour.'

The next few days saw contrary currents and hard winds from the northeast so that both ships beat up as close as they could. Chase called it sailing on a bowline and the *Pucelle* proved the better sailor and slowly, so slowly, she began to make up the lost ground. The ship smacked hard into the waves, shattering the seas across the decks and sails. Rain squalls sometimes blotted the *Revenant* from the *Pucelle*'s view, but she always reappeared and, through his telescope, Sharpe could see her pitching like the *Pucelle*. Once, gazing at the black and yellow warship, he saw strips of canvas flutter at her bow and she seemed to slew towards him for a few seconds, but in another few heartbeats the Frenchman had hoisted a new sail to replace the one that had blown out. 'Worn canvas,' the first lieutenant commented. 'Reckon that's why we're faster on the wind. His foresails are threadbare.'

'Or his stays aren't tight enough,' Chase muttered, watching as the *Revenant* resumed her previous course. 'But he made that sail change quickly,' he acknowledged ruefully.

'He probably had the new sail bent on ready, sir,' Haskell suggested.

'Like as not,' Chase agreed. 'He's good, our Louis, ain't he?'

'Probably got English blood,' Haskell said in all seriousness.

They passed the Cape Verde Islands which were mere blurs on a rain-smudged horizon and, a week later, in another rainstorm, they glimpsed the Canaries. There was plenty of local shipping about, but the sight of two warships sent them all scurrying for shelter.

There was just one more week, maybe a day less, to Cadiz. 'She'll make port on my birthday,' Chase said, staring through his glass, then he collapsed the telescope and turned away to hide his bitterness for, unless a miracle intervened, he knew he faced utter failure. He had one week to catch the Frenchman, but the wind had backed and for the next few days the *Revenant* kept her lead so that the sun-faded tricolour at her stern was a constant taunt to her pursuers.

'What will Chase do if we don't catch her?' Grace asked Sharpe that night.

'Sail on to England,' he said. Plymouth, probably, and he imagined landing on a wet autumn afternoon on a stone quay where he would be forced to watch Lady Grace going away in a hired four-wheeler.

'I shall write to you,' she said, reading his thoughts, 'if I know where.'

'Shorncliffe, in Kent. The barracks.' He could not hide his misery. The stupid dreams of a ridiculous love were fading into a grim reality, just as Chase's hopes of catching the *Revenant* were fading.

Grace lay beside him, gazing up at the deck, listening to the hiss of rain falling on the deadlight of the cabin's scuttle. She was dressed, for it was almost time for her to slip out of his door and go down to her own cabin, yet she clung to him and Sharpe saw the old sadness in her eyes. 'There is something,' she said softly, 'that I was not going to tell you.'

‘Not going to tell me?’ he asked. ‘Which means you will tell me.’

‘I was not going to tell you,’ she said, ‘because there is nothing to be done about it.’

He guessed what she was going to say, but let her say it.

‘I’m pregnant,’ she said and sounded forlorn.

He squeezed her hand, said nothing. He had known what she was going to say, but was now surprised by it.

‘Are you angry?’ she asked nervously.

‘I’m happy,’ he said, and laid a hand on her flat belly. It was true. He was filled with joy, even though he knew that joy had no future.

‘The child is yours,’ she said.

‘You know that?’

‘I know that. Maybe it’s the laudanum, but . . .’ She stopped and shrugged. ‘It’s yours. But William will think it’s his.’

‘Not if he can’t . . .’

‘He will think what I tell him!’ she interrupted fiercely, then began to cry and put her head on Sharpe’s shoulder. ‘It is yours, Richard, and I would give the world for the child to know you.’

But they would be home soon, and she would go away and Sharpe would never see the child for he and Grace were illicit lovers and there was no future for them. None. They were doomed.

And next morning everything changed.

It was a chill, wet day. The wind was north of northwest, so that the *Pucelle* sailed hard on her bowline. Rain squalls swept across the sea, seethed on the deck and dripped from the sails. The water was green and grey, streaked by foam and whipped by the wind. The officers on the quarterdeck looked unfamiliar for they were in thick oiled coats, and Sharpe, feeling the cold for the first time since he had gone to India, shivered. The ship bucked and shuddered, fighting sea and wind, and sometimes heeled far over as a gusting squall strained the sails. Seven men manned the double wheel and it needed all their combined strength to hold the heavy ship up into the wind's teeth. 'A touch of autumn in the air,' Captain Chase greeted Sharpe. Chase's cocked hat was covered with canvas and tied beneath his chin. 'Did you have breakfast?'

'I did, sir.' It was not much of a breakfast for supplies were getting low on the *Pucelle* and the officers, like the men, subsisted on short rations of beef, ship's biscuit and Scotch coffee which was a vile concoction of burnt bread dissolved in hot water and sweetened with sugar.

'We're gaining on him,' Chase said, nodding towards the distant *Revenant* which was evidently having as hard a time as the *Pucelle*, for she was shattering the seas with her bluff bow and smothering her hull in spray as she pushed as near northwards as her helmsman could manage. The *Pucelle* closed the gap relentlessly, as she always did when the ships were hard on the wind, but just after the second bell of the forenoon watch the breeze went into the south-south-west and the *Revenant* was no longer struggling into the wind, but could sail with her canvas spread to the treacherous wind's kindness and so keep her lead. Then, just a half-hour later, she unexpectedly turned to the east which meant she was heading towards the Straits of Gibraltar instead of Cadiz.

'Starboard, starboard!' Chase called to the helmsman.

Haskell ran up to the quarterdeck as the seven men spun the *Pucelle*'s wheel. Sail handlers ran about the deck, loosing sheets. The sails flapped, spattering rain-water across the deck. 'Has she blown out her foresails again?' Haskell shouted over the noise of the beating canvas.

'No,' Chase said. The Frenchman was travelling faster and easier now, sliding across the waves to leave a track of ragged white water at her stern. 'He's making for Toulon!' Chase decided, but no sooner had he spoken than the *Revenant* turned back onto her old course and the *Pucelle*'s watch, who had just loosened her sheets, had to haul them tight again.

'Follow him!' Chase called to the quartermaster and pulled out his glass again, unhooded the lens and stared at the Frenchman. 'What the devil is he doing? Is he taunting us? Knows he's safe and wants to mock us? Blast him!'

The answer came ten minutes later when a lookout called that a sail was in sight. Twenty minutes more and there were two sails out on the northern horizon and the closer of the two had been identified as a British frigate. 'Can't be the blockading squadron,' Chase said, puzzled, 'because we're too far south.' A moment later the second ship came into clearer view and she too was a Royal Navy frigate.

The *Revenant* had plainly changed course to avoid the two ships, fearing from her first glimpse of their topsails that they might be British ships of the line, but then, realizing that she was faced by two mere frigates, she had decided to fight her way through to Cadiz. 'She'll have no trouble brushing them aside,' Chase said gloomily. 'Their only hope of stopping her is by laying themselves right across her course.'

Signals were suddenly flying in the breeze. Sharpe could not even see the distant frigates, but Hopper, the bosun of Chase's crew, could not only see them, but could identify the nearer ship. 'She's the *Euryalus*, sir!'

'Henry Blackwood, by God,' Chase said. 'He's a good man.'

Tom Connors, the signal lieutenant, was halfway up the mizzen ratlines where he gazed through a glass at the *Euryalus* which was flying a string of bright flags from her mizzen yard. 'The fleet's out, sir!' Connors called excitedly, then amended his report. '*Euryalus* wants us to identify ourselves, sir. But she also says the French and Spanish fleets are out.'

'My God! Bless me!' Chase, his face suddenly stripped of all its tiredness and disappointment, turned to Sharpe. 'The fleet's out!' He sounded disbelieving and exultant at the same time. 'You're certain, Tom?' he asked Connors, who was now running up to the flag lockers on the poop. 'Of course you're sure. They're out!' Chase could not resist dancing two or three celebratory steps that were made clumsy by his heavy tarpaulin coat. 'The Frogs and Dons, they're out! By God, they're out!'

Haskell, normally so stern, looked delighted. The news was racing round the ship, bringing off-duty men up to the deck. Even Cowper, the purser, who normally stayed mole-like in the lower depths of the ship, came to the quarterdeck, hurriedly saluted Chase, then gazed northwards as though expecting to see the enemy fleet on the horizon. Pickering, the surgeon, who normally did not stir from his cot till past midday, lumbered on deck, glanced at the far frigates, then muttered that he was going out of range and went back below. Sharpe did not quite understand the excitement and surprise that had quickened the crew, indeed it seemed to him that the news was grim. Lieutenant Peel slapped Sharpe's back in his joy, then saw the confusion on the soldier's face. 'You don't share our delight, Sharpe?'

'Isn't it bad news, sir, if the fleet's out?'

'Bad news? Good Lord above, no! They won't be out without our permission, Sharpe. We keep 'em bottled up with a close blockade, so if they're out it means we let 'em out, and that means our own fleet's somewhere close by. Monsieur Crapaud and Señor Don are dancing to our tune now, Sharpe. Our tune! And it'll be a hot one.'

It seemed Peel was right, for when the *Pucelle* hoisted a string of flags that identified her and described her mission, there was a long wait while that message was passed on by the British frigates to other ships that evidently lay beyond the horizon, and if there were other ships across that grey skyline then it could only mean that the British fleet was also out. All the fleets were out. The battleships of Europe were out, and Chase's quarterdeck rejoiced. The *Revenant* sailed on, ignored by the two frigates which had bigger fish to fry than one lone French seventy-four. The *Pucelle* still dutifully pursued her, but then another flurry of colour broke out among the sails of the *Euryalus* and everyone on the quarterdeck stared at the signal lieutenant, who in turn gazed through a glass at the frigate. 'Hurry!' Chase said under his breath.

'Vice Admiral Nelson's compliments, sir,' Lieutenant Connors said, scarce able to conceal his excitement, 'and we're to bear north northwest to join his fleet.'

'Nelson!' Chase said the name with awe. 'Nelson! By God, Nelson!'

The officers actually cheered. Sharpe stared at them in astonishment. For over two months they had pursued the *Revenant*, using every ounce of seamanship to close on her, yet now, ordered to abandon the chase, they cheered? The enemy ship was just to sail away?

'We're a gift from heaven, Sharpe,' Chase explained. 'A ship of the line? Of course Nelson wants us. We add guns! We're in for a battle, by God, we are too! Nelson against the Frogs and the Dons, this is heaven!'

'And the *Revenant*?' Sharpe asked.

'If we don't catch her,' Chase asked airily, 'what does it matter?'

'It might matter in India.'

'That'll be the army's problem,' Chase said dismissively. 'Don't you understand, Sharpe? The enemy fleet's out! We're going to pound them to splinters! No one can blame us for abandoning a chase to join battle. Besides, it's Nelson's decision, not mine. Nelson, by God! Now we're in good company!' He danced another brief and clumsy hornpipe before picking up his speaking trumpet to call out the orders that would turn the *Pucelle* towards the British fleet that lay beyond the horizon, but before he could even draw breath a shout came from the main crosstrees that another fleet was visible on the northern horizon.

'Stand on,' Chase ordered the quartermaster at the wheel, then ran for the main shrouds, followed by a half-dozen officers. Sharpe went more slowly. He climbed the rain-soaked ratlines, negotiated the lubber's hole and trained his telescope north, but he could see nothing except a wind-broken sea and a mass of clouds on the horizon.

'The enemy.' Captain Llewellyn of the marines had arrived beside Sharpe on the maintop's grating. He breathed the words. 'My God, it's the enemy.'

'And the *Revenant* will join them!' Chase said. 'That's my guess. They'll be as glad of Montmorin's company as Nelson is of ours.' He turned and grinned at Sharpe. 'You see? We may not have lost her after all!'

The enemy? Sharpe could still see nothing but clouds and sea, but then he realized that what he had mistaken for a streak of dirty white cloud on the horizon was in fact a mass of topsails. A fleet of ships was on that horizon and sailing straight towards his glass so that their sails coalesced into a blur. God alone knew how many ships were there, but Chase had said that the combined navies of France and Spain had put out to sea. 'I see thirty,' Lieutenant Haskell said uncertainly, 'maybe more.'

'And they're coming south,' Chase said, puzzled. 'I thought the rascals were supposed to be going north to cover the invasion?'

'It's French navigators,' Lieutenant Peel, the rotund man who had sung so beautifully at the concert, said. 'They think Britain's off Africa.'

'They can sail to China so long as we catch them,' Chase said, then collapsed his telescope and disappeared down the futtock shrouds. Sharpe stayed in the maintop until a squall of rain blotted the far fleet from view.

The *Pucelle* turned westwards, but the fickle wind turned with her so that she had to beat her way out into the Atlantic, thumping the cold waves to spatter spray down the holy-stoned decks. The enemy fleet was soon lost to sight, but Chase's course took the *Pucelle* past two more frigates which formed the fragile chain connecting Nelson's fleet with the enemy. The frigates were the scouts, the cavalry, and, having found the enemy, they stayed with her and sent messages back down the long windy links of their chain. Connors watched the bright coloured flags and passed on their news. The enemy, he reported, was still sailing south and the *Euryalus* had counted thirty-three ships of the line and five frigates, but two hours later the total was increased by one ship of the line because the *Revenant*, as Chase had foreseen, had been ordered to join the enemy's fleet.

'Thirty-four prizes!' Chase said exultantly. 'My God, we'll hammer them!'

The last link in the chain was not a single-decked frigate, but a ship of the line which, to Sharpe's amazement, was identified even before her hull showed above the horizon. 'It's the *Mars*,' Lieutenant Haskell said, peering through his glass. 'I'd know that mizzen topsail anywhere.'

'The *Mars*?' Chase's spirits were flying high to the

heavens now. 'Georgie Duff, eh! He and I were midshipmen together, Sharpe. He's a Scotsman,' he added as though that were relevant. 'Big fellow, he is, big enough to be a prize fighter! I remember his appetite! Never had enough to eat, poor fellow.'

A string of flags appeared at the *Mars*'s mizzen. 'Our number, sir,' Connors reported, then waited a few seconds. 'What brings you home in such a hurry?'

'Give Captain Duff my compliments,' Chase said happily, 'and tell him I knew he'd need some help.' The signal lieutenant dragged flags from their lockers, a midshipman bent them on to the halliard and a seaman hauled them up.

'Captain Duff assures you, sir, that he will not permit us to come to any harm,' Connors reported after a moment.

'Oh, he's a good fellow!' Chase said, delighted with the insult. 'A good fellow.'

An hour later another cloud of sail appeared, only this one was on the western horizon and it grew from a blurred smear into the massed sails of a fleet. Twenty-six ships of the line, not counting the *Mars* or the *Pucelle*, were sailing northwards and Chase took his ship towards the head of the line while his officers crowded at the quarterdeck's lee rail and gazed at the far ships. Lord William and Lady Grace, both bundled in heavy cloaks, had come on deck to see the British fleet.

'There's the *Tonnant*!' Chase exulted. 'See her? A lovely ship, just lovely! An eighty-four. She was captured at the Nile. God, I remember seeing her come into Gibraltar afterwards, all her topmasts gone and blood crusted at her scuppers, but don't she look wonderful now? Who has her?'

'Charles Tyler,' Haskell said.

'What a good fellow he is, to be sure! And is that the *Swiftsure*?'

'It is, sir.'

'My God, she was at the Nile too. Ben Hallowell had her then. Dear Ben. She's under Willy Rutherford now,' he said to Sharpe, as though Sharpe would know the name, 'and he's a good fellow, a capital fellow! Look at that copper on the *Royal Sovereign*! New, eh? She'll be sailing quick as you like.' He was pointing to one of the bigger warships, a great brute with three gundecks and Sharpe, peering through his glass, could see the bright gleam of her newly coppered hull whenever she leaned to the wind. The other ships, when they tilted to the breeze, showed a band of copper turned green by the sea, but the *Royal Sovereign*'s lower hull shone like gold. 'She's Admiral Collingwood's flagship,' Chase told Sharpe, 'and he's a good fellow. Not as nice as his dog, but a good fellow.'

To Chase they were all good fellows. There was Billy Hargood who was sailing the *Belleisle*, a seventy-four that had been captured from the French, and Jimmy Morris of the *Colossus* and Bob Moorsom of the *Revenge*. 'Now there's a fellow who knows how to train a ship,' Chase said warmly. 'Wait till you see her in battle, Sharpe! She can fire broadsides faster than anyone.'

'The *Dreadnought*'s faster,' Peel suggested.

'The *Revenge* is much quicker!' Haskell said, irritated by the second lieutenant's comment.

'The *Dreadnought*'s quick, no doubt of it, she's quick.' Chase tried to mediate between his senior lieutenants. He pointed out the *Dreadnought* to Sharpe, who saw another three-decker. 'Her guns are quick,' Chase said, 'but she's painful slow on the wind. John Conn has her, doesn't he?'

'He does, sir,' Peel said.

'What a good fellow he is! I wouldn't like to bet a farthing on which of them is swifter with their guns. Conn or Moorsom. Pity the enemy ships that draw them as dancing partners, eh? Look! The *Orion*, she was at the Nile. Edward Codrington has her now. What a good fellow he is! And his wife Jane's a lovely woman. Look! Is that the *Prince*? It is. Sails like a haystack!' He was pointing to another three-decker that thumped her way northwards. 'Dick Grindall. What a first-rate fellow he is.'

Behind the *Prince* was another seventy-four that, even to Sharpe's untutored eye, looked just like the *Revenant* or the *Pucelle*. 'Is she French?' he asked, pointing.

'She is, she is,' Chase said. 'The *Spartiate*, and she's bewitched, Sharpe.'

'Bewitched?'

'Sails faster at night than she does by day.'

'That's because she's built of stolen timbers,' Lieutenant Holderby opined.

'Sir Francis Laforey has her,' Chase said, 'and he's a capital fellow. Look, there's a minnow! Which is she?'

'The *Africa*,' Peel answered.

'Only sixty-four guns,' Chase said, 'but she's under the command of Harry Digby and there isn't a finer fellow in the fleet!'

'Or a richer,' Haskell put in drily, then explained to Sharpe that Captain Henry Digby had been monstrous fortunate in the matter of prize money.

'An example to us all,' Chase said piously. 'Is that the *Defiance*? By God, it is! She was badly cut about at Copenhagen, wasn't she? Who's her captain now?'

'Philip Durham,' Peel said, then silently mouthed Chase's next four words.

'What a fine fellow!' Chase explained. 'And look, the *Saucy*!'

'The *Saucy*?' Sharpe asked.

'The *Temeraire*.' Chase dignified the vast three-decker with her proper name. 'Ninety-eight guns. Who has her now?'

'Eliab Harvey,' Haskell answered.

'So he does, so he does. Odd sort of name, eh? Eliab? I've never met him, but I'm sure he's a prime fellow, prime! And look! The *Achille*! Dick King has her, and what a splendid fellow he is. And look, Sharpe, the *Billy Ruffian*! All's well if the *Billy Ruffian* is here!'

'The *Billy Ruffian*?' Sharpe asked, puzzled by the name that was evidently attached to a two-decker seventy-four that otherwise looked quite unremarkable.

'The *Bellerophon*, Sharpe. She was Howe's flagship at the Glorious First of June and she was at the Nile, by God! Poor Henry Darby was killed there, God rest his soul. He was an Irishman and a capital soul, just capital! John Cooke has her now, and he's as stout a fellow as ever came from Essex.'

'He came into money,' Haskell said, 'and moved to Wiltshire.'

'Did he now? Good for him!' Chase said, then trained his glass on the *Bellerophon* again. 'She's a quick ship,' he said enviously, though his *Pucelle* was just as fast. 'A lovely ship. Medway-built. When was she launched?'

' 'Eighty-six,' Haskell answered.

'And she cost £30,232 14s and 3d,' Midshipman Collier interjected, then looked ashamed for his interruption. 'Sorry, sir,' he said to Chase.

'Don't be sorry, lad. Are you sure? Of course you're sure, your father's a surveyor in the Sheerness dockyard, ain't he? So what was the threepence spent on?'

'Don't know, sir.'

'A ha'penny nail, probably,' Lord William said acidly. 'The peculation in His Majesty's dockyards is nothing short of scandalous.'

'What is scandalous,' Chase retorted, stung to the protest, 'is that the government permits ill-founded ships to be given to good men!' He swung away from Lord William, frowning, but his good spirits were restored by the sight of the British fleet's black and yellow hulls.

Sharpe just gazed at the fleet in awe, doubting he would ever see a sight like this again. This was the majesty of Britain, her deep-sea fleet, a procession of majestic gun batteries, vast, ponderous and terrible. They moved as slowly as fully laden harvest waggons, their bluff bows subduing the seas and the beauty of their black and yellow flanks hiding the guns in their dark bellies. Their sterns were gilded and their figureheads a riot of shields, tridents, naked breasts and defiance. Their sails, yellow, cream and white, made a cloud bank, and their names were a roll call of triumphs: *Conqueror* and *Agamemnon*, *Dreadnought* and *Revenge*, *Leviathan* and *Thunderer*, *Mars*, *Ajax* and *Colossus*. These were the ships that had cowed the Danes, broken the Dutch, decimated the French and chased the Spanish from the seas. These ships ruled the waves, but now one last enemy fleet challenged them and they sailed to give it battle.

Sharpe watched Lady Grace standing tall beside the mizzen shrouds. Her eyes were bright, there was colour in her cheeks and awe on her face as she stared at the stately line of ships. She looked happy, he thought, happy and beautiful, then Sharpe saw that Lord William also watched her, a sardonic expression on his face, then he turned to gaze at Sharpe who hastily looked back to the British fleet.

Most of the ships were two-deckers. Sixteen of those, like the *Pucelle*, carried seventy-four guns, while three, like the *Africa*, only had sixty-four guns apiece. One two-decker, the captured French *Tonnant*, carried eighty-four guns, while the other seven ships of the fleet were the towering triple-deckers with ninety-eight or a hundred guns. Those ships were the brute killers of the deep, the slab-sided gun batteries that could hurl a slaughterous weight of metal, but Chase, without showing any alarm at the prospect, told Sharpe there was a famous Spanish four-decker, the largest ship in the world, that carried over a hundred and thirty guns. 'Let's hope she's with their fleet,' he said, 'and that we can lay alongside her. Think of the prize money!'

'Think of the slaughter,' Lady Grace said quietly.

'It hardly bears contemplation, milady,' Chase said dutifully, 'hardly bears it at all, but I warrant we shall do our duty.' He put his telescope to his eye. 'Ah,' he exclaimed, staring at the leading British ship, a three-decker with ornate giltwork climbing and wreathing her massive stern. 'And there's the best fellow of them all. Mister Haskell! A seventeen-gun salute, if you please.'

The leading ship was the *Victory*, one of the three hundred-gun ships in the British fleet and also Nelson's flagship, and Chase, gazing at the *Victory*, had tears in his eyes. 'What I wouldn't do for that man,' he exclaimed. 'I never fought for him myself and thought I'd never have the chance.' Chase cuffed at his eyes as the first of the *Pucelle*'s guns banged from the weather deck in salute of Lord Horatio Nelson, Viscount and Baron Nelson of the Nile and of Burnham Thorpe, Baron Nelson of the Nile and of Hilborough, Knight of the most Honourable Order of the Bath and Vice Admiral of the White. 'I tell you, Sharpe,' Chase said, still with tears on his cheeks, 'I would sail down the throat of hell for that man.'

The *Victory* had been signalling to the Mars, which, in turn, was passing the messages on down the chain of frigates to the *Euryalus*, which lay closest to the enemy, but now the flagship's signal came down and a new ripple of bright flags ran up her mizzen. The *Pucelle*'s guns still fired the salute, the shots screaming out to fall in the empty ocean to starboard.

'Our numeral, sir!' Lieutenant Connors called to

Captain Chase. 'He makes us welcome, sir, and says we are to paint our mast hoops yellow. Yellow?' He sounded puzzled. 'Yellow, sir, it does say yellow, and we are to take station astern of the *Conqueror.*'

'Acknowledge,' Chase said, and turned to stare at the *Conqueror*, a seventy-four which was sailing some distance ahead of a three-decker, the *Britannia.* 'She's a slow ship,' Chase muttered of the *Britannia*, then he waited for the last of the seventeen guns to sound before seizing the speaking trumpet. 'Ready to tack!'

He had some tricky seamanship ahead, and it would have to be done under the eyes of a fleet that prized seamanship almost as much as it valued victory. The *Pucelle* was on the starboard tack and needed to go about so that she could join the column of ships which sailed north on the larboard tack, yet as she turned into the wind she would inevitably lose speed and, if Chase judged it wrong, he would end up becalmed and shamed in the wind-shadow of the *Conqueror.* He had to turn his ship, let her gather speed and slide her smoothly into place and if he did it too fast he could run aboard the *Conqueror* and too slow and he would be left wallowing motionless under the *Britannia*'s scornful gaze. 'Now, quartermaster, now,' he said, and the seven men hauled on the great wheel while the lieutenants bellowed at the sail handlers to release the sheets. 'Israel Pellew has the *Conqueror*,' Chase remarked to Sharpe, 'and he's a fine fellow and a wonderful seaman. Wonderful seaman! From Cornwall, you see? They seem to be born with salt in their veins, those Cornish fellows. Come on, my sweet, come on!' He was talking to the *Pucelle* which had turned her bluff bows into the wind and for a second it seemed she would hang there helplessly, but then Sharpe saw the bowsprit moving against the cavalcade of British ships, and men were running across the deck, seizing new sheets and hauling them home. The sails flapped like demented things, then tightened in the wind and the ship leaned, gathered speed and headed docilely into the open space behind the *Conqueror*. It had been done beautifully.

'Well done, quartermaster,' Chase said, pretending he had felt no qualms during the manoeuvre. 'Well done, Pucelles! Mister Holderby! Muster a work party and break out some yellow paint!'

'Why yellow?' Sharpe asked.

'Every other ship has yellow hoops,' Chase said, gesturing back down the long line, 'while ours are like the French hoops, black.' Only the upper masts were made from single pine trunks while the lower were formed from clusters of long timbers that were bound and seized by the iron hoops. 'In battle,' Chase said, 'maybe that's all anyone will note of us. And they'll see black hoops and think we're a Frog ship and pour two or three decks of good British gunnery into our vitals. Can't have that, Sharpe! Not for a few slaps of paint!' He turned like a dancer, unable to contain his elation, for his ship was in the line of battle, the enemy was at sea and Horatio Nelson was his leader.

CHAPTER 9

The British fleet tacked after dark, the signal passed on from ship to ship by lanterns hung in the rigging. Now, instead of sailing northwards, the fleet headed south, staying parallel to the enemy ships, but out of their sight. The wind had dropped, but a long swell ran from the western darkness to lift and drop the ponderous hulls. It was a long night. Sharpe went on deck once and saw the stern lanterns of the *Conqueror* reflecting from the seas ahead, then he gazed eastwards as a brilliant flame showed briefly on the horizon. Lieutenant Peel, bundled against the cold, reckoned it was one of the frigates setting off a firework to confuse the enemy. 'Keeping them awake, Sharpe, keeping them worried.' Peel slapped his gloved hands together and stamped his feet on the deck.

'Why are they sailing south?' Sharpe asked. He was shaking. He had forgotten just how the cold could bite.

'The good Lord alone knows,' Peel said cheerfully, 'and He ain't telling me. They aren't going to cover an invasion force in the Channel, that's for certain. They're probably heading for the Mediterranean which means they'll keep on south until they're clear of the shallows off Cape Trafalgar, then they can run east towards the Straits. Does your chess improve?'

'No,' Sharpe said, 'too many rules.' He wondered whether Lady Grace would risk coming to his cabin, but he doubted it, for the night-shrouded ship was unnaturally busy as men readied themselves for the morning. A seaman brought him a cup of Scotch coffee and he drank the bitter liquid, then chewed on the sweetened bread crumbs that gave the coffee its flavour.

'This will be my first battle,' Peel admitted suddenly.

'My first at sea,' Sharpe said.

'It makes you think,' Peel said wistfully.

'It's better once it starts,' Sharpe suggested. 'It's the waiting that's hard.'

Peel laughed softly. 'Some clever bugger once remarked that nothing concentrates the mind so much as the prospect of being hanged in the morning.'

'I doubt he knew,' Sharpe said. 'And besides, we're the hangmen tomorrow.'

'So we are, so we are,' Peel said, though he could not hide the fears that gnawed at him. 'Of course nothing might happen,' he said. 'The buggers might give us the slip.' He went to look at the compass, leaving Sharpe to stare into the darkness. Sharpe stayed on deck until he could abide the cold no longer, then went and shivered in his confining cot that felt so horribly like a coffin.

He woke just before dawn. The sails were flapping and he put his head out of his cabin door and asked Chase's steward what was happening. 'We're wearing ship, sir. Going north again, sir. There's coffee coming, sir. Proper coffee. I saved a handful of beans because the captain does like his coffee. I'll bring you shaving water, sir.'

Once he had shaved, Sharpe pulled on his clothes, draped his borrowed cloak about his shoulders and went on deck to find that the fleet had indeed turned back to the north. Lieutenant Haskell now had the watch and he reckoned that Nelson had been running southwards to keep out of the enemy's sight so that they would not use the excuse of his presence to return to Cadiz, but as the first grey light seeped along the eastern horizon the admiral had turned his fleet in an attempt to get between the enemy and the Spanish port.

The wind was still light so that the line of great ships lumbered northwards at less than a man's walking pace. The sky brightened, burnishing the long swells with shifting bands of silver and scarlet. *Euryalus*, the frigate which had dogged the enemy fleet ever since it had left harbour, was now back with the fleet, while to the east, almost in line with the burning sky where the sun rose, was a streak of dirty cloud showing against the horizon. That streak was the topsails of the enemy, blurred by distance.

'Good God.' Captain Chase had emerged on deck and spotted the far sails. He looked tired, as though he had slept badly, but he was dressed for battle, doing honour to the enemy by wearing his finest uniform which was normally stored deep in a sea chest. The gold on the twin epaulettes gleamed. His tasselled hat had been brushed till it shone. His white stockings were of silk, his coat was neither faded by the sun nor whitened by salt, while his sword scabbard had been polished, as had the silver buckles on his clean shoes. 'Good God,' he said again, 'those poor men.'

The decks of the British ships were thick with men, all staring eastwards. The *Pucelle* had seen the French and Spanish fleet on the previous day, but this was the first glimpse for the other crews of Nelson's ships. They had crossed the Atlantic in search of this enemy, then sailed back from the West Indies and, in the last few days, they had tacked and worn ship, sailed east and west, north and south, and some had wondered if the enemy was at sea at all, yet now, as if summoned by a demon of the sea, thirty-four enemy ships of the line showed on the horizon.

'You'll not see its like again,' Chase told Sharpe,

nodding towards the enemy fleet. His steward had brought a tray with mugs of proper coffee onto the quarterdeck and Chase gestured that his officers should be served first, then took the last cup. He looked up at the sails which alternately stretched in the wind then slackened as the fitful gusts passed. 'It will take hours to come up with them,' he said moodily.

'Maybe they'll come to us,' Sharpe said, trying to raise Chase's spirits that seemed dampened by the dawn and the pitiful wind.

'Against this sorry excuse for a breeze? I doubt it.' Chase smiled. 'Besides, they won't want battle. They've been stuck in harbour, Sharpe. Their sail handling will be poor, their gunnery rusty, their morale down in the mud. They'd rather run away.'

'Why don't they?'

'Because if they run east from here they'll end up on the shoals of Cape Trafalgar, and if they run north or south they know we'll intercept them and beat them to smithereens, and that means they have nowhere to go. Nowhere to go, Sharpe. We have the weather gauge, and that's like having the higher ground. I just pray we catch them before dark. Nelson fought the Nile in the dark and that was a triumph, but I'd rather fight in daylight.' He drained his coffee. 'Is that really the last of the beans?' he asked the steward.

'It is, sir, except for those that got wetted in Calcutta, sir, and they're growing fur.'

'They might grind, though?' Chase suggested.

'I wouldn't feed 'em to a pig, sir.'

The *Victory* had been flying a signal which ordered the British column to form their proper order, which was little more than an encouragement for the slower ships to press on more sail and close the intervals in the line, but now that signal was hauled down and another flew in its place.

'Prepare for battle, sir,' Lieutenant Connors reported, though it was scarcely necessary, for every man aboard except the landlubbers like Sharpe had recognized the signal. And the *Pucelle*, like the other warships, was already preparing, indeed the men had been readying their ship all night.

Sand was scattered on the decks to give the bare-footed gunners a better grip. The men's hammocks, as they were every morning, were rolled tight and brought on deck where they were laid in the hammock nettings that surmounted the gunwale. The packed hammocks, secured in the net trough and lashed down under a canvas rain cover, would serve as a bulwark against enemy musket fire. Up aloft a bosun was leading a dozen men who were securing the ship's great yards, from which the vast sails hung, with lengths of chain. Other men were reeving spare halliards and sheets so that heavy coils of rope were forever tumbling through the rigging to thump on the decks. 'They like slashing our rigging to bits,' Captain Llewellyn told Sharpe. 'The Dons and the Frogs both, they like to fire at the masts, see? So the chains stop the yards falling and the spare sheets are there if the others are shot through. Mind you, Sharpe, we'll lose a stick or two before the day's out. It rains blocks and broken spars in battle, it does!' Llewellyn anticipated that dangerous downpour with relish. 'Is your cutlass sharp?'

'It could do with a better edge,' Sharpe admitted.

'Forrard on the weather deck, ' Llewellyn said, 'by the manger, there's a man with a treadle wheel. He'll be glad to hone it for you.'

Sharpe joined a queue of men. Some had cutlasses, others had boarding axes while many had fetched down the boarding pikes which stood in racks about the masts on the upper decks. The goats, sensing that their routine had changed, bleated piteously. They had been milked for the last time and now a seaman rolled up his sleeves before slaughtering them with a long knife. The manger, with its dangerously combustible straw, was being dismantled and the goats' carcasses would be packed in salt for a future meal. The first beast struggled briefly, then the smell of fresh blood cut through the ship's usual stench.

Some of the men invited Sharpe to go to the head of the queue, but he waited his turn as the nearby gunners teased him. 'Come to see a proper battle, sir?'

'You'd never win a scrap without a real soldier, lads.'

'These'll win it for us, sir,' a man said, slapping the breech of his twenty-four-pounder on which someone had chalked the message 'a pill for Boney'. The mess tables, on which the gunners ate, were being struck down into the hold. As much wooden furniture as possible was removed from the decks above water so that they could not be reduced to splinters that whirled lethally from every strike of enemy shot. Sharpe's cot and chest were already gone, as was all the elegant furniture from Chase's quarters. The precious chronometers and the barometer had been packed in straw and taken down to the hold. Some ships hoisted their more valuable furniture high into the rigging in hopes that it would be safe, while others had entrusted it to the ships' boats that were being launched and towed astern to keep them from enemy gunnery.

A gunner's mate sharpened the cutlass on the wheel, tested its edge against his thumb, then gave Sharpe a toothless grin. 'That'll give the buggers a shave they'll never forget, sir.'

Sharpe tipped the man sixpence, then walked back down the deck just in time to see the panelled walls of Chase's quarters being manoeuvred down the quarterdeck stairs on their way to the hold. The simpler wooden bulkheads from the officers' cabins and the wardroom at the stern of the weather deck had already been struck down so that now, for the first time, Sharpe could see the whole length of the ship, from its wide stern windows all the way to where men swept up the last straw of the manger in the bows of the ship. The *Pucelle* was being stripped of her frills and turned into a fighting machine. He climbed to the quarterdeck and saw that was similarly empty. The wide space beneath the long poop, instead of holding cabins, was now an open sweep of deck from the wheel to the windows of Chase's day cabin. The dining cabin had vanished, Sharpe's quarters were gone, the pictures had been taken below and the only remaining luxury was the black-and-white chequered canvas carpet on which the two eighteen-pounder guns stood.

Connors, stationed on the poop to watch for the flagship's signals which were being repeated by the frigate *Euryalus*, called down to Chase. 'We're to bear up in succession on the flagship's course, sir.' Chase just nodded and watched as the *Victory*, leading the line, swung to starboard so that she was now heading straight for the enemy. The wind, such as it was, came from directly behind her and Captain Hardy, doubtless on Nelson's orders, already had men up on his yards to extend the slender poles from which he would hang his studdingsails.

Nine ships behind the *Pucelle* another three-decker swung to starboard. This was the *Royal Sovereign*, the flagship of Admiral Collingwood, Nelson's second-in-command. Her bright copper gleamed in the morning light as the ships behind followed her eastwards. Chase looked from the *Victory* to the *Royal Sovereign*, then back to the *Victory* again. 'Two columns,' he said aloud, 'that's what he's doing. Making two columns.'

Even Sharpe could understand that. The enemy fleet

formed a ragged line that stretched for about four miles along the eastern horizon and now the British fleet was turning directly towards that line. The ships turned in succession, those at the front of the fleet curling round to make a line behind the *Victory* and those at the back following in the *Royal Sovereign*'s wake, so that the two short lines of ships were sailing straight for the enemy like a pair of horns thrusting at a shield.

'We'll set studdingsails when we've turned, Mister Haskell,' Chase said.

'Aye aye, sir.'

The *Conqueror*, the fifth ship in Nelson's column and the one immediately ahead of the *Pucelle*, turned towards the enemy, showing Sharpe her long flank which was painted in stripes of black and yellow. The *Conqueror*'s gunports, all on the yellow bands, were painted black to give her a half-chequered appearance.

'Follow her, quartermaster,' Chase said, then walked to the table behind the wheel where the ship's log lay open. He dipped the pen in ink and made a new entry. '6.49 AM. Turned east towards the enemy.' Chase put the pen down, then took a small notebook and a stub of pencil from his pocket. 'Mister Collier!'

'Sir?' The midshipman looked pale.

'I will trouble you, Mister Collier, to take this notebook and pencil and to make a copy of any signals you see this day.'

'Aye aye, sir!' Collier said, taking the book and pencil from Chase.

Lieutenant Connors, the signal lieutenant, overheard the order from his place on the poop deck. He looked offended. He was an intelligent young man, quiet, red-haired and conscientious, and Chase, seeing his unhappiness, climbed to him. 'I know that logging the signals is your responsibility, Tom,' he said quietly, 'but I don't want young Collier brooding. Keep him busy, eh? Let him think he's doing something useful and he won't worry so much about being killed.'

'Of course, sir,' Connors said. 'Sorry, sir.'

'Good fellow,' Chase said, slapping Connors's back, then he ran back down to the quarterdeck and stared at the *Conqueror* which had just completed her turn. 'There goes Pellew now!' he cried. 'See how well his fellows spread their wings?' The *Conqueror*'s studdingsails, projecting far outboard on either side of her huge square sails, fell to catch the small wind and were sheeted home.

'It's a race now,' Chase said, 'and the devil take the foremost. Lively now! Lively!' He was shouting at the men on the main yard who had been slow to release the *Pucelle*'s studdingsail yards, and doubtless Chase was thinking that Israel Pellew, the Cornishman commanding the *Conqueror*, would be watching him critically, but the yards were run out handily enough and, the eastwards turn completed, the sails fell with a great slap and flap before the men on deck hauled them tight. The enemy was still hull down on the horizon and the wind scarce more than a whisper. 'It'll be a long haul,' Chase said ruefully, 'a long, long haul. Are you sure there are no more coffee beans?' he asked his steward.

'Only the furry ones, sir.'

'Try them, try them.'

The British ensigns broke out at the sterns of the ships. Today, respecting Nelson's wishes, every ship flew the white ensign. Chase had been ready to hoist the red up his mizzen, for the commander of the East Indian station had been a rear admiral of the red, but when he saw the white break at the *Conqueror*'s stern he ordered that flag brought up from the storeroom. Even Collingwood, Vice Admiral of the Blue, had hoisted Nelson's beloved white at the mizzen of the huge three-decked *Royal Sovereign*. Union flags were hoisted to the fore topgallant mast and to the main topmast stay so that every ship flew three flags. Two masts might be shot away, but the British colours would still fly.

The marines were coiling down the lines of the grapnels that they had hung on the hammock nettings. The grapnels were triple-barbed hooks that could be hurled into an enemy's rigging to drag her close for boarding. The wooden tubs on the deck, in which the sail sheets were usually coiled, were being carried down below. Some ships had jettisoned theirs, but Chase deemed that a waste of money. 'Though by sundown, God willing, we'll be the owners of enough French and Spanish chandlery to fit out a couple of warships.' He turned and took off his hat to greet Lady Grace who had appeared on deck with her husband. 'I apologize, milady, that your cabin has been dismantled.'

'It seems Britain has a better use for the space today,' she said, amused.

'We shall restore your privacy as soon as we have dealt with those fellows,' Chase said, nodding towards the enemy fleet, 'but once we are within gunshot, milady, I shall have to insist that you go below the water line.'

'I would prefer to offer my services to the surgeon,' Lady Grace said.

'The cockpit can come under fire, ma'am,' Chase said, 'especially if the enemy depress their guns. I would be remiss if I did not insist you shelter in the hold. I shall have a place made ready for you.'

'You will go to the hold, Grace,' Lord William said, 'as the captain orders you.'

'As must you, my lord,' Chase said.

Lord William shrugged. 'I can fire a musket, Chase.'

'Doubtless you can, my lord, but we must gauge whether you are more valuable to Britain alive than dead.'

Lord William nodded. 'If you say so, Chase, if you say so.' Was he relieved? Sharpe could not tell, but certainly Lord William was making no great effort to persuade Chase to let him stay on deck. 'How long till you close on them?' Lord William asked.

'Five hours at least,' Chase said, 'probably six.' A seaman was casting the log that brought ill news with every throw. Two knots slipped through his fingers, sometimes three, but it was slow going even though Chase was cramming every sail onto the masts. Sharpe stood ten paces from Lady Grace, not daring to look at her, but acutely aware of her. Pregnant! He felt his heart leap with a strange happiness, then he flinched as he realized that they must soon be parted and what would happen to his child then? He stared fixedly down into the weather deck where two gunners were attaching the flintlocks to the guns. Another gunner received permission to come to the quarterdeck to arm the twelve eighteen-pounder cannons and the four thirty-two-pounder carronades. Two more of the brutal carronades squatted on the forecastle. They were short-barrelled and wide-mouthed, capable of belching a terrible onslaught of musket and cannon balls at an enemy's deck.

A dozen gunners were now in Chase's quarters, marvelling at the gilded beams and delicately carved windows. Small tubs of water for swabbing the guns or slaking the men's thirst were placed beside every cannon, while other men threw water on the decks and the ship's sides so that the dampened timber would be slow to catch fire. Match tubs were readied, half filled with water and capped with a pierced lid through which a slow match hung in case a flintlock should break. Down in the orlop deck men coiled an anchor cable to make a gigantic bed on which the wounded could be laid as they waited to see Pickering, the surgeon, who was singing as he laid out his knives, saws, probes and pincers. The carpenter was putting shot plugs all about the orlop deck. The plugs were great cones of wood, thickly smeared with tallow, that could be rammed into any hole punched close to the water line. Relieving ropes were laid for the rudder so that if the wheel was shot away, or the tiller rope severed by a round shot, the ship could be steered from the weather deck. Leather fire buckets, most filled with sand, stood in clusters. The powder monkeys, small boys of ten or eleven, brought up the first charges from the magazines. Chase had ordered blue bags, which were the middle size of charge. The biggest powder charges, in black bags, were used when firing at long range, the blue were more than adequate for a close-range fight, while even the red bags, which had the smallest charge and were usually used for signalling, could smash a shot through an enemy ship's side at point-blank range. 'By day's end,' Chase said wistfully, 'we'll probably be double-loading reds.' He suddenly brightened. 'My God, it's my birthday! Mister Haskell! You owe me ten guineas! You recall our wager? I said, did I not, that we should come up with the *Revenant* on my birthday?'

'I shall pay gladly, sir.'

'You'll pay nothing, Mister Haskell, nothing. If Nelson hadn't been here then the *Revenant* would have escaped us. It ain't fair for a captain to win a bet with an admiral's help. This coffee tastes good! The fur adds piquancy, don't you think?'

The galley cooked a last burgoo, a generous one, with great chunks of pork and beef floating in the greasy oats. It would be the last hot meal the men would enjoy before battle, for the galley fires would have to be doused in case an enemy shot struck the oven and scattered fire across a gundeck where the powder bags waited to be loaded. The men ate the meal sitting on the deck, while the bosun's mates took round a double ration of rum. A band began playing on the *Conqueror.* 'Where's our band?' Chase demanded. 'Have them play! Have them play! I'd like some music.'

But before the band could gather, the *Victory* signalled to *Pucelle*, a signal that was repeated by the *Euryalus.* 'Our number, sir!' Lieutenant Connors shouted, then watched the frigate that sailed wide out on the larboard side of Nelson's column. 'You're invited to take breakfast with the admiral, sir.'

'I am?' Chase sounded delighted. 'Inform his lordship I'm on my way.'

The barge crew was summoned while the barge itself, which was already on tow behind the ship, was hauled up to the starboard side. Lord William stepped forward, plainly expecting to accompany Chase to the *Victory*, but the captain turned to Sharpe instead. 'You'll come, Sharpe? Of course you will!'

'Me?' Sharpe blinked in astonishment. 'I'm not dressed to meet an admiral, sir!'

'You look fine, Sharpe. Ragged, perhaps, but fine.' Chase, blithely ignoring Lord William's ill-concealed indignation, dropped his voice. 'Besides, he'll expect me to bring a lieutenant, but if I take Haskell, Peel will never forgive me and if I take Peel, Haskell will feel slighted, so you'll have to do.' Chase grinned, pleased with the idea of introducing Sharpe to his beloved Nelson. 'And you'll divert him, Sharpe. He's a perverse man, he likes soldiers.' Chase drew Sharpe forward as the barge crew, led by the huge Hopper, scrambled down the steps built into the *Pucelle*'s side. 'You go first, Sharpe,' Chase said. 'The boys will make sure you don't get a bath.'

The side of a warship leaned steeply inwards, for the ships were built to bulge out close to the water line, and that generous slope made the first few steps easy enough, but the nearer Sharpe came to the water line the steeper the narrow steps became and, though there was scarcely any wind, the *Pucelle* was rising and falling in the big swells, while the barge was falling and rising, and Sharpe could feel his boots sliding on the lower wooden ledges that were slimy with growth. 'Hold it there, sir,' Hopper growled at him, then shouted, 'Now!' and two pairs of hands unceremoniously grasped Sharpe by his breeches and jacket and hauled him safe into the barge. Clouter, the escaped slave, was one of his helpers and he grinned as Sharpe found his feet.

Chase came nimbly down the steps, glanced once at the pitching barge, then stepped gracefully onto the rear thwart. 'It'll be a stiff pull, Hopper.'

'It'll be easy enough, sir, easy enough.'

Chase took the tiller himself while Hopper sat at an oar. It was indeed a hard pull and a long one, but the barge crept past the intervening ships and Sharpe could stare up at their massive striped sides. From the white and red barge, low down among the swells, the ships looked vast, cumbersome and indestructible.

'I also brought you,' Chase grinned at Sharpe, 'because your inclusion will annoy Lord William. He doubtless thinks he should have been invited, but bless me, how he would bore Nelson!' Chase waved to an officer high on the stern of a seventy-four. 'That's the *Leviathan*,' he told Sharpe, 'under Harry Bayntun. He's a prime fellow, prime! I served with him in the old *Bellona*. I was only a youngster, but they were happy days, happy days.' The swell lifted the *Leviathan*'s stern, revealing an expanse of green copper and trailing weed. 'Besides,' Chase went on, 'Nelson can be useful to you.'

'Useful?'

'Lord William don't like you,' Chase said, not bothering that he was being overheard by Hopper and Clouter who had the two stroke oars nearest the stern, 'which means he'll try and obstruct your career. But I know Nelson's a friend of Colonel Stewart, and Stewart's one of your strange riflemen, so perhaps his lordship will put in a word for you? Of course he will, he's the very soul of generosity.'

It took a half-hour to reach the flagship, but at last Chase steered the barge into the *Victory*'s starboard flank and one of his men hooked onto its chains so that the small boat was held just beneath another ladder as steep and perilous as the one Sharpe had descended on the *Pucelle*. A gilded entryway was halfway up the ladder, but its door was closed, meaning Sharpe must climb all the way to the top. 'You first, Sharpe,' Chase said. 'Jump and cling on!'

'God help me,' Sharpe muttered. He stood on a thwart, twisted the cutlass out of his way, and leaped for the ladder when the barge was heaved up by a wave. He clung on desperately, then climbed past the entryway's gilded frame. A hand reached down from the weather deck and hauled him through the entry port where a line of bosun's mates waited to welcome Chase with their whistles.

Chase was grinning as he scrambled up the side. A lieutenant, immaculately uniformed, saluted him, then inclined his head when Sharpe was introduced. 'You're most welcome, sir,' the lieutenant told Chase. 'Another seventy-four today is a blessing from heaven.'

'It's good of you to let me join the celebrations,' Chase said, removing his hat to salute the quarterdeck. Sharpe hurriedly followed suit as the bosun's whistles made their strange twittering sound. The *Victory*'s upper decks were crowded with gunners, sail-handlers and marines who ignored the visitors, though one older man, a sailmaker, judging from the big needles thrust into his grey hair which was bundled on top of his head, did bob down as Chase was led towards the quarterdeck. Chase stopped, clicked his fingers. 'Prout, isn't it? You were on the *Bellona* with me.'

'I remembers you, sir,' Prout said, tugging the hair over his forehead, 'and you was just a boy, sir.'

'We grow old, Prout,' Chase said. 'We grow damned old! But not too old to give the Dons and Frenchmen a drubbing, eh?'

'We shall beat 'em, sir,' Prout said.

Chase beamed at his old shipmate, then went to the quarterdeck, which was thickly crowded with officers who politely removed their hats as Chase and Sharpe were ushered aft past the great wheel and under the poop to the admiral's quarters, which were guarded by a single marine in a short red jacket crossed by a pair of pipe-clayed belts. The lieutenant opened the door without knocking and led Chase and Sharpe through a small sleeping cabin which had been stripped of its furniture and then, again without knocking, into a massive cabin that stretched the whole width of the ship and was lit by the wide array of stern windows. This cabin had also been emptied of its furniture, so that only a single table was left on the black and white chequered canvas floor. Two massive guns, already equipped with their flintlocks, stood on either side of the table.

Sharpe was aware of two men silhouetted against the stern window, but he could not distinguish which was the admiral until Chase put his hat under his arm and offered a bow to the smaller man who was seated at the table. The light was bright behind the admiral and Sharpe still could not see him clearly and he hung back, not wanting to intrude, but Chase turned and gestured him forward. 'Allow me to name my particular friend, my lord. Mister Richard Sharpe. He's on his way to join the Rifles, but he paused long enough to save me from an embarrassment in Bombay and I'm monstrous grateful.'

'You, Chase? An embarrassment? Surely not?' Nelson laughed and gave Sharpe a smile. 'I'm most grateful to you, Sharpe. I would not have my friends embarrassed. How long has it been, Chase?'

'Four years, my lord.'

'He was one of my frigate captains,' Nelson said to his companion, a post captain who stood at his shoulder. 'He commanded the *Spritely* and took the *Bouvines* a week after leaving my command. I never had the chance to congratulate you, Chase, but I do now. It was a creditable action. You know Blackwood?'

'I'm honoured to make your acquaintance,' Chase said, bowing to the Honourable Henry Blackwood who commanded the frigate *Euryalus.*

'Captain Blackwood has been hanging onto the enemy's apron strings ever since they left Cadiz,' Nelson said warmly, 'and you've drawn us together now, Blackwood, so your work's done.'

'I trust I shall have the honour of doing more, my lord.'

'Doubtless you will, Blackwood,' Nelson said, then gestured at the chairs. 'Sit, Chase, sit. And you, Mister Sharpe. Tepid coffee, hard bread, cold beef and fresh oranges, not much of a breakfast, I fear, but they tell me the galley's been struck.' The table was set with plates and knives amongst which the admiral's sword lay in its jewelled scabbard. 'How are your supplies, Chase?'

'Low, my lord. Water and beef for two weeks, maybe?'

' 'Twill be long enough, long enough. Crew?'

'I pressed a score of good men from an Indiaman, my lord, and have sufficient.'

'Good, good,' the admiral said, then, after his steward had brought coffee and food to the table, he questioned

Chase about his voyage and the pursuit of the *Revenant*. Sharpe, sitting to the admiral's left, watched him. He knew the admiral had lost the sight of one eye, but it was hard to tell which, though after a while Sharpe saw that the right eye had an unnaturally large and dark pupil. His hair was white and tousled, framing a thin and extraordinarily mobile face that reacted to Chase's story with alarm, pleasure, amusement and surprise. He interrupted Chase rarely, though he did stop the tale once to request that Sharpe carve the beef. 'And perhaps you'll cut me some bread as well, Mister Sharpe, as a kindness? My fin, you understand,' and he touched his empty right sleeve that was pinned onto a jacket bright with jewelled stars. 'You're very kind,' he said when Sharpe had obeyed. 'Do go on, Chase.'

Sharpe had expected to be awed by the admiral, to be struck dumb by him, but instead he found himself feeling protective of the small man who emanated a fragile air of vulnerability. Even though he was sitting, it was clear he was a small man, and very thin, and his pale, lined face suggested he was prone to sickness. He looked so frail that Sharpe had to remind himself that this man had led his fleets to victory after victory, and that in every fight he had been in the thick of the battle, yet he gave the impression that the slightest breeze would knock him down.

The admiral's apparent frailty made the most immediate impression on Sharpe, but it was the admiral's eyes that had the stronger effect, for whenever he looked at Sharpe, even if it was merely to request a small service like another piece of buttered bread, it seemed that Sharpe became the most important person in the world at that moment. The glance seemed to exclude everything and everyone else, as though Sharpe and the admiral were in collusion. Nelson had none of Sir Arthur Wellesley's coldness, no condescension, and gave no impression of believing himself to be superior; indeed it seemed to Sharpe that at that moment, as the fleet lumbered towards the enemy, Horatio Nelson asked nothing from life except to be seated with his good friends Chase, Blackwood and Richard Sharpe. He touched Sharpe's elbow once. 'This talk must be tedious to a soldier, Sharpe?'

'No, my lord,' Sharpe said. The discussion had moved on to the admiral's tactics this day and much of it was beyond Sharpe's comprehension, but he did not care. It was enough to be in Nelson's presence and Sharpe was swept by the little man's infectious enthusiasm. By God, Sharpe thought, but they would not just beat the enemy fleet this day, but pound it into splinters, hammer it so badly that no French or Spanish ship would ever dare sail the world's seas again. Chase, he saw, was reacting the same way, almost as though he feared Nelson would weep if he did not fight harder than he had ever fought before.

'Do you put your men in the tops?' Nelson asked, clumsily attempting to remove the peel of an orange with his one hand.

'I do, my lord.'

'I do fear that the musket wads will fire the sails,' the admiral said gently, 'so I would rather you did not.'

'Of course not, my lord,' Chase said, immediately yielding to the modest suggestion.

'Sails are only linen, after all,' Nelson said, evidently wanting to explain himself further in case Chase had been offended by the order. 'And what do we put inside tinderboxes? Linen! It is horribly flammable.'

'I shall respect your wishes gladly, my lord.'

'And you comprehend my greater purpose?' the admiral asked, referring to his earlier discussion of tactics.

'I do, my lord, and applaud it.'

'I shall not be happy with less than twenty prizes, Chase,' Nelson said sternly.

'So few, my lord?'

The admiral laughed and then, as another officer entered the cabin, stood. Nelson was at least a half-foot shorter than Sharpe who, standing like the others, had to stoop beneath the beams, but the newcomer, who was introduced as the *Victory*'s captain, Thomas Hardy, was a half foot taller than Sharpe again and, when he spoke to Nelson, he bent over the little admiral like a protective giant.

'Of course, Hardy, of course,' the admiral said, then smiled at his guests. 'Hardy tells me it is time to strike down these bulkheads. We are being evicted, gentlemen. Shall we retreat to the quarterdeck?' He led his guests forward, then, seeing Sharpe hang back, he turned and took his elbow. 'Did you serve under Sir Arthur Wellesley in India, Sharpe?'

'I did, my lord.'

'I met him after his return and enjoyed a notable conversation, though I confess I found him rather frightening!' The admiral's tone made Sharpe laugh, which pleased Nelson. 'So you're joining the 95th, are you?'

'I am, my lord.'

'That is splendid!' The admiral, for some reason, seemed particularly pleased by this news. He ushered Sharpe through the door, then walked him across to the hammock nettings on the larboard side of the quarterdeck. 'You're fortunate indeed, Mister Sharpe. I know William Stewart and count him among my dearest and closest friends. You know why his rifle regiment is so good?'

'No, my lord,' Sharpe said. He had always thought that the new-fangled 95th was probably made of the army's leavings and was dressed in green because no one wanted to waste good red cloth on its soldiers.

'Because they're intelligent,' the admiral said enthusiastically. 'Intelligent! It is a quality sadly despised by the military, but intelligence does have its uses.' He looked up at Sharpe's face, peering at the tiny blue-flecked marks on Sharpe's scarred cheek. 'Powder scars, Mister Sharpe, and I note you are still an ensign. Would I offend you by suspecting that you once served in the ranks?'

'I did, my lord.'

'Then you have my warmest admiration, indeed you do,' Nelson said energetically, and his admiration seemed entirely genuine. 'You must be a remarkable man,' the admiral added.

'No, my lord,' Sharpe said, and he wanted to say that Nelson was the man to admire, but he did not know how to phrase the compliment.

'You're modest, Mister Sharpe, and that is not good,' Nelson said sternly. To Sharpe's surprise he found he was alone with the admiral. Chase, Blackwood and the other officers stood on the starboard side while Nelson and Sharpe paced up and down under the larboard hammock nettings. A dozen seamen, grinning at their admiral, had begun collapsing the panelled bulkheads so that no enemy shot could turn them into lethal splinters that could sweep the quarterdeck. 'I am not in favour of modesty,' Nelson said, and once again the admiral was overwhelming Sharpe with a flattering intimacy, 'and you doubtless find that surprising? We are told, are we not, that modesty is among the virtues, but modesty is not a warrior's virtue. You and I, Sharpe, have been forced to rise from a lowly place and we do not achieve that by hiding our talents. I am a country clergyman's son and now?' He waved his one hand at the far enemy fleet, then unconsciously touched the four brilliant stars, the jewelled decorations of his orders of knighthood, that glinted on the left breast of his coat. 'Be proud of what you have done,' he said to Sharpe, 'then go and do better.'

'As you will, my lord.'

'No,' Nelson said abruptly, and for a moment he looked desperately frail again. 'No,' he repeated, 'for in bringing these two fleets together, Sharpe, I will have done my life's work.' He looked so forlorn that Sharpe had a ridiculous urge to comfort the admiral. 'Kill those ships,' Nelson went on, gesturing at the enemy fleet filling the eastern horizon, 'and Bonaparte and his allies can never invade England. We shall have caged the beast in Europe, and what will be left for a poor sailor to do then, eh?' He smiled. 'But there will be work for soldiers, and you, I know, are a good one. Just remember, though, you must hate a Frenchman like the very devil!' The admiral said this with a venomous force, showing his steel for the first time. 'Never let go of that sentiment, Mister Sharpe,' he added, 'never!' He turned back to the waiting officers. 'I am keeping Captain Chase from his ship. And it will be time for you to go soon, Blackwood.'

'I shall stay a while longer, if I may, my lord?' Blackwood said.

'Of course. Thank you for coming, Chase. I'm sure you had more important business to attend to, but you have been kind. Will you accept some oranges as a gift? They're fresh out from Gibraltar.'

'I should be honoured, my lord, honoured.'

'You do me honour by joining us, Chase. So lay alongside and hit away. Hit away. We shall make them wish they had never seen our ships!'

Chase descended into his barge in a kind of trance. A net of oranges, enough to feed half a regiment, lay on the barge's bottom boards. For a time, as Hopper stroked back down the line of warships, Chase just sat silent, but then he could contain himself no longer.

'What a man!' he exclaimed. 'What a man! My God, we're going to do some slaughter today! We shall murder them, murder them!'

'Amen,' Hopper said.

'Praise the Lord,' Clouter volunteered.

'What did you think of him, Sharpe?' Chase asked.

Sharpe shook his head, almost lost for words. 'What was it you said, sir? That you would follow him into the throat of hell? By God, sir, I'd follow that man into the belly of hell and down to its bowels too.'

'And if he led us,' Chase said reverently, 'we would win there, just as we shall win this day.'

If they ever got into battle. For the wind was still light, desperately light, and the fleet sailed slow as haystacks. It seemed to Sharpe that they could never reach the enemy, and then he was sure of it, for an hour after he and Chase regained the *Pucelle*'s deck, the combined enemy fleet turned clumsily around to sail back northwards. They were heading for Cadiz in a last attempt to escape Nelson whose ships, their white wings spread, ghosted towards hell in a wind so light that it seemed the very heavens were holding their breath.

The *Pucelle*'s band, more enthusiastic than it was skilled, played 'Hearts of Oak', 'Nancy Dawson', 'Hail Britannia', 'Drops of Brandy' and a dozen other tunes, most of which Sharpe did not know. He did not know many of the words either, but the sailors bellowed them out, not bothering to disguise the coarsest verses even though Lady Grace was on the quarterdeck. Lord William, when one particularly obscene song echoed up from the weather deck, remonstrated with Captain Chase, but Chase pointed out that some of his men were about to be silenced for ever and he was in no temper to bridle their tongues now. 'Your ladyship can go to the hold now?' he suggested.

'I am not offended, Captain,' Lady Grace said. 'I know when to be deaf.'

Lord William, who had chosen to wear a slim sword and had a long-barrelled pistol holstered at his waist, stalked to the starboard rail and stared at Admiral Collingwood's column that lay a little more than a mile southwards. Collingwood's big three-decker, the *Royal Sovereign,* newly come from England with her freshly coppered bottom, was sailing faster than the other ships so that a gap had opened between her and the rest of Collingwood's squadron.

The French and Spanish seemed no nearer, though when Sharpe extended his glass and looked at the enemy fleet he saw that their hulls were now above the horizon. They showed no flags yet and their gunports were still closed, for the battle, if one ever ensued, was still two or three hours away. Some of the ships were painted black and yellow like the British fleet, others were black and white, two were all black, while some were banded with red. Lieutenant Haskell had commented that they were attempting to form a line of battle, but their attempts were clumsy, for Sharpe could see great gaps in the fleet which looked like clumps of ships strung along the horizon. One ship did stand out, for, maybe a third of the way from the front of the line, there was a towering vessel with four gundecks. 'The *Santisima Trinidad,*' Haskell told Sharpe, 'with at least one hundred and thirty guns. She's the largest ship in the world.' Even at such a distance the Spaniard's hull looked like a cliff, but a cliff pierced with gunports. Sharpe tracked the French line, looking for the *Revenant,* but there were so many black-and-yellow two-decked ships that he could not distinguish her.

Some of the men were writing letters, using their guns as desks. Others wrote wills. Few could write, but those who could took the dictation of others and the letters were taken down to the safety of the orlop deck. The wind stayed feeble; indeed it seemed to Sharpe that the great swells coming from the west heaved the ships on with more effect than the wind. Those seas were monstrously long, looking like great smooth hills that ran silent and green towards the enemy. 'I fear,' Chase said, coming to Sharpe's side, 'that we are in for a storm.'

'You can tell?'

'I hate those glassy swells,' Chase said, 'and the sky has an ominous cast.' He looked behind the ship where the sky was darkening, while overhead the blue was crossed by bands of feathered white streaks. 'Still,' he continued, 'it should hold off long enough for this day's business.'

The band on the forecastle came to the end of one of its more ragged efforts and Chase went to the quarterdeck rail and held up a hand to keep them silent. The captain had still not ordered the drummer to beat to quarters, so most of the lower-deck men were on the weather deck and that great throng now looked up at Chase expectantly, then stood respectfully when he doffed his hat. The officers copied him. 'We shall be handing out a drubbing to the Frenchies and Dons today, men,' Chase said, 'and I know you will make me proud!' A murmur of agreement sounded from the men crowded about the guns. 'But before we go about our business,' Chase went on, 'I would like to commend all our souls to Almighty God.' He took a prayer book from his pocket and leafed through its pages, seeking the Prayer to Be Said Before a Fight at Sea Against Any Enemy. He was not an outwardly religious man, but the captain had a blithe faith in God that was almost as strong as his trust in Nelson. He read the prayer in a strong voice, his fair hair lifting to the small wind. 'Stir up thy strength, O Lord, and come and help us. Let not our sins cry against us for vengeance, but hear us, thy poor servants, begging mercy and imploring thy help, that thou would'st be a defence unto us against the enemy. O Lord of Hosts, fight for us. Suffer us not to sink under the weight of our sins or the violence of the enemy. O Lord, arise, help us, and deliver us for thy name's sake.' The men called out amen and some of them crossed themselves. Chase put his hat on. 'We shall have a glorious victory! Listen to your officers, don't waste shot! I warrant you I shall lay us alongside an enemy and then it is up to you and I know the wretches will regret the day they met the *Pucelle*!' He smiled, then nodded at the band. 'I think we could suffer "Hearts of Oak" once more?'

The men cheered him and the band struck up again. Some of the gunners were dancing the hornpipe. A woman appeared on the weather deck, carrying a can of water to one of the gun crews. She was a stocky young woman, pale after being concealed below decks for so long and raggedly dressed in a long skirt and a threadbare shawl. She had red hair that hung lank and filthy and the men, pleased to see her, teased her as she threaded her way across the crowded deck. The officers pretended not to notice her.

'How many women are aboard?' Lady Grace had come to stand beside Sharpe. She was wearing a blue dress, a wide-brimmed hat, and a long black boat cloak.

Sharpe glanced guiltily towards Lord William, but his lordship was deep in conversation with Lieutenant Haskell. 'Chase tells me there are at least a half-dozen,' Sharpe said. 'They hide themselves.'

'And they will shelter in the battle?'

'Not with you.'

'It doesn't seem fair.'

'Life isn't fair,' Sharpe said. 'How do you feel?'

'Healthy,' she said, and indeed she looked glowing.

Her eyes were bright and her cheeks, that had been so pale when Sharpe first saw her in Bombay, were full of colour. She touched his arm briefly. 'You will take care, Richard?'

'I shall take care,' he promised, though he doubted that his life or death were in his own keeping this day.

'If the ship is taken . . .' Lady Grace said hesitantly.

'It won't be,' Sharpe interrupted her.

'If it is,' she said earnestly, 'I do not want to meet another man like that lieutenant on the *Calliope*. I can use a pistol.'

'But you have none?' Sharpe asked. She shook her head and Sharpe drew out his own pistol and held it towards her. They were standing close together at the quarterdeck rail and no one behind could see the gift which Lady Grace took, then pushed into a pocket of the heavy cloak. 'It's loaded,' Sharpe warned her.

'I shall take care,' she promised him, 'and I doubt I will need it, but it gives me a comfort. It's something of yours, Richard.'

'You already have something of mine,' he said.

'Which I will protect,' she said. 'God bless you, Richard.'

'And you, my lady.'

She walked away from him, watched by her husband. Sharpe stared doggedly forward. He would borrow another pistol from Captain Llewellyn whose marines were lining the forecastle rails and sometimes leaning outboard to see the distant enemy.

Chase had gathered his officers and Sharpe, curious, went to listen as the captain outlined what Nelson had told him on board the *Victory*. The British fleet, Chase said, was not going to form a line parallel to the enemy, which was the accepted method of fighting a sea battle, but intended to sail its two columns directly into the enemy's line. 'We shall chop their line into three pieces,' Chase said, 'and destroy them piecemeal. If I fall, gentlemen, then your only duty is to stand on, pass through their line, then lay the ship alongside an enemy.'

Captain Llewellyn shuddered, then drew Sharpe to one side. 'I don't like it,' the Welshman said. 'It's none of my business, of course, I am merely a marine, but you will have noticed, Sharpe, surely, that we have no guns to speak of in the bow of the ship?'

'I had noticed,' Sharpe said.

'The foremost guns can fire somewhat forward, but not directly forward, and what the admiral is proposing, Sharpe, is that we sail straight towards the enemy who will have their broadsides pointing at us!' Llewellyn shook his head sadly. 'I don't have to spell that out to you, do I?'

'Of course not.'

Llewellyn spelt it out nonetheless. 'They can fire at us and we cannot return the fire! They will rake us, Sharpe. You know what raking is? You rake an enemy when your broadside faces his defenceless stern or bow, and it is the quickest way to reduce a ship to kindling. And for how long will we be defenceless under their guns? At this speed, Sharpe, for at least twenty minutes. Twenty minutes! They can pour round shot into us, they can tear our rigging to pieces with chain and bar, they can dismast us, and what can we do in return?'

'Nothing, sir.'

'You have grasped the point,' Llewellyn said, 'but as I said it is none of my business. But the fighting tops, Sharpe, they are my business. Do you know what the captain has ordered?'

'No men in the tops,' Sharpe said.

'How could he order such a thing?' Llewellyn demanded indignantly. 'The Frogs, now, they'll have men in the rigging like spiders in a web, and they'll be pouring nastiness on us, and we must just cower on the deck? It isn't right, Sharpe, it isn't right. And if I cannot put men up the masts then I cannot use my grenades!' He sounded aggrieved. 'They are too dangerous to keep on deck, so I've left them in the forward magazine.' He stared at the enemy fleet which was now less than two miles away. 'Still,' Llewellyn went on, 'we shall beat them.'

The *Britannia,* which followed the *Pucelle,* was a slow ship and so a long gap had opened between the two. There were similar gaps in both columns, but none so wide as the gap between Collingwood's *Royal Sovereign* and the rest of his squadron. 'He'll be fighting alone for a time,' Llewellyn said, then turned because Connors, the signal lieutenant, had called that the flagship was signalling.

It was an immensely long signal, so long that when the *Euryalus* repeated the message the flags needed to be flown from all three of the frigate's masts where the pennants made bright splashes of colour against the white sails. 'Well?' Chase demanded of Connors.

The signal lieutenant waited for the feeble wind to spread some of the flags, then paused as he tried to remember the flag code. It was a recent code, and simple enough, for each flag corresponded to a letter, but some combinations of flags were used to transmit whole words or sometimes phrases, and there were over three thousand such combinations to be memorized and it was evident that this long signal, which required no less than thirty-two flags, was using some of the more obscure words of the system. Connors frowned, then suddenly made sense of it. 'From the admiral, sir. England expects that every man will do his duty.'

'I should damn well think so,' Chase said indignantly.

'What about the Welsh?' Llewellyn asked with an equal indignation, then smiled. 'Ah, but the Welsh need no encouragement to do their duty. It's you bloody English who have to be chivvied.'

'Pass the message on to the men,' Chase ordered his officers and, in contrast to the resentful reception the message had received on the quarterdeck, it provoked cheers from the crew.

'He must be bored,' Chase said, 'sending messages like that. Is it in your notebook, Mister Collier?'

The midshipman nodded eagerly. 'It's written down, sir.'

'You noted the time?'

Collier reddened. 'I will, sir, I will.'

'Thirty-six minutes past eleven, Mister Collier,' Chase said, inspecting his pocket watch, 'and if you are uncertain of the time of any message you will find the wardroom's clock has been conveniently placed under the poop on the larboard side. And by consulting that clock, Mister Collier, you will be hidden from the enemy and so might stop them from removing your head with a well-aimed round shot.'

'It's not a very big head, sir,' Collier said bravely, 'and my place is near you, sir.'

'Your place, Mister Collier, is where you can see both the signals and the clock, and I suggest you stand under the break of the poop.'

'Yes, sir,' Collier said, wondering how he was expected to see any signals while standing in the shelter of the poop deck.

Chase was staring at the enemy, drumming his fingers on the rail. He was nervous, but no more so than any other man on the *Pucelle.* 'Look at the *Saucy*!' Chase said, pointing ahead to where the *Temeraire* was trying to overtake the *Victory*, but the *Victory* had unfurled her topgallant studdingsails and so held onto her lead. 'He really shouldn't go first through their line,' Chase said, frowning, then turned. 'Captain Llewellyn!'

'Sir?'

'Your drummer can beat to quarters, I think.'

'Aye aye, sir,' Llewellyn replied, then nodded to his drummer boy who hitched his instrument up, raised his sticks, then beat out the rhythm of the song 'Hearts of Oak'.

'And God preserve us all,' Chase said as the men crowding the weather deck began to disappear down the hatchways to man the lower-deck guns. The drummer kept on beating as he went down the quarterdeck steps. The boy would beat the call to arms all about the ship, though not one sailor aboard needed the summons. They had long been ready.

'Open gunports, sir?' Haskell asked.

'No, we'll wait, we'll wait,' Chase said, 'but tell the gunners to load another shot on top of the first, then put in a charge of grape.'

'Aye aye, sir.'

The *Pucelle*'s guns would now be double-shotted, with a cluster of nine smaller balls ahead of the bigger round shot. Such a charge, Chase explained to Sharpe, was deadly at close range. 'And we can't fire till we're in the thick of them, so we might as well hurt them badly with our opening broadside.' The captain turned to Lord William. 'My lord, I think you should go below.'

'Not yet, surely?' It was Lady Grace who answered. 'No one has fired.'

'Soon,' Chase said, 'soon.'

Lord William scowled, as if disapproving of his wife questioning the captain's orders, but Lady Grace just stared ahead at the enemy as if she was memorizing the extraordinary sight of an horizon filled by ships of the line. Lieutenant Peel was surreptitiously sketching her in his notebook, trying to capture the tilt of her profiled face and its expression of intent fascination. 'Which is the enemy admiral's ship?' she asked Chase.

'We can't tell, my lady. They haven't put out their flags.'

'Who is the enemy admiral?' Lord William asked.

'Villeneuve, my lord,' Chase answered, 'or so Lord Nelson believes.'

'Is he a capable man?' Lord William asked.

'Compared to Nelson, my lord, no one is capable, but I am told Villeneuve is no fool.'

The band had gone to their stations so the ship was oddly quiet as she heaved forward on the big swells. The wind just filled the sails, though in every lull, or when the waves drove the ship faster, the canvas sagged before lazily stretching again. Chase stared southwards at the *Royal Sovereign* which was now far ahead of Collingwood's other ships as, under every possible sail, she headed towards a lonely battle in the thick of the enemy fleet. 'How far is she from the enemy?' he asked.

'A thousand yards?' Haskell guessed.

'I'd say so,' Chase said. 'The enemy will open on her soon.'

'Bounce won't like that,' Lieutenant Peel said with a smile.

'Bounce?' Chase asked. 'Oh! Collingwood's dog.' He smiled. 'It hates gunfire, doesn't it? Poor dog.' He turned to stare beyond his own bows. It was possible to estimate now where the *Pucelle* would meet the enemy line and Chase was working out how many ships would be able to batter him while he sailed his defenceless bows towards them. 'When we come under fire, Mister Haskell, we shall order the crew to lie down.'

'Aye aye, sir.'

'It won't be for three quarters of an hour yet,' Chase said, then frowned. 'I hate waiting. Send me wind! Send me wind! What's the time, Mister Collier?'

'Ten minutes of twelve, sir,' Collier called from under the poop.

'So we should meet their fire at half past midday,' Chase said, 'and by one o'clock we'll be among them.'

'They've opened!' It was Connors who shouted the words, pointing towards the southern part of the enemy line where one ship was wreathed in grey and white smoke which blossomed to hide her hull entirely.

'Make a note in the log!' Chase ordered, and just then the sound of the broadside came like a ripple of thunder across the sea. White splashes punctured the swells ahead of the *Royal Sovereign*'s bows, showing that the enemy's opening salvo had fallen short, but a moment later another half-dozen ships opened fire.

'It sounds precisely like thunder,' Lady Grace said in amazement.

The *Victory* was still too far from the northern part of the enemy's fleet to be worth firing at, and so the vast majority of the French and Spanish ships stayed silent. Just the six ships kept firing, their shots whipping the sea to foam ahead of Collingwood's flagship. Perhaps it was the sound of those guns that prompted the enemy to reveal their colours at last for, one by one, their ensigns appeared so that the approaching British could distinguish between their enemies. The French tricolour appeared brighter than the Spanish royal flag which was dark red and white. 'There, my lady,' Chase said, pointing forward, 'you can see the French admiral's flag? At the masthead of the ship just behind the *Santisima Trinidad*.'

The *Royal Sovereign* must have been taking shots, for she suddenly fired two of her forward guns so that their smoke would hide her hull as it drifted with the feeble wind. Sharpe took out his telescope, trained it on Collingwood's flagship, and saw a sail twitch as a round shot whipped through the canvas, and now he could see other holes in the sails and he knew the enemy must be firing at her rigging in an attempt to stop her brave advance. Yet she stood on, studdingsails set, widening the gap between her and the *Belleisle*, the *Mars* and the *Tonnant* which were the next three ships astern. The splashes of the enemy gunfire began to land about those ships now. None could fire back, and none could expect to open fire for at least twenty minutes. They must simply endure and hope to repay the battering when they reached the line.

Chase turned. 'Mister Collier?'

'Sir?'

'You will escort Lord William and Lady Grace to the lady hole. Use the aft hatchway in the gunroom. Your maid will accompany you, my lady.'

'We are not under fire, Captain,' Lady Grace objected.

'You will oblige me, my lady,' Chase insisted.

'Come, Grace,' Lord William said. He still wore his sword and pistol, but made no attempt to stay on deck. 'May I wish you well, Captain.'

'Your sentiments are much appreciated, my lord. I thank you.'

Lady Grace gave Sharpe a last look, and he dared not answer it with a smile for Lord William would see it, but he met her gaze and held it till she turned away. Then she was gone down the quarterdeck steps and Sharpe felt a horrid pang of loss.

The *Pucelle* was catching up with the *Conqueror* now and Chase took her towards that ship's starboard side. He stared at the enemy through his glass and suddenly called Sharpe. 'Our old friend, Sharpe.'

'Sir?'

'There, look.' He pointed. 'You see the *Santisima Trinidad*? The big ship?'

'Yes, sir.'

'Six ships back. It's the *Revenant*.'

Sharpe trained his telescope and counted the ships

astern of the vast four-decked Spanish battleship, and there, suddenly, was the familiar black and yellow hull and as he gazed he saw the ports open and the guns appear. Then the *Revenant* vanished in smoke.

And the *Victory* was under fire, and the enemy could not hope to escape to Cadiz because, despite the fickle wind, there would be a battle. Thirty-four enemy ships would take on twenty-eight British. Two thousand five hundred and sixty-eight enemy guns, manned by thirty thousand French and Spanish seamen would face two thousand one hundred and forty-eight guns crewed by seventeen thousand British tars.

'To your places, gentlemen,' Chase said to the officers on his quarterdeck. 'To your places, please.' He touched the prayer book in his pocket. 'And may God preserve us, gentlemen, preserve us each and every one.'

For the fighting had begun.

CHAPTER 10

Sharpe's place was on the forecastle. Captain Llewellyn and his young lieutenant commanded forty of the ship's marines stationed on the poop and quarterdeck, while Sharpe had twenty, though in truth the score of forecastle men were led by Sergeant Armstrong, a man as squat as a hogshead and stubborn as a mule. The sergeant came from Seahouses in Northumberland where he had been imbued with a deep distrust of the Scots. 'They're thieves to a man, sir,' he confidently assured Sharpe, but still contrived that every Scotsman among Llewellyn's marines serve in his squad. 'Because that's where I can keep an eye on the thieving bastards, sir.'

The Scots were content to serve under Sergeant Armstrong, for, if he distrusted them, he hated anyone from south of the River Tyne. So far as Armstrong was concerned only men from Northumberland itself, raised to remember the cattle-raiders from north of the border, were true warriors while the rest of mankind was composed of thieving bastards, cowardly foreigners and officers. France, he seemed to believe, was a populous county somewhere so far south of London as to be execrable, while Spain was probably hell itself. The sergeant possessed one of Captain Llewellyn's precious seven-barrel guns that he had propped against the foremast. 'You can take your eyes off that, sir,' he had told Sharpe when he saw the officer's interest in the weapon, ''cos I'm saving it for when we board one of the bastards. There's nothing like a volley gun for clearing an enemy deck.' Armstrong was instinctively suspicious of Sharpe for the ensign was not a marine, not from Northumberland and not born into the officer class. Armstrong was, in short, ugly, ignorant, prejudiced and as fine a soldier as Sharpe had met.

The forecastle was manned by the marines and by two of the ship's six thirty-two-pounder carronades. The one to larboard was under the command of Clouter, the escaped slave who was in Chase's barge crew. The huge black man, like his gunners, was naked to the waist and had a scarf tied around his ears. 'Going to be lively, sir,' he greeted Sharpe, nodding towards the enemy line that was now barely a mile away. A half-dozen ships were firing at the *Victory*, just as another half-dozen were hammering the *Royal Sovereign* a little more than a mile to the south. That ship, by far the closest to the French and Spanish line, looked bedraggled, for her studdingsail yards had been shot away and the sails hung like broken wings beside her rigging. She could still not return the enemy's fire, but in a few minutes she would be among them and her three decks of guns could begin to repay the beating she endured.

The sea ahead of the *Pucelle* was being pockmarked by shot, flicked by white spray or whipped by round shots skimming the waves, though so far none of those shots had come close to the *Pucelle* herself. The *Temeraire*, which had failed to overtake the *Victory* and was now sailing off her starboard quarter, was taking shots through her sails. Sharpe could see the holes appear like magic, making the ship's whole spread of canvas quiver. A broken line whipped and flew wide. To Sharpe it seemed as though the *Victory* and *Temeraire* were sailing directly towards the *Santisima Trinidad* with its four smoke-wreathed decks of death. The sound of the enemy guns was loud now, punching over the water, sometimes in thunderous groups, more often single gun by single gun. 'It'll be ten or fifteen minutes before we're in range, sir,' Clouter said, answering Sharpe's unspoken question.

'Good luck, Clouter.'

The tall man grinned. 'Ain't a white man alive that can kill me, sir. No, sir, they done all they can to me, and now it's me and my smasher's turn.' He patted his carronade, his 'smasher', which was as ugly a weapon as any Sharpe had seen. It resembled an army mortar, though it was slightly longer in the barrel, and it squatted in its short carriage like a deformed cooking pot. The carriage had no wheels, but instead allowed the barrel to slide back, wood on greased wood. The gun's wide muzzle gaped and its belly was crammed with one thirty-two-pound round shot and a wooden cask of musket balls. It was no pretty thing, nor was it accurate, but bring it within yards of an enemy ship and it could belch a flail of metal that could have torn the guts out of a battalion.

'A Scotsman invented it.' Sergeant Armstrong had appeared beside Sharpe. The sergeant sniffed as he looked at the vast pot on its carriage. 'Heathen gun, sir. Heathen gunner, too,' he added, looking at Clouter. 'If we boards an enemy, Clouter,' he said sternly, 'you stay close to me.'

'Yes, Sergeant.'

'Why close to you?' Sharpe asked Armstrong as they walked away from the carronade.

'Because when that black heathen starts to fight, sir, there ain't a man born who dares stand in his way. A fiend, he is.' Armstrong sounded disapproving, but then, Clouter was palpably not a Northumbrian. 'And you, sir?' Armstrong asked suspiciously. 'Will you board with us?' What the sergeant really wanted to know was whether Sharpe planned to usurp his authority.

Sharpe could have insisted on commanding the marines, but he suspected they would fight better if Armstrong gave them their orders. Which meant Sharpe had little to do on the forecastle other than set an example, which was what most junior officers were doing when they were killed in battle. Armstrong knew what had to be done, the marines had been superbly trained by Llewellyn, and Sharpe had no mind to pace the forecastle showing a gentlemanly disdain for enemy fire. He would rather fight. 'I'm going below,' he told Armstrong, 'to draw a musket from stores.'

The enemy shots were still falling well short of the *Pucelle* as Sharpe went down the companionway and forward into the covered bow portion of the weather deck where he found the galley – usually a place where men gathered – empty, cold and deserted. The fires in the vast iron oven had all been doused and two of the ship's cats were rubbing themselves against the blackened metal as if curious as to why their source of warmth was gone. The gunners sat by their guns. Once in a while a man would lift a gunport, letting in a bright wash of light, and lean out to peer towards the enemy.

Sharpe went on down to the lower deck which was as dim as a cellar, though some light seeped from the wide windows of the stripped wardroom that lay at the stern. The ship's biggest guns squatted here like tethered beasts behind their closed ports. The cannons were usually stored with their barrels fully elevated and then drawn tight to the ship's sides, but now the barrels had been lowered to the fighting position and the carriages were standing well back from the ports. The sound of the enemy gunfire was muted so that it was little more than a dull grumble. Sharpe dropped down one more companionway to the orlop deck which was lit by shielded lanterns. He was below the water line now, and it was here that the ship's magazines were guarded by marines armed with muskets, bayonets and orders to stop any unauthorized person from going through the double leather curtains that were dripping with sea water. Powder monkeys, some in felt slippers, but most barefooted, waited by the outer curtain with their long tin canisters and Sharpe asked one of the boys to fetch him a pouch of musket ammunition and another of pistol shot while he went forrard to the small arms store and took a musket and pistol from the racks. The weight of the pistol made him think of Grace, safe now in the deep after hold. He tested both flints, found them secure.

He took the two pouches, thanked the boy, and climbed back to the lower deck where he paused to hang the cartridge pouches from his belt. The ship swooped up on a long swell, making him stagger slightly, then subsided into the trough, and suddenly a terrible crash echoed through the timbers, making the deck beneath Sharpe's feet quiver, and he realized that a round shot must have hit the upperworks. 'Froggies have our range,' a man said in the gloom.

'For what we are about to receive,' another man intoned, but before he could finish the prayer Lieutenant Holderby's voice interrupted him. Holderby was at his station by the aft companionway.

'Open ports!' the fifth lieutenant shouted, and petty officers repeated the order to the forward part of the deck.

The lower deck's thirty gunports were all raised, letting the daylight stream in to reveal the ship's masts like three gigantic pillars about which was a seething mass of half-naked men. The long guns were all in their recoil position, hard back against their breeching ropes.

'Run them out!' Holderby ordered. 'Run them out!'

Gunners heaved on the tackles and the thick deck

quivered as the huge guns were hauled forward so that their barrels protruded beyond the ship's sides. Holderby, elegant in silk stockings and gilded coat, ducked under the deck beams. 'You're to lie down between the guns. Between the guns! Lie down! Have a rest, gentlemen, before proceedings commence. Lie down!'

Chase had ordered his crew to lie down because the enemy's shot, coming from directly forward, could scream down these decks and each one could easily knock down a score of men, but if the gun crews were in the intervals between the heavy cannons then they would be mostly protected. Up on the quarterdeck Chase shuddered and when Haskell raised an eyebrow, the captain smiled. 'She's going to be knocked to pieces, ain't she?'

Haskell rapped a knuckle on the quarterdeck rail. 'French-built, sir, well built.'

'Aye, they do make good ships.' Chase stood on tiptoes to see across the barrier of the hammock netting to where the *Royal Sovereign* was almost up to the enemy line. 'She survived,' he said admiringly, 'and she's been under fire for twenty-three minutes! Dreadful gunnery, wouldn't you say?'

The tip of the British right horn was about to tear into the enemy, but the *Pucelle* was in the left horn and that was still well short of the line, and the enemy could still fire without fear of any reply. Chase winced as a round shot smacked through his sails to open a succession of holes. The *Pucelle*'s ordeal had begun, and all he could do now was sail slowly on into an ever-increasing storm of gunnery. A fountain spewed up on the starboard side, spattering one of the carronade crews. 'Water's cold, eh, lads?' Chase remarked to the bare-chested gunners.

'We won't be swimming in it, sir.'

A topsail shivered as a high shot slashed through. The ships ahead of the *Pucelle* were taking a more serious pounding, but the *Pucelle* was drawing closer and closer, heaved by the big swells and wafted by the ghosting wind, and every second took her nearer to the guns and soon, Chase knew, he would be under a much heavier cannonade, and just as he thought that so a heavy round shot struck the starboard cathead and whirled a wicked splinter of oak across the forecastle. Chase was suddenly aware that his fingers were drumming nervously against his right thigh and so he forced his hand to be still. His father, who had fought the French thirty years before, would have been appalled by these tactics. In Chase's father's day the ships of the line edged together, broadside to broadside, taking exquisite care never to expose their vulnerable bows and sterns to a raking, but this British fleet went bull-headed at the enemy. Chase wondered whether his father's memorial stone had been delivered from the masons, and whether it had been placed in the church choir, and then he touched the prayer book in his pocket. 'Hear us and save us,' he said under his breath, 'that we perish not.'

'Amen.' Haskell had overheard him. 'Amen.'

Sharpe climbed back to the forecastle where he found the marines crouching by the hammock netting and the carronade crews squatting behind their barrels. Sergeant Armstrong was standing by the foremast, scowling at the enemy line which suddenly seemed much nearer. Sharpe looked to his right and saw the *Royal Sovereign* had reached the enemy line. Her crew had hauled the fallen studdingsails inboard and her guns were at last firing as the vast ship pierced the enemy's formation. A ripple of filthy smoke was travelling from her bows to her stern as she emptied her larboard broadside into the stern of a Spanish ship and her starboard guns into the bows of a Frenchman. One of the *Royal Sovereign*'s topmasts had fallen, but she had broken the enemy line and now she would be swallowed into their fleet. The next ship in Collingwood's column, the two-decked *Belleisle*, was still a long way behind which meant the *Royal Sovereign* must fight the enemy single-handed until help arrived.

A slap overhead made Sharpe look up to see that a hole had been punched through the *Pucelle*'s foresail. The ball had then pierced all the lower sails, one after the other, before vanishing astern. Another crash, close to his feet, made him spin round. 'Low on the bows, sir,' Armstrong said. 'They hit the cathead earlier.' That would have been the first crash Sharpe had heard and he saw that the starboard cathead, a stout timber that jutted from the bows and from which the anchor was lowered and raised, was gouged almost halfway through.

His heart was thumping, his mouth was dry and a muscle twitched in his left cheek. He tried clamping his jaws shut to still the muscle, but it kept quivering. A shot landed close by the *Pucelle*'s bows and spattered water back over the beak and forecastle. The sprit-topsail yard under the reaching bowsprit twitched, one end flying into the air, then fell, broken, to hang close to the sea. This was worse than Assaye, Sharpe reckoned, for at least on land a soldier had the illusion that he could step left or right and so try to avoid the enemy's shot, but here a man could only stand as the ship crawled towards the enemy line which was a row of massive batteries, each ship carrying more artillery than had marched with Sir Arthur Wellesley's army. Sharpe could see the cannon balls looking like short pencil lines that flickered in the sky, and each pencil line meant a ball was coming more or less straight towards the *Pucelle*. A dozen enemy were firing at

Nelson's ships now. Another hole appeared in the *Pucelle*'s foresail, a studdingsail boom was shot away, a crash sounded close to the larboard water line and another enemy shot bounced across the swells to leave a trail of foam close on the starboard side. An odd whistling sound, almost a moan, but with a curious sharp rhythm, came from near the ship, then went silent. 'Chain shot, sir,' Sergeant Armstrong said. 'Sounds like the devil's wings beating, it does.'

The *Royal Sovereign* had vanished, her position marked only by a vast cloud of smoke out of which the rigging and sails of a half-dozen ships stood against the cloudy sky. The noise of that battle was a continuous thunder, while the sound from the ships ahead of the *Pucelle* was of gun after gun, close together, unending, as the French and Spanish crews took this chance of firing at an enemy who could not fire back. Two shots struck the *Pucelle* close to the water line, another ricocheted from her larboard flank, gouging a splinter as long as a boarding pike, a fourth struck the mainmast and broke apart one of the newly painted hoops, a fifth screamed past the forward starboard carronade, decapitated a marine, threw two others back in a spray of blood, then whipped overboard to leave a trail of red droplets glistening in the suddenly warm air.

'Throw him overboard!' Armstrong screamed at his marines who appeared paralysed by their comrade's sudden death. Two of them took hold of the decapitated body and carried it to the rail beside the carronade, but before they could heave it overboard Armstrong told them to take the man's ammunition. 'And see what's in his pockets, lads! Didn't your bloody mothers teach you to waste not and want not?' The sergeant paced across the deck, picked up the severed head by its bloody hair and dropped it over the side. 'Are they kicking?' He looked at the two men who lay like rag dolls in the sheet of blood that covered a quarter of the deck.

'Mackay's dead, Sergeant.'

'Then get rid of him!'

The third marine had lost an arm and the shot had also opened his chest so that his ribs showed in a jelly-like mass of torn muscle and blood. 'He won't live,' Armstrong said, stooping over the man, who was blinking through a mask of blood and breathing in juddering gasps. A round shot scattered the hammock netting, turned the quarterdeck rail to splinters and punched out through the stern without doing any injury to the crew. Another broke a topsail yard just as two shots banged through the weather deck to leave the ship's waist strewn with timber scraps. A round shot banged into one of the lower-deck guns, throwing the three-ton barrel clean off its carriage, crushing two gunners and filling the ship with a sound like a vast hammer striking a giant anvil.

The enemy ships ahead were shrouded in smoke, but because the small wind was blowing from the west, that smoke was shredding through their rigging and sails like a bank of fog drifting before a sea breeze, yet the fog was fed continually and Sharpe could see the pulses of fresh grey, white and black smoke, and he could also see the dark brightness of the cannon flames appear like evanescent spear-heads in the fog. The flames would stab, momentarily lighting the interior of the smoke bank, then vanish and the fog flowed over the enemy decks and the shots whipped out to thump into the *Victory* and the *Temeraire* and the *Neptune* and the *Leviathan* and the *Conqueror* and the *Pucelle*, and after those ships there was a gap before the lumbering three-decked *Britannia* which was still not under fire.

'Heave him over!' Armstrong commanded two of his men, gesturing at the third marine who had died. The man's arm, its torn tendons, flesh and muscle trailing like wet offal from the red sleeve, lay forgotten under the small structure that held the ship's bell and Sharpe picked it up, carried it to the larboard rail and hurled it into the sea. He could hear men singing from a gundeck below. One of the marines was kneeling in prayer, 'Mary, Mother of God,' he said over and over again, crossing himself. Clouter spat a wad of chewed tobacco over the gunwale, then cut himself another plug. The carronade's thirty-two-pound balls, each as large as a man's head, were stored on a grating.

Sharpe went back to stand beside the foremast and suddenly remembered he had forgotten to load either of his weapons, and was grateful for the lapse, for it gave him something to do. He bit open the cartridge and saw a body being thrown off the *Conqueror*'s quarterdeck. He primed the musket as a round shot went close enough to his head to punch his scalp with the wind of its passing. The shot hit nothing, threading the *Pucelle*'s rigging to splash far aft. Three hammering blows in quick succession shuddered the ship's timber as balls ploughed through the twin layers of oak that formed her hull. Seamen scrambled up the ratlines to reeve broken lines. The mainsail had six great holes in it now, and shook as a seventh appeared. Chase was standing at the shattered quarterdeck rail, appearing as calm as though he were sailing the *Pucelle* into an empty inland sea. Sharpe rammed the musket and, between his feet, there appeared a trickle of blood, spilling from the flood released by the shot that had killed the three marines. The trickle looked very red against the white of the scrubbed timber. When the ship tilted slightly to larboard the trickle veered to the left, when the stern was raised by a following sea the trickle dashed ahead and when the bows raised to the swell it hesitated, then the red rivulet slid to the right as the ship leaned to starboard, and Sharpe scrubbed the trickle into oblivion with his foot, then pushed the ramrod back into its hoops. He loaded the pistol. A shot hit the foremast, making the rigging shake; a silver-painted splinter whirled into the sea as Joan of Arc was struck on her belly. The guns were loud enough to hurt Sharpe's eardrums. There was blood on the weather deck where a ricocheting round shot had struck a crew and the air was filled with a shrieking, whistling, tearing noise that was chain shot and bar shot whipping through the masts to slice lines and rip sails. A rending crash sounded as a heavy shot tore up the poop deck and Sharpe could see Captain Llewellyn dragging a body towards the stern rail. Another thump from below, a second, a third, then screams made a shrill descant to the battering noise of the enemy guns. The enemy ships ahead were still in clumps, and where they were close together they looked like islands of guns. Or islands of smoke speared by gun-flames. Another gouging, tearing noise erupted from the starboard side and Sharpe leaned over to see a bright splinter of timber jutting from a band of black-painted hull. A body appeared in a gunport and was pushed overboard. A second body followed. The insides of the gunports were painted red and one of them was hanging from a single hinge until a man tore it away and let it drop.

A ball gouged through the wet blood on the forecastle, bounced up to tear a gap in the forecastle's after rail and punched through the lower edge of the mainsail. Three of the studdingsails were now hanging from the yards and Chase's seamen were trying to haul them inboard. A bar shot, two lumps of iron joined by a short iron rod, banged into the foremast close to the deck and stuck there, driven deep into the wood by the force of the impact. The *Victory* was close to the smoke cloud now, but she seemed to Sharpe to be sailing straight into a wall of smoke, flame and noise. The *Royal Sovereign* was lost in cloud, surrounded by the enemy, fighting desperately as the limp wind brought help so slowly. A portion of the forward rail of the forecastle suddenly vanished into splinters, sawdust and whirling slivers of wood. A marine fell backwards, struck through the lungs by one of the splinters. 'Hodgkinson! Take him below!' Armstrong shouted.

Another marine had an arm torn open by a splinter, but though his sleeve was soaked with blood and more blood dripped from his wrist, he refused to go. 'Ain't but a scratch, Sergeant.'

'Move your fingers, boy.' The man obediently wriggled his fingers. 'You can pull a trigger,' Armstrong allowed. 'But bind it up, bind it up! You ain't got nothing to do for the next few minutes, so bind it up. Don't want you dripping blood on a nice clean deck.'

A shot whipped out the timberhead which held the fore staysail sheets. Another struck the ship's beakhead, whistling a shred of wood high into the air, then a tearing, ripping, rustling sound made Sharpe look up to see that the *Pucelle*'s main topgallant mast, the slenderest and highest portion of the mainmast, was falling to bring down a tangle of rigging and the main topgallant sail with it. Heavy wooden blocks thumped on the deck. Some ships had rigged a net across the quarterdeck to save heads from being stove in by such accidental missiles, but Chase did not like such '*sauve-têtes*', for, he claimed, they protected the officers on the quarterdeck while leaving the men forrard unprotected. 'We must all endure the same risks,' he had told Haskell when the first lieutenant had suggested the netting, though it seemed to Sharpe that the officers on the quarterdeck ran more risk than most for they were made distinctive to the enemy by their unprotected position and by the brightness of their gold-encrusted uniforms. Still, Sharpe supposed, they were paid more so they must risk more. A staysail halliard parted and the sail drifted down to drag in the sea until a rush of seamen went forrard along the bowsprit to pull it in and attach a new halliard. One, two, three more strikes on the hull, each making the *Pucelle* tremble, and Sharpe wondered how the enemy could even see to aim their guns for the powder smoke lay so thickly along their hulls. The seamen chanted as they raised the staysail again.

More sail-handlers were up the mainmast trying to secure the wreckage of the topgallant mast. The mainsail had at least a dozen holes in it now. The ships ahead of the *Pucelle* were similarly wounded. Masts were shattered, yards broken, sails hung in folds, but enough canvas remained to drive them slowly onwards. Three bodies floated beside the *Pucelle*, heaved overboard from the *Temeraire* or *Conqueror*. Splashes whipped up from the sea all about the leading ships.

'There goes His Majesty!' Armstrong called. The sergeant was evidently confused about Nelson's true rank and exempted the admiral from all dislike, regarding him as an honorary Northumbrian who was now taking his flagship into the enemy's line, and Sharpe heard the sound of her broadsides and saw the flames flickering down her starboard flank as she crashed three decks of double-shotted guns into the bows of one of the French ships that had been tormenting her for so long. The Frenchman's foremast, all of it, right down to the deck, swayed left and right, then toppled slowly. The *Victory*'s guns would have recoiled inboard and men would be swabbing and reloading, ramming and heaving, breathing smoke and dust, and slipping on fresh blood as they hauled the guns out.

The *Pucelle*'s fore topgallant sail collapsed, the chains holding the yard shot through. The *Conqueror* was suffering as well. Her studdingsails trailed in the water, though Pellew's men were working to drag them inboard. Her fore topmast was bent at an unnatural angle and there were scars on her painted flank. The British ships, now that their gunports were opened, were studded with red squares that broke the black and yellow stripes. The air quivered with the sound of guns, whistled with the passage of shots, and the long Atlantic swell lifted and drove the slow ships straight into the enemy fire.

Sharpe watched one ship dead ahead. She was a Spaniard and her red and white ensign was so huge that it almost trailed in the water. A gust of wind freed her of smoke and when she rolled to a long sea Sharpe could see daylight clean through her gunports, but then she rolled back and a half-dozen of those gunports stabbed flame. The shots screamed through the *Pucelle*'s rigging, shivering the sails and severing lines. The Spaniard's red and black hull was hidden by smoke that thickened as more guns fired. A shot ploughed into the forecastle, another struck high on the foremast and a third smacked into the water line on the larboard side. Sharpe was counting, watching the stern of the Spaniard where the first guns had fired. One minute passed and the smoke there was thinning. Two minutes, and still the guns had not fired again. Slow, he thought, slow, but a slow gunner could still kill. Sharpe could see men with muskets in the enemy rigging. A shot howled overhead and vanished astern. The *Britannia*'s bluff bows, bright with the figurehead of Britannia holding her shield and trident, were suddenly pushing through a curtain of spray where an enemy round shot had fallen short. The marine still prayed, calling on Christ's mother to protect him, making the sign of the cross again and again.

The *Victory* had almost disappeared in smoke. She

was through the enemy line now and the gun smoke seemed to boil around her, though Sharpe could just see the flagship's high gilded stern reflecting a weak daylight through the man-made fog. It seemed to him that the enemy ships were gathering round Nelson and the sound of their guns was quivering the sea, rattling Sharpe's teeth, deafening him. The *Temeraire*, second in Nelson's column, forced her ponderous way through a gap in the enemy line and opened fire, pouring her broadside into the stern of a Frenchman. Sharpe looked right and saw that the first ships behind Collingwood's *Royal Sovereign* had at last reached the enemy. The sea there seemed to seethe with steam. A mast toppled into smoke. A huge gap was opening in the enemy's line north of where Collingwood had attacked, which showed that the British ships were snaring and pounding the enemy south of the *Royal Sovereign*, but the French and Spanish ships to the north of Collingwood's flagship just sailed on towards the place where Nelson's *Victory* was setting up a second snare.

Everything happened so slowly. Sharpe found that hard to bear. It was not like a land battle where the cavalry could pound across the field to leave a plume of dust and horse artillery slewed about in a spray of earth. This battle was taking place at a lethargic speed and there was a strange contrast between the stately slow beauty of the full-rigged ships and the noise of their guns. They went to their deaths so gracefully, in the full beauty of tensioned masts and spread sails above painted hulls. They crept towards death. The *Leviathan* and *Neptune* were in the battle now, piercing the enemy line a little to the south of the *Victory*. A shot gouged a furrow through the *Pucelle*'s forecastle deck, another struck the mizzenmast, shaking it, a third hammered the length of the weather deck, piercing bows and stern and miraculously touching nothing in the flight between. The men were still crouched between the guns. Chase was standing by the mizzenmast, hands clasped behind his back. The *Pucelle* was three ship lengths away from the enemy line and Chase was choosing the place where he would sail her through. 'Starboard a point,' he called, and the wheel creaked as the quartermaster hauled the spokes. Screams sounded from the lower deck as an enemy shot punched through the oak and ricocheted from the mainmast to strike a crouching gun crew. 'Steady,' Chase said, 'steady.'

A buzz whipped past Sharpe's ear and he thought it was an insect, then he saw a small splinter fly out of the deck and knew that it was musket fire coming from the rigging of the ships ahead. He willed himself to stand still. The Spanish ship that had been straight ahead had gone into smoke and there was a Frenchman there instead, and close behind her was another ship, though whether she was French or Spanish Sharpe could not tell, for her ensign was hidden by the mass of her undamaged sails. The sails looked dirty. She was a two-decker, smaller than the *Pucelle*, and her figurehead showed a monk with an uplifted hand holding a cross. A Spaniard, then. Sharpe looked for the *Revenant*, but could not see her. Chase seemed to be aiming across the smaller Spaniard's bows, taking the *Pucelle* through the shrinking gap between her and the Frenchman ahead, while the Spaniard was trying to cut the *Pucelle* off, trying to lay his smaller ship right across her bows and he was so close to the Frenchman that his jib boom, the outer part of his bowsprit, almost touched the French mizzen. French guns poured round shot into the *Pucelle*'s hull. Musket balls pattered on the sails. The French rigging was spotted with powder smoke, her hull was sheathed in it.

Chase gauged the gap. He could haul the ship round and take on the French ship broadside to broadside, but his orders were to pass through the line, though the gap was narrowing dangerously. If he misjudged, and if the Spaniard succeeded in laying his hull athwart the *Pucelle*'s bows then the Dons would seize his bowsprit, lash it to their own ship and hold him there while they raked, pounded and turned his ship into bloody splinters. Haskell recognized the danger and turned on Chase with a raised eyebrow. A musket ball struck the deck between them, then a round shot splintered the edge of the poop deck just above Chase before scattering the flag lockers built against the taffrail so that the *Pucelle* suddenly trailed a bright stream of gaudy flags. A musket bullet buried itself in the wheel, another broke the binnacle lantern. Chase stared at the shrinking gap and felt the temptation to head across the Spaniard's stern, but he would be damned if he let the Spanish captain dictate his battle. 'Stand on!' he said to the quartermaster. 'Stand on!' He would tear the bowsprit clean out of the Spaniard's hull before he gave way. 'The gun crews will stand up, Mister Haskell!' Chase said.

Haskell shouted down to the weather deck. 'Stand up! Stand up! Stand to your guns!'

Midshipmen and lieutenants repeated the order to the lower deck. 'Stand up! Stand up!' Men gathered round their guns, peered through the open ports, eyed the ragged holes that had already been punched in the hull's double-planked oak timbers. The cannons' flintlocks were cocked and the gunners crouched to the side, lanyards held ready.

A marine cursed and staggered on the forecastle as a musket bullet drove down through his shoulder into his belly. 'Make your own way to the surgeon,' Armstrong told him, 'and don't make a fuss.' He stared up at the Frenchman's mizzenmast where a knot of men were firing muskets down onto the *Pucelle*. 'Time to teach those bastards some manners,' he growled. The

Pucelle's bowsprit, ragged with its broken yard, pushed into the gap between the two ships. The gunners below decks could not yet see the enemy, but they knew they were close for the smoke of the enemy guns lay across the sea like mist, then thickened as the enemy fired again, though now the *Pucelle* was so close that they were firing at the ships behind her.

'Push on through!' Chase shouted at his ship. 'Push on through!'

For now was the glorious moment of revenge. Now was the moment when, if the *Pucelle* could force her passage, she would carry her broadsides within feet of an unprotected enemy stern and an unprotected enemy bow. Then, having taken the punishment for so long, she could rake two ships at once, ripping blood and bone and timber with her own fire-driven metal. 'Make the shots tell!' Chase called. 'Make them tell!'

Make the bastards bleed, he thought vengefully. Make the bastards sorry they had ever been born and damn them to a fiery hell for the damage they had already done to his ship. There was a ripping, splintering sound as the *Pucelle*'s bowsprit tangled with the Spanish bowsprit, but then the Spaniard's jib boom broke off altogether and the *Pucelle*'s shot-battered bows were in the gap, her broken sprit topsail yard was ripping the French ensign, and the first of her guns could bear. 'Now kill them!' Chase shouted, relief flooding through him because at last he could fight back. 'Now kill them!'

Lord William Hale had refused to allow his wife's maid to take refuge in the lady hole, peremptorily telling the girl to find a place further forward in the *Pucelle*'s hold. 'It is bad enough,' he told his wife, 'that we are forced to this place, let alone that we should share it with servants.'

The lady hole was the aftermost corner of the *Pucelle*'s hold, a triangular space made where the hull supported the rudder. Its forward bulkhead was formed by the shelves where the officers' empty dunnage was stored and where Malachi Braithwaite had sought the memorandum on the day of his death, and the floor of the hole was made by the steeply sloping sides of the ship, and though Captain Chase had ordered that a patch of old sailcloth be placed in the hole to provide a rudimentary comfort, Lord William and Lady Grace were still forced to perch uncomfortably against the plank slopes beneath the small hatch that led to the gunroom on the orlop deck above. It was in the gunroom that the cannons' flintlocks were usually stored and where the ship's small weapons could be repaired. It was empty now, though the surgeon might use it as a place to put the dying.

Lord William had insisted on having two lanterns which he hung from rusting hooks in the lady hole's ceiling. He drew his pistol and lay it on his lap, using it as a prop for the spine of a book he drew from his coat pocket. 'I am reading the *Odyssey*,' he told his wife. 'I thought I should have the leisure for much reading on this voyage, but time has flown. Have you found the same?'

'I have,' she said dully. The sound of the enemy guns was very muted down below the water line.

'But I was pleased to discover,' Lord William went on, 'in the few moments I have been able to devote to Homer, that my Greek is as fresh as ever. There were a few words that escaped me, but young Braithwaite recalled them. He was not much use, Braithwaite, but his Greek was excellent.'

'He was an odious man,' Lady Grace said.

'I did not realize you had remarked him,' Lord William said, then shifted the book so that the lantern light fell on the page. He traced the lines with his finger, mouthing the words silently.

Lady Grace listened to the guns, then started when the first shot struck the *Pucelle* and made all the ship's timbers quiver. Lord William merely raised an eyebrow, then went on with his reading. More shots struck home, their sound dulled by the decks above. Opposite Lady Grace, where the hull's inner planking was joined to a rib, water wept through a seam and every time a swell passed under the hull the water would bulge in the seam, then run down to vanish into the hold beyond the dunnage shelves. She restrained an urge to press a finger against the seam which was stuffed with a narrow strip of frayed oakum, and she remembered Sharpe telling her how, as a small child in the foundling home, he had been forced to pick apart great mats of tarred rope that had been used as fenders on London's docks. His job had been to extract the hemp strands which were then sold to the shipyards to be used as caulking for planks. His fingernails were still ragged and black, though that, he said, was the result of firing a flintlock musket. She thought of his hands, closed her eyes and wondered at the madness that had swamped her. She was still in its thrall. The ship shook again, and she had a sudden terror of being trapped in this cramped space as the *Pucelle* sank.

'I am reading about Penelope,' Lord William said, ignoring the frequent crashes as the enemy shot hacked into the *Pucelle.* 'She is a remarkable woman, is she not?'

'I have always thought as much,' Lady Grace said, opening her eyes.

'The quintessence, would you not say, of fidelity?' Lord William asked.

Grace looked into her husband's face. He was sitting to her left, perched on the opposite side of the narrow space. He seemed amused. 'Her fidelity is always praised,' she said.

'Have you ever wondered, my dear, why I took you to India?' Lord William asked, closing the book after carefully marking his place with what appeared to be a folded letter.

'I hoped it was because I could be of use to you,' she answered.

'And so you were,' Lord William said. 'Our necessary visitors were entertained most properly and I have not one single complaint about the manner in which you organized our household.'

Grace said nothing. The rudder, so close behind them, creaked in its pintles. The enemy gunfire was a constant succession of dull thumps, sometimes rising to a thunderous crescendo, then lulling again into the steadier banging.

'But of course,' Lord William went on, 'a good servant can run a household quite as well as a wife, if not better. No, my dear, I confess it was not for that reason that I wished you to accompany me, but rather, forgive me, because I feared you would find it hard to imitate Penelope if I were to leave you at home for such a long period.'

Grace, who had been watching the water well and spill from the seam, looked at her husband. 'You are offensive,' she said coldly.

Lord William ignored her words. 'Penelope, after all,' he went on, 'stayed faithful to her husband through all the long years of his exile, but would a modern woman show the same forbearance?' Lord William pretended to mull over this question. 'What do you think, my dear?'

'I think,' she said acidly, 'that I would need to be married to Odysseus to answer such a question.'

Lord William laughed. 'Would you like that, my dear? Would you like to be married to a warrior? Though is

Odysseus such a great warrior? It always seems to me that he is a trickster before he is a soldier.'

'He is a hero,' Grace insisted.

'As, I am sure, all husbands are to their wives,' Lord William said placidly, then looked up at the deck beams as a double blow shook the ship. A wave heaved up the stern, making him reach out a hand to steady himself. Feet scraped on the deck above, where the ship's first wounded were going under the surgeon's knife. Then a particularly loud crash, sounding very close by, made Lady Grace cry aloud. There was the ominous sound of gushing water that stopped abruptly as the carpenter, finding the hole in the ship's water line, hammered a shaped plug into the shot hole. Lady Grace wondered how far beneath the water line they were. Five feet? Captain Chase had been certain that no shot could penetrate the lady hole, explaining that the sea water slowed the cannon balls instantly, but the terrible sounds suggested that every part of the *Pucelle* could be wounded. The ship's pumps clattered, though once the *Pucelle* opened fire the men would be too busy at the guns to bother with the pumps. The ship was full of noises: the creaking of the mast roots in the hold, the gurgle of water, the sucking gulps of the pump, the groanings of strained timbers, the shriek of the rudder on its metal hangings, the banging of the enemy guns and the tearing crashes of the shots striking home. Lady Grace, assaulted by the cacophony, had one hand at her mouth and the other clasped to her belly where she carried Sharpe's child.

'We are entirely safe here,' Lord William calmed his wife. 'Captain Chase assures me that no one dies beneath the water line. Though when I come to think of it, my dear, poor Braithwaite did just that.' Lord William put his hands together in mock piety. 'He was killed beneath the water line,' he intoned.

'He fell,' Lady Grace said.

'Did he?' Lord William asked, his tone suggesting how much he was enjoying this discussion. A thunderous blow shook the ship, then something scraped quick and hard against the hull. Lord William settled himself more comfortably. 'I must confess I have wondered whether he did indeed fall.'

'How else could he have died?' Grace asked.

'And what a cogent question that is, my dear.' Lord William pretended to think about it for a while. 'Of course, a quite different construction could be placed on the unfortunate man's death if we were to discover that he was particularly disliked by anyone aboard. Like you? You told me he was odious.'

'He was,' Lady Grace said bitterly.

'But I do not think you could have killed him,' Lord William said with a smile. 'Perhaps he had other enemies? Enemies who could make his death appear an accident? Odysseus, in the unlikely event that he could ever have encountered young Braithwaite, would surely have had no trouble disguising such a murder?'

'He fell,' Lady Grace insisted tiredly.

'And yet, and yet,' Lord William said, frowning in thought. 'I confess I did not much like Braithwaite. His pathetic ambition was too naked for my tastes. He lacked subtlety and could not disguise his ridiculous envy of privilege. Once in England I should have been forced to relinquish his services, but he must have had a higher opinion of me than I of him, for he chose to confide in me.'

Lady Grace watched her husband. The swaying lanterns made the shadows either side of his body shift ominously. A cannon ball thumped into the lower deck above them and the ship's ribs carried the harsh sound down into the lady hole, but for once Lady Grace did not flinch at the noise. She was scratching at a shred of oakum with her right hand, trying to imagine how it felt to a small child in a cold foundling home.

'Perhaps he did not exactly confide in me,' Lord William said pedantically, 'for, naturally, I did not encourage intimacy, yet he did have a premonition of his death. Do you think, perhaps, he was possessed of some prophetic powers?'

'I know nothing of him,' Grace said distantly.

'I almost feel sorry for him,' Lord William said, 'for he lived in fear.'

'A sea voyage can engender nervousness,' Lady Grace said.

'So much fear,' Lord William went on, blithely ignoring his wife's words, 'that before he died he left a sealed letter among my papers. "To be opened," the letter said, "in the event of my death."' He sneered. 'Such a very dramatic ascription, wouldn't you say? So dramatic that I hesitated to obey it, for I expected it to contain nothing more than his pathetic resentments and self-justifications. Indeed, I was so aghast at the thought of hearing from Braithwaite beyond the grave that I very nearly threw the letter overboard, but a Christian sense of duty made me pay him attention, and I confess he did not write uninterestingly.' Lord William smiled at his wife, then delicately took the folded paper from between the pages of his *Odyssey*. 'Here, my dear, is young Braithwaite's legacy to our connubial happiness. Please read it, for I have been so looking forward to your construal of its contents.' He held the letter towards her and though Lady Grace hesitated, her heart sinking, she knew she must obey. It was either that or listen as her husband read the letter aloud and so, without a word, she took the paper.

Her husband closed his hand about the hilt of his pistol.

The *Pucelle*'s bowsprit tore the jib boom from the Spanish ship.

And Lady Grace read her doom.

The stern of the French ship was so close that Sharpe felt he could have reached out and touched it. Her name was written in golden letters placed on a black band between two sets of the stern's lavishly gilded windows. *Neptune*. The British had a *Neptune* in the fight, a three-decked ship with ninety-eight guns, while this *Neptune* was a two-decker, though Sharpe had the impression she was bigger than the *Pucelle*. Her stern was a foot or more higher than the *Pucelle*'s forecastle and it was lined with French marines armed with muskets. Their bullets banged on the deck or buried themselves in the hammock nettings. Just beneath the enemy's gun smoke a shield was carved into the taffrail. The shield was surmounted by an eagle and on either side of the crest were sheaves of wooden flags, all of them, like the shield itself, painted with the French tricolour, but the paint had weathered and Sharpe could see faded gold traces of the old royalist fleur-de-lys beneath the red, white and blue. He fired his musket, obliterating the view with smoke, then Clouter, who had deliberately waited until his carronade could fire directly down the centre line of the French *Neptune*, pulled the lanyard.

It was the first of the *Pucelle*'s guns to fire, and it shrieked back on its carriage in a cloud of black smoke. The French marines vanished, shredded to a bloody mist by the cask of musket balls that had been loaded on top of the massive round shot that shattered the painted shield and then struck the *Neptune*'s mizzen-mast with a crack that was drowned by the first guns firing from the *Pucelle*'s lower decks.

These guns were double-shotted and each had a

bundle of grape rammed on top of the twin cannon balls, and they were being fired straight into the Frenchman's stern windows. The glass panes and their frames disappeared as the heavy missiles whipped down the lengths of the *Neptune*'s two gundecks. Cannon barrels were hurled from their carriages, men were eviscerated, and still the shots came, gun after gun, as the *Pucelle* slowly, so slowly, travelling at an old man's walking pace, inched past the stern to bring the successive larboard gunports to bear. The guns on the starboard side were firing into the Spaniard's bow, breaking the heavy timber apart to send their murderous shots down her gundecks. The *Pucelle* was dishing out slaughter and the smoke billowed from her sides, starting at the bows and working down to her stern.

The *Neptune*'s mizzenmast went overboard. Sharpe heard the screams of the marksmen in her rigging, watched them fall, then rammed a new ball down his musket. The starboard carronade, loaded like Clouter's with musket balls and a vast round shot, had swept the Spaniard's forecastle clean of men. Blood dripped from the forecastle scuppers while the figurehead of the monk with a cross had been turned into matchwood. A big crucifix was fastened to the Spanish ship's mizzenmast, but when Chase's stern carronades blasted down the smaller ship's length the hanging Christ's left arm was torn away and then his legs were broken.

The *Pucelle* had ripped away a part of the Frenchman's ensign, while the rest was in the water with the fallen mizzenmast. Chase wanted to turn his ship to larboard and lay her alongside the *Neptune* and batter her hull into bloody ruin, but the smaller Spanish ship rammed the *Pucelle* and inadvertently turned her to starboard. There was a tearing, grating, grinding sound as the two hulls juddered together, then the Spanish captain, fearing he would be boarded, backed his topsails and the smaller ship fell away astern. Her starboard gunports had been closed, but now a few opened as the surviving gunners crossed from larboard. The guns fired into the *Pucelle.* Captain Llewellyn's marines were firing up into the Spanish rigging. Smoke obscured the smaller ship. Chase thought about putting his helm hard down and closing on her, but he was already past and so he shouted at the quartermaster to turn the ship north towards the cauldron of fire and smoke that surrounded the *Victory.* The flagship's hull could not be seen amidst that stinking fog, but, judging from the masts, Chase reckoned there was a Frenchman on either side of her. 'Pull in the studdingsails,' he ordered. The sails, which projected either side of the ship, were only useful in a following wind and now the *Pucelle* would turn to place the small wind on her larboard flank. The sail-handlers streamed out along the yards. One, struck by a musket ball, collapsed over the mainyard, then fell to leave a long trail of blood down the mainsail.

The French *Neptune* was slowed by her trailing mizzenmast. Her crew slashed at the fallen rigging with axes, trying to lose the broken mast overboard. The *Pucelle* was off her quarter now and Chase's larboard gunners had reloaded and poured shot after shot into the Frenchman, firing through the lingering smoke of their first broadside. The noise of the guns filled the sky, made the sea quiver, shook the ship. Clouter had reloaded the larboard carronade, a slow job, but there was no target close and he would not waste the giant shot on the *Neptune* which had at last released the wreckage of its mast and was drawing away. He rammed another cask of musket balls into the short barrel, then waited for another target to come within the short gun's range.

But the *Pucelle* was suddenly in a patch of open sea

with no enemy near. She had pierced the line, but the *Neptune* had gone north while the Spaniard had disappeared in smoke astern and there were no ships in front except for an enemy frigate that was a quarter-mile off and ships of the line did not stoop to fight frigates when there were battleships to engage. A long line of French and Spanish battleships was coming from the south, but none was in close range and so Chase continued towards the churning smoke, lit by gun-flashes, that marked where Nelson's beleaguered flagship lay. There was honour to be gained in defeating a flagship and the *Victory*, like the *Royal Sovereign*, was drawing enemy ships like flies. Four other British ships were in action close to the *Victory*, but the enemy had seven or eight, and no more help would arrive for a time because the *Britannia* was such a slow sailor. The French *Neptune* looked to be going to join that mêlée, and so Chase followed. The sail-handlers, short numbered because so many were manning the guns, sheeted home the sails as the *Pucelle* swung round. The sea was littered with floating wreckage. Two bodies drifted past. A seagull perched on one, sometimes pecking at the man's face which had been torn open by gunfire and washed white by the sea.

The *Pucelle*'s wounded were carried below and the dead jettisoned. The cannon barrel that had been thrown off its carriage was lashed tight so that it would not shift with the ship's rolling and crush a man. Lieutenants redistributed gunners among the crews, making up the numbers where too many had died or been injured. Chase stared aft at the Spanish ship. 'I should have laid alongside her,' he told Haskell ruefully.

'There'll be others, sir.'

'By God I want a prize today!' Chase said.

'Plenty to go round, sir.'

The nearest enemy ship now was a two-decker that

was laid alongside the bigger *Victory*. Chase could see the smoke of the *Victory*'s guns spewing out from the narrow space between the two ships and he imagined the horror in the Frenchman's lower decks as the three tiers of British guns mangled men and timber, but he also saw that the French upper decks were crowded. The French captain appeared to have abandoned his gundecks altogether and assembled his whole crew on the forecastle, open weather deck and quarterdeck where they were armed with muskets, pikes, axes and cutlasses. 'They want to board *Victory*!' Chase exclaimed, pointing.

'By God, sir, so they do.'

Chase could not see the French ship's name, for the powder smoke curled round her stern, but her captain was plainly a bold man, for he was willing to lose his own ship if, thereby, he could capture Nelson's flagship. His seamen had grappled the bigger *Victory* and dragged her close, his gunners had closed their ports and seized their cutlasses and now the French sought a way across to Nelson's deck. The *Victory* was higher than the Frenchman, and the two ships' tumblehomes meant that even when their hulls were touching, the rails were still thirty or more feet apart. The *Victory*'s guns were pounding the Frenchman's hull, while the French ship had scores of men in the rigging, and those men were pouring a lethal musket fire down onto the flagship's exposed decks. They had almost cleared those decks, so that now the British fought from their lower decks while the French sought a way to cross to the flagship's virtually unguarded upper decks. The French captain planned to pour hundreds of men onto the *Victory*. He would make his name, be an admiral by nightfall and carry Nelson as a prisoner back to Cadiz.

Chase had climbed a few feet up the mizzen shrouds to see what was happening, and what he saw appalled him. He could not see the admiral, or Captain Hardy. A few red-coated marines crouched under the cover of the carronades and put up a feeble fire to counter the lashing musketry that still ripped down from the French masts, while on the *Victory*'s farther side another enemy ship fired into her hull.

Chase dropped down the rigging. 'Starboard a point,' he said to the helmsman, then took a speaking trumpet from the shattered rail. 'Clouter! Have you got musket balls loaded?'

'Full of them, sir!'

The enemy ship was a hundred yards away. The *Victory*'s cannon fire was ripping upwards through her decks now as Hardy's gunners elevated their barrels as high as they could. Holes were being punched high in the French two-decker's starboard side as round shot, fired into the ship's larboard flank, hammered clean through her. Yet the British gunners were firing blind and the boarders were gathering on the side nearest the *Victory* where the British guns could not reach. The French captain shouted at his men to drop the main-yard, for that would serve as their bridge to glory. His rigging was tangled with the *Victory*'s rigging, but his was filled with men and the *Victory*'s was empty. The sound of the muskets crackled like thorn burning. The *Victory*'s guns made deep booms. Wood splintered from the French deck and side as the shots punched out.

Fifty yards to go. The wind was foully light. The sea was covered in patches of smoke like breaking fog. The swells heaved the *Pucelle* eastwards. 'Larboard a point, John,' Chase said to the quartermaster, 'larboard. Take me by his quarter.' The smoke at the French ship's stern thinned and Chase saw the name of the two-decker which threatened to board the *Victory*. The *Redoutable*. Death to the *Redoutable*, he thought, and just then the French seamen released the *Redoutable*'s mainyard halliards and the great spar dropped to crash onto the *Victory*'s shattered hammock netting. It lay like a canvas-wrapped log across the *Redoutable*'s waist, but its larboard end jutted out over the *Victory*'s weather deck. It was a slender bridge, but it was sufficient for the French.

'*A l'abordage*!' the French captain shouted. He was a small man with a very loud voice. He had his sword drawn. '*A l'abordage*!'

His men cheered as they swarmed up the yard. The *Pucelle* lifted on a wave.

'Now!' Chase shouted to the forecastle. 'Now, Clouter, now!'

And Clouter hesitated.

CHAPTER 11

His lordship should know, Malachi Braithwaite had written in a careful copperplate hand, that his wife was conducting an adulterous affair with Ensign Sharpe. He had overheard the two of them in Sharpe's quarters aboard the *Calliope* and, painful though it was to relate, the sounds emanating – that was the word he used, emanating – from the cabin suggested that her ladyship had quite forgotten her high station. Braithwaite had written in a cheap ink, a faded brown that had bled into the damp paper, and was hard to read in the dim lady hole. At first, the confidential secretary related, he had not believed the evidence of his own ears, and scarce even dared credit it when he had glimpsed the Lady Grace leaving the lower-deck steerage in the darkness before dawn, so he had thought it his duty to confront Sharpe with his suspicions. 'But when I taxed Ensign Sharpe with my accusations,' he wrote, 'and upbraided him for taking advantage of her ladyship, he did not deny the circumstances, but instead threatened me with murder.' Braithwaite had underlined the word 'murder'. 'It was that circumstance, my lord, which constrained my cowardly tongue from its bounden duty.' It gave him no pleasure, Braithwaite concluded the letter, to inform his lordship of these shameful events, especially as his lordship had ever shown him such excessive kindnesses.

Lady Grace let the letter fall into her lap. 'He lies,'

she said, 'he lies.' There were tears in her eyes.

The lady hole was suddenly filled with noise. The *Pucelle*'s own guns had started to fire and the shock of the cannon reverberated through the ship, shaking the twin lanterns. The noise went on and on, becoming louder as the firing drew nearer to the stern of the ship. Then there was a terrible crash as the Spanish ship's bows collided with the *Pucelle*'s side, followed by a groaning screech as tons of wood ground and scraped against the hull. A man shouted, a gun fired, then three more. The sound of the reloaded guns being hauled forward was like bursts of brief thunder.

Then there an odd silence.

'He did lie,' Lord William said placidly in the silence, and reached over to take the letter from his wife's lap. Grace made an effort to snatch it back, but Lord William was too quick. 'Of course Braithwaite lied,' his lordship went on. 'It must have provided him with an exquisite pleasure to tell me of your disgusting behaviour. One detects his enjoyment throughout the letter, don't you think? And I certainly did him no excessive kindnesses! The thought is as ludicrous as it is offensive.'

'He lies!' Lady Grace said more defiantly. A tear quivered at her eye, then rolled down her cheek.

'Showed him excessive kindnesses!' Lord William said scathingly. 'Why would I do such a thing? I paid him a small salary commensurate with his services, and that was all.' Lord William carefully pocketed the folded letter. 'One circumstance did puzzle me, though,' he went on. 'Why did he confront Sharpe? Why not come straight to me? I have thought about that, and still it puzzles me. What was the point of seeing Sharpe? What did Braithwaite expect of him?'

Lady Grace said nothing. The rudder squealed in its pintles, and an enemy shot struck the *Pucelle* with a deep booming sound, then there was silence again.

'Then I remembered,' Lord William went on, 'that Sharpe deposited some valuables with that wretched man Cromwell. I thought it an odd circumstance, for the man is palpably poor, but I suppose he could have plundered some wealth in India. Could Braithwaite have been attempting blackmail? What do you think?'

Lady Grace shook her head, not in answer to her husband's question, but as if to shake off the whole subject.

'Or perhaps Braithwaite tried to blackmail you?' Lord William suggested, smiling at his wife. 'He used to watch you with such a pathetically yearning face. It amused me, for it was plain what he was thinking.'

'I hated him!' Lady Grace blurted out.

'An extravagant waste of emotion, my dear,' Lord William said. 'He was an insignificant thing, scarce worth disliking. But, and this is the point of our conversation, was he telling the truth?'

'No!' Lady Grace wailed.

Lord William lifted the pistol and examined its lock in the lantern light. 'I noted,' he said, 'how your spirits revived after we boarded the *Calliope*. I was pleased, naturally, for you have been over-nervous in these last months, but once aboard Cromwell's ship you seemed positively happy. And indeed, in these last few days, there has been a vivacity in you that is most unnatural. Are you pregnant?'

'No,' Lady Grace lied.

'Your maid tells me you vomit most mornings?'

Grace shook her head again. Tears were running down her cheeks. Partly she cried from shame. When she was with Sharpe it seemed so natural, so comforting and exciting, but she could not plead that in her defence. He was a common soldier, an orphan from the London rookeries, and Grace knew that if society ever learned of her liaison then she would become a laughing stock. A part of her did not care if she was mocked, another part cringed under the lash of Lord William's scorn. Grace was deep in a ship, down among the rats, lost.

Lord William watched her tears and thought of them as the first trickles of his revenge, then he looked up at the planks of the orlop deck and frowned. 'It's oddly silent,' he said, trying to keep her off balance by momentarily talking of the battle before torturing her with his sharp tongue once more. 'Perhaps we have run away from the fighting?' He could hear the grumbling of some distant gunnery, but no cannons were being fired close to the *Pucelle*. 'I remember,' he said, laying the pistol on his knees, 'when we first met and my uncle suggested I should marry you. I had my doubts, of course. Your father is a wastrel and your mother a garrulous fool, but you possess, Grace, a classical beauty and I confess I was drawn to it. I was concerned that you boasted an education, though it has proved scantier than you think, and I feared you might possess opinions, which I rightly suspected would be foolish, but I was prepared to endure those afflictions. I believed, you see, that my apprehension of your beauty would overcome my distaste for your intellectual pretensions, and in return I asked very little of you, save that you gave me an heir and upheld the dignity of my name. You failed in both things.'

'I gave you an heir,' Grace protested through her tears.

'That sickly whelp?' Lord William spat, then shuddered. 'It is your other failure that concerns me now, my dear. Your failure of taste, of behaviour, of decency, of fidelity' – he paused, seeking the right insult – 'of manners!'

'Braithwaite lied!' Grace screamed. 'He lied.'

'He did not lie,' Lord William said angrily. 'You, my lady, made the beast with two backs with that common soldier, that lump of ignorance, that brute.' His voice was cold now, for he could no longer hide his long-cosseted rage. 'You fornicated with a peasant, and you could not have sunk lower had you put yourself on the streets and lifted your skirts.'

Lady Grace rested her head on the planking. Her mouth was open, gasping for breath and the tears were dripping onto her cloak. Her eyes were red, unseeing, as she wept.

'And now you look so ugly,' Lord William said, 'which will make this much easier.' He lifted the pistol.

And the ship echoed again to the sound of a shot.

Clouter did not pull the carronade's flintlock lanyard when Chase ordered him to fire. He waited. It seemed to Sharpe, and to everyone else who watched, that Clouter was waiting too long and that the French would reach the *Victory*'s weather deck, but the *Pucelle* had heaved up on a swell and Clouter was waiting for the ship to roll to larboard on the back of the wave. She did, and on that down roll Clouter fired and the shot was perfectly timed so that its barrelful of musket balls and round shot slashed into the Frenchmen clambering up the spar that would have carried them onto the *Victory*'s unprotected deck. One moment there was a boarding party, the next there was a butcher's yard. The fallen yard and sail were drenched with blood, but the Frenchmen had disappeared, snatched into oblivion by the storm of metal.

The *Pucelle* now glided past the *Redoutable*'s quarter. She was a pistol shot away and the big guns of Chase's larboard broadside began to work on the devastated enemy. Chase had ordered the gunners to raise their barrels so that the shots cracked through the Frenchman's side and tore their way upwards through the deck which was thronged with men. Shot after shot spat from the *Pucelle* in a fire that was deliberate, slow and lethal. Men were lifted from the enemy deck, snatched upward by the round shot. Some shots passed through the *Redoutable* to strike the *Victory*'s weather-deck rail. It took more than a minute for the *Pucelle* to pass the doomed French ship, and for all of that minute the guns ripped into her, and then it was the turn of the quarterdeck carronades that could look down on the bloody mess left on the enemy deck and the two smashers finished the work, emptying their squat barrels into the squirming mass.

The *Redoutable* had no cannons manned. The French captain had gambled everything on boarding the *Victory*, and his boarders were now dead, wounded or dazed, but the ship's rigging was still filled with the marksmen who had emptied the upper decks of Nelson's flagship and those men had turned their muskets onto the *Pucelle*. The balls rained down, smacking on the quarterdeck like metal hail. Grenades were hurled, exploding in gouts of smoke and whistling shards of glass and iron.

The *Pucelle*'s marines did their best, but they were outnumbered. Sharpe fired up into the dazzling light, then hurriedly reloaded. The deck about his feet was being pockmarked with bullet strikes. A ball clanged off Clouter's empty carronade and struck a man in the thigh. A marine reeled back from the rail, his mouth opening and closing. Another, pierced through the throat, knelt by the foremast and gazed wide-eyed at Sharpe. 'Spit, boy!' Sharpe shouted at him. 'Spit!'

The man looked vacantly at Sharpe, frowned, then obediently spat. There was no blood in the spittle. 'You'll live,' Sharpe told him. 'Get yourself below.' A bullet hit a mast hoop, scraping away fresh yellow paint.

Sergeant Armstrong fired his musket, swore as a bullet drilled his left foot, limped to the rail, picked up another musket and fired again. Sharpe rammed his bullet, primed the gun, lifted it to his shoulder and aimed at the knot of men on the Frenchman's maintop. He pulled the trigger. He could see musket flashes up there. A grenade landed on the forecastle and exploded in a sheet of flame. Armstrong, wounded by shards of glass, smothered the flames with a bucket of sand, then began to reload. Blood was trickling from the scuppers of the *Redoutable*'s weather deck, trickling under the shattered rail and dribbling red across her closed gunports. The *Pucelle*'s foremost guns, reloaded, fired into the Frenchman's bows and there was a crack like the gates of hell being shut as the vast anchor was struck by a round shot. More round shot from the *Victory* was breaking out of the enemy's side and some struck the *Pucelle.* A dozen more muskets fired from the enemy's maintop and Sergeant Armstrong was on his knees, cursing, but still reloading. More muskets flickered from the enemy's mast and Sharpe threw down his musket and picked up Sergeant Armstrong's volley gun. He looked up at the enemy maintop and reckoned it was too far away and that the seven bullets would spread too wide before they reached the platform that was built where the Frenchman's lower mast was jointed to the upper.

He went to the starboard rail, slung the big gun on his shoulder and pulled himself up the foremast shrouds. He could see a marine lying on the *Pucelle*'s quarterdeck with a rivulet of blood seeping from his body along the planks. Another marine was being carried to the rails. He could not see Chase, but then a bullet struck the shroud above him, making the tarred rope tremble like a harp string and he climbed desperately, his ears buffeted by the sound of the big guns.

Another bullet whipped close by, a second struck the mast and, bereft of force, thumped against the volley gun's stock. He reached the futtock shrouds and, without thinking, hurled himself upwards and outwards, the quickest way to the maintop. There was no time to be frightened; instead he scrambled up the ratlines as nimbly as any sailor and then rolled onto the grating to find that he was now level with the Frenchmen in their maintop. There were a dozen men there, most reloading, but one fired and Sharpe felt the wind of the ball whipping past his cheek. He unslung the volley gun, cocked and aimed it.

'Bastards,' he said, and pulled the trigger. The recoil of the gun hurled him back against the topmast shrouds. The volley gun's smoke filled the sky, but no shots came from the Frenchman's maintop. Sharpe slung the empty gun on his shoulder and lowered himself off the grating. His feet flailed for a heartbeat, then found the inward-sloping futtock shrouds and he went back down to the *Pucelle*'s deck and, when he looked back up, all he could see at the *Redoutable*'s maintop was a body hanging off the edge. He threw the volley gun down, picked up a musket and walked to the larboard rail.

A dozen marines were left. The others were dead or wounded. Sergeant Armstrong, his face bleeding from three cuts and his trousers a deep red from a bullet wound, was sitting with his back against the foremast. He had a musket at his shoulder and, though his right eye was closed by blood, he did his best to aim the musket, then fired. 'You should go below, Sergeant!' Sharpe shouted.

Armstrong gave a monosyllabic opinion of that advice and pulled a cartridge from his pouch. A bullet had grazed Clouter's back leaving a bloody welt like the stroke of a lash, but the big man was paying it no heed.

He was stuffing another cask of musket balls into the carronade, though by now the *Pucelle* had gone beyond the *Redoutable* and the Frenchman was out of Clouter's range.

Captain Chase still lived. Connors, the signal lieutenant, had lost his right forearm to a cannon ball and was down in the cockpit, while Pearson, a midshipman who had twice failed his lieutenant's examination, had been killed by the musketry. The marine lieutenant was wounded in the belly and had been taken below to die. A dozen gunners were dead and two marines had been thrown overboard, but Chase reckoned the *Pucelle* had still been lucky. She had destroyed the *Redoutable* just as that ship had been on the point of boarding the *Victory*, and Chase felt an exultation as he looked back to see the terrible damage his guns had done. They had filleted her, by God! Chase had half considered laying alongside the *Redoutable* and boarding her, but she was already lashed to the *Victory* and doubtless the flagship's crew would take her surrender, then he saw the French *Neptune* ahead and he shouted at the helmsman to steer for her. 'She's ours!' he told Haskell.

The first lieutenant was bleeding from a bullet wound in his left arm, though he refused to have it treated. The arm hung useless, but Haskell claimed it did not hurt and, besides, he said, he was right-handed. Blood dripped from his fingers. 'At least get the arm bandaged,' Chase suggested, staring at the *Neptune*, which was making surprising speed despite the loss of her mizzenmast. She must have sailed clean round the western edge of the mêlée while the *Pucelle* passed to its east, and now the Frenchman was heading landwards as though trying to escape the battle.

'I'm sure Pickering is quite busy enough without having to be detained by scratched lieutenants,' Haskell answered testily.

Chase took off his white silk stock and beckoned to Midshipman Collier. 'Tie that round Lieutenant Haskell's arm,' he ordered the midshipman, then turned to the quartermaster. 'Starboard, John,' he said, gesturing, 'starboard.' The *Neptune* was threatening to cross the *Pucelle*'s bows and Chase needed to avoid that, but he reckoned he had speed enough to catch the Frenchman, lay her alongside and fight her muzzle to muzzle, and, because she carried eighty-four guns and he only had seventy-four, his victory would be all the more remarkable.

Then disaster struck.

The *Pucelle* had sailed past the *Victory* and the *Redoutable*, leaving a thick cloud of smoke that drifted after her, and out of that cloud there appeared the bows of an undamaged ship. Her figurehead showed a ghostly skeleton, scythe in one hand and a French tricolour in the other, and she was crossing behind the *Pucelle*, not a pistol's length away, and the whole of her larboard broadside was facing the *Pucelle*'s decorated stern.

'Hard to starboard!' Chase shouted at the quartermaster who had already begun the turn which would bring the *Pucelle*'s larboard broadside to face the *Neptune*, but then the new enemy fired and the very first shot ripped away the tiller ropes so that the wheel spun uselessly in the quartermaster's hands. The rudder, no longer tensioned by the ropes, centred itself and the *Pucelle* swung back to larboard, leaving her stern naked to the enemy guns. She would be raked.

A shot screamed down the weather deck, killing eight sailors and wounding a dozen more. The shot left a spattering trail of blood the whole length of the deck, and the next shot cut Haskell in half, leaving his torso on the starboard rail and his legs hanging from the quarterdeck's forward rail. Collier, still holding the silk stock, was smothered in Haskell's blood. The fourth shot shattered the *Pucelle*'s wheel and impaled the quartermaster on its splintered spokes. Chase leaned on the broken quarterdeck rail. 'Tiller ropes!' he shouted. 'Mister Peel! Tiller ropes! And hard to starboard!'

'Aye aye, sir! Hard to starboard!'

More shots broke through the stern. The *Pucelle* was shaking from the impact. Musket bullets cracked on her poop. 'Walk with me, Mister Collier,' Chase said, seeing that the boy seemed close to tears, 'just walk with me.' He paced up and down the quarterdeck, one hand on Collier's shoulder. 'We are being raked, Mister Collier. It is a pity.' He took the boy under the break of the poop, close to the mangled remains of the wheel and the quartermaster. 'And you will stay here, Harold Collier, and note the signals. Watch the clock! And keep an eye on me. If I fall you are to find Mister Peel and tell him the ship is his. Do you understand?'

'Yes, sir.' Collier tried to sound confident, but his voice was shaking.

'And a word of advice, Mister Collier. When you command a ship of your own, take great care never to be raked.' Chase patted the midshipman's shoulder, then walked back into the musket fire that pitted the quarterdeck. The enemy's cannons still raked the *Pucelle*, shot after shot demolishing the high windows, throwing down cannon and spraying blood on the deck beams overhead. The remains of the mizzenmast were cut through below the decks and Chase watched appalled as the whole mast slowly toppled, tearing itself out of the poop deck as it collapsed to starboard. It went slowly, the shrouds parting with sounds like pistol shots, and the mainmast swayed as the stay connecting it to the mizzen tightened, then that cable parted and the mizzen creaked, splintered and finally fell. The enemy cheered. Chase leaned over the broken quarterdeck rail to see a dozen men hauling on one of the spare tiller lines that had been rove before the battle. 'Pull hard, lads!' he shouted, bellowing to be heard above the sound of the enemy's guns that still hammered into the *Pucelle*. A twenty-four-pounder cannon lay on its side, trapping a screaming man. One of the starboard carronades on the quarterdeck had been punched off its carriage. The great white ensign trailed in the water. None of the *Pucelle*'s guns could answer, nor could they until the ship turned. 'Pull hard!' Chase shouted and saw Lieutenant Peel, hatless and sweating, add his weight to the tiller rope. The ship began to turn, but it was the mizzenmast, with its sail and rigging that lay in the water off the *Pucelle*'s starboard quarter, that did most to drag the ship around. She came slowly, still being punished by the French ship that had sailed out of the mêlée's smoke.

She was the *Revenant*. Chase recognized her, saw Montmorin standing coolly on his quarterdeck, saw the smoke of the Frenchman's guns sweeping up into her undamaged rigging and heard the terrible sounds of his ship being battered beneath his feet, but at last the *Pucelle* responded to the drag of the mizzen and the tug of the tiller and Chase's starboard broadside could begin to respond, though some of his guns had been dismounted and others had dead crews and so his first broadside was feeble. No more than seven guns fired. 'Close the larboard ports,' Chase called down the weather deck. 'All crews to starboard! Lively now!'

The *Pucelle* slowly came to life. She had been stunned by her raking, but Chase led a score of seamen up to the poop to cut away the mizzen's wreckage, and below decks the surviving gunners from the larboard cannon went to make up the crews of the starboard broadside. The *Revenant* turned to larboard, plainly intending to run alongside the *Pucelle*. Her forecastle was crowded with men armed with cutlasses and boarding pikes, but the remaining starboard carronade on Chase's quarterdeck ripped them away. John Hopper, the bosun of Chase's barge crew, commanded that gun. Chase slashed through a last shroud with a boarding axe, left a petty officer to clear the mess on the poop deck and went back to his quarterdeck as the *Revenant* crept closer and closer. The *Pucelle*'s starboard guns were firing properly now, their crews reinforced at last, and the shots were splintering holes in the *Revenant*'s side, but then the first of the Frenchman's guns were reloaded and Chase watched their blackened muzzles appear in the gunports. Smoke billowed. He saw the *Revenant*'s sails quiver to the shock of her guns, felt his own ship tremble as the balls struck home, saw young Collier standing at the starboard rail staring at the approaching enemy. 'What are you doing here, Mister Collier?' Chase asked.

'My duty, sir.'

'I told you to watch the clock in the poop, didn't I?'

'There ain't no clock, sir. It went.' The boy, in mute proof, held up the twisted enamel of the clock's face.

'Then go down to the orlop deck, Mister Collier, and don't disturb the surgeon, but in his dispensary there is a net of oranges, a gift from Admiral Nelson. Bring them up for the gun crews.'

'Aye aye, sir.'

Chase looked back and saw the *Victory*. A signal flew from her rigging and Chase did not need a signal lieutenant to translate the flags. 'Engage the enemy more closely.' Well, he was about to do that, and he was engaging a virtually undamaged enemy ship while his own had been grievously hurt, but by God, Chase thought, he would make Nelson proud. Chase did not blame himself for being raked. In this kind of battle, a wild mêlée with ships milling about in smoke, it would be a miracle if any captain was not raked, and he was proud that his men had turned the ship before the *Revenant* could empty her whole broadside into the *Pucelle*'s stern. She could still fight. Beyond the *Victory*, beyond the smoke that lay about her, beyond the embattled ships, some dismasted, he could see the undamaged rigging of the British vessels that formed the rearmost part of each squadron and those ships, not yet committed, were only just entering the battle. The *Santisima Trinidad*, towering over both fleets like a behemoth, was being raked and pounded by smaller ships that looked like terriers yapping at a bull. The French *Neptune* had vanished, and the *Pucelle* was threatened by the *Revenant* alone, but the *Revenant* had somehow escaped the worst of the fighting and Montmorin, as fine a captain as any in the French navy, was determined to pluck some honour from the day.

Two seamen dragged the *Pucelle*'s soaking white ensign onto the quarterdeck, smearing Haskell's blood with the sopping folds of the heavy flag. 'Run it up to the main topsail yard, larboard side,' Chase ordered. It would look odd there, but by God he would fly it to show that the *Pucelle* was undefeated.

Musket balls began striking the deck. Montmorin had fifty or sixty men in his upperworks and they would now try to do what the *Redoutable* had done to the *Victory*. He would clear the *Pucelle*'s decks and Chase desperately wanted to retreat into the shelter of the damaged poop, but his place was here, in full view, and so he put his hands behind his back and tried to look calm as he paced up and down the deck. He resisted the temptation to extend each length of the deck until he was under the poop, but forced himself to turn a few paces short, though he did stop once to stare in fascination at the mangled remains of the binnacle and its compass. A musket ball thumped the deck by his feet and he turned and paced back. He should have summoned a lieutenant from below decks to replace Haskell, but he decided against it. If he fell then his men knew what to do. Just fight. That was all there was to do now. Just fight, and Chase's life or death would make small difference to the outcome, whereas the lieutenants, commanding the guns, were doing something useful.

The crews of the two larboard carronades, which had no targets, were levering the fallen starboard carronade out of the way so that they could drag one of their two guns to replace it. Chase skipped out of their way, then saw Midshipman Collier on the weather deck where he was handing out oranges from his huge net. 'Throw one here, lad!' he called to the boy.

Collier looked alarmed at the order, as though he feared to throw something at his captain, but he tossed the orange underhand as if he was bowling a cricket ball and Chase had to lunge to one side to catch it single-handed. Some gunners cheered the catch and Chase held the orange aloft like a trophy, then tossed it to Hopper.

Captain Llewellyn's marines were firing at the French in their fighting tops, but the French were more numerous and their lashing fire was thinning Llewellyn's ranks. 'Shelter your men as best you can, Llewellyn,' Chase ordered.

'If I can take some to the maintop, sir?' the Welshman suggested.

'No, no, I gave my word to Nelson. Shelter them. Your time will come soon enough. Under the break of the poop, Llewellyn. You can fire from there.'

'You should come with us, sir.'

'I feel like taking the air, Llewellyn,' Chase said with a smile. In truth he was terrified. He kept thinking of his wife, his house, the children. In her last letter Florence had said that one of the ponies had a sickness, but which one? The cob? Was it better? He tried to think of such domestic things, wondering if the apple harvest was good and whether the stable yard had been repaved and why the parlour chimney smoked so bad when the wind was in the east, but in truth he just wanted to dash into the poop's shadow and so be protected from the musketry by the deck planks above. He wanted to cower, but his job was to stay on his quarterdeck. That was why he was paid four hundred and eighteen pounds and twelve shillings a year, and so he paced up and down, up and down, made conspicuous by his cocked hat and gilded epaulettes, and he tried to divide four hundred and eighteen pounds and twelve shillings by three hundred and sixty-five days and the Frenchmen aimed their muskets at him so that Chase walked a strip of deck that became ever more lumpy and ragged from bullet strikes. He saw the ship's barber, a one-eyed Irishman, hauling on a weather-deck gun. At this moment, Chase reckoned, that man was more valuable to the ship than its captain. He paced on, knowing he would be hit soon, hoping it would not hurt too badly, regretting his death so keenly and wishing he could see his children one more time. He was frightened, but it was unthinkable to do anything else but show a cool disdain for danger.

He turned and stared westwards. The mêlée about the *Victory* had grown, but he could distinctly see a British ensign flying above a French tricolour, showing that at least one enemy ship had struck. Farther south there was a second mêlée where Collingwood's squadron had cut off the rear of the French and Spanish fleet. Away to the east, beyond the *Revenant*, a handful of enemy ships shamefully sailed away, while to the north the enemy vanguard had at last turned and was lumbering southwards to help their beleaguered comrades. The battle, Chase reckoned, could only get worse, for a dozen ships on either side had yet to engage, but his fight was with Montmorin now.

The *Pucelle* shuddered as the *Revenant* slammed into her side. The force of the collision, broadside to broadside, two thousand tons meeting two thousand tons, drove the two ships apart again, but Chase shouted at the few remaining men on his top decks to throw the grapnels and make the *Revenant* fast. The hooks flew into the enemy's rigging, but the enemy had the same idea and her crew was also hurling grappling hooks, while seamen in the Frenchman's rigging were tying the *Pucelle*'s lower yards to their own. To the death, then. Neither ship could escape now, they could only kill each other. The rails of the two ships were thirty feet apart because their lower hulls bulged out so greatly, but Chase was close enough to see Montmorin's expression and the Frenchman, seeing Chase, took off his hat and bowed. Chase did the same. Chase wanted to laugh and Montmorin was smiling, both men struck by the oddity of such courtesies even as they did their best to kill each other. Beneath their silver-buckled feet the great guns gouged and hammered. Chase wished he had an orange to throw to Montmorin who, he was sure, would appreciate the gesture, but he could not see Collier.

Chase did not know it, but his presence on the deck was directly useful, for the French marksmen in the fighting tops were obsessed by his death and so ignored the carronade crews which, seeing French seamen gather in the *Revenant*'s waist, fired down into the mass. The Frenchmen had been snatching boarding pikes from their racks about the mainmast, while others held axes or cutlasses, but one carronade forward and one aft provided a tangling crossfire that destroyed the boarding party. The French had no carronades, relying on the men in their fighting tops to clear an enemy's deck with musket fire.

Ten marines were left on the *Pucelle*'s forecastle. Sergeant Armstrong, bleeding to death, still sat by the foremast and clumsily fired his musket up into the enemy rigging. Clouter, his black torso streaked and spattered by other men's blood, had taken command of the starboard carronade after half its crew was killed by a grenade thrown from the *Revenant*'s foremast. Sharpe was firing up into the maintop, hoping his bullets would gouge through its timbers to kill the French marksmen perched on the platform. The wind seemed to have died completely so that the sails and flags hung limp. Powder smoke thickened between the ships, rising to hide and protect the *Pucelle*'s bullet-lashed deck. Sharpe was deaf now, his ears buffeted by the big guns and his world shrunken to this small patch of bloody deck and the smoke-wreathed enemy rigging soaring above him. His shoulder was bruised by the musket so that he flinched every time he fired. An orange rolled across the deck at his feet, its skin dimpling the blood on the planks. He brought the musket's brass-bound stock hard down on the orange, squashing and bursting the fruit, then stooped and scooped up some of the pulped flesh. He ate some, grateful for the juice in his parched mouth, then scooped some more which he put into Armstrong's mouth. The sergeant's unbloodied eye was glassy, he was scarce conscious, but he was still trying to reload his musket. He coughed hoarsely, mingling bloody spittle with the orange juice that trickled down his chin. 'We are winning, aren't we?' he asked Sharpe earnestly.

'We're murdering the bastards, Sergeant.'

The dead lay where they fell now, for there were not enough men to throw them overboard, or rather the men who remained were too busy fighting. The worst of that fight was below decks where the two ships, matched gun to gun, mangled each other. The lower deck was dark now, for the *Revenant* blotted out the daylight on the starboard side and the larboard gunports were closed. Smoke filled the low deck, curling under beams splashed with blood from the *Revenant*'s first raking broadside. Now the Frenchman's shots broke open the hull, screamed across the deck and crashed out to leave patches of newly created daylight where they holed the larboard side. Thick dust and thicker smoke drifted in the shafts of light. The *Pucelle*'s guns returned the fire, roaring back on their breeching ropes to fill the deck with thunder. The ships touched here, their gunports almost coinciding so that when a British gunner tried to swab his cannon a French cutlass half severed his arm, then the lambswool swab on its staff was seized and carried aboard the French ship. The French shots were heavier, for they carried larger guns, but larger guns took longer to reload and the British fire was noticeably quicker. Montmorin's crew was probably the best trained in all the enemy's fleet, yet still Chase's men were faster, but now the enemy tossed grenades through the open gunports and fired muskets to slow the British guns.

'Fetch marines!' Lieutenant Holderby shouted at a midshipman, then had to go right up to the boy and cup his hands over the midshipman's ear. 'Fetch marines!' A round shot killed the lieutenant, spewing his intestines across the gratings where the thirty-two-pound round shots were stored. The midshipman stayed still for a second, disoriented. Flames were rising to his left, then a gunner threw sand across the remnants of the grenade and another tossed a cask of water to douse the fire. Another gunner was crawling on the deck, vomiting blood. A woman was hauling on a gun tackle, spitting curses at the French gunners who were only a cutlass length away. A gun recoiled, filling the deck with noise and breaking its breeching rope so that it slewed round and crushed two men whose shrieks were lost in the din. Men heaved and rammed, their naked torsos gleaming with sweat that trickled through the powder residue. They all looked black now, except where they were spotted or streaked or sheeted with blood. The *Revenant*'s powder smoke belched into the *Pucelle*, choking men who struggled to return the favour.

The midshipman scrambled up the companionway to the weather deck that shook from the recoil of its twenty-four-pounder guns. Wreckage of the rigging lay across the central part of the deck which was so thick with smoke that the midshipman climbed to the forecastle instead of to the quarterdeck. His ears were ringing with the sound of the guns and his throat was as dry as ash. He saw an officer in a red coat. 'You're wanted below, sir.'

'What?' Sharpe shouted.

'Marines, sir, needed below.' The boy's voice was hoarse. 'They're coming through the gunports, sir. Lower deck.' A bullet smacked into the deck beside his feet, another ricocheted off the ship's bell.

'Marines!' Sharpe bellowed. 'Pikes! Muskets!'

He led his ten men down the companionway, stepped over the body of a powder monkey who lay dead though there was not a mark on his young body that Sharpe could see, then down to the hellish dark and thick gloom of the lower deck. Only half of the starboard cannons were firing now, and they were being impeded by the French who slashed through the gunports with cutlasses and pikes. Sharpe fired his musket through a gunport, glimpsed a Frenchman's face dissolve into blood, ran to the next and used the butt of the empty musket to hammer an enemy's arm. 'Simmons!' he shouted at a marine. 'Simmons!'

Simmons stared at him, wide-eyed. 'Go to the forward magazine,' Sharpe shouted. 'Fetch the grenades!'

Simmons ran, grateful for a chance to be beneath the water line even if only for an instant. Three of the *Pucelle*'s heavy guns fired together, their sound almost stunning Sharpe, who was going from gunport to gunport and stabbing at the French with his cutlass. A huge crash, dreadful in its loudness and so prolonged that it seemed to go on for ever, broke through Sharpe's deafened ears and he reckoned a mast had gone overboard, though whether it was another of the *Pucelle*'s or one of the *Revenant*'s he could not tell. He saw a Frenchman ramming a cannon, half leaning out of the opposing gunport, and he skewered the man's arm with the cutlass. The Frenchman sprang back and Sharpe skipped aside for he could see the gunner holding the linstock to the touch-hole. Sharpe registered that the French did not use flintlocks, was surprised to have noticed such a thing in battle, then the gun fired and the rammer, left in the barrel, disintegrated as it was driven across the *Pucelle*'s deck. A midshipman fired a pistol into an enemy gunport. A flintlock sparked and the sound of the heavy gun pounded Sharpe's ears. Some of the men had lost the scarves they had tied about their heads and their ears dribbled blood. Others had bleeding noses caused by nothing more than the sound of the guns.

Simmons reappeared with the grenades and Sharpe took a linstock from one of the remaining water barrels, lit its fuse, then waited until the vagaries of the ocean swells brought a French gunport into view. The fuse sputtered. He could see the *Revenant*'s yellow planking, then the opposing ship ground against the *Pucelle*'s hull and a gunport came into sight and he hurled the glass ball into the *Revenant*. He dimly heard an explosion, saw flames illuminate the black smoke filling the enemy's gundeck, then he left Simmons to throw the other grenades while he went back down the deck, stepping past bodies, avoiding the gunners, checking each gunport to make sure no more Frenchmen were trying to reach through with cutlass or pike. The big capstan in the middle of the deck, used to haul the ship's anchor cables, had an enemy round shot buried in its wooden heart. Blood dripped from the deck above. A gun, crammed with grapeshot, recoiled across his path and Frenchmen screamed.

Then another scream pierced Sharpe's ringing ears. It came from above, from the weather deck that was slick with so much blood that the sand no longer gave men a secure footing. 'Repel boarders! Repel boarders!'

'Marines!' Sharpe shouted at his few men, though none heard him in the noise, but he reckoned some might follow if they saw him climb the companionway. He could hear steel striking steel. No time to think, just time to fight.

He climbed.

Lord William frowned at the sound of the carronade, then flinched as the *Pucelle*'s larboard broadside began to fire, the sound rolling down the ship to fill the lady hole with thunder. 'I perceive we are still in action,' he said, lowering the pistol. He began to laugh. 'It was worth pointing a gun at your head, my dear, just to see your expression. But was it remorse or fear that actuated your misery?' He paused. 'Come! I wish an answer.'

'Fear,' Lady Grace gasped.

'Yet I should like to hear you express remorse, if only as evidence that you possess some finer feelings. Do you?' He waited. The guns fired, the sound becoming louder as the nearer cannon recoiled two decks above their refuge.

'If you had any feelings,' Grace said, 'any courage, you would be on deck sharing the dangers.'

Lord William found that very amusing. 'What a strange idea you do have of my capabilities. What can I do that would be useful to Chase? My talents, dearest, lie in the contrivance of policy and, dare I say, its administration. The report I am writing will have a profound influence on the future of India and, therefore, on the prospects of Britain. I confidently expect to join the government within a year. Within five years I might be Prime Minister. Am I to risk that future just to strut on a deck with a pack of mindless fools who believe a brawl at sea will change the world?' He shrugged and looked up at the lady hole's ceiling. 'Towards the end of the fight, my dear, I shall show myself, but I have no intention of running any unnecessary or extraordinary risks. Let Nelson have his glory today, but in five years I shall dispose of him as I wish and, believe me, no adulterer will gain honour from me. You know he is an adulterer?'

'All England knows.'

'All Europe,' Lord William corrected her. 'The man is incapable of discretion and you too, my dear, have been indiscreet.' The *Pucelle*'s broadside had stopped and the ship seemed silent. Lord William looked up at the deck as if he expected the noise to begin again, but the guns were quiet. Water gurgled at the stern. The ship's pumps began again. 'I might not have minded,' Lord William went on, 'had you been discreet. No man wishes to be a cuckold, but it is one thing for a wife to take a genteel lover and quite another to lie down with the servant classes. Were you mad? That would be a charitable excuse, but the world does not see you as mad, so your action reflects upon me. You chose to rut with an animal, a lump, and I suspect he has made you pregnant. You disgust me.' He shuddered. 'Every man on the ship must have known you were rutting. They thought I did not know, they sneered at me, and you went on like a tuppenny whore.'

Lady Grace said nothing. She stared up at one of the lanterns. Its candle was guttering, spewing a dribble of smoke that escaped through the lantern's ventilation holes. She was red-eyed, exhausted from crying, incapable of fighting back.

'I should have known all this when I married you,' Lord William said. 'One hopes, one does so hope, that a wife will prove a woman of fidelity, of prudence and quiet good sense, but why should I have expected it? Women have ever been slaves to their grosser appetites. "Frailty,"' he quoted, '"thy name is woman!" The feeble sex, and by God how true that is! I found it hard to credit Braithwaite's letter at first, but the more I thought about it, the more true it rang, and so I observed you and found, to my disappointment, that he did not lie. You were rutting with Sharpe, wallowing in his sweat.'

'Be quiet!' she pleaded with him.

'Why should I be quiet?' he asked in a reasonable voice. 'I, my dear, am the offended party. You had your moment's filthy pleasure with a mindless brute, why should I not have my moment of pleasure now? I have earned it, have I not?' He raised the pistol again, just as the whole ship shook with a terrible blow, then another, blows so loud that Lord William instinctively ducked his head, and still the blows went on, rending the ship and crashing through the decks and making the *Pucelle* shudder. Lord William, his anger momentarily displaced by fear, stared up at the deck as if expecting the ship to fall apart. The lanterns quivered, noise filled the universe and the guns kept firing.

The crash Sharpe had heard when he was on the lower deck had been the *Revenant*'s mainmast collapsing across both ships and, when he reached the weather deck, he saw Frenchmen running across the mast that, together with the *Revenant*'s fallen main yard, served as a bridge between the two ships' decks. The *Pucelle*'s gunners had abandoned their cannon to fight the invaders with cutlasses, handspikes, rammers and pikes. Captain Llewellyn was bringing marines from the poop, but taking them along the starboard gangway which ran above the weather deck beside the ship's gunwale. A dozen Frenchmen were on that gangway and trying to reach the *Pucelle*'s stern. More Frenchmen were in the waist of the ship, screaming their war cry and hacking with cutlasses. Their attack, as sudden as it was unexpected, had succeeded in clearing the centre section of the weather deck where the invaders now stabbed at fallen gunners, as a bespectacled French officer hurled overboard the cannons' rammers and swabs. Still more Frenchmen ran along the fallen mainmast and yard to reinforce their comrades.

The *Pucelle*'s crew began to counterattack. A seaman flailed with one of the handspikes used to shift the cannon, a vast club of wood that crushed a Frenchman's skull. Others seized pikes and speared at the French. Sharpe drew the long cutlass and met the invaders under the break of the forecastle. He slashed at one, parried another, then lunged at the first to spit the man on his cutlass blade. He kicked the dying Frenchman off the steel, then swung the bloody blade to drive two more boarders back. One of them was a huge man, thick-bearded, carrying an axe, and he chopped the blade at Sharpe who stepped back, surprised by the bearded man's long reach, and his right foot slid in a pool of blood and he fell back and twisted aside as the axe split the deck next to his head. He stabbed up, trying and failing to rake the Frenchman's arm with the cutlass point, then rolled to his left as the axe slammed down again. The Frenchman kicked Sharpe hard in the thigh, wrenched the axe free and raised it a third time, but before he could deliver the killing stroke he uttered a scream as a pike slid into his belly. There was a roar above Sharpe as Clouter, letting go of the pike, seized the axe from the Frenchman's hand and charged on in a frenzy. Sharpe stood and followed, leaving the bearded Frenchman twisting and shaking on the deck, the pike still buried in his guts.

Thirty or forty Frenchmen were in the ship's waist now, and more were streaming along the mast, but just then a carronade blasted from the quarterdeck and emptied the makeshift bridge. One man, left untouched on the mast, jumped down to the *Pucelle*'s deck and Clouter, almost underneath him, brought the axe up between the man's legs. The scream seemed to be the loudest noise Sharpe had heard in all that furious day. A tall French officer, hatless and with a powder-stained face, led a charge towards the *Pucelle*'s bows. Clouter knocked the man's sword aside then punched him in the face so hard that the officer recoiled into his own men, then a swarm of British gunners, screaming and stabbing, swept past the black man to hack at the invaders.

The guns pounded below, grinding and mangling the two ships. Captain Chase was fighting on the weather deck, leading a group of men who assailed the French from the stern. Captain Llewellyn's marines had recaptured the gangway and now guarded the fallen mast, shooting down any Frenchman who tried to cross, while the remaining invaders were caught between the attack from the stern and the assault from the bows. Clouter was back in the front rank, chopping the axe in short hard strokes that felled a man each time. Sharpe trapped a Frenchman against the ship's side, beneath the gangway. The man lunged his cutlass at Sharpe, had it effortlessly parried, saw death in the redcoat's face and so, in desperation, squirmed through a gunport and threw himself down between the ships. He screamed as the seas drove the two hulls together. Sharpe leaped the gun, looking for an enemy. The *Pucelle*'s waist was filled with hacking, stabbing, shouting seamen who ignored the desperate shouts for quarter from the French whose impetuous attempt to capture the *Pucelle* had been foiled by the carronade. The bespectacled enemy officer still tried to render the *Pucelle*'s guns useless by jettisoning their rammers, but Clouter threw the axe and its blade thumped into the man's skull like a tomahawk and his death seemed to still the frenzy, or perhaps it was Captain Chase's insistent voice shouting that the *Pucelle*s should stop fighting because the remaining Frenchmen were trying to surrender. 'Take their weapons!' Chase bellowed. 'Take their weapons!'

Only a score of Frenchmen were still standing and, disarmed, they were shepherded towards the stern. 'I don't want them below,' Chase said, 'they could make mischief. Buggers can stand on the poop instead and be shot at.' He grinned at Sharpe. 'Glad you sailed with me?'

'Hot work, sir.' Sharpe looked for Clouter and hailed him. 'You saved my life,' he told the tall man. 'Thank you.'

Clouter looked astonished. 'I didn't even see you, sir.'

'You saved my life,' Sharpe insisted.

Clouter gave a strange, high-pitched laugh. 'But we killed some, didn't we? Didn't we just kill some?'

'Plenty left to kill,' Chase said, then cupped his hands. 'Back to the guns! Back to the guns!' He saw the purser peering nervously from the forward companionway. 'Mister Cowper! I'll trouble you to find rammers and swabs for this deck. Lively now! Back to the guns!'

Like two bare-knuckled boxers, deep in their thirtieth or fortieth round, both bleeding and dazed, yet neither willing to give up, the two ships pounded each other. Sharpe climbed to the quarterdeck with Chase. To the west, where the long swells came so high, the sea was all battle. Nearly a dozen ships fought there. To the south another score blazed at each other. The ocean was thick with wreckage. A mastless hulk, its guns silent, drifted away from the mêlée. Five or six pairs of ships, like the *Pucelle* and the *Revenant*, were clasped together, exchanging fire in private battles that took place beyond the bigger mêlée. The towering *Santisima Trinidad* had lost her foremast and most of her mizzen and still she was being hammered by smaller British ships. The powder smoke now spread across two miles of ocean, a man-made fog. The sky was darkening to the north and west. Some of the enemy ships, not daring to come close to the fighting and looking to escape, bombarded the brawling fleets from a distance, but their shots were as much a danger to their own side as to the British. The very last of the British ships, the slowest of the fleet, were only just entering the fray and opening fresh gunports to add their metal to the carnage.

Capitaine Montmorin looked across at Chase and shrugged, as if to suggest that the failure of his boarders was regrettable but not serious. The Frenchman's guns were firing still, and Sharpe could see more boarders gathering on the *Revenant*'s weather deck. He could also see Captain Cromwell, peering from the shelter of the poop, and Sharpe seized a musket from a nearby marine and aimed at the Englishman who, seeing the threat, ducked back out of sight. Sharpe handed the musket back. Chase found a speaking trumpet amidst the wreckage on the deck. 'Captain Montmorin? You should yield before we kill more of your men!'

Montmorin cupped his hands. 'I was going to offer you the same chance, Captain Chase!'

'Look there,' Chase shouted, pointing beyond his own stern, and Montmorin climbed up his mizzen ratlines to see over the *Pucelle*'s poop and there, ghosting across the swells, untouched, was the *Spartiate*, a British seventy-four, the French-built ship that was rumoured to be bewitched because she sailed faster by night than by day and now, coming late to the battle, she opened her larboard gunports.

Montmorin knew what was about to happen and he could do nothing to stop it. He was going to be raked and so he shouted at his men to lie down between the guns, though that would not save them from the *Pucelle*'s gunfire, then he stood in the centre of his quarterdeck and waited.

The *Spartiate* gave Montmorin's ship a full broadside. One after another the guns crashed back and their balls smashed the high gallery windows of the *Revenant*'s stern and screamed down her decks, just as the *Revenant* had raked the *Pucelle* earlier. The *Spartiate* was painfully slow, but that only gave her gunners more time to aim properly, and the broadside drove deep wounds into the *Revenant*. Her mizzen shrouds parted with a sound like Satan's harp strings snapping, then the whole mast toppled, splintering like a monstrous tree to carry yards, sails and tricolour overboard. Sharpe heard the French musketeers screaming as they fell with the mast. Guns were thrown off carriages, men were mangled by round shot and grapeshot, and still Montmorin stood unmoving, even when the wheel was shot away behind him. Only when the last of the *Spartiate*'s guns had sounded did he turn and look at the ship that had raked him. He must have feared that she would put up her helm and lay alongside his starboard flank, but the *Spartiate* sailed grandly on, seeking a victim all her own.

'Yield, *Capitaine*!' Chase shouted through the speaking trumpet.

Montmorin gave his answer by cupping his hands and shouting down to his weather deck. '*Tirez*! *Tirez*!' He turned and bowed to Chase.

Chase looked about the quarterdeck. 'Where's Captain Llewellyn?' he asked a marine.

'Broken leg, sir. Gone below.'

'Lieutenant Swallow?' Swallow was the young marine lieutenant.

'Think he's dead, sir. Badly wounded, anyway.'

Chase looked at Sharpe, paused as the *Revenant*'s guns opened fire again. 'Assemble a boarding party, Mister Sharpe,' Chase said formally.

It was always going to be a fight to the finish, right from the moment the *Pucelle* had first seen the *Revenant* off the African coast. And now Sharpe would finish it.

CHAPTER 12

Lord William listened to the guns, but it was impossible to tell how the battle went from their sound alone, though it was plain that the fighting had reached a new level of fury. '*Si fractus inlabatur orbis*,' he said, raising his eyes to the deck above.

Grace said nothing.

Lord William chuckled. 'Oh, come, my dear, don't tell me you have forgotten your Horace? It is one of the things that most annoys me about you; that you cannot resist translating my tags.'

'If the sky should break,' Lady Grace said dully.

'Oh come! That is hardly adequate, is it?' Lord William asked sternly. 'I grant you sky for *orbis*, though I would prefer universe, but the verb demands falling, does it not? You were never the Latinist you thought you were.' He looked up again as a dolorous thump echoed through the ship's timbers. 'It does indeed sound as though the broken sky falls. Are you frightened? Or do you feel yourself to be entirely safe here?'

Lady Grace said nothing. She felt bereft of tears, gone to a place of abject misery that was beset by guns, horror, spite and hate.

'I am safe here,' Lord William went on, 'but you, my dear, are beset by fears, so much so that in a moment you will seize my pistol and turn it on yourself. You feared, I shall say, a repetition of that amusing episode on the *Calliope* when your lover so bravely rescued you, and I shall claim it was impossible to prevent you from destroying yourself. I shall, of course, demonstrate an abject though dignified sadness at your demise. I shall insist that your precious body is carried home so that I may bury you in Lincolnshire. Black plumes shall crown your funerary horses, the bishop will pronounce the obsequies and my tears shall moisten your vault. All will be done properly, and your tombstone, cut from the very finest marble, will record your virtues. It will not say that you were a sordid fornicator who opened her legs to a common soldier, but rather that you combined wisdom with understanding, grace with charity and possessed a Christian forbearance that was a shining example of womanhood. Would you like the inscription in Latin?'

She gazed at him, but did not speak.

'And when you are dead, my love,' Lord William went on, 'and safely buried beneath a slab recording your virtues, I shall set about destroying your lover. I shall do it quietly, Grace, subtly, so that he will never know the source of his misfortunes. Having him removed from the army will be simple, but what then? I shall think of something, indeed it will provide me with pleasure to contemplate his fate. A hanging, don't you think? I doubt I shall be able to convict him for poor Braithwaite's death, which he undoubtedly caused, but I shall contrive something, and when he is dangling there, twitching, and pissing in his breeches, I shall watch and I shall smile and I shall remember you.'

She still stared at him, her face expressionless.

'I shall remember you,' he said again, unable to hide the hatred he felt for her. 'I shall remember that you were a common whore, a slave to your filthy lusts, a slut who let a commoner roger her.' He raised the pistol.

The guns, two decks above, began to fire again, their recoil shaking the timbers clear down to the lady hole.

But the pistol shot sounded much louder than the great guns. Its sound echoed in the confined space, filling it with thick smoke as bright blood splashed up the lady hole's planking. *Si fractus inlabatur orbis.*

The swells were getting bigger, the sky darker. The wind had risen a little, so that the smoke patches streamed eastwards, flowing round disabled ships that trailed masts and fallen rigging. The guns still punctured the air, but fewer now, for more enemy ships were yielding. Gigs, barges and longboats, some grievously damaged by shot, rowed between the combatants carrying British officers who went to accept an enemy's surrender. Some French and Spanish ships had struck their flags, but then, in the vagaries of battle, their opponents had moved on and those ships rehoisted their colours, hung what sail they could on their fractured masts and headed eastwards. Far more stayed as captured prizes, their decks a shambles, their hulls riddled and their crews stunned by the ferocity of the British gunfire. The British fired faster. They were better trained.

The *Redoutable*, still lashed to the *Victory*, was French no longer. She was scarcely even a ship, for all her masts were gone and her hull was mangled by cannon fire. A portion of her quarterdeck had collapsed and a British flag now hung over her counter. The *Victory*'s mizzen was gone, her fore- and mainmasts were mere stumps, but her guns were still manned and still dangerous. The vast *Santisima Trinidad* was silent, her ensign struck. The fiercest battle now was to the north of her where a few of the enemy vanguard had risked coming back to help their comrades and now opened fire on the battle-weary British ships that loaded and fired and rammed and fired again. To the south, where Collingwood's *Royal Sovereign* had opened the battle, a ship burned. The flames leaped twice as high as the masts and the other ships, fearing the firebrands that must be spewed when her magazines exploded, set sail to move away from her, though some British ships, knowing what horrors the crew of the burning ship endured, sent small boats to pluck them to safety. The burning ship was French, the *Achille*, and the sound of her explosion was a dull thump that rolled across the wreckage-littered sea like the crack of doom. A cloud of smoke, black as night, boiled where the burning ship had floated while scraps of fire seared to the clouds, fell to the sea, hissed in the ocean, died.

Nelson died.

Fourteen enemy ships had struck so far. A dozen more still fought. One was burned and sunk, the rest were fleeing.

Captain Montmorin, knowing that Chase intended to board him, had sent men with axes to cut away the fallen mainmast. Other men chopped through the grapnel lines that tied the *Revenant* to the *Pucelle.* Montmorin was trying to cut himself free, hoping he could limp away to Cadiz and live to fight another day.

'I want those carronades busy!' Chase shouted, and the gunners who had helped repel the boarders now ran to the squat weapons and levered them round to fire at the men trying to free the *Revenant*, which now had more troubles, for her foresail had caught fire. The flames spread with extraordinary swiftness, engulfing the great spread of shot-punctured canvas, but Montmorin's men were just as swift, cutting the halliards that held the sail's spar and so dropping it to the deck where they risked the fire to hurl the burning sail over the side. 'Let them be!' Chase bellowed at those of his men who were aiming muskets at the struggling French sailors. He knew the fire could spread to the *Pucelle* and both ships would then burn together and explode in horror. 'Well done! Well done!' Chase applauded his opponent's crew as they tipped the last burning wreckage overboard. Then the carronades recoiled on their slides and spat casks of musket balls which cut down the axemen still trying to free the two ships from their mutual embrace. A gun exploded on the *Revenant*, the sound echoing horribly as scraps of the shattered breech cut down Montmorin's lower-deck gunners. There were more British guns firing now, for the *Revenant* had lost a dozen when she was raked, and the *Pucelle* was hurting the Frenchman relentlessly. A midshipman, commanding the *Pucelle*'s lower-deck guns, saw that the two hulls were so close together that the muzzle flames of his thirty-two-pounders were setting fire to the splintered wood of the *Revenant*'s lower hull, so he ordered a half-dozen men to throw buckets of water at the small fires in case the flames caught and spread to the *Pucelle*.

'Marines!' Sharpe was shouting. 'Marines!' He had gathered thirty-two marines and supposed the rest were dead, wounded or else guarding either the magazines or the French prisoners on the poop. These thirty-two would have to suffice. 'We're boarding her!' Sharpe shouted over the bellow of the guns. 'You want pikes, axes, cutlasses. Make sure your muskets are loaded! Hurry!' He turned as he heard the sound of a sword scraping from a scabbard and saw Midshipman Collier, bright-eyed and still drenched in Lieutenant Haskell's blood, standing under the fallen French mainmast that would be the boarding bridge. 'What the hell are you doing here, Harry?' Sharpe asked.

'Coming with you, sir.'

'Like hell you are. Go and watch the bloody clock.'

'There isn't a clock.'

'Then just go and watch something else!' Sharpe snapped. The weather-deck gunners, bare-chested, blood-streaked and powder-blackened, were assembling with pikes and cutlasses. The lower-deck guns still fired, shaking both ships with every shot. A few French guns answered, and one ball smashed through the gathering boarders, driving a path of blood across the *Pucelle*'s deck. 'Who's got a volley gun?' Sharpe shouted, and a marine sergeant held up one of the stubby weapons. 'Is it loaded?' Sharpe asked.

'Yes, sir.'

'Then give it here.' He took the gun, exchanging it for his musket, then made sure his cutlass was not blood-crusted to its scabbard. 'Follow me up to the quarterdeck!' Sharpe shouted.

The fallen mast jutted across the weather deck, but was too high to be reached unless a man stood on a hot gun barrel and hauled himself up. It would be easier, Sharpe reckoned, to go to the quarterdeck, then return along the *Pucelle*'s starboard gangway. From there a man could step onto the mast. He would then have to run, balancing himself on the broken pine spar, before jumping down onto the *Revenant*'s deck, and because the two ships were moving unequally in the long high swells, the mast would be pitching and rolling. Jesus, Sharpe thought, sweet Jesus, but this was a terrible place to be. Like going through the breach of an enemy fortress, he reckoned. He ran up the quarterdeck steps, turned down the gangway and tried not to think of what was about to happen. There were French marines on the opposing gangway, and a horde of armed defenders waiting in the *Revenant*'s blood-drenched waist. Montmorin knew what was coming, but just then the forward carronade sent a shattering cask of musket balls into the *Revenant*'s belly and belched a pall of smoke above the ship.

'Now!' Sharpe said, and clambered up onto the mast, but a hand held him back and he turned, cursing, to see that it was Chase.

'Me first, Sharpe,' Chase chided him.

'Sir!' Sharpe protested.

'Now, boys!' Chase had his sword drawn and was running across the makeshift bridge.

'Come on!' Sharpe shouted. He ran behind Chase, the heavy seven-barrelled gun in his hands. It was like traversing a tightrope. He looked down to see the sea churning white between the two hulls and he felt dizzy and imagined falling to be crushed to death as the two hulls banged together, then a bullet spat past him and he saw Chase had jumped from the shattered stump of the mast and Sharpe followed, screaming as he leaped through the smoke.

Chase had gone left, jumping into a space cleared by the carronade, though it was still cluttered with twitching bodies and the deck was slick with new blood. He stumbled on the corpses and the Frenchmen saw him, his gold braid bright in the smoke, and they shouted as they charged, but then Sharpe fired the volley gun from the spar and the bullets twitched the French back in a cloud of smoke. Sharpe jumped down, threw the volley gun aside and drew his cutlass. He had leaped into the smoking madness of battle, not the deliberate calm of disciplined fighting when battalions fired volleys or when stately ships exchanged cannon fire, but the visceral horror of the gutter fight. Chase had fallen between two of the Frenchman's starboard guns, and they protected him, but Sharpe was exposed and he screamed at the enemy, flicked a pike aside with the cutlass, lunged at a man's eyes, missed, then a marine jumped onto the Frenchman's back, throwing him forward, and Sharpe stamped on the man's head as the marine was piked in the back. He swung the cutlass to the right, inadvertently foiling another pike thrust, then reached and seized the French seaman's shirt and pulled him forward, straight onto the cutlass blade. Sharpe twisted the steel in the man's belly, wrenched it free. He was shrieking like a fiend. He used both hands to swing the cutlass back to his left, driving away a French officer who stumbled over the dying British marine and fell back out of range. The dead were making a barricade to protect Sharpe and Chase, but a French marine was climbing over one of the guns. Chase scrambled to his feet, lunged his slender sword at his attacker, then fired a pistol across the other cannon. Sharpe swung the cutlass again, then cheered as a rush of British marines and seamen dropped to the deck.

'This way!' Sharpe leaped the dead, carrying the fight towards the *Revenant*'s bows. The French defenders were numerous, but the way aft was blocked by just as many men. Muskets cracked from the quarterdeck and more fired from the forecastle and at least one defender was killed by his own side in that wild fire. The *Revenant*'s men far outnumbered the boarders, but the British numbers increased every second and the *Pucelle*'s crewmen wanted revenge for the raking the *Revenant* had given them. They slashed and lunged and screamed and hit and battered men down. A gunner was swinging a handspike, swatted aside a sword, crushed a Frenchman's skull, then he was pushed on by the men behind. Chase was shouting at men to follow him aft towards the quarterdeck while Sharpe was leading a swarm of crazed men forward. 'Kill them!' he shrieked. 'Kill them!'

Afterwards he would remember little of that fight, but he rarely remembered such brawls. They were too confused, too loud, too full of horror, so full of horror, indeed, that he was ashamed when he remembered the joy of it, but there was a joy there. It was the happiness of being released to the slaughter, of having every bond of civilization removed. It was also what Richard Sharpe was good at. It was why he wore an officer's sash instead of a private's belt, because in almost every battle the moment came when the disciplined ranks dissolved and a man simply had to claw and scratch and kill like a beast. You did not kill men at long range in this kind of fighting, but came as close as a lover before you slaughtered them.

To go into that kind of fighting needed a rage, or a madness or a desperation. Some men never found those qualities and they shrank from the danger, and Sharpe could not blame them, for there was little that was admirable in rage, insanity or despair. Yet they were the qualities that drove the fight, and they were fuelled by a determination to win. Just that. To beat the bastards down, to prove that the enemy were lesser men. The good soldier was cock of a blood-soaked dunghill, and Richard Sharpe was good.

His rage went cold in a fight. The fear might harass him before the fighting began, and for two blunt pins he might have found an excuse not to cross the trembling mast bridge that would drop him into a crowd of the enemy, but once there he fought with a precision that was lethal. It seemed to him that the very passage of time slowed, so that he could see clearly what every enemy intended. A man to his right was drawing back a pike, so that threat could be ignored because it would take at least a heartbeat for the pike to come forward, and meanwhile a bearded man in front was already swinging down a cutlass and Sharpe twisted the point of his own blade into that man's throat, then whipped the cutlass to his right, parrying the pike thrust, though Sharpe himself was looking to his left. He saw no imminent danger, looked back to the right, flicked the blade up into the pikeman's face, looked front again, then shoulder charged the pikeman, driving him back so that he fell against a cannon and Sharpe could raise the cutlass and, with both hands, drive it down into the man's belly. The point stuck in the gun's timber carriage and Sharpe wasted a second wrenching it free. British seamen pounded past him, forcing the French another two or three paces back down their deck, and Sharpe climbed the cannon and jumped down its other side. A Frenchman tried to surrender to him there, but Sharpe dared not leave a man in his rear so he slashed at the Frenchman's wrist so he could not use the axe he had dropped, then kicked him in the groin before climbing the next cannon. The spaces between the cannon served as refuges for the French and Sharpe wanted to break them out and drive them onto the pikes and blades of the boarders.

Captain Chase's barge crew had followed him aft, fighting their own battle towards the quarterdeck steps, but Clouter had come late to the fight, for he had been the man who fired the *Pucelle*'s forward starboard carronade down into the mass of defenders just as Chase had led the charge across the mast. The big black man came across the fallen mainmast, leaped to the deck and headed aft, howling to be let through the crowded seamen. Once he was in the front rank he cleared the larboard side of the *Revenant*'s weather deck while Sharpe led the charge along the starboard side. Clouter was using an axe, swinging it one-handed, ignoring the men who tried to surrender, but just cutting them down in an orgy of killing. Men were surrendering now, throwing down axes or swords, holding up their hands or just throwing themselves to the deck where they pretended to be dead. Sharpe slashed a pike aside, cut his blade across a Frenchman's eyes, then found no one to oppose him, but a musket ball plucked at the hem of his jacket as he turned to look for his marines. 'Fire at those bastards!' he shouted, pointing up at the forecastle deck where some of Montmorin's crew still fought back. One of the marines aimed a seven-barrelled gun, but Sharpe snatched it from him. 'Use a musket, lad.'

He sheathed the cutlass, forcing the blood-clotted blade into the scabbard's throat, then ran through the defeated Frenchmen to where the forward companionway led down to the lower deck. The *Revenant* was the *Pucelle*'s sister ship, indeed it felt to Sharpe that he was fighting on the *Pucelle*, so alike were the two vessels. He pushed his way through the enemy, going into the shadow of the forecastle. A gunner half-heartedly rammed a cannon swab at Sharpe, who thumped the volley gun's butt onto the man's head, then shouted at the bastards to get out of his way. Marines were following him. Two Frenchmen cowered in their galley where the big iron stove had been torn apart by gunfire. Sharpe could hear the big guns firing below, filling the ship with their thunderous pounding, though whether it was the *Revenant*'s guns that fired or the *Pucelle*'s, he could not tell. He swung down the companionway into the lower deck's gloom.

He slid down on his backside, landed with a thump and just pointed the volley gun down the lower deck. He pulled the trigger, adding to the smoke that writhed under the beams, then he drew the cutlass. 'It's over!' he shouted. 'Stop firing! Stop firing!' He wished he knew French. 'Stop firing, you bastards! Stop firing! It's over!' A gunner, deaf to Sharpe's shouts, and half blinded by the smoke, pushed a powder-filled reed into a cannon's touch-hole and Sharpe slashed him with the cutlass. 'Stop it, I said! Stop firing!'

Two shots from the *Pucelle* hammered through the ship. Sharpe drew his pistol. The nearest French gunners just stared at him. Dozens of dead lay on the deck, some with great wooden splinters jutting from their bodies. The mainmast had a great bite gouged from one side. The deck was scorched where the cannon had exploded. 'It's over!' Sharpe screamed. 'Get away from that gun. Get away!' The Frenchmen might not speak English, but they understood the pistol and cutlass well enough. Sharpe went to a gunport. '*Pucelle*! *Pucelle*!'

'Who is it?' a voice called back.

'Ensign Sharpe! They've stopped firing! Hold your fire! Hold your fire!'

One last cannon belched smoke and flame into the *Revenant*'s belly, then there was silence at last as the big guns ceased. A gunner crawled out of one of the *Pucelle*'s lower gunports and scrambled into the *Revenant* where Sharpe was walking down the deck, stepping over corpses, climbing a fallen cannon, gesturing that the French gunners should kneel or lie down. Three marines followed him, bayonets fixed. 'Down!' Sharpe snarled at the wild-eyed, powder-blackened enemy. 'Down!' He turned to see more marines and British seamen coming down the companionway. 'Disarm the bastards,' he shouted, 'and get them on deck.' He stepped over the splintered remains of one of the ship's pumps. A French officer faced him with a drawn sword, but he took one look at Sharpe's face and let the blade clatter on the deck. More of the *Pucelle*'s gunners were crawling out of the British ship's gunports and clambering into the French ports, coming to plunder what they could.

Sharpe crossed a patch of blackened deck where one of his grenades had exploded. The French watched him warily. He pushed a man aside with his cutlass blade, then turned down the aft companionway into the ship's cockpit which was lit with a dozen lanterns.

He almost wished he had not come down the ladder for here there were scores of men bleeding and dying. This was death's kingdom, the red-wet belly of the ship, the place where foully wounded men came to face the surgeon and, in all likelihood, eternity. It smelt of blood and excrement and urine and terror. The surgeon, a white-haired man with a beard that was streaked with blood, looked up from the table where, with hands red to the wrists, he was delving into a man's belly. 'Get out of here,' he said in good English.

'Shut your face,' Sharpe snarled. 'I haven't killed a surgeon yet, but I don't mind starting with you.'

The surgeon looked startled, but said nothing more as Sharpe walked into the gunroom where an officer and six men lay bandaged on the floor. He forced the cutlass into its scabbard, gently moved one wounded man aside, then seized the ring of the hatch leading into the *Revenant*'s lady hole. He hauled it up and pointed the pistol down into the lantern-lit space.

A man and a woman were there. The woman was Mathilde, and the man was Pohlmann's so-called servant, the man who claimed to be Swiss, but who was in truth a subtle enemy of Britain. Above Sharpe, up in the smoky daylight, cheers sounded as the *Revenant*'s tricolour, which had been draped over her shattered taffrail, was bundled up and presented to Joel Chase. The ghost had been hunted and the ship was taken. 'Up,' Sharpe said to Michel Vaillard. 'Up!' They had pursued this man across two oceans and Sharpe felt a livid anger at the betrayal of the *Calliope*.

Michel Vaillard showed empty hands, then peered through the hatch. He blinked, plainly recognizing Sharpe, but unable to place him. Then he remembered exactly who Sharpe was, and in an instant understood that the *Calliope* must have been retaken by the British. 'It's you!' he sounded resentful.

'It's me. Now up! Where's Pohlmann?'

'On deck?' Vaillard suggested. He climbed the ladder, dusted his hands, then stooped to help Mathilde climb through the hatch. 'What happened?' Vaillard asked Sharpe. 'How did you get here?'

Sharpe ignored the questions. 'You will stay here, ma'am,' Sharpe told Mathilde. 'There's a surgeon out there who needs help.' He pushed Vaillard's arms aside and plucked back the Frenchman's coat to see a pistol hilt. He pulled the pistol free and tossed it back into the lady hole. 'You come with me.'

'I am merely a servant,' Vaillard said.

'You're a lump of treacherous French shit,' Sharpe said. 'Now go!' He pushed Vaillard in front of him, forcing him up the companionway to the lower deck where the great guns, hot as pots on a stove, now stood abandoned. The French dead and wounded were left, and a dozen British seamen were searching their bodies.

Vaillard refused to go any further, but turned instead to face Sharpe. 'I am a diplomat, Mister Sharpe,' he said gravely. His face was clever and his eyes gentle. He was dressed in a grey suit and had a black cravat tied in the lacy collar of his white shirt. He looked calm, clean and confident. 'You cannot kill me,' he instructed Sharpe, 'and you have no right to take me prisoner. I am not a soldier, not a sailor, but an accredited diplomat. You might have won this battle, but in a day or two your admiral will send me into Cadiz because that is how diplomats must be treated.' He smiled. 'That is the rule of nations, Ensign. You are a soldier, and you can die, but I am a diplomat and I must live. My life is sacrosanct.'

Sharpe prodded him with the pistol, forcing him aft towards the wardroom. Just as in the *Pucelle* all the bulkheads had been taken down, but the bare deck suddenly gave way to a painted canvas carpet that was smeared with blood, and the beams here were touched with gold paint. The great gallery windows had been shattered by the *Spartiate*'s guns so that not a pane was left and what remained of the elegantly curved window seat was smothered in broken glass. Sharpe pulled open a door on the wardroom's starboard side and saw that the quarter gallery, which held the officers' latrine, had been shot clean away by the *Spartiate*'s broadside so that the door opened onto nothing but ocean. Far off, almost hull down, the few enemy ships that had escaped the battle sailed towards the coast of Spain. 'You want to go to Cadiz?' Sharpe asked Vaillard.

'I am a diplomat!' the Frenchman protested. 'You must treat me as such!'

'I'll treat you as I bloody want,' Sharpe said. 'Down here there are no bloody rules, and you're going to Cadiz.' He seized Vaillard's grey coat. The Frenchman struggled, pulling away from the opened door beyond which the remnants of the latrine hung above the sea. Sharpe cracked him across the skull with the pistol barrel, then swung him to the door and shoved him towards the open air. Vaillard clung to the door's edges with both hands, his face showing as much astonishment as fear. Sharpe smashed the pistol against the Frenchman's right hand, then kicked him in the belly and slammed the gun against the knuckles of Vaillard's left hand. The Frenchman let go, shouting a last protest as he fell back into the sea.

A British sailor, his pigtail hanging almost to his waist, had watched the murder. 'Were you supposed to do that, sir?'

'He wanted to learn to swim,' Sharpe said, holstering the pistol.

'Frogs should be able to swim, sir,' the seaman said. 'It's their nature.' He stood beside Sharpe and stared down into the water. 'But he can't.'

'So he's not a very good Frog,' Sharpe said.

'Only he looked rich, sir,' the sailor reproved Sharpe, 'and we could have searched him before he went swimming.'

'Sorry,' Sharpe said, 'I didn't think.'

'And he's drowning now,' the sailor said.

Vaillard splashed desperately, but his struggles only drove him under. Had he told the truth about his protected status as a diplomat? Sharpe was not sure, but if Vaillard had spoken the truth then it was better that he should drown here than be released to spread his poison in Paris. 'Cadiz is that way!' Sharpe shouted down at the drowning man, pointing eastwards, but Vaillard did not hear him. Vaillard was dying.

Pohlmann was already dead. Sharpe found the Hanoverian on the quarterdeck where he had shared the danger with Montmorin and had been killed early in the battle by a cannon ball that tore his chest apart. The German's face, curiously untouched by blood, seemed to be smiling. A swell lifted the *Revenant*, rocking Pohlmann's body. 'He was a brave man,' a voice said, and Sharpe looked up to see it was Capitaine Louis Montmorin. Montmorin had yielded the ship to Chase, offering his sword with tears in his eyes, but Chase had refused to take the sword. He had shaken Montmorin's hand instead, commiserated with the Frenchman and congratulated him on the fighting qualities of his ship and crew.

'He was a good soldier,' Sharpe said, looking down into Pohlmann's face. 'He just had a bad habit of choosing the wrong side.'

As had Peculiar Cromwell. The *Calliope*'s captain still lived. He looked scared, as well he might, for he faced trial and punishment, but he straightened when he saw Sharpe. He did not look surprised, perhaps because he had already heard of the *Calliope*'s fate. 'I told Montmorin not to fight,' he said as Sharpe walked towards him. Cromwell had cut his long hair short, perhaps in an attempt to change his appearance, but there was no mistaking the heavy brows and long jaw. 'I told him this fight was not our business. Our business was to reach Cadiz, nothing else, but he insisted on fighting.' He held out a tar-stained hand. 'I am glad you live, Ensign.'

'You? Glad I live?' Sharpe almost spat the words into Cromwell's face. 'You, you bastard!' He seized Cromwell's blue coat and rammed the man against the splintered gunwale planking beneath the poop. 'Where is it?' he shouted.

'Where's what?' Cromwell rejoined.

'Don't bugger me, Peculiar,' Sharpe said. 'You bloody well know what I want, now where the hell is it?'

Cromwell hesitated, then seemed to crumple. 'In the hold,' he muttered, 'in the hold.' He winced at the thought of this defeat. He had sold his ship because he believed the French would rule the world, and now he was in the middle of shattered French hopes. Near a score of French and Spanish ships had been taken and not a British ship had been lost, but Peculiar Cromwell was lost.

'Clouter!' Sharpe saw the blood-streaked man climbing to the quarterdeck. 'Clouter!'

'Sir?'

'What happened to your hand?' Sharpe asked. The tall black man had a blood-soaked rag twisted about his left hand.

'Cutlass,' Clouter said curtly. 'Last man I fought. Took three fingers, sir.'

'I'm sorry.'

'He died,' Clouter said.

'You can hold this?' Sharpe asked, offering Clouter the hilt of his pistol. Clouter nodded and took the gun. 'Take this bastard down to the hold,' Sharpe said, gesturing at Cromwell. 'He's going to give you some bags of jewels. Bring the stones to me and I'll give you some for saving my life. There's also a watch that belongs to a friend of mine, and I'd like both those, but if you find anything else, it's yours.' He pushed Cromwell into the black man's embrace. 'And if he gives you any trouble, Clouter, kill the bastard!'

'I want him alive, Clouter.' Captain Chase had overheard the last words. 'Alive!' Chase said again, then stood aside to let Cromwell pass. He smiled at Sharpe. 'I owe you thanks again, Richard.'

'No, sir. I have to congratulate you.' Sharpe stared at the two ships, still lashed together, and saw wreckage and smoke and blood and bodies, and in the wider sea there were floating hulks and tired ships, but all now were under British flags. This was the image of victory, splintered and smoke-stained, tired and blood-streaked, but victory. The church bells would ring in Britain's villages for this, and then families would anxiously wait to discover whether their menfolk would come home. 'You did well, sir,' Sharpe said, 'you did well.'

'We all did well,' Chase said. 'Haskell died, did you know? Poor Haskell. He so wanted to be a captain. He was married last year. Only last year, just before we left for India.' Chase looked as weary as Montmorin, but when he looked up he saw his old red ensign hoisted above the French tricolour on the *Revenant*'s foremast, the only mast left to the French ship. The white ensign flew from the *Pucelle*'s mainmast and its white cloth was smeared with Haskell's blood. 'We didn't let him down, did we?' Chase said, tears in his eyes. 'Nelson, I mean. I could not have lived with myself had I let him down.'

'You did him proud, sir.'

'We had some help from the *Spartiate*. What a good fellow Francis Lavory is! I do hope he's taken a prize for himself.' A wind lifted the ensigns and dragged the thinning smoke fast across the sea. The long swells were rippling with wind while white foam splashed about the floating wreckage that littered the sea. There were only a dozen ships in sight which still retained their masts and rigging intact, but Nelson had started the day with twenty-eight ships and now there were forty-six in his fleet, and the rest of the enemy had fled. 'We must look for Vaillard,' Chase said, suddenly remembering the Frenchman.

'He's dead, sir.'

'Dead?' Chase shrugged. 'Best thing, I suppose.' The wind filled the ragged sails of the two ships. 'My God,' Chase said, 'there's wind at last, and not just a little, I fear. We must be about our work.' He gazed at the *Pucelle*. 'Doesn't she look battered? Poor dear thing. Mister Collier! You survive!'

'I'm alive, sir,' Harold Collier said with a grin. He had his sword still drawn, its blade smeared with blood.

'You can probably sheathe the sword, Harry,' Chase said gently.

'Scabbard was hit, sir,' Collier said, and lifted the scabbard to show where a musket ball had bent it.

'You did well, Mister Collier,' Chase said, 'and now you'll muster men to separate the ships.'

'Aye aye, sir.'

Montmorin was taken aboard the *Pucelle*, but the rest of his crew were imprisoned below the *Revenant*'s decks. The wind was moaning in the torn rigging now, and the sea was breaking into whitecaps. A midshipman and twenty men were put aboard the captured *Revenant* as a prize crew, then the two ships were cut apart. A tow line had been rigged from the *Pucelle*'s stern so that her prize could be towed to port. Lieutenant Peel had a score of men laying new cables to the *Pucelle*'s remaining masts, trying to brace them against the promised storm. The gunports were closed, the flintlocks dismounted from the cannons' breeches, and the guns lashed up. The galley fires were relit and their first job was to heat great vats of vinegar with which the bloody decks would be scoured, for it was believed that only hot vinegar could draw blood from timber. Sharpe, back on board the *Pucelle*, found some oranges in the scupper and ate one, filling his pockets with the others.

The dead were jettisoned. Splash after splash. Men moved slowly, bone weary from an afternoon of blood and thirst and fighting, but the fall of night and the rising wind brought the worst news of the day. A boat from the *Conqueror* pulled past and an officer shouted the news up to Chase's shattered quarterdeck. Nelson had died, the officer said, struck down by a musket ball on the *Victory*'s deck. The *Pucelle*'s seamen scarcely dared believe the news, and Sharpe first heard of it when he saw Chase weeping. 'Are you hurt, sir?' he asked.

Chase looked utterly bereft, like a man defeated instead of a captain with a rich prize. 'The admiral's dead, Sharpe,' Chase said. 'He's dead.'

'Nelson?' Sharpe asked. 'Nelson?'

'Dead!' Chase said. 'Oh, good God, why?'

Sharpe just felt an emptiness inside. The whole crew looked stricken, as if a friend, not a commander, had died. Nelson was dead. Some did not believe it, but the commander-in-chief's flag flying above the *Royal Sovereign* confirmed that Collingwood now commanded the victorious fleet. And if Collingwood commanded then Nelson was dead. Chase wept for him, cuffing away his tears only when the last body was thrown overboard.

There was no ceremony for that final corpse, but then no one who had died that day had received any ceremony. The corpse was brought to the quarterdeck and, in the deepening dusk, thrown into the sea. It seemed cold suddenly. The wind had a cutting edge and Sharpe shivered. Chase watched the body float away on the waves, then shook his head in puzzlement. 'He must have decided to join the fight,' Chase said. 'Can you credit it?'

'Every man was expected to do his duty, sir,' Sharpe said stolidly.

'So they were, and so they did, but no one expected him to fight or to fetch a bullet in the head. Poor fellow. He was braver than I ever thought. Does his wife know?'

'I shall tell her, sir.'

'Would you?' Chase asked. 'Yes, of course you will. No one better, but I'm grateful to you, Richard, grateful.' He turned to watch the fleet, its stern lanterns already lit, struggling under half sail in the rising wind. Only the *Victory* was dark, with not a single light showing. 'Oh, poor Nelson,' Chase lamented, 'poor England.'

Sharpe, as soon as he was back aboard the *Pucelle*, had gone down to the cockpit which was as foetid and bloody as the one on the *Revenant*. Pickering had been sawing at a man's thigh bone, sweat dripping from his face into the mangled flesh. The patient, a leather pad between his teeth, was twitching as the blunt saw grated on bone. Two seamen held him down, and neither they nor the surgeon had noticed Sharpe go through to the gunroom where he lifted the lady-hole hatch to see blood spattered on its underside. Lord William lay sprawled in the narrow space, his skull gaping bloodily where the pistol bullet had exited. Grace had been huddled with her arms about her knees, shaking, and she half screamed as the hatch was opened, then she shuddered with relief when she saw it was Sharpe. 'Richard? It is you?' She was crying again. 'They're going to hang me, Richard. They're going to hang me, but I had to shoot him. He was going to kill me. I had to shoot him.'

Sharpe had dropped down into the lady hole. 'They ain't going to hang you, my lady,' he said. 'He died on deck. That's what everyone will think. He died on deck.'

'I had to do it!' she wailed.

'The Frogs did it.' Sharpe took the pistol from her and shoved it into a pocket, then he put his hands under Lord William's armpits and heaved him up, trying to push the corpse through the hatch, but the body was awkward in the narrow space.

'They'll hang me,' Grace cried.

Sharpe let the corpse drop, then turned and crouched beside her. 'No one will hang you. No one will know. If they find him down here, I'll say I shot him, but with a little luck I can get him up on deck and everyone will think the Frogs did it.'

She put her arms round his neck. 'You're safe. Oh, God, you're safe. What happened?'

'We won,' Sharpe said. 'We won.' He kissed her, then held her tight for an instant before he went back to struggle with the corpse. If Lord William was found here then no one would believe he had been killed by the enemy and Chase would be honour bound to hold an enquiry into the death, so the body had to be taken up above the orlop deck, but the hatch was narrow and Sharpe could not get the corpse through, but then a hand reached down and took hold of Lord William's bloody collar and heaved him effortlessly upwards.

Sharpe had cursed under his breath. He cursed because someone else now knew that Lord William had been shot in the lady hole, and when he had clambered up into the dimly lit gunroom he found it was Clouter who, one-handed, was proving as able as most men with two hands. 'I saw you come down here, sir,' Clouter said, 'and was going to give you these.' He had held out Sharpe's jewels, all of them, and Major Dalton's watch, and Sharpe had taken them and then tried to return some of the emeralds and diamonds to Clouter.

'I did nothing,' the big man protested.

'You saved my life, Clouter,' Sharpe said and folded the big black fingers round the stones, 'and now you're going to save it again. Can you get that bastard up on deck?'

Clouter grinned. 'Up where he died, sir?' he asked and Sharpe scarce dared believe that Clouter had so quickly understood the problem and its solution. He just stared at the tall black man who grinned again. 'You should have shot the bastard weeks ago, sir, but the Frogs did it for you and there ain't a man aboard who won't say the same.' He stooped and hauled the corpse onto his shoulder as Sharpe helped Lady Grace up through the hatch. He told her to wait while he went with Clouter to the quarterdeck and there, in the gathering dusk and rising wind, Lord William had been heaved overboard.

No one had taken any notice of the body being carried through the ship, for what was one more corpse being brought up from the surgeon's knife? 'He was braver than I thought,' Chase had said.

Sharpe went back to the cockpit where Lady Grace stared white-faced and wide-eyed as Pickering tied off blood vessels, then sewed the flap of skin over the newly made stump. Sharpe took her arm and led her into one of the midshipmen's tiny cabins at the rear of the cockpit. He closed the door, though that hardly gave them privacy for the doors were made of wooden slats through which anyone could have seen them, but no one had eyes for the cabin.

'I want you to know what happened,' Lady Grace said when she was alone with Sharpe in the midshipman's cabin, but then she could say no more.

'I know what happened,' Sharpe said.

'He was going to kill me,' she said.

'Then you did the right thing,' Sharpe said, 'but the rest of the world thinks he died a brave man's death.

They think he went on deck to fight, and he was shot. That's what Chase thinks, it's what everybody thinks. Do you understand?'

She nodded. She was shivering, but not with cold. Her husband's blood flecked her hair.

'And you waited for him,' Sharpe said, 'and he did not come back.'

She turned to look at the gunroom door that hid the lady-hole hatch. 'But the blood,' she wailed, 'the blood!'

'The ship is full of blood,' Sharpe said, 'too much blood. Your husband died on deck. He died a hero.'

'Yes,' she said, 'he did.' She gazed at him, her eyes huge in the dark, then held him fiercely. He could feel her body shaking. 'I thought you must be dead,' she said.

'Not even a scratch,' Sharpe replied, stroking her hair.

She shuddered, then pulled her head back to look at him. 'We're free, Richard,' she said with a note of surprise. 'Do you realize that? We're free!'

'Yes, my lady, we're free.'

'What are we going to do?'

'Whatever we want,' Sharpe said, 'whatever we can.'

She held him and he held her and the ship leaned to the weather and the wounded moaned and the last scraps of smoke vanished in the night as the storm wind rose from the darkening west to batter ships already pounded past endurance. But Sharpe had his woman, he was free, and he was at last going home.

Historical Note

Sharpe really had no business being at Trafalgar, but he had to travel home from India and Cape Trafalgar lies not far from the route he would have taken and he might well have passed it on or about 21 October 1805. But if Sharpe had no business being there, then Admiral Villeneuve, commander of the combined French and Spanish fleets, had even less.

The great fleet had been gathered to cover the invasion of Britain, for which Napoleon had assembled his Grand Army near Boulogne. The British blockade and the weather combined to keep the enemy in port, except for a foray across the Atlantic by which Villeneuve hoped to draw Nelson away from the English coast. The foray failed, Villeneuve had put into Cadiz, and there he was trapped. Napoleon abandoned his invasion plans and marched his army east towards its great victory at Austerlitz. The French and Spanish fleet was now an irrelevance, but Napoleon, furious with Villeneuve, sent a replacement admiral and it seems likely that Villeneuve, knowing that he faced disgrace and eager to justify his existence before his replacement reached Cadiz, put to sea. Ostensibly he was taking the fleet to the Mediterranean, but he must have hoped he could fight the British ships blockading Cadiz, win a victory and so restore his reputation. After just a day at sea he discovered that the blockading fleet was much larger than he had thought and so turned his ships back northwards in hope of escaping battle. It was already too late; Nelson was in sight and the combined fleet was doomed.

There was no *Pucelle*, nor a *Revenant*. Nelson fought Trafalgar with twenty-seven ships of the line, while the combined French and Spanish fleet had thirty-three. By day's end seventeen of those enemy ships had struck their colours and one had been destroyed by fire, making Trafalgar the most decisive naval battle until Midway. The British lost no ships but paid, of course, the price of Nelson's life. He was the matchless hero of the Napoleonic wars, as beloved by his men as he was feared by the enemy. He was also, of course, a famous adulterer, and his last request of his country was that Britain should look after Lady Hamilton. The granting of that request lay in the power of politicians, and politicians do not change, so Lady Hamilton died in miserable penury.

On the night after the battle a huge storm blew up and all but four of the seventeen prizes were lost. Many were being towed, but the storm was too fierce and the tows were cast off. Three of the prizes sank, two were deliberately set afire and five were wrecked. Another three captured ships, manned by prize crews too small to cope with the storm, were handed back to their original crews and sailed to safety, but they were so damaged by battle and storm that none was fit to sail again. Of the fifteen enemy ships that escaped capture in battle, four were taken by the Royal Navy and one was wrecked in the next two weeks. Many of the British ships were as badly damaged as the French or Spanish, but superb seamanship brought them all safe into port.

The *Pucelle*, when it raked the ship alongside the *Victory*, was stealing the *Temeraire*'s thunder. The *Redoutable* was commanded by a fiery Frenchman called Lucas, probably the ablest French captain at Trafalgar, who had trained his crew in a novel technique aimed solely at boarding and capturing an enemy ship. When the *Victory* closed on his much smaller ship he shut his gunports and massed his men on deck. His rigging was filled with marksmen who rained a dreadful fire onto the *Victory*, and it was one of those men who shot Nelson. Lucas virtually cleared the *Victory*'s upper decks of men, but just as he was assembling his crew to board the British flagship, the *Temeraire* sailed past and emptied her carronades into the boarders. The '*Saucy*' also raked Lucas's ship which was, anyway, being pounded by the *Victory*'s lower-deck guns. That finished Lucas's fight. The *Redoutable* was captured, but had been so damaged by gunfire that she sank in the subsequent storm. The *Victory* lost 57 men dead, including Nelson, and had 102 wounded. The *Redoutable*, in contrast, had 22 of her 74 guns dismounted and, from a crew of 643, had 487 killed and 81 wounded. That extraordinarily high casualty rate (88%) was caused by gunnery, not musketry. Other enemy ships suffered similar high casualty rates. The *Royal Sovereign*'s opening broadside (double-shotted) raked the French *Fougueux* and killed or injured half her crew in that one blow. When the *Victory*, later in the battle, raked Villeneuve's flagship, the *Bucentaure*, she dismounted twenty of her eighty guns and again killed or wounded half the crew.

The disparity in casualty rates was extraordinary. The British lost 1,500 men, either killed or wounded, while the French and Spanish casualties were about 17,000; testimony to the horrific effectiveness of British gunnery. Several British ships were raked, as the fictional *Pucelle* was, but none recorded the high casualties suffered aboard the enemy ships that found themselves bow or stern on to a British broadside. The *Victory* suffered the highest casualty list of the British fleet, while probably the most battered of all the British ships, the

Belleisle, which sailed into the southern mêlée and was raked more than once, losing all her masts and bowsprit, suffered only 33 men killed and 93 wounded. Fourteen of the enemy ships lost more than a hundred men killed, while only fourteen British ships had ten or more men killed. One British ship, HMS *Prince,* she who 'sailed like a haystack', had no casualties at all, probably because her slow speed kept her from battle until late in the afternoon when few enemies were capable of putting up much resistance. The imbalance of casualties disguises the tenacity with which most of the enemy fought. They were being decimated by superior British gunnery, yet they stubbornly stuck to their guns. Most of the French and Spanish crews were ill-trained, some had no prior experience of fighting at sea, yet they did not lack for courage.

The *Victory*'s high casualty rate was partly caused by Lucas's tactics of drenching her with musket fire and partly because she was the first British ship into the northern part of the enemy's fleet and so fought alone for a brief time. She was also flying the admiral's pennant and so became a target for several enemy ships. Collingwood's flagship, the *Royal Sovereign,* first into the southern part of the enemy fleet and also flying an admiral's pennant, lost 47 men dead and had 94 wounded, the greatest casualties of any ship in Collingwood's squadron. Admirals led from the front.

The battle was truly decisive. It so shocked the morale of the French and Spanish navies that neither recovered for the remainder of the Napoleonic wars. British sea power was supreme, and stayed so until the beginning of the twentieth century. Nelson, more than any man, imposed Britain on the nineteenth-century world. It is often said that his tactics were revolutionary, and so they were in the context of eighteenth-century naval warfare where the accepted mode of fighting one fleet against another was to form parallel lines of battle and fight it out broadside to broadside. Yet, in 1797, off Camperdown, Admiral Duncan had formed his fleet of sixteen British battleships into two squadrons that he sailed straight into the broadsides of eighteen Dutch ships of the line, and by battle's end he had captured eleven of those ships and lost none of his own. This is not to denigrate Nelson, who had proved his resourcefulness time and again, but it suggests the Royal Navy was open to innovative thinking in those desperate years. It was also extraordinarily confident. By sailing his squadrons directly at the enemy line, Nelson, like Duncan before him, was gambling that his ships could survive continuous raking. They did, and proceeded to mangle the enemy. At Trafalgar, for at least twenty minutes at the opening of the battle, the British ships could not fire a single shot, while a dozen of the enemy could fire at will. Nelson knew that, risked that and was certain he could win despite that. It was not until the Royal Navy fought the US Navy in the war of 1812 that British gunnery met its equal, but the US Navy did not deploy battleships and so could only be a minor nuisance to a worldwide fleet which was by then globally pre-eminent.

Did any man serve at both Trafalgar and Waterloo? I know of only one. Don Miguel Ricardo Maria Juan de la Mata Domingo Vincente Ferre Alava de Esquivel, mercifully known as Miguel de Alava, was an officer in the Spanish navy in 1805 and served aboard the Spanish admiral's flagship, the *Principe de Asturias.* That ship fought nobly at Trafalgar and, though she was hurt badly, managed to avoid capture and escaped back to Cadiz. Four years later Alava had become an officer in the Spanish army. Spain had changed sides by then, and the Spanish army was allied with the British army under Sir Arthur Wellesley, the future Duke of Wellington, as it fought in the Peninsula, and General de Alava was appointed Wellington's Spanish liaison officer and the two became extremely close friends, a friendship that endured till their deaths. De Alava stayed with Wellington until the end of the Peninsular War when he was appointed the Spanish ambassador to the Netherlands and so was able to join the allies at the Battle of Waterloo where he remained at Wellington's side throughout the day. He had no need to be there, yet his presence was undoubtedly a help to Wellington who trusted de Alava's judgement and valued his advice. Nearly all of Wellington's aides were killed or wounded, yet he and de Alava survived unhurt. So Miguel de Alava fought against the British at Trafalgar and for them at Waterloo, a strange career indeed. Sharpe joins de Alava in surviving that remarkable double.

I am enormously grateful to Peter Goodwin, the Historical Consultant, Keeper and Curator of HMS *Victory*, for his notes on the manuscript, and to Katy Ball, Curator at Portsmouth Museums and Records Office. The errors which survive are all my own, or can be blamed on Richard Sharpe, a soldier adrift in a strange nautical world. He will be back on land soon, where he belongs, and will march again.

Also by Bernard Cornwell

The SHARPE series
(in chronological order)

SHARPE'S TIGER

SHARPE'S TRIUMPH

SHARPE'S FORTRESS

SHARPE'S PREY

SHARPE'S RIFLES

SHARPE'S EAGLE

SHARPE'S HAVOC

SHARPE'S GOLD

SHARPE'S ESCAPE

SHARPE'S FURY

SHARPE'S BATTLE

SHARPE'S COMPANY

SHARPE'S SWORD

SHARPE'S ENEMY

SHARPE'S HONOUR

SHARPE'S REGIMENT

SHARPE'S SIEGE

SHARPE'S REVENGE

SHARPE'S WATERLOO

SHARPE'S DEVIL

The GRAIL QUEST Series

HARLEQUIN

VAGABOND

HERETIC

STONEHENGE: A NOVEL OF 2000 BC

The STARBUCK Chronicles

REBEL

COPPERHEAD

BATTLE FLAG

THE BLOODY GROUND

The WARLORD Chronicles

THE WINTER KING

THE ENEMY OF GOD

EXCALIBUR

GALLOWS THIEF

THE LAST KINGDOM

THE PALE HORSEMAN

THE LORDS OF THE NORTH

By Bernard Cornwell and Susannah Kells

A CROWNING MERCY

FALLEN ANGELS